Praise for *Before We Arrived*

"Pine tackles difficult topics with subtlety and tenderness ... Immersive storytelling ... poignant ... The diverse cast brings depth and richness to the themes of loss and renewal ... a remarkable novel. Highly recommended read for fans of emotive, inspirational, and immersive literary fiction. 5/5."

—Readers' Favorite

"Jodie Pine's *Before We Arrived* spins a beautiful tapestry of interconnected lives across time, grief, and healing. It's about holding sorrow in one hand and still reaching out with the other. The prose is warm and alive ... like someone left the light on for you. For anyone who's ever been broken open ... deeply moving. 5/5."

—Literary Titan

"A transformative novel ... Pine addresses heavy topics directly but with immense care ... The (characters') stories will rock you ... an inspiring journey."

—Independent Book Review

"At the heart of Pine's narrative are the questions about how to live with trauma, both personal and collective ... distilling uneasy truths about race, displacement, and the myths that people construct to make sense of our origins ... the novel embraces the often turbulent nature of healing ... an invitation to reflect on the stories we inherit and those we choose to rewrite."

—BookLife

"Set over a myriad of time and place in combination with an appealing cast of characters, *Before We Arrived* is original in its focus on individual histories while still probing universal themes of belonging, healing, and identity. Readers will be captivated by how their stories intertwine."

—BookLife Prize

"An intimate and tangled novel that delicately dissects grief and the difficulties of healing, *Before We Arrived* is a nuanced and emotionally charged character-driven drama. This generation-spanning story explores a range of existential turning points and contemporary crises with unflinching honesty, which is both heartrending and inspiring."

—SPR

Before We Arrived

JODIE PINE

BEFORE WE ARRIVED

Library of Congress # TXu 2-481-223

ISBN 979-8-9923195-0-7 paperback
ISBN 979-8-9923195-1-4 large print paperback
ISBN 979-8-9923195-2-1 eBook

For My Father

CONTENTS

AUTHOR'S NOTE

Dear Readers,

Some of you may notice the lack of capitalization of 'Black' and 'Indigenous' within the text of the novel. The *Before We Arrived* story arcs take place between 1971–2005, long before capitalization of these terms was adopted for common usage. I made every effort to keep the language in sync with the timeline and locations of the story. There is certainly no disrespect intended toward any individual or community of people.

Please also note that a few racist and antisemitic remarks, spoken by bigoted minor fictional characters, have been watered down a bit with an asterisk. I was not censored as of pre-publication (for better or worse I did my own editing and proofreading); I simply figured the point would get across without the full spelling of venomous words.

Having been personally targeted on numerous occasions, these issues carry an extra layer of sensitivity for me, above and beyond consideration of moral codes and basic human decency.

I hope you enjoy reading *Before We Arrived* as much as I enjoyed writing it. Rest assured, there's plenty of levity and fun stuff.

Jodie Pine
(she/her)
2025

I shall
Gather up
All the lost souls
That wander this earth
All the ones that are alone
All the ones that are broken
All the ones that never really fitted in
I shall gather them all up
And together we shall find our home

— Athey Thompson

1. AN OPPORTUNITY

The only courage that matters is the kind that gets you from one moment to the next. —Mignon McLaughlin

HENRY Friday, June 24, 2005 Western Massachusetts

- **Okay, Henry, your hand is looking good. Now that the stitches are out there's a horizontal divot where your index finger used to be, so keep it bandaged up for the next ten days so it'll stay clean and dry. I'll put one on for you now, remove it when you shower, and put a fresh one on afterwards, okay? I'm glad we were able to repair most of the puckering on the dorsal side. The numbness in your middle finger may lessen over time, but don't count on it. The best thing you can do now is to start using your hand and fingers as normally as possible, and to keep doing the exercises the OT gave you to regain strength. Any questions?**

- No, I don't think so. Thank you, Dr. Patel.

- You're welcome, Henry. Oh, Jean from Social Services wants to touch base with you before you leave the building, let me page her.

Jean has been my caseworker since before the second surgery in 2001. She's always been helpful with practical matters, and what I guess would be considered emotional
situations; she seems to know what I'm thinking and feeling
before I even know it myself. There should be more people
like her in the world.

> **— Jean's upstairs in Geriatrics and says to meet her
> at her office in five minutes. You'll probably get
> there at the same time.**

> **— Okay, thank you.**

> **— No problem. Call my office if you have any issues.
> Take care, Henry.**

I picked up my backpack, the strap of the bike helmet clipped
to it, and made my way to the elevators. I know this hospital
like the back of my hand—ha! I made a silly little joke for
myself. This has been my life for the last eight years: aimlessly
zigzagging through a murky stream of misery, trying so hard
to keep things light. I guess under the circumstances I'm doing
okay though and shouldn't complain.

> **— Hi Henry, come on in, nice to see you!**

Jean was carrying a large stack of file folders. She pushed the
door open with her elbow and made her way to the rolling chair
behind her desk. I planted myself in one of the two chairs facing her. It was a small room with a tiny window just below the
seven-foot ceiling. A set of old metal filing cabinets lined the
adjacent wall, and a box of tissues took its usual place on the
desk; I imagine lots of people use them, I certainly have.

> **— How did it go with Dr. Patel?**

> **— Fine, I guess this is as good as it's going to get.**

I showed her my mangled left hand.

- **It does look substantially better, she did a great job.**

- **Someone told me recently that she's the best reconstructive hand surgeon in the region, so I guess I lucked out.**

- **I know luck is a relative term, but for what you needed you got the best.**

- **Oh, and thank you for helping me get the reduced fees for the last two surgeries. Most of my savings are gone now, but at least the medical procedures are finished.**

- **Yes, the costs are exorbitant, glad you got through all of this.**

There was a framed picture I hadn't noticed before of two teen-agers, a boy and a girl, on the narrow shelf next to Jean's desk.

- **Those are your kids?**

- **Yes, they're all grown up now, the oldest is about your age.**

I looked down at my hand, which was resting on my lap, its usual place, away from prying eyes.

- **I, um, I used to think I'd meet a nice, smart girl and get married some day and maybe even have a child, but I don't think anyone will want to see this weirdness every day.**

- **Henry, we all have flaws. Would you really want to be with someone who cares about what your hand looks like?**

– Uh, no, I guess not.

– Alright. Well I wanted to talk to you about an opportunity that I think you should seriously consider. There's a marvelous place—a local animal sanctuary, and they currently have an opening in their Volunteer Work Program. You don't have to have any previous experience with animals, they train you there. You work full time in exchange for room and board. There are several casitas on site that they use for housing …

What is she talking about? I don't know anything about animals—I don't understand what this has to do with me—and what the heck is a casita?

– … they rehabilitate farm animals that have been abused or neglected. There are communal meals for the staff and volunteers. You'd be around good people, Henry. I'm on the board there, and I've known the director for many years.

– But my hand—it's kind of weak and useless, and I have to keep it clean.

– They'll give you gloves. You do what you're able to do. It's not a factory, it's a relaxing, supportive environment, and I think you'd enjoy it. The sanctuary is off Route 5 as you're heading toward West Hatfield, not far from that nice furniture store.

– Just north of here, on this side of the river?

– Yes.

I've been crashing at the home of college friends for the last few months, and that can't go on forever, so maybe this would be a way to move forward, at least for the interim.

— **Okay, so please explain this to me again. How long would I be there?**

— **The work volunteers stay up to six months, and then you can apply for a paid job there if there's an opening, which is unlikely, and in any case you'd have to find your own place to live after the six months. It's a small nonprofit, they rely on grants and donations and volunteers to keep things going.**

— **So ... there's a bunch of cows there that need to be taken care of?**

— **Actually there are no cows. They have goats, and some other odd, interesting creatures, but no cows.**

— **Okay, well, um, I guess I could give it a try. If it's too much for me I wouldn't be obligated to stay, right?**

— **Right. There's a long waiting list, so your space would be filled immediately if you left.**

— **Oh! So how did you get me in?**

— **I've had you on the waiting list a while, without having given your name, I used mine, so we'll need to call now to confirm.**

— **Okay—can I ask you one more question?**

— **Of course.**

Jean is so patient; anyone else would be exasperated with me by now.

— Uh … do you know if I'd be the only black guy there?

— I'm not sure who the other work volunteers are right now, but in any case I guarantee you won't be the only minority. The regular group of staff is small but diverse.

— Oh, okay.

— Is that a yes?

I nodded in assent and she made the call.

— Hi Suzy, it's Jean, how's it going … good … I'm checking about that volunteer slot … alright, I have someone for you. Is Rivka around? … Can you get her on the line?

A minute or so passed, and Jean was quickly filling out some sort of form.

— Hello-hello! … busy as usual, yes. I'm here in my office with a thirty-one- year-old gentleman named Henry Carter, and he's interested in participating in the Volunteer Work Program … yes … well he's a bit nervous because he hasn't worked with animals before … right, that's what I told him. Actually he has a background in landscape design … alright, let me try and remember which buttons to push … I think you're on speaker now.

— Hi Henry, can you hear me okay?

— Yes, ma'am.

— This is Rivka Solomon. That's great that you're willing to give it a try. Can you be here on Monday, late morning, around elevenish?

— This coming Monday??

— Yes, the twenty-seventh.

— Uh, yes? I could do that.

— Okay, good. Jean will give you the address and all that. Check in with Suzy as soon as you arrive. Jean will fax over your referral papers, and Suzy will show you around and you'll join us for lunch. Then you can get settled in and you would start work on Tuesday, okay?

— Um, okay. Sounds good.

— Okay, looking forward to meeting you, Henry. Have a good weekend.

— You too, thank you, ma'am.

I wasn't quite sure what I'd just gotten myself into, though I didn't think Jean would steer me wrong. Rivka sounds like a nice lady, and has that oh-so-familiar no-nonsense New York manner of speaking. But goats?

I guess I need to hang tough and give this place a try. Jean handed me a pamphlet and business card and directions. I was tired and overwhelmed, would have to look at the papers later.

— Well thank you for everything.

— You're welcome, Henry. Let me know how it goes. I think you'll do well.

— Thank you, ma'am.

— Henry, we've known each other for over four years now, it's certainly alright to call me Jean.

— Yes, ma'am.

2. A PACT

The best way out of a difficulty is through it. —Will Rogers

JAYCE Tuesday, July 15, 1975 Western Massachusetts

We just buried my little sister. She died a few days ago at the age of sixteen. Word must have gotten out, because a few members of the Aquinnah Wampanoag were present at the ceremony and chanted some prayers. My father, Elan, who has been mostly absent from our lives over the last few months, also stood with us at the grave. Only my mother and I would be returning to her apartment.

My life had been getting back on track. I've been living in a large, old rental house in upstate New York. I have a steady, trustworthy housemate named Simon, also a Cornell student, who is quiet like me, and at times we have a third person living with us. In 1973, when I was twenty-one, I applied and was accepted with a partial scholarship into the Accelerated Archaeology Program, where after five years of continuous academic study, plus field work in the summers, I would graduate with both a Bachelor's and Master's. It's intense and fascinating and what I've always wanted to do. The summer digs count as academic credit, and also serve to offset some of my tuition; I took out a student loan to cover living costs. Had just completed Year Two when all hell broke loose. Again. I'm supposed to be on a dig right now, but obviously had to rush across state lines to be with my mother. I don't know what's going to happen. Not only did my sister die; her baby is in the hospital and he has no parents.

My mother has always been stoic; I must have inherited her forbearance. I'm not sure if that's a good thing, it's just the way we're built. My sister was light and merry for most of her short life. I wonder what the baby will be like as he grows up; hopefully he'll be cheerful like his mother used to be.

We've been silent for most of the day. My mother spoke briefly at the grave, while clutching her blouse with her entwined hands over her heart:

— **My precious girl was born of the air … she lived in the spirit of the sky. Mother Earth will reclaim her body and the Creator will bring her spirit back to its place of origin, where she will be free of pain and suffering. She will always be a part of us.**

I drove us back to her place in my car. She's forty-five years old and has never learned to drive; when my father was around he would take us shopping or wherever we needed to go. He has the car now so my mother has to get to work and the hospital and the store either by walking or by asking other people to take her. There's no public transportation to speak of; the PVTA started running a bus service a few months ago, but they only make trips between the colleges. There are no trains or taxis. Her neighbor Doreen helps out in emergencies, but my mother hates asking for assistance with anything. Something to add to my list of Things I Need To Talk To My Mother About: get a damn license and a used car so you can get around on your own. But there were other, more immediate, priorities.

I made us some coffee and sliced the pound cake that Doreen had dropped off this morning. Nice woman. She wanted to come to the cemetery with us but couldn't find any-one to watch her kids. I brought everything over to the table in front of the couch, where my mother was sitting in a partially-numb state. I'm sure she hasn't had any restful sleep in months, and now this.

— So what are we going to do, ma?

— I'm going to raise my grandson. You're going to go back to New York.

— But how can you possibly manage? You're working, and the baby is going to need so much—your time, your energy—and expenses …

— I know, I've been thinking about it, that's all I do is think about it. I will manage. Look, Jayce, you're my only living child now. You MUST finish your degree so you can get work that will be good for your soul. No crappy jobs like I have. You already got a crib for the baby. There are enough diapers, and Doreen gave me a bunch of nappy pins she doesn't need anymore. When the baby's ready to come home from the hospital I'll ask them for some formula to get us started. Even though his lip is deformed he's been able to suck out of a bottle okay.

— But ma …

— Listen to me, Jayce. You're going to fulfill your purpose, just like before. You are NOT going to stop your life, like you did when you got drafted. Your sister would want you to get on with your plans. Think about that. When you finish school in three years you will get a good job. Then, and only then, will you help me a little if you are able. Make a promise. You will continue to work hard in school. You will graduate. You will get a job that holds meaning for you. You'll come visit when you are able and be a good uncle to the baby because you've carried out your dream and are full and complete inside. This is important, Jayce. Promise me now.

— Okay, ma … I promise to do those things, as long as you promise to tell me if you need me, and if you change your mind …

— Okay, but I won't change my mind—it is done.

My mother has never been particularly affectionate but is warm nonetheless, as long as she knows you and trusts you. I took her hand and held it for a while. She eventually squeezed mine back. I stood and cleared the mugs and plates from the table, worried about all that was pressing on her and how she'll manage. And I prayed for my sweet sister, who has flown away with the other graceful little birds.

3. A CASE OF INTRIGUE

Somewhere, something incredible is waiting to be known. —Carl Sagan

RIVKA Monday, July 21, 1975 Western Massachusetts

- **Morning, Jean.**

- **Morning. Good weekend?**

- **Not bad. Slept in on Saturday, did a ten hour shift yesterday at the group home. Do we have a slew of new cases since Friday?**

- **Yes, a couple of frequent flyers and a bunch of new people in Geri and Med-Surg. But I've prioritized a home visit that needs to happen ASAP.**

She handed me the intake-sheet, which contains basic information obtained upon admission or shortly thereafter and is what we use as a reference to get started on a new case.

Patient name: **BABY BOY KING** dob: **7/11/75**
Physician: **Lambert**

- **Preemie?**

- **Yes, thirty-four weeks.**

Late preterm, not too bad. I glanced at the intake-sheet. **5 lbs 7 oz** at birth. Jean continued …

— Cleft lip, unilateral complete. Palate is okay but he'll need the surgery. The big piece of this is that mom died right after the birth.

— Oh my god. C-section?

— No, Lambert wasn't able to because mom came in fully dilated with close contractions. Evidently she didn't take care of herself during the pregnancy, she was a teenager. No known pre-natal visits. She delivered about an hour after she got here.

— Okay. Baby's father in the picture?

— Not that we know of. Default caretaker is the maternal grandmother.

— Do we know if Lambert spoke to her at all about surgery?

— My understanding is that he mentioned it the day after birth, but didn't push it given that she had just lost her daughter.

— Yeah, I get it, but is there some reason he didn't call us in before discharge? Did he forget?

— Probably. The baby was here until Friday night, the eighteenth. It was Linda who made the referral to us this morning.

Kudos to his on-the-ball nurse. I glanced down again.

— No pediatrician on record.

— Right. So your mission, should you choose to accept it, is to go talk to the grandmother and see if you can get her on board for the surgery.

— **Shriner's, right? Looks like there's no insurance either. I'll bring a Medicaid application.**

— **Good idea.**

— **No phone number listed, so I'll just go. You'll be okay here until I return?**

— **I'll have to be. Don't worry about it, I'll see you later. We can only do what we can do.**

Right. I gathered some documents, a legal pad to take notes, and a fresh file folder, and stuffed everything into my large cross-body bag, which I use as a combo pocketbook-briefcase. When I got back out to the parking lot the sky was darkening, thick clouds rolling in quickly. I was wearing one of my usual summer work outfits: a plain T-shirt over a long, loose skirt, and a thin cotton overshirt to help shield me from the dreadful air-conditioning of some indoor buildings. Canvas sneakers. I scanned the parking lot and jogged over to my car while the rain began in large, intermittent drops. Reaching for my umbrella from the floor behind the driver's seat so it would be handy in the front when I'd need it, I remembered that the metal ribs were broken—useless. I drove out and headed toward Florence, a subdivision of Northampton. Two minutes in and a heavy downpour ensued. My windshield wipers function at one speed: slow, and it was difficult to see more than a few yards ahead. I didn't know exactly how to get to this woman's place, but was somewhat familiar with the main roads.

I had seen on the intake-sheet that the grandmother's name was **Nina King**, and **Amer.Ind.** had been typed into the 'Race' box on the form. I was aware of how poorly Native Americans have been treated by the white Europeans who came to this country and took over. Terrible killings, their land stolen from them (their home!), loss of their languages, their culture and traditions. Forced assimilation into white culture. Generations of indigenous children taken away from their parents and placed with white foster parents, some of whom abused these poor kids, who couldn't possibly understand why they weren't living with their loving, natural families. And many forced into government and church-run boarding schools, where most barely survived the horrid conditions. Thousands of those children died of mistreatment and neglect. There is no rational explanation for all of the unnecessary cruelty in this world, yet here it is. So while I don't know the history of this particular family, I'm anticipating some possible reluctance on the part of the grandmother to engage with me. I wouldn't blame her one iota. And her daughter just died—I can't even begin to imagine what she's going through.

I circled back around to West Elm but couldn't find the side street I was looking for. I couldn't even see the road signs through the lashing rain. I pulled into a gas station on the next block, and proceeded to get drenched during the five second sprint to the cashier's office. There was no one behind the counter, but I managed to get directions from a gentleman who was standing around waiting to pay. I was only about three blocks from my destination. I sure hoped that Mrs. King was at home.

A few minutes later I found the apartment and parked out front. It was part of a complex of one-level units, about sixty in all, arranged in groups of five. I was pretty sure some of these were Section 8s. The assistance program launched last year and has quickly become an excellent alternative to public housing. It's beneficial to low-income renters and landlords alike. Well, except for slumlords, who can't deal with the regular safety inspections. I dashed over to the front door. There were neat piles of old wooden slats on the ground next to the entrance, perhaps from a porch that used to exist along the front? Currently there was no covering. I knocked a couple of times, getting wetter by the second. No answer. I resorted to a stronger knock and yelled out her name, which I don't normally do out of respect for people's privacy amidst sometimes-nosy neighbors.

– Mrs. King?!?

The door finally opened a bit and a petite middle-aged woman with long black hair glared at me. She was a tad shorter than my five-foot-five bony frame. Wearing light cords and a simple dark-green tunic, she gave me what my Bubbe would have called The Evil Eye. Well, not outright hostile, but extremely wary.

- **Hi. I'm Rivka Solomon. From Hampshire Memorial? Dr. Lambert sent me—he wanted me to talk to you about getting the cleft repair surgery for the baby.**

- **He doesn't need surgery. He's taking to the bottle just fine.**

- **Yes, but there are other complications, and I'd like to discuss it all with you. Please, Mrs. King. I'm not here to do any harm, I just want to talk with you. Inside, if possible? It's pretty wet out here. And I don't want to keep shouting over the rain.**

She slowly opened the door wider; I crossed over the threshold and stepped inside. A large, gold nubby cloth armchair was to my left and Mrs. King nodded for me to sit while she shut the door. Progress. My hair was plastered to my face and the soggy sneakers chilled my feet. She left the room for what I assumed was just a moment, perhaps to check on the baby, who must be somewhere in the back. I unwound the bag from my torso and placed it on the brownish carpet.

I took stock of my surroundings. The living room extended from the front door to a large cased opening leading to a small kitchen, most of which I could see: all the usual appliances plus a small table with three mismatched chairs over khaki linoleum flooring. There must be a bathroom and at least one bedroom beyond that. The furniture was old and shabby, not unlike much of my own. A gold couch ran the length of the side wall to my left. A large, generic lamp filled most of the square side table's surface. A carved wooden sculpture of a fox sitting atop a tree stump was positioned in front of it. The little fox radiated a warm forcefield of energy and dispatched a gentle, slow-swirling mist in my direction.

I resumed the scan. Behind me a window faced the street, and a low rectangular table filled the space in front of the couch. The white walls were barren except for a colorful tapestry centered above the couch. I wanted to get a closer look but it's not right to snoop around without permission. Part of my job is to conduct a needs assessment, but not get distracted by interesting decor or a magical fox. Everything overall was sparse and clean. Mrs. King returned, handed me a towel, and sat down on the couch. I dried my face, squeezed some of the wet out of my hair, and placed the open towel across my lap, figuring it might absorb some of the moisture from my skirt.

— **Thank you. I know this is a difficult time, and I appreciate you letting me talk with you. I'm very sorry for your loss, Mrs. King … that must have come as quite a shock—did your daughter have a difficult pregnancy?**

– Yes.

No details. Blood from a stone.

– Have you named the baby yet?

– David. His name is David.

– That's a good name, a strong name.

I wanted to meet the baby, but that would have to wait until she was more comfortable with me, if that were ever to happen.

– Okay, so here's the thing. It's great that David is able to drink from the bottle right now. But as he grows, he's most likely going to have difficulty eating solid food. The shape of his mouth will prevent him from eating properly and getting the nutrients he needs. It's fortunate that it's only his lip and not the palate that's affected. But still, the surgery will easily correct it and will curtail potential problems down the road. Aside from eating issues, kids with this condition are also more susceptible to ear and speech problems if they don't get the surgery.

I paused for a moment so that she could take it all in. I didn't want to overwhelm her any more than she probably already was.

– I don't think I want him to go through surgery. They would have to put him to sleep?

– Yes, but they tailor the type and amount of anesthesia to the baby's size and weight and the kind of surgery he's having, so it's precise. Shriner's Hospital will do it at no cost to you, Mrs. King. They do these cleft surgeries all the time, the doctors over there are very skillful ...

I reached into my bag for the pamphlet with the before-and-after pictures and passed it to her.

— **They need to do it when the baby is about sixteen weeks old to ensure the best results. They used to do it at the twenty-four-month mark but now they prefer to do it sooner. If you wait until he's older, when he's starting to have problems … well that makes the surgery more complicated. Also, when David reaches school-age he may experience bullying from classmates. Look. The surgery takes about two hours. He would stay over at Shriner's one or two nights, then you would take him back home. It will take about three weeks for the incisions to heal, then the stitches are removed. I know this is a lot to absorb right now, but it's obviously important enough for Dr. Lambert to send me here. If you're agreeable, I can get this scheduled for late October/early November.**

She seemed to be mulling this over. I'm glad I remembered to bring the photos, which she's been perusing. My clothing was still wet but I wasn't as chilled as I had been. In any case, I needed to be patient.

— **Even if I agree, I don't have a car to bring him to Springfield.**

— **Well, don't worry about that right now. I can get this scheduled, and then if you can't find a ride I'd be happy to drive you and David myself.**

— **You can do that?**

— **Sure. I'm here to help you sort things out, Mrs. King.**

— Ah. Well … I guess it's okay then. I can stay with him at Shriner's?

— Of course. I mean they won't let you in the operating suite, but they'll expect you to be nearby, just like you were for the eight days he was in the NICU. This will be a lot quicker. He'll be in good hands. And we can ask them to set up a cot for you in his room for the overnight.

A couple of moments passed. She looked at the photos again.

— Okay … okay.

— Okay, great. Now a couple of other things. We need to get Medicaid for David so he'll have coverage for his medical visits. And we need to get him set up with a pediatrician for his regular outpatient check-ups, which should begin as soon as possible. I'm not officially allowed to recommend a particular doctor, but we can go through the list together and I'll tell you what I know, and we'll sort out where they're located and narrow it down to two or three. Then when I get back to the hospital I can make some calls and see who's taking on new Medicaid patients and so forth.

— That would be helpful.

We moved into the kitchen and spent the next hour at the table completing the Medicaid application and related paperwork. I apologized several times for asking the many intrusive questions necessary to get through the process. I learned that David's mother's name was Chilali. That she got pregnant when she was fifteen, when the family lived in

Bridgeport. '**Terrible schools there.**' They moved to this area just a few months ago, I suspect when Chilali started showing. I asked about the father of the baby and Mrs. King shut me down immediately. I explained that I was asking not only for the Medicaid but also to find out if there was a possibility he might someday come out of the woodwork and try to make a claim for David. Mrs. King assured me that was never going to happen. Okay then. A thorny story was probably tangled up in there, but today was not the day I'd be hearing it.

I learned that Mrs. King's husband became (understandably) unglued about his daughter's pregnancy, that '**he couldn't hold on**', and that he moved here with the family from Connecticut but spent more and more time away from them to the point where he doesn't come around anymore. Mrs. King thinks he's turned to drink to drown his sorrows. She doesn't know where he's been staying, probably with someone from work. They have a grown son, about my age, who lives in upstate New York, and '**is a good young man, unusually smart and of strong character.**' I asked about extended family; there is no one she's in touch with anymore and definitely no one nearby. I wondered how Mrs. King was going to manage raising the baby. She told me about her two part-time jobs, one at a local laundromat and the other at a small mom-and-pop grocery store, also within walking distance. Both employers know about her situation and each gave her some unpaid time off and would try to be flexible with her hours in the future, but she would still be expected to show up regularly. I would look into daycare options; hopefully there was a program nearby. Oy gevalt—this was going to be a rough road ahead for her.

Mrs. King gave me her neighbor Doreen's phone number in case I needed to get a message through. I in turn explained how she could have me paged at the hospital.

The baby started making noises as he woke up; Mrs. King rose and went to him. I remained seated in case my presence back there was unwanted; I didn't want to push it. After a couple of minutes of cooing and calming sounds, Mrs. King walked in with David in her arms and began doing something at the sink.

— **I used to babysit infants a lot when I was a teenager, can I help with anything? Would you like me to get the bottle ready?**

— **Is your shirt dry now?**

— **Yes.**

— **You take the baby, I'll do the bottle.**

I stood up slowly, and as she transferred David to me I saw the prominent cleft that formed at the left side of his upper lip and extended to the base of his nostrils. I was happy to hold this sweet baby, just ten days old. He had a full head of dark-brown hair and smelled like baby powder; Mrs. King must have changed his diaper. I gently patted his bare back while murmuring softly, his warm, pliant body melting into my chest and neck. I stayed close so Mrs. King would know he was safe. The baby felt small and was still a little sleepy.

— **Did they tell you his weight when he was discharged on Friday night?**

— **Just over six pounds.**

– **That's good. I'll make those pediatrician calls, and when you start going they'll weigh him at each visit.**

– **Yes, that's what they did at the Indian Health Service clinic when my kids were little. Not the same doctor, though, my kids were born seven years apart.**

Mrs. King now had the bottle ready and was watching me and David.

– **He's grabbing onto your curls.**

– **Aww … I'm glad someone doesn't mind the crazy hair.**

She gave me a soft smile. I was already smiling, content to hold the baby.

The storm had cleared by the time I left to head back to the hospital. Our office was temporarily housed in a double-wide trailer, along with the Medical Records staff. 'Temporarily' meaning for the last twelve years and counting, according to Jean. The trailer was connected to the main building with a ramp, a short version of the kind they have at airport terminals to board the plane. Social Services existed to support patients and families; we didn't generate any income for the hospital and therefore were treated as peons by the administrators. The nurses and most of the physicians appreciated us, so that's something.

I'm not a breakfast person, and missed the cafeteria lunch break while out at the home visit, so I wolfed down a couple of Fig Newtons from the emergency stash in my desk drawer, while simultaneously picking off the dead leaves of Jean's philodendron. I scribbled a quick note letting her know

I was back, in case I didn't run into her soon upstairs. It was getting close to two, so I picked up the intake-sheets that Jean had left for me and headed to the elevators. I would take care of the surgery appointment and the pediatrician search tomorrow morning. I'd get the Medicaid packet ready before leaving work tonight, so that it could go out in tomorrow's mail. I was filled with relief that Mrs. King was agreeable to the medical treatment for her grandson. And that she trusted me enough to hold him. I said a little prayer for both of them: Yivarechecha adonai v'yishmerecha. May god bless you and protect you.

4. AN INFORMATIVE LESSON

When the father's generation eats salt, the child's generation thirsts for water. —Vietnamese Proverb

HENRY Saturday, June 25, 2005 Western Massachusetts

I've spent most of the day trying to organize my thoughts, and my belongings. I don't own much, but since I don't have a vehicle I'd have to ask Toni and Heather if I can leave some things here with them for now. I had moved to New York City with my family when I was eleven, and there was no need for a car. Ample public transportation throughout the five boroughs, an appalling lack of parking spaces, and inconvenient and expensive garages made it impractical to own a vehicle. Plus the fact that the idea of learning to drive makes me nervous. That was quite a while back though, and I've been living in small towns and suburbs of Massachusetts. If I can overcome my fears and get a driver's license and vehicle, that would greatly help my fledgling business. But first things first.

- **Hey Henry, how's it going?**

- **Good—I have some news for you guys. But I don't want to interrupt your conversation.**

— No, it's okay, we'll finish later. Is it good news?

— Uh … well I think so, but not sure yet. My caseworker at the hospital told me yesterday about an animal farm that needs live-in volunteers, and she thinks it'll be good for me, because she knows I've been kind of depressed, so I'm going to give it a try. I have to report there on Monday morning.

— Wow, that's exciting. What's the name of the place?

— I've got the pamphlet here … King Solomon Sanctuary.

— Oh, I've heard good things about them. They involve the community with some of their projects. I think they have alpacas.

— What's an alpaca?

— It's like a mini-llama, in the camel family. This is big news, Henry. We'll miss you, but I'm excited for you. It'll be a new adventure.

Heather and Toni have been a couple for ten years, and although they're certainly distinct women, they often speak as one. I find it both bewildering and amusing that they're so in tune with each other that they can finish each other's sentences. Toni and I know each other from UMass Amherst; we started as freshmen in the early nineties. Heather went to Smith but took some classes at our school; they met and fell in love.

— I want to thank you both for letting me crash in your den all these months—it's been a big help.

— You're welcome, Henry, you've been an easy housemate. You pick up after yourself, and you've contributed to the rent, you're quiet, it's been our pleasure. And we expect you to keep us informed about your new goings on.

— Okay, I will. Hey, what were you guys talking about when I walked in?

— Oh yeah. Remember Ms. Lipski from Euro Lit?

— Yeah, nice lady. I liked that class.

— Me too. Well a few days ago I was in the cafeteria, because I'm taking that Women's Studies summer class. She was eating lunch with another professor, I think the Art Department director, the one with all those colorful batik outfits and bangles? So I asked if I could join them, and they said yes. They were talking about this thing called epigenetics.

— Epigenetics? I don't think I've ever heard of that.

— I hadn't either. So, well let me back up a bit. Did you know that both of Ms. Lipski's parents were Holocaust survivors?

Lord, have mercy.

— I didn't know that. Go on.

I'd been standing but now joined them at the table.

— Okay. So you know how there's individual/personal trauma, and then there's collective/historical trauma, like the Holocaust, and other genocides, like the Armenians, and Native Americans and other indigenous groups? And systemic racism, slavery, all that stuff. And people who have lived through a famine, or extreme poverty.

– Yes. Go on.

– So epigenetics is a relatively new field. There are a bunch of studies starting to come out now that track how trauma affects the genes of the next generation, and the generation after that. It's incredible. They're finding that trauma survivors, whether it's personal or collective, produce less cortisol in their body, but also have lower levels of the enzyme that breaks down the cortisol, probably to compensate so that the internal organs can survive. And when a woman is carrying a fetus, even if it was only the father who experienced some sort of trauma, the placenta develops higher than normal levels of the enzyme, as if to biologically prepare the child for the same traumatic conditions that the mother and/or father endured. But in reality those children end up with a higher risk for PTSD and metabolic issues than people who don't have parents that are trauma victims. There's this whole DNA thing, this theory of epigenetic inheritance. The DNA codes themselves don't change, but they express themselves differently, creating this transgenerational trauma. It had been widely believed that stress-related stuff could not be passed on through DNA, but they're finding out now that it can. They used to think that the children of Holocaust survivors, for example, had their specific set of issues caused only by environmental factors, like how their parents raised them, or talked about what they experienced, or didn't talk about those experiences, which is usually the case. But now there's evidence that there's also this genetic transmission, and they're trying to understand exactly how it happens. The trauma experienced by one or both parents doesn't cause the DNA to mutate, but it does leave a chemical mark and changes the way the genes convert into functioning proteins, and that gets passed on in utero. Interesting, huh? The research is new and therefore controversial, but I'll bet a lot more studies will get done over the next few years and we'll know more.

– Wow. Thank you for explaining all this, Toni. Lots to think about.

– Yeah.

Lots and lots to think about as I get ready for what will probably be the next phase of my life.

5. A HOLDING PATTERN

We can do no great things; only small things with great love.
—Mother Teresa Bojaxhiu

RIVKA Thursday, October 30, 1975 Western Massachusetts

It was crisp and sunny on the day of David's scheduled surgery, hopefully a good omen. I wore a turtleneck over jeans, a wool jacket I found at Goodwill last fall for a dollar, and dark sunglasses, because my eyes have always been acutely sensitive to light. I crave the warmth of the sun but am blinded by its blaze.

After a cracker-cheese-apple dinner last night, I grabbed my small stash of nickels and walked to the phone booth down the street from my apartment building. I left a message with Doreen, Mrs. King's neighbor-friend, to please remind her that I'd be picking them up at seven-fifteen in the morning. Doreen had told me a couple of weeks ago that she wouldn't be available to drive them.

I was a bit worried that Mrs. King might back out. I haven't seen her in three months but did speak with her a couple of times on Doreen's phone regarding the Medicaid (processed quickly at my request—thank god for small favors) and the new pediatrician. Hopefully she'll have the baby ready when I get there. It was going to be a long day for her, even if everything goes without a hitch.

She walked out with David as soon as I pulled up. The entire front facade had been rebuilt, providing not only a cover over the entryways but also a good- sized porch beside each entrance. Fresh white paint. Mrs. King carried her grandson down the four steps to the pathway. He wore a thick, navy sweater, which I later learned she had hand-knitted for him.

- **Morning! Oh my gosh, he's gotten so big! How are you, sweetheart?**

- **Yeah, he's been guzzling that formula down like there's no tomorrow. Thirteen pounds now.**

- **Fantastic! Okay, you'll have to hold him on your lap in the front, there are no working seat belts in the back.**

I drive a 1970 grey Toyota Corolla, which I bought used last year. It's relatively safe, decent on gas, and the heater usually works. I held my arms out for David while Mrs. King got herself buckled into the passenger seat, then placed him on her lap. He was alert and seemed curious about this new experience. Somebody ought to invent some sort of safety apparatus for transporting infants in cars. They started making booster seats for toddlers, but there's nothing for babies. I sprinted around to the driver's side, buckled up, and started the engine. Our appointment was for eight and I wanted to arrive early if possible.

- **I noticed the landlord got the front all fixed up.**

- **Yes, the porch is even nicer than it had been before they tore it down.**

— Good. I've always liked porches, never had one growing up. You got the food stamps and childcare vouchers in the mail, right?

— Yes, thank you. I went to Color Wheel Daycare and they're going to start taking him for the three days a week I work at the store. The laundromat lets me bring him with me.

— Okay, good. How far is the daycare center from your place?

— Only half a mile, and Jayce took me shopping for a stroller when he was here last month. It's lightweight and has a cover for when it rains.

— Like a little awning?

We both giggled, amused by modern versions of old devices. She told me about the bulky wicker carriage and wooden cradleboard her mother had used for her when she was little. We were more than halfway to Shriner's, and I was thankful we could converse easily rather than both of us outwardly worried about the upcoming surgery. David looked over at me and seemed content.

— May I ask you something?

— Of course.

— Where does the name Rivka come from?

— It's Hebrew—she was one of the matriarchs in biblical times. The name means 'connection, to join'. The mystical interpretation means 'captivating and transformative'.

— You're Jewish.

— Yes, 100 percent. The eyes and hair come from my father's side. They're mostly Turkish and Spanish, with some Polish and Lithuanian mixed in. My small, round nose is from my mother's side, they're mostly Russian as far as we know.

— So many places. The name suits you well.

— Thank you, Mrs. King.

— The hospital lets you drive patients to appointments like this?

— Well, not technically, because there could potentially be liability issues if I were on duty. But my supervisor is letting me use a vacation day, so it's fine.

She frowned and seemed a little upset. I didn't tell her that I was also working weekends at a group home for 'emotionally disturbed' violent teenagers. While I could have used a real day off, I wanted to make sure the baby got the operation and to provide whatever support I could to Mrs. King, who has had more on her plate than anyone should ever have. And she's probably terrified about the surgery.

— Please … it's not a problem at all—really, it's fine. Okay, we're here. I'm coming in with you, so let's see if we can find a space not too far from the south entrance—that's where they said to go.

She pointed to a **Patient Parking** sign in the distance and I pulled in. Excellent. David was wide awake and gazing alternately at me and his grandmother. She was teaching him to call her Nana, so I reinforced that when I spoke to him.

— Okay bubbeleh, I'm going to hold you while Nana gets out of the car. Mrs. King, he's so much heavier. What a sweetie you are.

He patted my shoulder and gave a barely perceptible cleft-version of a smile. The surgery will fix that. We walked up to the entrance and I transferred David to her before opening the door for them. I had her take the lead in getting him registered, and she remembered to ask for a cot for herself for the overnight(s). The receptionist said they provide that automatically, so that was reassuring. We were directed to sit in the waiting area, which was situated off the main lobby, until the nurse came to take the baby. Mrs. King removed his sweater and then debated about changing his diaper, as it was possibly a little wet. I told her not to bother, the hospital staff would take care of it; they were certainly used to babies peeing in their diaper. She made an effort to smile but was clearly getting anxious now that we were actually here. There was a young bleary-eyed couple sitting on the far side holding hands, and an older, dapper gentleman pacing back and forth who seemed nervous enough for all of us put together.

— I know it's scary, especially because he's so small. They're fantastic here, tons of experience with this kind of surgery, he'll be in good hands.

She nodded slowly, and just then a nurse in a starchy white uniform and one of those funny little hats walked over to us. She confirmed the baby was David King, and explained that they would be prepping him for surgery, that it would take about two or three hours in all, and then Dr. Carmel would come out and talk to us. Mrs. King gave the baby a kiss on his forehead and gingerly handed him over. Oy—now it would be a waiting game. The man had stopped pacing and was sitting near us, offering a reassuring smile to Mrs. King. She ignored him.

- **I'm going to look for the cafeteria and see if they have any hot tea. Would you like to come with?**

- **No, someone has to be here when the doctor comes.**

- **Mrs. King, that won't be for at least another couple of hours.**

She sighed and gave me one of those glares. Okay then.

- **How do you like your coffee?**

I remember having seen a coffee maker on her kitchen counter when I was there over the summer.

- **Black, a little sugar, but don't bother, I'm okay for now.**

I gave her a raised eyebrow-slight head tilt; she replied with a half-smile in spite of herself and extended a subtle 'go ahead, you're dismissed' hand gesture. Tough woman, some softness inside if she lets you in. I was liking her more and more by the minute.

After a brief stop in the restroom and a somewhat lengthy visit to the cafeteria to browse the offerings, I returned with some tepid tea for myself, and a hot coffee and sugar packets for Mrs. King. She fixed it up and drank slowly and appreciatively. The guy sitting near her was chatting away about his granddaughter, who evidently was being treated for burns on her arm caused by some sort of explosion in her science class a few days ago. Mrs. King nodded from time to time but wasn't

in the mood to reciprocate. Nevertheless, perhaps it was comforting for her to know that there were other families here, also
filled with worry about their loved ones.

— **They have eggs and waffles and stuff until nine.
   If you want to go I can stay here in case there's
   any news.**

— **No, I'm fine. Thank you for the coffee.**

— **You're welcome.**

I had brought a book with me: *Five Smooth Stones*, an interesting
novel by Ann Fairbairn, who used to be a tour manager for a
jazz musician and his band. The story is about a mixed-race
couple in the backdrop of the civil rights movement, which we
had just lived through. What a fucking mess things have been
in this country. I fished it out of my bag to give Mrs. King
some space. I'm a fast reader and figured I'd get through a few
more chapters while we waited. Mrs. King seemed fine leafing
through some magazines that were lying around and pretending she wasn't listening to the nice guy talking about his family
and the restaurant business he owns. He was taking a shine to
her, even though I'm pretty sure she hasn't spoken more than
two words to him.

— **King family?**

It was ten-thirty and Dr. Carmel had come to speak with us.
We raised our hands like schoolchildren and sprung out of our
seats. He reported that the surgery had gone well, there were
no complications, and David would be in post-op for about an
hour. Then he'd be transferred to a regular room where Mrs.
King could see him after checking in at the nurse's station. We
thanked him and breathed a sigh of relief. I asked Mrs. King

if it would be okay if I left now, and she said yes, she never expected me to stay this long, she never expected me to stay at all. I advised that she check with the nurses if she had any questions or concerns during the afternoon or overnight, and to get the stitch-removal scheduled before leaving the hospital. She nodded and told me that Doreen would be able to get them back home when the baby is discharged, whether that would be tomorrow or Saturday.

— **Okay, Mrs. King, let me know if you need anything.**

— **Thank you, Rivka. You've helped us a lot … you of the 'joining' and 'transformation'. And it's Nina. You can call me Nina.**

— **Nina. Okay. I'll be in touch.**

Okay then. Nina King, a woman to be reckoned with. And David, sweet boy. Refuah shle'mah. May you make a full recovery.

6. A REFUGE

Everything new must have its roots in what was before.
—Sigmund Freud

HENRY Monday, June 27, 2005 Western Massachusetts

It was nine-thirty in the morning, fairly warm with a light rain. I didn't know what to expect as I rode my bicycle toward the animal sanctuary with my duffel strapped to my back, helmet on my head, and a thin windbreaker that wasn't doing a great job of keeping me dry. My mother had ordered the green jacket from L.L.Bean and had it sent to me after she moved back to Louisiana; my initials were near the bottom zipper stop. I got an early start because I wasn't sure how long it would take me. That's what I tell myself, anyway; I'm always early for appointments. Toni and Heather were fine about letting me store some of my belongings with them until I had a better idea what I'd be doing over the next few months. It was a large suitcase and a couple of boxes that were left back at their place.

Anxiety tends to grip me in new situations. It wasn't always like that, but the last few years have been tough. I turned right at the large wooden **King Solomon Sanctuary** sign and started up the unpaved road. It was just wide enough for two vehicles to pass each other with lots of untamed brush and weeds on both sides. The bike tires started getting stuck in the dirt, which was turning to mud. I dismounted and began climbing the slightly inclined path, not yet able to see any buildings up ahead. When I heard a vehicle approaching from behind I turned to see an old, dark-blue pickup. The driver pulled up next to me and lowered the passenger window.

— **Dude! You going up to the farm?**

— **Uh … yes?**

— **Let's load your bike into the back and I'll take you the rest of the way.**

The driver got out and opened the tailgate latch. He helped me get the bike in quickly and shut the latch. Smiling brightly, he seemed to have an abundance of energy. He was medium height, shorter than me, thin and fit, about my age. His skin was golden, like the blossom honey Toni uses for baking her fancy Greek desserts. He wore blue jeans, a thin button-down plaid flannel open over a crisp white T-shirt, and brown sneaker-boots, a newer version of the pair I packed last night.

— **Hop in!**

As soon as we were seated he put the truck in gear and we continued up the road. A bunch of overflowing Trader Joe's paper grocery bags filled the space behind our seats in the cab. I removed my helmet and clipped it to the duffel. He offered his hand to shake.

— **David.**

— **Henry.**

— **Good to meet you. You're the new volunteer?**

— **Uh, yes. I've never worked on a farm … or with any animals.**

— **Dude. It'll be fine. First time for everything, right?**

— **Right.**

— **Okay, I'll drop you off at the front entrance, I need to go around the side and get this food to Peter. Go check in with Suzy, she'll tell you what's what. Don't worry about your bike, I'll take care of it. See you later, Henry.**

— **Okay, thank you, see you later.**

It had taken a couple of minutes to get here once he picked me up; the dirt drive must have been at least half a mile and I was grateful for the lift. I exited the truck with my duffel and walked to the wide covered area in front of the entrance. Two low wooden steps led up to a large door, or you could use the cement ramp off to the right. On the other side was a bike rack—nice. Everything looked fairly new. The exterior had the appearance of a log cabin. A couple of buggies sat off to the side. I don't think there's a golf course here but what do I know? The building looked like a smaller version of that spacious upscale lodge-like rest stop off of Interstate 91 when you cross into Vermont. I stepped inside into a large room with an open-beamed vaulted ceiling, wide-plank wooden flooring, and some marvelous music coming from somewhere on the left—African drumming and singing? I didn't know what I had gotten myself into, but was starting to feel better already.

A long rectangular table sat parallel to the left wall, and a doorframe led to a back room (a kitchen?). A few small round tables with plastic chairs and a picnic table with benched seating filled the rest of the space. Some smaller rooms were off to the right; that must be the office area. I headed over to the sign on the open door that said **Suzy Sanchez, Office Manager** under the name, and a few feet beyond was another door with a sign that read **Rivka Solomon, Director.** That must be the lady I spoke with on the phone in Jean's office a few days ago. I knocked on Suzy's door and she motioned me in as she hung up the phone.

— **Hi, I'm Henry Carter.**

— **Good timing, Henry, just finished the supply orders. Have a seat, hon. Let me pull up your file—I'll need your signature on a couple of docs here. It's the standard stuff for all volunteers: no drugs, no craziness.**

— **Yes, ma'am.**

— **It's Suzy, we don't do formal here.**

— **Oh, okay … Suzy.**

— **I'll show you around in a few minutes, and then I'll bring you to your casita.**

— **Okay.**

— **So here are the basics. David's going to need your help with the animals. He has the other guys working on the fencing this month.**

— **I just met him on my way in here. I don't have any experience with animals though—**

— **No problem, David will teach you. So unless he tells you otherwise, you report to him at eight-thirty every morning after breakfast. You get six days off each calendar month, and you work out with David how you want to do that. The animals need care every day, so he'll need to know ahead**

of time if you're going to take a day off so he can pull someone else in to help, depending on what's going on, like if there's a new four-legged creature that needs a lot of one-on-one. They're like his babies.

She leaned in to whisper that last part and returned my smile.

— **Now, about food. For us humans, I mean. There are three buffet-style meals a day: breakfast from seven-thirty to eight-thirty, light continental style but you can cook up something hot for yourself if you want. Peter usually gets here around nine and starts prepping for lunch, which is from noon til one-thirty. Dinner's at six-thirty. You bring your tray up to a shelf near the kitchen when you're done. Rivka doesn't allow meat, but there are plenty of veggies and dairy, sometimes fish. Pete makes a mean lentil salad and tasty roasted potatoes, I must say. All the on-site work volunteers rotate kitchen duty, so we'll get you on the roster. There are six of you, so every six days you help Yusef clean up after the lunch and dinner for that day. Yusef is here four days a week, he tends to the vegetable garden and helps Pete in the kitchen with the food prep and cleaning.**

— **Okay.**

— **Alright, leave your bag here for now and come with me.**

She stood up cautiously. Suzy is a white middle-aged woman with spiky dark hair, plump and on the short side. She had a slow gait and a bit of a limp.

— My knees are killing me. Had surgery last year on the right one. It's better but now the left one is bad. Hector's been trying to get me on the golf course and I keep telling him I don't want to stand around all day swinging metal sticks—not my idea of fun.

— Hector is your husband?

— Yeah. Together eleven years. Second marriage for both of us.

— Oh, that's nice. You mentioned golf—are those golf carts outside?

— Yes, the yellow one is mine, so don't touch it.

— Yes, ma'am. Suzy.

— The white one anyone can use. They're for if we need to get a message to someone who's out in the barn or the pastures, or to haul small equipment from one area to another. We've got about nine acres here, so it's not super-huge like a Montana ranch or anything, but it's big enough that it gets tiring for the guys if they have to schlep heavy buckets or tools back and forth on foot. And a waste of time. So the carts are fun but they also serve a practical purpose.

— Yes, I can see how they would save time and effort.

— David uses his pickup for some of the big hauls, like fencing. Okay, hon, here's the kitchen. Between Pete and Rivka they've probably got the entire Putamayo collection. I used to think the music was weird, but it's kind of grown on me.

— I think it's wonderful.

— **Well then you're going to fit in just fine. Pete! Turn that down for a minute and meet Henry.**

Peter was tall like me, fortyish, with thick, sandy-colored hair sticking out from under a ball cap worn backwards. A faded black-and-white checkered apron wrapped around his torso, and the tattoo on his upper right arm looked like an anchor and *ANG* …the rest was covered by the sleeve of his T-shirt. *ANGIE?* *ANGEL?* Or perhaps something else entirely.

— **It smells good in here.**

— **Fish stew today. And rice. David says you're going to help with the animals?**

— **Uh, yes, that's the plan.**

— **This place is a trip, man. In a good way. I was a volunteer myself when the farm first opened a couple of years ago, helped me get back on my feet, you know? Now I'm working as a chef here, paying it forward while getting paid. It's a good gig here, Henry.**

— **Thank you for the welcome. Good to meet you, Peter. And I like the music, by the way.**

Peter laughed, gave me a thumbs up as he swiveled around to ramp the volume back up and resume his cooking. I followed Suzy to David's office, on the same side of the building as the kitchen, in the far corner. The sign read **David King** with **Operations Manager** beneath it. The large room had dark wainscoting, and a pegboard on one wall with all sorts of tags and keys and small tools. A door led out to a wide porch and the fields, which I could see through the window. Horizontal shelving housed a long row of thick binders.

— **This serves as a mudroom as well as David's office. Nicole uses that other desk over there, she's the Outreach Coordinator. Most of the animal supplies are in the barn. This is where David keeps a book for each animal and records everything. Medical, behavioral, everything. If one of the donkeys lets out a sneeze, he writes it down. I swear he has more information on each of them than I ever had for my three kids combined.**

— **But that's good, right? He obviously cares about them.**

— **He sure does. I tease him because he's constantly having me order more plastic sleeves and paper for those books. Alright, so check here first in the mornings, if David's not here then go out to the barn.**

— **Okay.**

— **There are two restrooms behind here. Rivka and I have one on the other side just for us. And of course you'll have your own bathroom in your casita. But when you're working outside all day and smell like hay and animal poop, you'll want to wash your hands before lunch, so you come through here.**

— **Yes, of course.**

On the other side, beyond the two offices, was a small conference room. Inside were a few chairs surrounding a round table, and a sizable glass window facing the main interior space of the building. In the corner, directly across from David's office, was a cozy space with some bookshelves filled with paperbacks and hardcovers, a couch, and some comfy-looking mismatched upholstered chairs. A few metal folding chairs leaned against the wall. There was a window adjacent to the porch, the same porch that ran across the building behind David's office. A TV sat on top of an end table in one corner, a VCR/DVD player on the shelf beneath it, and a large colorful area rug covered most of the floor.

— **Rivka calls this the library-slash-den. The volunteers usually gather here after dinner and watch TV, or chat, or read, or all three. When Rivka's daughter is in town, they sometimes have Music Night.**

— **Music Night?**

— **Yes. She plays guitar and sings. Talented girl.**

— **Sounds delightful.**

— **It is. Okay, hon, my knees are getting worn out, let's get you over to your little place. Grab your bag from my office and we'll take my cart. Then you can get yourself back here for lunch.**

We walked out the front entrance, and as we boarded the buggy I noticed my bike parked in the rack; David's a man of his word, and he had even dried it off for me. The sky had cleared, the sun emerging. I felt simultaneously overwhelmed, exhilarated, and full of anticipation. I'm not sure how a person can feel all of this at once, but I did, and was pleased to be feeling *some*thing. We bopped along a hundred yards away from the main building toward a string of attached wood-framed units. Suzy pointed to another out-building close by and said it's where we can do our laundry. And a designated smoking shed on the other side. She also said that David lives on the premises in an RV at the far corner of the farm.

We stepped out of the buggy. Suzy unlocked the door to unit #2 and gave me the key. The room was about two hundred and fifty square feet, modest and clean. There was a single bed, all made up, a small dresser, and an extra blanket on a shelf in the closet. A decent full bathroom with soap and folded towels, and a kitchenette with a tiny sink and trash can. Cleaning supplies were in a plastic tub under the sink, and a mini-fridge sat on a wooden pallet. A window next to the door faced the fields. In the back was another window, small and horizontal, high above the bed. A large, vintage painting of horses by a meadow hung on the adjacent wall. It felt homey and simple. Suzy explained that I would have to purchase my own electric kettle if I wanted one, but I could get coffee or tea every morning at breakfast in the main building, which everyone calls the lodge. She said that all the volunteers are expected to clean up after themselves, it's not a hotel.

— **Of course, thank you, Suzy, for showing me around.**

— **You're welcome. Any questions?**

— **Um … I was wondering if it would be okay if I walk around the property after lunch, since I won't be starting work until tomorrow?**

— **Sure, hon. Just don't open any of the gates until you've been trained. David would have a FIT if any of those animals got loose.**

— **Okay, yes, of course.**

— **Alright, I'm going back now for lunch, see you there. Rivka should be returning from her meetings soon so you'll probably meet her a little later.**

— **Okay, great, thank you.**

I was alone now in the room, my new home. I opened my duffel and transferred the small pile of clothes to the top of the dresser. I brought my toiletry kit to the bathroom, set it down behind the sink faucet, and removed the bandage from my left hand. After washing up I taped a new one on. The problems with my injury were dissipating, or at least the time and energy I'd been expending on them seemed wasteful to me in this moment. It was a new day, a good day.

The lunch selection was a pleasant surprise. Then again, everything's been a pleasant surprise since I made that turn at the sanctuary sign a couple of hours ago. There was the fish stew and rice, a green salad, a hot bean dish, some good quality bread, butter, and cheese. And homemade fruit pie for dessert. There were bottles of ginger ale, seltzer, and regular water with lemon slices in a large carafe to choose from. Everything looked and smelled fantastic. Peter's music was emanating at a low volume from the kitchen.

I sat down with my food and drink at one of the small tables and was immediately joined by a couple of men in their forties who were also in the Volunteer Work Program. One of them told me he had served a year in prison for a check-fraud scheme he'd been involved in. He was getting close to his six-month 'graduation' from the farm and planned to get a job with a construction crew in the Westfield area putting up drywall.

— I know drywall, man. And now I know how to install fencing—wood fencing, metal fencing, post-and-rail—I can do all that now! Skills, man, that's what I need, makes it easy to keep my nose clean and out of jail. They've been real nice to me here, that's for damn sure. They even gave me a reference for the court and for the Westfield boss to say I showed up for work on time every day here and did my job.

The other guy was mostly quiet but did say that David has him help out with the animals sometimes and that he enjoys it, especially the alpacas. He told me that when they got a new alpaca a couple of months ago she was '**practically starving to death**', and he had to bottle-feed her. Her name is Rose and he visits her most days when their fencing work is finished, before he goes to his casita to shower for supper. I was filled with curiosity as I took it all in.

Peter came over with his own meal and asked if I was enjoying the lunch. I told him it was delicious. He smiled approvingly and said that most of the vegetables are grown right here on the farm, all organic, and that over the rest of the summer there will be more to harvest. In addition to working here, he fixes cars on the side at his brother-in-law's shop. I told him about some landscaping jobs I've done and he said that it sounds like that's my forte. He was easy and fun to talk with.

The other tables were filled with people who I'm guessing were other volunteers or staff, and Suzy was at her own table eating lunch and reading a romance novel, if the cover was any indication. People acknowledged each other with friendly hand gestures or nods, and everyone looked relaxed and, well … downright cheerful.

A three-foot-high wall separated the entrance from the eating area, and extended around that corner a few feet, providing a sense of division and semi-privacy within the spacious main room. A woman about my mother's age, with dark curly hair and a large briefcase strapped over her shoulder, walked into the director's office. The briefcase must have been heavy, because she bent sideways to let it ease down slowly onto a chair. She immediately made a phone call with one hand while removing her jacket with the other. Within seconds of hanging up, David came out of his office and walked quickly across the large room into hers. They exchanged a few words, and did what looked like a happy- dance followed by a brief hug. I would find out a few days later that an important grant had come through for the sanctuary, which indeed was happy news.

I watched where the others brought their trays after eating and followed suit. It was a low ledge at a pass-through, with plastic bins for dirty silverware, glasses, and so forth and could be reached from the kitchen. When I turned back around, David was coming toward me with the woman I'd seen in the office.

— **Riv, this is Henry. Henry, this is our director, Rivka.**

— **So nice to meet you in person, ma'am.**

— **Rivka would be fine. Are you settling in okay?**

— **Yes, ma'am … Rivka. Suzy gave me a tour of the building, and this afternoon I was planning to walk around a little outside, if that's okay.**

— **Yes, go ahead and get the lay of the land. David and I are going to grab some lunch while there's still some food left. We're so glad you're here, we need as much help as we can get.**

— Thank you, glad to be here.

— Okay, we'll see you later.

I decided to go back to the casita first, to wash up and get my bearings. There was no phone that I could see, but would later learn that I could freely use the phone in David's office, or the conference room when it's vacant. I usually speak to my mother when she returns from church on Sundays, and I wanted to let her know where I was.

Looking out the window, in the far distance someone was leading a bunch of animals from the gargantuan rust-colored barn into the fields, two or three at a time. I was eager to get out there and see what was happening. I did a couple of hand stretches and made sure the bandage was still intact. My hand was still sore but I could probably start using a regular Band-Aid in a day or so.

The sun warmed my skin as I wandered over to a good-sized vegetable garden, edged by low chicken-wire fencing. The largest section was filled with beets, onions, spinach, several varieties of peppers and lettuce, cherry tomatoes, heirloom tomatoes, kale, broccoli, cucumbers, beans, and several rows of carrot tops. Squash and cabbage as well, not quite ready to harvest. Seedlings were breaking through the dirt in another section. Quite impressive. I knew from my grandmother's garden, when I was a kid in the south, that if the growing season was long enough you could do a second round of planting and harvesting for some things, like lettuce and peas and spinach.

Sunlight reflected off the metal barn roof. I approached and introduced myself, over the four-foot fence, to the woman handling the animals. She had light skin, large eyes, and ash-brown hair pulled into a loose topknot, probably in her mid-twenties.

— **Hi, I'm Nicole.**

— **Oh, you're the Outreach Coordinator, right?**

— **Yes. I normally work here on Wednesdays, but David asked if I could come in today because, after the grocery run, he spent the rest of the morning working with one of the horses, and now he's at the feed store. Someone has to be here at all times to make sure everyone's okay. Rivka helps out in emergencies, but she's usually busy with meetings and other vital director stuff, like funding, to keep this place going. The fencing and vet bills cost a fortune, let alone everything else. All the animals stayed inside the barn this morning because they don't like the rain. Well, except for the horses, they don't mind it much as long as it's not cold or muddy.**

I pointed at an apricot-colored horse in the big field.

— **That's Ginger, in horse-talk she's a chestnut. She's doing fine. Pretty, isn't she?**

— **Yes. And there's another horse here?**

— **Yes, a bay named Cody. He came to us about three weeks ago from a nearby farm when his previous owner died. Poor guy is having a hard time adjusting. He was well taken care of but hasn't eaten much since he arrived. David thinks he's depressed, and has been trying to** get him out and about. We have a covered, open-air corral on the far side of the barn over there, and David finally got him in there this morning and got him to do a few laps, actually a lot of laps, to kind of walk off some of the sad energy, and to stretch his legs. It was successful in that Cody ate well after that, more than he has been. He's resting in his stall now. So hopefully this morning was a turning point, but these things take time.

— Hmm … just like for humans?

— Just like for humans.

— I didn't mean to interrupt your work for so long, but I'm curious about all of these animals. David's going to start training me tomorrow.

— No problem. So the pasture I'm in now is the largest. It's the main area for the horses, goats, and donkeys to graze in decent weather. The alpacas get along with everyone but they have to have their own pasture over there, because they can't really defend themselves if someone starts playing rough, they're more delicate than these other guys. Also, it's better health-wise for them to be separate because they have different nutritional and medical needs. Right now we have five alpacas, two donkeys, seven goats, and the two horses. And on that side we have a couple of smaller pastures, which we use to safely introduce a new animal to the others—they can see and smell each other through the fencing, and get used to each other for a week or so before we let them mix in the same space. We also sometimes use those areas for temporary breathers to keep everyone safe. One of the goats wouldn't stop head-butting the others a few weeks ago—we got the tips of his horns shaved down an inch so they wouldn't be quite as pointy, and as you can see we're using the foam floaty-tubes in case he starts getting rambunctious again. And we have to keep an eye out that the horns don't get caught in the fencing.

— Oh my, so much to know about all these guys. And it sounds like they each have their own personality.

— You bet. David will teach you how to approach them. And it'll be good if you can learn their names as soon as possible. They all know their own name and will respond if you call them.

— How will I learn all their names?!

— The same way you learn new names in a work or school situation, it gets easier each day. Also, you can always look through the binders over at the lodge. There's a color photo of each animal on the first page.

— Oh! Okay, that's very helpful, thank you. And what are those structures out there?

— Well the animals need shelter options, even if it's a nice day. That large lean-to will protect from the western winds, and even the horses could fit in there if they wanted to. Or if it starts getting too hot or begins to rain, some of them will head over there until we can get them back in the barn. The structure over there with the ramp is mainly for the goats—they can use the bottom part as a shelter, but usually they just go up and down the ramp for fun because they're natural climbers and like to explore.

— But that ramp looks so steep!

— Oh, that's nothing. They hail from mountain areas. Some goats can actually climb trees, like in the argan fields of Morocco. We need to build another climbing structure for them, they only have that ramp and the big boulder at the far end of the pasture.

— Lordy, lordy, so many things I knew nothing about before. May I ask you one more question?

— Sure.

— I was wondering how you got involved with the farm?

— Oh, well I was in Vet Tech school with David. We stayed in touch after graduation, and when this place was getting set up he recruited me to help out part-time with the animals and to do community outreach. We started an educational program last year for local school groups. The kids come the first and third Wednesday of each month. Sometimes we're able to coordinate the timing with a non-urgent vet visit, so the vet can

explain what he or she is doing, and why. It's a learning experience for all of us.

— That's fantastic. Well, sorry to hold you up, Nicole, thank you for explaining all of this to me.

— No problem. Good to meet you, Henry—see you later.

I was almost dizzy with all of the new information and sensory experiences. And I only just arrived today! For years I've been trapped in a dull, gloomy fog … and now the world was in full color; I was Dorothy transported to *Oz*.

I continued strolling and waved to the guys I had met at lunch as I passed by. They were working on the perimeter fencing, digging holes for the large wooden posts, difficult work even with the proper tools. Piles of heavy cylindrical poles lay nearby, along with rolls and rolls of metal meshing. They were building the fencing up to seven feet, which I found out at supper would most likely keep out the bears, foxes, coyotes, and deer, but not the bobcats, who evidently can climb anything. There was really nothing that could be done about the occasional roaming bobcat.

A large red oak stood majestically near the back of the property, about an acre's distance from the barn. Some shade plants like hostas and ferns would look nice there, far enough out from the expanding roots of the oak but close enough to be under its canopy. It could extend to a large perennial garden into the sun, anchored by a large dogwood on the other side. I visualized a multitude of bushes and flowering plants, thinking how delightful they might look. So many possibilities. But I wasn't here to design a garden. I was here to work with the animals and whatever else they needed me to do.

After a pleasant supper, which included bits of conversation with the other volunteers, I headed over to David's office and acquainted myself with some of the animal names. Later, back in the casita, I set my watch alarm for seven, and dreamt of grazing horses, and masses upon masses of flowers.

7. ADAGIO

We bereaved are not alone. We belong to the largest company in all the world—the company of those who have known suffering.
—Helen Keller

RIVKA Wednesday, November 26, 1975
Western Massachusetts

- We were dispatched yesterday to the Holyoke side of the mountain road. Car crash—some middle-aged Indian guy. One vehicle, three trees. He was gone by the time we got there—most likely died on impact.

- That's probably a good thing.

- Yeah. The police were able to identify him. Turns out the guy's daughter died right here in the hospital a few months ago.

- Christ.

- I know. They had to close the road down for a few hours—y'know, for the tow guys to get the car out of there. It was sticking out too much for anyone to safely pass.

— They should've built that damn road wider to make room for a full shoulder on at least one side.

— Yeah.

Shit. It was late morning as I rode the elevator with two ambulance staff, both of whom I was familiar with from my work in the ER and the Geri unit. While they know who I am, I wish they'd keep these confidential conversations to themselves. Chances were close to 100 percent they were referring to Nina's estranged husband. I've been meaning to get in touch with her, to see how she and the baby are doing. David was no longer officially my patient or client, so this would be a social call. I didn't feel right divulging what I'd overheard, but then again it will be posted in the Hampshire Gazette within the next couple of days. In any case, there was no way I wasn't going to offer Nina my support. I had helped arrange for her to get a phone and service a couple of weeks after the cleft surgery. I still didn't have a home phone of my own, so I called from work and asked if I could come over this evening. Nina said yes and that six-thirty or so would be good.

I left work at five-forty and stopped at the grocery store to pick something up for her, I didn't know what. I settled on a small banana bread, the ones they bake in foil pans. I also purchased a colorful teething ring for David, figuring he'd need it soon if not already. After paying I was left with less than three dollars in my wallet and five dollars in my bank account, but my paychecks would be coming in a couple of days so it would be alright.

— Hello bubbeleh, look at you … such a big boy! Nina, his mouth looks great. Is he still drinking the formula okay?

— Oh yeah, even more diaper changes than before. The stitches were removed just two days ago.

— Such a precious boy you are! You're doing a lot of gurgling now, aren't you? Nina, I got him a teething ring, is that okay?

— Sure, let me see it.

— It's in that paper bag, on top of the little bread loaf I got for you.

— Thank you, Rivka, you didn't need to get anything for us.

— Are you kidding? For the sweetest boy in all of Massachusetts? Nina, maybe rinse that with some hot soapy water first, since it's going in his mouth. God only knows how many hands touched it between the factory and the store.

— Good idea.

— Did your fingers get stuck in my hair, bubbeleh? Yeah, it happens to me too—all the time! Nina, the scar will get smoother and lighter as he gets older.

— I have to admit it looks better than I thought it would, and I can see that it will help avoid problems later on.

— Exactly. What's Nana doing? Is she washing something for you?

David had one chubby hand in my hair while the other patted my paisley scarf with gusto. He smiled and babbled, the way babies do. Nina gave him the teething ring, which he stared at briefly before putting in his mouth. After a few more minutes of chatting she said he needed to go down for the night. I carried him to the back room. The adjacent bathroom bore the distinct smell of bleach from the diaper-soaking and washing; a bunch were on the drying rack she had set up in the tub, and some were draped over the shower curtain rod.

> — **Holy mackerel, Nina, you weren't kidding about him going through a lot of diapers.**

> — **Those are all just from the last two days. It's a never-ending cycle.**

I placed David gently in his crib, which was situated in what had been his mother's room. A twin bed topped with a pur-ple-flowered quilt was on the other side. Some nature photos, probably ripped from an inexpensive calendar, were taped to the wall: a butterfly on a pink coneflower, hummingbirds, a fox. A few tchotchkes befitting an adolescent girl sat on a small desk along with some well-used pencils and a pile of fancy *Living Bird* magazines. On the floor in front of the closet was an empty cardboard box. Nina probably has all intentions of clearing things out; she's too practical to leave the room as a shrine to her dead daughter. Directly across the tiny hallway was another small bedroom with a double bed—that must be where Nina sleeps.

> — **I had the crib in my room until last week.**

> — **Yeah, it makes sense to have him in here now. Does he sleep through the night?**

> — **Not always, but he's usually out for about four hours at a stretch.**

- Oh, that's good, Nina. At least you can get some rest from time to time. I know that 'rest' is a relative term.

- You've got that right. But he doesn't fuss much, I have no complaints.

Nina turned his light off and left the door ajar. She made some hot tea for me, from a small unopened box, and coffee for herself. We both doctored our drinks with sugar. She removed the saran wrap cover from the banana loaf and sliced it up. I grabbed a couple of napkins and we brought everything to the living room. I moved into the big chair that faces the kitchen while she sat on the adjacent couch, just like the first time we met. We were both able to reach the coffee table.

- Nina. I heard there was a bad accident on the mountain road yesterday?

- Yes, it was Elan. The police said they didn't think he necessarily had been drinking, that the road was icy in spots, as it always is in winter. They said they could request an autopsy but I said no. Whether he had been drinking or not doesn't matter. He wanted to die and saw to it. He was forty-eight years old.

- I'm sorry, Nina.

- The only time Jayce and I had seen him in the last few months was at Chilali's funeral … and a few times when he dropped off money.

Jayce must be their son, Chilali's brother. Nina had said they were seven years apart, so that would make him a year older than me. I sipped the tea and waited for her to continue telling me whatever she wanted to tell me.

> — Elan and I were content for most of our marriage. It wasn't a big, deep love, but we were compatible. He provided for us and was good with the kids. He worked for many years at the Warnaco factory. Then everything changed when we found out Chilali was pregnant. Well, actually before then. It wasn't just that she was pregnant, it was the circumstances surrounding the pregnancy …

I watched her intently as she took a couple of slow breaths, as if preparing herself for the telling of the rest. She placed her mug on the table.

> — She was fifteen years old, had just started tenth grade at the high school in Bridgeport. She was a sweet girl, Rivka. Did her homework every night, and her report cards were always As and Bs. She liked drawing, was always sketching at home, mostly birds and butterflies, that sort of thing. She had talent, but needed some guidance and instruction. The school had only one art class, and she couldn't get in because it was limited, so it was usually just the seniors, and maybe a few younger kids whose parents were on the school board, you know how that goes.

> — Yes, I do. And whenever a school district has to make cuts, they always manage to keep football, and they cut music and art.

> — That's right. It was a big, crowded school, mostly white kids in all the grades. A few blacks, and

maybe one other Native kid. Chilali didn't have any close friends there, pretty much kept to herself—she was shy around people she didn't know well. There were a few rough white boys that hung out together. They were mostly in eleventh grade I think, and they started bothering her. She told me that they called her 'In*un Sq*aw' and would make vile noises whenever they passed her in the hallways. It started becoming a regular occurrence, and she was getting scared. Elan went over to the school to try and talk to the principal. He ended up talking to the vice principal, who told him 'Well, y'know, boys will be boys, they probably like her, that's why they tease her. But I'll keep an eye out, nothing to worry about. Have a good day'. The taunting didn't stop. Chilali said she had always tried her best to ignore them, but on this one day, in October of last year, five of them were following her in the main hallway and calling her names like they always did. She was fed up and turned around and yelled at them: 'Leave me the hell alone you stupid, stupid boys!' It was the first and only time she stood up to them. She must have said it loudly, because she and one of the boys, the ringleader, were sent to the principal's office. The other boys had dispersed. So Chilali and the main bully were both given detention, can you believe it? For yelling, for being 'disruptive'. Chilali, disruptive—yeah, right. They were actually sent to sit in the same empty classroom, with no teacher there, for an hour after school that same day. Chilali told me she sat way on the other side of the room from that disgusting boy, and tried to do some homework while he was aiming spitballs at her. When the hour was up some teacher walked in and said he hoped they had learned their lesson and that they could both go home now. Well of course Chilali had missed the bus, and Elan and I were both at our jobs, and there was no way for her to contact us, so she started walking home. It was about a mile. The ringleader must have told his buddies to wait for him after school, because there were three of them, including the main bully, that followed her. She knew she couldn't outrun them, so she walked as fast as she could while they continued to taunt her. There's a shortcut through a field, but you have to pass between a chain link fence and a dense row of evergreens to get there, and Chilali told me afterwards that she hesitated for a second, because it would be away from the main road and might put her in further danger. But she wanted to reach home so badly that she decided to risk it. And as soon as she turned that corner the boys ran up from behind and attacked her. They pushed her under the trees where they couldn't be seen and pulled her pants and underwear down.

— She was GANG-RAPED?!?

— Yes. One of the boys held her down while the other two took turns. Then they switched places.

— **Oh my god, Nina.**

My level of anguish and nausea had been rising steadily since the beginning of the story. My eyes welled up and I could hardly breathe.

I knew from personal experience, coincidentally with that very same police department five years ago, that the cops would most likely not have been helpful, but had to ask anyway:

— **Was there any police involvement?**

She emitted a short guttural sound, a cry-snicker.

— **The fathers of two of those three boys were on the Bridgeport PD force, probably still are.**

— **Oh, Nina.**

— **Yeah. So there was no point.**

— **No.**

— **She never went back to school after that. Her spirit was broken, Rivka. She didn't want to go to the clinic. She didn't want to go anywhere. She hardly ate. She was just … numb. I tried to get her to eat. I tried to get her to go shopping with me. I tried to get her to draw again. She just wouldn't … couldn't. Jayce drove down from Ithaca a few times, and he would sit with her for hours, but he couldn't get through to her. None of us could. Jayce said that her eyes were vacant, like she wasn't there anymore. It's true. Elan was going out of his mind—he wanted to hurt or kill those boys but knew that would create more problems than it would solve. So he started staying out after**

work, going to a bar in the evenings. Before this he had never had more than one or two beers over the course of a weekend. But it got to the point where he couldn't bear being in the house, seeing his daughter like that, feeling he should have but couldn't protect her. Knowing what had happened to his sweet, innocent girl broke his heart. I'm not sure where he was sleeping, but it usually wasn't with us. I know he was still going to work, but he wasn't well. And this was all before we realized that Chilali was pregnant from those bastards.

I fished a packet of tissues out of my bag and we wiped our eyes and noses.

— **So she told me when she missed her period. I don't think she fully understood what was happening.**

— **How could she? She was so young and had been the target of a horrific attack. How the hell do you even begin to process any of that?**

— **Right. She had been menstruating for about two years, but it was never regular, plus she wasn't getting good nutrition, so it was hard to tell what was happening to her body. But she said her chest hurt, and she placed her palms over her small breasts, and that's when I knew. We took her to the Indian Health Service clinic, I insisted she go. Elan found someone to cover his shift and we drove almost two hours to Rhode Island—that was the closest. They didn't have a gynecologist working there at the time, but the regular internist confirmed the**

pregnancy from the urine sample and gave her some pre-natal vitamins, which she took for about a week when I reminded her each day. Then she stopped. And was still barely eating. She wanted to get an abortion but there wasn't anyone at the clinic to do it, and she was too scared to go to a white clinic.

Nina was quiet for a couple of minutes. We both needed a break. Thankfully David was still sleeping quietly in the back. I wondered what Nina would tell him when he got older and started asking who his father was. Perhaps she would give him a simplified version of the truth. Or maybe she would shut down and refuse to tell him anything. It was possible he wouldn't ask until he was much older. In any case, I knew she was devoted to him and would raise him as best she could. She didn't ask for this responsibility, but was willing and able. She's a tough cookie.

— **Before I finish the story … I'm going to put some more water up to boil. But first I want to show you something.**

She reached under the corner side table and pulled out a paper bag.

— **The police brought this to me last night when they told me about the crash—what's left of a man after he dies … they found these things in his car. A couple of shirts … some underwear and socks … twenty-one dollars. And this was in his jacket pocket.**

She held up a leather pouch, the color of mocha. It was about five-by-eight with a belt loop on the back. She handed it to me; it was worn and supple, the edges sewn together with thick black thread in precise, evenly-spaced diagonal stitches. A flap covered the opening and tucked into a narrow strip of the same leather across the front to secure it.

> **— It's so soft, did he have this for a long time?**

> **— Yes, I made it for him when we were married in 1950.**

> **— Wow, nice work, Nina. How did you get the thread through?**

> **— I used a leather hole-punch, and then a special needle.**

> **— What a beautiful gift you made for him.**

I handed it back to her. She opened the flap and removed a small photo, one of those Polaroids with the annoying pinkish tint. She passed it to me.

> **— He used the pouch as a wallet, and for receipts and notes and such. That picture—well it's the only one of all three of us together. I'm glad to have it back. Elan borrowed the camera from someone at work, just for that weekend. It was the end of summer last year, just a couple of months before the rape. We were at Seaside Park and it was a good day. Look how happy Chilali was.**

I studied the photo. Some blue sky on top, then their faces and bodies down to their shins. All of them had shades of golden-brown skin, warm and smooth. Nina was on the right in the picture, looking straight into the camera. She looked the same as she does now, but with a softer expression. On the left was Jayce, tall and slender, with thick black hair like his mother's that rested below his shoulders. An earnest, serious air about him … and that face—my god—a bit Gregory Peck, a bit Ellison Brown, his own unique version of staggering male beauty. Chilali was in the middle, slightly shorter than Nina, and looking up at her much taller brother, grinning and perhaps trying to get Jayce to laugh. Chilali's right arm was around her brother's waist and the left was around her mother's. She had soft, round features and was petite like her mom. A lively, hopeful girl, full of promise. I wished the photo were larger; I couldn't take my eyes off of it. I was so preoccupied that when I finally looked up, Nina was in the kitchen and had already prepared our hot drinks. I walked over.

> — **Nina, thank you for showing this to me. You raised two gorgeous kids. Chilali looks so at ease and full of joy.**

> — **That's who she was, Rivka, smiling and joking and happy to be alive. She adored Jayce, looked up to him, confided in him. He was the one who encouraged her to pursue the drawing. He would bring her pictures of birds and small animals from leaflets and magazines for her to copy. He took her to the library and showed her where the Audubon books were. She loved spending time with him, and he indulged her. She was devastated when he was drafted into the army. She was twelve and Jayce was nineteen. Neither of them were the same after that.**

> — **And you and Elan?**

> — **Yeah, I guess we weren't the same after that either. Of course we had no way of knowing that the worst was yet to come.**

We moved back to the living room, and Nina continued:

- So in January we got a letter from the school administration saying that Chilali was 'truant'. Truant! God-almighty. Something about needing to give them a doctor's letter explaining her absence for all of those weeks, or they would be pressing formal charges with the juvenile court. Elan and I were so disgusted, but we decided we couldn't tell them why Chilali had not been in school.

- Understandable, from the dismissive attitude of the vice principal when Elan tried to talk to him, there's no doubt the school would have launched a massive coverup, with their union lawyers and the police department, if you had told them what those horrible boys had done. They would have kept on victimizing the victim.

- Yes, that's what we figured. Around that same time, I decided to try and talk some sense into Chilali. I was a little harsh with her, the gentle approach wasn't working. I told her that if she was going to get a safe abortion, we needed to get her to a white clinic immediately. Like the next day. If she wasn't going to get an abortion, then she needed to start eating better and take those vitamins every day. I know she heard what I was saying but she kept silent, tears running down her face. She slept through most of the next day, and the following evening I asked her if she had made a decision, and she shook her head no, said 'I can't'. I said you can't do the abortion or you can't make a decision? She said she couldn't make a decision. She didn't want to be pregnant but was terrified of a white man touching her, even though I tried to reassure her we could request a female doctor. I got her to eat part of a peanut butter sandwich, but when I started trying to talk to her again she got up, said 'I'm sorry, mama', and went back to her room and closed the door.

— She was too young and distraught to have to make that kind of decision, but she was the only one who could make it. Her body, her life. An impossible situation for her and for you.

— Yes. So time kept passing, and soon it would be too late to do anything. At the end of February, right after Chilali's sixteenth birthday, which she refused to celebrate, Elan and I packed up all of our belongings and moved out of our rental in Connecticut and came up here. Elan's family are Narragansett, and my people are Nipmuck and Wampanoag. We both used to have relations in this area. They're all gone now, either dead or moved elsewhere, but at least we were somewhat familiar with the region and figured we'd be safer here than if we stayed in Bridgeport. And we'd be close to the river and the mountains. It's pretty here, easy to find quiet places.

— Yes, and the people are more laid back and inclusive than in some of the big cities. But tell me the rest, Nina.

— Okay, so Elan had given notice at Warnaco and figured he'd find work here, which he did. It wasn't easy, because some of the Springfield plants were closing, but he was able to get a decent job at Smith College in their maintenance department. He was always good at fixing things, and that's mostly what he does there—did there—along with the regular janitorial work. He said that each day was different, so he wasn't bored. They would have him go adjust seating in the lecture hall, another day he fixed their mimeograph machine, sometimes moved desks or file cabinets, whatever they needed. I miss him, Rivka. He couldn't stick it out when our lives unraveled, but he was a decent man.

— You were together more than twenty-five years.

— Yes. I knew Chilali was going to need a lot of help with the baby, and I was preparing myself for that, figuring Elan would also do what he could, or at least be by my side. But then she died. She died while they were stabilizing the baby, cleaning him up and getting him on oxygen. I'm not sure she would have wanted to hold him, but she didn't even have that chance. I watched the whole thing unfold—it happened so quickly but it felt like the pace of a tortoise. So I buried my girl four months ago, and now I have to bury my husband.

Nina and I settled in silence. She was submerged in the worst form of tsuris—big, complicated troubles, an enormous, distressing mess. At some point I stood, while everything was spinning in slow motion, and placed myself next to her, close to her, on the couch. We continued to sit quietly for a long time, shrouded in resignation and solidarity.

There are some events that cannot be imagined or prepared for. The gang-rape of a child for which there would never be any accountability or punishment. A father who loved his family but couldn't cope when everything skidded sideways. A fatal car crash. A mother who has lost her child and her husband and is now left to raise her grandson while juggling minimum-wage jobs. A baby who will never know his mother. Lives lost. A marriage ruined, a family destroyed. A school system that doesn't give a shit about protecting the children they're supposed to be educating and keeping safe. Cops who raise cruel, violent kids. Surely we can do better.

Most cultures have created words or phrases for the many dimensions of sorrow. Devastating loss. Consuming sadness. Tragedy. Affliction. Catastrophe. Despair. Heartache and heartbreak. Anguish. Relentless grief. Deep and mournful sadness. Agony. Misery and gloom. Heaviness. Woe. Regret. Tears of sorrow and suffering. Despondency. Sad pain—trista pena. Dolor. Bron agus gradh. Lupe. Yagon. In Vietnam it's called phi muon. Nigeria also has a multitude of expressions in the language of Yoruba; ibanuje tai ibinuje means sorrow and grief. The Filipinos say pighati and kalungkutan. The Japanese call it kanashimi. The Polish say zal.

In the end there are too many words, and not nearly enough.

8. A JOLT OF WONDER

You can't blame gravity for falling in love. —Albert Einstein

JAYCE November, 1980 Western Massachusetts

The first time I met Rivka I was elbow deep in hot sudsy water. I was visiting my mother Nina for the weekend, and we had just finished an early dinner. She had cooked, and I was cleaning with my sleeves rolled up. My boisterous five-year-old nephew David had eaten earlier and was next door playing with a couple of the neighborhood kids. My mother appreciated any break she could get; working outside jobs and raising her grandson sometimes took its toll. I had spent a few hours with him today and was tired out.

There was a knock on the door. I figured it was David and anticipated spending the next hour or so calming him down from a sugar high or his natural high and trying to get him off to bed at a reasonable hour. But when my mother opened the door to the outside chill, a blast of a different shape blew in.

— **Nina!!**

They instantaneously hugged each other. I had a clear view from the kitchen sink when I looked to my left and could not believe my eyes. I had never seen my mother hug anyone over the age of six except, occasionally, a family member.

— Let me get my boots off. How are you?

— Good, Jayce is here.

She immediately focused on me with a friendly smile and lightly-raised hand.

— Hi. I'm Rivka.

— Hi. Just finishing the dishes here.

— Okay.

From fifteen feet away I watched her lithe movements as she removed her mittens, hung her coat, and deposited her slush-covered boots on the mat. She wore a flowy purple skirt that reached the floor and a loose-fitting black sweater. Silver dangly earrings peeked out from a wild mass of long dark-brown curly hair. She looked like she had arrived directly from the Woodstock music festival, had it been held in winter. Upon straightening herself up she looked over at me again. My intrigue was heightened by the hint of sorrow in her eyes, incongruous with her ebullience.

Having lost the ability to think straight, the dish I'd been washing suddenly broke in my hands. I was thankful for the noise of the running water, saving me from a moment of potential embarrassment. What was happening? It was time to get out of the kitchen. The dish was one of many inexpensive porcelain plates that came with the apartment from the previous tenant, so I threw the pieces in the trash, pulled up the sink drain, quickly dried my hands on the towel, and went to lean against the cased opening between the two rooms. I was acutely aware of the mere eight-foot distance from this woman who my mother said had been immensely kind to her when David was a baby.

— So you're in from Ithaca?

— Yes.

- It's great to finally put an in-person-face to the name.

- Yes. You too. My mother told me how helpful you were. Have been.

- Well, your mom is a very special person. As is David. So I hear you're an archaeologist, what is that like?

- It's not as glamorous as some people might think, but I enjoy it.

- You're doing research work for your doctorate but also go on digs?

- Yes. The digs are exhilarating, although a lot of our time is spent wrapping found fragments and labelling everything.

- Ah … so lots of bagging and tagging. Oh, god— sorry. Shit. I didn't mean—I'm sorry, Jayce. Sometimes I say really stupid things.

- It's okay.

My mother must have told her I had served in Nam. No one said anything for a few beats. Rivka continued staring at me.

- You might be bleeding … your hand, Jayce. I probably have a Band-Aid, hold on a sec—

Huh? I uncrossed my arms and looked down—sure enough there was a cut on the side of my right hand between the wrist and base of the little finger, doubtless from the dish breaking in the sink when my attention had been elsewhere. Rivka must have seen the blood seeping into my white thermal shirt, and was now riffling quickly through her gigantic black purse or bag or whatever it was …

– Got it! Do you have any hydrogen peroxide?

She started to approach as I shook my head slowly, knowing that my mother doesn't keep things like that on hand, and I stepped back to the sink to rinse off the blood in cold water, a quick dry with a paper towel, and back to the jamb. Rivka removed the Band-Aid from its paper sheath—didn't bother with the red pull-string, just ripped it open—while I offered my hand to her, palm up. When she lowered her head a bit, a large plastic tortoiseshell clip that barely contained her hair came into view. I'd forgotten to roll my sleeve back down but she didn't flinch at the sight of my ugly scar, didn't even blink. I breathed in a subtle, comforting lavender scent, and in that moment while she was wrapping my hand I thought I could stand there forever, if only to be near her. In my peripheral vision was Nina, sitting on the couch and stifling a laugh. It was over too quickly and Rivka smiled up at me with vivid green eyes the color of moss, a shade so deep and striking I knew they would enter my dreams. She had dense, dark lashes, smooth skin, full lips, perfect teeth, and up close was a bit exotic and completely captivating—a rare, complex crystal. I'm a few inches taller and had the impulse to protect her somehow, which is ridiculous because we just met and I imagine she's perfectly capable of taking care of herself. Even knowing that the impulse probably stems from my failure to be in the right place at the right time to protect other people I've loved, the urge remained.

Rivka resettled herself in the chair and spoke to my mother about something regarding the development of a new program to assist working people who can't afford health insurance. Rivka's voice was low, throaty, and inviting. My heart continued to race. Who the heck carries Band-Aids around with them, anyway?

Another knock on the door. My mother got up to greet the neighbor, Doreen, delivering David. We all said hello, Nina thanked her, and the door was closed as Doreen retreated. David had barely finished tearing off his boots when he realized that Rivka was there. He could barely contain himself.

— RIVERRR!!!

— Hello sweetheart, did you have fun today?

He gave a quick nod as he climbed up onto her lap. He started gently playing with her hair and she put an arm around his tiny back while he half-sat-half-kneeled on her legs. He quieted himself and was all over her, didn't say a word while Rivka and my mother continued to chat. I had never seen David calm down so quickly. He was mesmerized by Rivka's earrings and I found myself in awe of the easy love between them. I was as transfixed as he was.

A few minutes later my mother told David it was time to close the day. Rivka helped David get ready for bed at his request: teeth brushed, face and neck washed, into pajamas and under the covers for a story. Clearly she knew the routine and had done this before. My mother told me a couple of years ago that Rivka sometimes sings him Ladino lullabies. And that she's brought over books and sensible toys. While they were in the other room I wanted to learn more, so I spoke in low murmurs to my mother:

— Interesting woman.

— Yes.

— What's with the sad eyes?

— I know, she didn't used to be like that. I think there may be trouble in the marriage.

— Have you met the guy?

— No, she doesn't bring him here. He's from Portugal, she met him there when she was backpacking around Europe after finishing her graduate studies.

— Do you think he's hurting her?

— It's possible. She's not as confident or free-spirited as she used to be. And since he came to live with her she never stays for more than an hour when she visits us. I've asked her a couple of times if she's okay, and she says everything's fine and then changes the subject. I don't think there's anything we can do, Jayce. If she *is* in trouble, it seems she's not confiding in anyone.

We resumed speaking in our normal voices, about David, about when I needed to head back to New York, about food supplies, about regular stuff. Rivka emerged from the back and announced that David was all tucked in and that it's late and she needed to get back home. She put on her coat and boots without tying them properly, told me she was glad to meet me while avoiding my gaze. I was certain she hadn't overheard the earlier conversation but clearly she was anxious and was shutting down. I told her we appreciated everything she's done for David, and that if she ever needs anything … she averted her eyes and said 'okay, sure, thank you'. She hugged Nina and was out the door and gone. As deeply as I had felt her presence, her absence left me with pangs of confusion and regret.

9. A WILD RIDE

Blessed are the cracked, for they shall let in the light. —Groucho Marx

HENRY Tuesday, June 28, 2005 Western Massachusetts

- Hello?

- I'm in the tack room, Henry. Morning! You're early.

- Is that okay?

- You bet. Lots to cover, you'll be shadowing me all day.

- Okay, that sounds good, because I have no experience—

- Dude! It'll be fine!

Pen in hand, David was sitting at a small desk, reviewing what appeared to be checklists on a clipboard. Shafts of sunlight streamed into the huge room through a sizable window situated about twenty feet above the wooden floor. Rectangular clouds of dust motes hovered above us. Deep shelves held stacks of metal and plastic food bins, folded blankets and towels, an array of brushes, oversized sponges, boxes of baking soda, and what David explained were bridles, halters, and hoof picks. Large green buckets that could be plugged in to prevent the water from freezing in winter. Bales of hay in an open loft, everything orderly and packed full. The earthy scent of manure, hay, and wood permeated the air. David stood and grabbed a bunch of leashes from the pegboard. Like yesterday, he was spirited and upbeat, his arms in constant motion.

— **This is quite a setup.**

— **Yeah. The essentials were all here when we got the property, but we had to fix it up a bit. And add more shelving. And buy all of these supplies of course, it's never-ending. The only animal that came with the property was Ginger.**

— **The tangerine horse?**

— **Yeah, she's a sweetie. I'll introduce you to everyone, and then we'll get them outside, and then we'll come back in here and clean up the stalls.**

— **Okay.**

— **First things first. Oh, there's a pile of gloves over there, help yourself any time. Okay, so here are the basics: You approach the animals slowly. It's helpful to speak gently to them as you're getting closer. They'll get used to your voice and your scent, and eventually they'll come to you once you learn their names. The horses can actually read facial expressions, but we don't generally look at them straight in the eye. You move toward the horses from the front whenever possible, at an angle or in loops. They've got exceptional hearing but binocular vision, so they have blind spots and we don't wanna startle them. Once you know they see you, you can get closer, and then place both** hands on their upper shoulder. I'll show you with Ginger when we get to that end of the barn. We'll skip over Cody for now because he's been a little unsettled.

— Nicole told me a little about him yesterday.

— Yeah, poor guy. I'm gonna try to get him into the corral later today. Okay, so the alpacas are interesting. And pretty. We've got five of them. They don't generally like being held or petted until you've earned their trust—well, except for Rose, because she was mostly raised by us here.

— Oh, that's the one who had to be bottle-fed, right?

— Yes! Very good, Henry. Yeah, Larry's good with her, she likes when he comes around. So … approach the alpacas slowly from the front or side. Soon they'll let you pet them gently on their necks. As for the goats and donkeys: they're all super-smart. Actually all of the animals here are, but especially the donkeys and goats, more on that later. Okay, so you approach them from the side and from a distance if possible. Obviously when they're in the barn we don't always have that option, so just go slow, but with relaxed confidence. And you can pet the goats and donkeys, mostly on their necks and backs. Don't worry, dude, you'll get the hang of it soon, this is only your first official training day. I'll fill you in on the feeding once we get back in here.

— Okay, sounds good.

— Just follow my lead. Saddle up, Henry! Ready?

Boy, was I ever. The foyer and tack room were at one end of the barn, the corral at the other. In between were the large enclosures: one for the donkeys, and two for the horses near the corral. On the other side of the wide corridor, which David refers to as the 'aisle', were the large goat and alpaca pens. We came to the alpacas first. David opened the low gate, which swings out into the aisle. The alpacas stood about four-and-a-half feet tall, except for Rose, who was shorter and a bit scrawny. Her fleece was oatmeal with tan splotches. The others were named Esther, Willow, Freida, and Pearl. Goofy, curious faces, furry heads, long thin necks, short fluffy tails, and each one with its own distinct coloring. David explained that professional shearers come every spring to do a gentle, cruelty-free shaving, and then the fleece is sold to people who have the machines to make beautiful yarn out of it. Luxurious scarves and gloves and so forth are sewn from the hypoallergenic fiber. He said that for safety reasons, and as a precaution for cross-contamination of diseases, the perimeter of their pen was thicker, enforced with plastic panels in addition to the wood that made up the rest of the stalls.

— **What's that noise they're making?**

— **Yeah, they hum. Usually they're just talking to each other, sometimes to us when they wanna be fed, or they're just happy because they know we're about to get them outside. The sound changes if they think they're in danger, but usually it's just this low hum like they're doing now. Okay, here's how to put on their little halter and hook up the leash.**

Like horses, alpacas breathe through their nose, so the nose-band has to be placed on the bone, not the cartilage, so as not to block their nasal passages. The crown piece of the halter should be snug behind their ears. I led one of the alpacas out to their special pasture, following David, who handled two of them. I made efforts to memorize all the names as we walked. Returning to the barn, David had me take the remaining two alpacas out while he started rounding up the goats.

He showed me how to double-latch the gates surrounding the main pasture, explaining that given enough time, the goats could figure out how to dismantle just about anything. Astonishing, the ability to climb trees and the wherewithal to unlatch gates? Lordy, lordy, these goats could get mischievous. I remembered a couple of names from the binders last night, and now I would learn them all: George, Violet, Adam, Lily, Kevin, Julia, and Awuchee. What amusing names! Kevin had long ears, Lily was brown with lots of white spots, George had a noticeable beard, and Adam was the one with the big horns. Violet, George, and Julia had horns as well, but they were smaller and evidently not problematic.

I asked David about average lifespans, and he answered immediately—goats: fifteen years, donkeys: twenty-five to forty-five years, alpacas: fifteen to twenty, horses: twenty-five to thirty.

— **But that's if they're healthy. Most of these animals were neglected or abused at some point before we got them, so even though we build them back to physical and emotional health, their lifespans may be a little less than average. But let's hope not. These guys are my life now.**

— **May I ask you something?**

— **Of course.**

— **What were you doing before the sanctuary?**

— **I was in a Vet Tech program. And before that ... well ... I was selling houses and condos in New Jersey. But I grew up in this area.**

— **Oh! What brought you back here?**

— **I lost someone I loved in the Twin Towers—just couldn't stay down there after that.**

Lord, have mercy.

— **I'm sorry, David.**

— **Thanks.**

We continued walking the animals out and neither of us spoke for a couple of minutes. What a horror 9/11 was. I remember that at the time of the terrorist attacks I had immediately thought of my father, who used to work in an office on the eighty-eighth floor of the South Tower. But he had moved back to Texas by then. Did one tragedy inadvertently stave off another kind of tragedy for my family?

I looked over at David. In the bright light of the sun more details were visible than yesterday. He had a thick mop of dark-brown wavy hair, neatly trimmed around his ears and neck. There was a faint scar above his lip, almost imperceptible. He was a good looking guy, so affable, and buzzing with energy. I started up the conversation again, about something else.

— **I think we're about the same age? I was born February seventy-four.**

— **Yeah, we're close, dude. I'm July seventy-five. They didn't even have disposable diapers when we were babies!**

— **I know, yuck!**

We chuckled while heading back to the barn to get the rest of the animals. We led the remainder of the goats out. Then the donkeys: Liz and Luke. Liz and Luke! Liz was dark-brown with a white nose and belly; Luke had a lighter greyish-tan coloring and white circles around his eyes. They both had a black stripe down their backs, and were so much larger and heftier than I vaguely remembered from pictures I'd seen as a child.

I followed David to the horse stalls. He introduced me to Ginger, who initially didn't seem to care one way or the other that I was there. After David demonstrated how to touch the side of her neck, she was a little friendlier. And then she ate a piece of apple from my ungloved hand; she really liked that!

— **You're doing well, Henry. You're gentle and respectful, they know you mean no harm. After you all get used to each other you'll become part of the herd, so to speak.**

— **Oh, that's good. I like the idea of being part of the herd.**

David nodded, we both smiled and led Ginger out to the pasture. She nudged my shoulder with her velvety nose as we walked, looking for another treat I suppose.

— **Okay, so everyone gets neutered as soon as they get here.**

— **WHAT?!?**

> — **The animals, Henry, the animals! Oh dude, you look panic-stricken!**

David was laughing hysterically. He had already released Ginger and was doubled over. I joined him in the spirit of the moment.

> — **I'm never going to live this down, am I?**

> — **Never!**

> — **Lordy, lordy. This is quite the day.**

> — **Oh, dude. We're only halfway through the morning.**

We giggled all the way back to the barn, where David showed me how to rake up the dung in each stall, transferring the piles into large, wheeled bins to be brought to an area outside behind the corral. This would all make fantastic compost for a garden. Then he showed me how to hose down the cement floors into the drains, and lay fresh straw for the bedding.

> — **We add extra straw in the winter, it helps keep them warm. And we have a couple of radiant gas heaters. The animals don't need as much heat as we do, as a matter of fact it can be dangerous for them. We've insulated the areas that could cause a big draft, but we have to keep an air flow going. It's a balance, you know?**

> — **So many details to think about.**

> — **You bet. But it's worth it, keeping everyone safe and healthy. And happy.**

> — **Yeah, and happy. You're completely devoted to this place. May I ask how all of this came about?**

— Well, Rivka came up with the idea about ten months before we opened. When she makes a decision about something she moves fast ...

— Go on.

— Okay. Well she knew about this property up for sale, and talked to me about putting on my realtor hat to make a deal, and I did. We bounced some ideas around and came up with a plan. We're both animal lovers, obviously. She knew how to write grant proposals, and a mission statement, and we were able to get nonprofit status. We kind of figured out the details as we went along. Suzy was Riv's assistant back in the old days, and was willing to get on board fairly quickly. Nicole, Peter and Yusef came on a little later.

— Wow. So you've known Rivka a while?

— Oh yeah. She's been like an auntie to me since I was born, our families are close. And since I've grown up we've stayed good friends and now we're also business partners.

— Wow, that's quite remarkable. Oh! So 'King-Solomon' ...

— Yeah, it's coincidental, but we decided the names sounded cool together.

— Nice. And you're both such good people.

— Well thank you, Henry, we've learned to try and live each day as best we can, you know?

- **Yeah. I do know … well, am just learning how to do that. I'm glad to be here. To be truthful, I haven't laughed this much in a long time. Oh my, did I say that out loud?**

- **You did, it's okay, dude. Come on, let me show you how to clean and refill the feeding bins and water troughs.**

- **Okay, sounds good.**

We worked together, taking turns at the sink, while I learned which feed belonged to which type of animal. The horses each consume twenty pounds a day of grass or hay, plus grain legume pellets, and fruit and veggies as treats. David said they especially like apples and carrots, and that Ginger loves watermelon. Watermelon! The alpacas also eat grasses and hay, as well as bark, stems, and some plants. They get a special grain and mineral supplement, and enjoy the same treats as the horses. The donkeys consume barley, straw, grass, and hay. He said the goats are picky eaters; they feed on pasture grass but only the tips that are new and tender. The pastures get rotated. The goats can eat alfalfa and peanut hay, bark, twigs, dead leaves, and brush. They get hay supplements in winter, but it all has to be super-clean without any mold. And they like banana peels as treats. Peter and Yusef make sure they don't get thrown into the compost pile. I asked David if it would be okay to add some bin and shelving labels, to remind me what's where and which stall it goes to.

- **Go for it, dude. Here are some Post-its, and Suzy probably has some real labels in her office over at the mothership.**

**– Great, thanks. I'll have you check everything when
I'm done.**

– Good plan.

David had been going out periodically to monitor the animals.
He also checked on Cody a couple of times in his stall. He
explained that horses take multiple power naps during the day
while standing up that last only a few minutes. The major joints
in its legs lock up so the horse won't fall. It's called a 'stay
apparatus' involving the tendons and ligaments. He said that
elephants and giraffes have this ability as well. The horse raises
one back leg a bit to rest while they doze. They do need to
lie down to get their deep sleep, usually for short periods of
time. If they stay down too long and don't want to rise, they
may be sick or injured. David told me that all of the animals
get examined by a vet on a regular basis, and that we need to
be constantly on the alert for any changes in their habits or
behavior. I soaked up all of this information and couldn't wait
to learn more.

Lunch was an entertaining affair, just like yesterday. The
Gipsy Kings accompanied the flavorful food. I chatted with
Peter briefly, and met Yusef, who was as amiable as everyone else here. He's a bit shorter than me with dark hair and
olive skin. Perhaps the age of my parents, and wears a wedding band. He calls me On-Ree, having grown up in Lebanon
speaking both French and Arabic. David sat with me initially
but then got up to check with the volunteers at another table
about the status of the fencing project. Rivka joined me and
asked how things were going. We chatted about the NYBG—
previously known as the Bronx Botanical Garden—where,
surprisingly, she had also taken a bunch of horticulture classes

when she lived in the city, way back when I was just a small boy in Louisiana. She told me about some of the eccentric teachers she encountered there and was extremely knowledgable, even remembering some of the Latin names of various plant and tree species.

— I used to know so much more, Henry. It's true that you lose it if you don't use it. But it was a fun experience, even though I had to take a thousand buses back and forth between Manhattan and the Bronx, and then a long hike up to the grounds.

— Yes, I heard there was no interborough bus stop there until the nineties. That seems a little ridiculous.

— It was. But when I was young and strong I didn't care as much about those kinds of inconveniences. So are you enjoying things so far?

— Oh yes, ma'am—sorry—Rivka. I didn't recognize what an alpaca was until I got here.

— I know, they're adorable, right? We have only female alpacas, because even though we get them fixed if they're not already, the males would go after them, which can cause persistent UTIs. Urinary tract infections.

— Even if the males are fixed?

— Yes. They can't get neutered until they're about two, and by then they're so used to mating they usually don't stop. Then the females need lots of medical follow-up and it's a constant battle trying to keep them healthy. Thankfully David checked

with some alpaca farmers before we set up, so we knew what to avoid right from the start.

— That's interesting. David is exceptionally devoted and knows so much about each animal. I'm grateful for the learning experience, and getting to know them all.

— Yeah, they're a lot of work but also lots of fun, and once you get to know each one you'll probably form some strong bonds. Oh, and don't underestimate the donkeys and goats. They're all wicked smart and have amazing memories.

Rivka smiled warmly at me as she stood and brought her tray up, signaling the end of our lunch break. After finishing my water and returning the tray, I headed straight outside to the pastures, where David was attempting to straighten out a lengthy water hose. A couple of the alpacas, I think Willow and Pearl, were lying on their sides; he said it was their sunbathing siesta. I assisted with the hose as he relayed the story he'd heard about the alpaca rescue, an operation handled by another agency before they came under our care.

— It was four of them, all except Rose, who's a relatively recent arrival. The four had been part of a work farm in Pennsylvania. The property, along with lots of cattle and a few smaller groups of other animals, changed hands a couple of times. The alpacas got lost in the shuffle—a few of them got loose and were killed by wildlife. Someone who lived nearby called the SPCA, and their staff people were able to round up seven of them. They were all reportedly in bad shape from

not having been taken care of over the course of a couple of months, and one of them died shortly thereafter. They found a family willing to adopt two, and the remaining four were trucked here to us. I guess no one else out there was interested or able to take them. They're mellow and travel well. It didn't take long for them to regain their health and get into the routine here. After a few weeks of TLC the vet said they were in good shape and that what we've been doing is working. So that was reassuring. Even when you think you're doing everything correctly, things can go awry.

– Yes, I can imagine. They're awfully cute, and Willow's fleece is the prettiest pale-grey. I see now why they're safer in their own space, given they're not as hardy as the other animals.

– Exactly.

We walked over to the other side of the alpaca pasture, where a couple of them were standing around.

– You may not wanna get too close to—

– Ughhh!!!

– Tried to warn you, dude …

My face was covered in something wet and disgusting. David was roaring with laughter. Again! I whipped off my glasses.

– What just happened?!?

– Oh, dude, that was Esther. She spits at new people. She needs a lot of personal space and gets a little

insecure sometimes, and she may think she's protecting an imaginary cria, a baby.

— **Did she have a baby?**

— **Not that we know of, but it's possible she had one before she arrived here, we don't usually get a full history.**

— **But she was fine with me this morning when we were taking them out of the barn!**

— **I know, she just gets weirded out sometimes without warning. And she's sort of the dominant one of the herd. You didn't do anything wrong, she just needs to get used to you.**

— **And I wasn't even that close!**

— **I know, but they can spit up to ten feet. Go get yourself cleaned up.**

— **Ughhh …**

He was still chuckling as I trotted over to the lodge. Lordy, lordy.

The rest of the afternoon went smoothly. I spent some time with David in the main pasture getting to know the goats and donkeys, who let me pet them on their backs and sides. David explained that while donkeys have a reputation for being 'stubborn', it's actually just their strong self-preservation instinct; they contemplate your instructions and cues and will hesitate to move if they don't think it's in their best interest. He told me that the donkeys and goats get bored sometimes and he hopes to acquire or build an additional structure to keep them entertained.

— They have a scratching station over there, but it would be nice to have a bigger one, like the kind they have at car washes but with stiffer bristles. And some sort of sturdy jungle gym.

— What's that over there?

— That's a Jolly Ball. The donkeys pick it up by the handle with their mouth. The horses can too, but so far they haven't been particularly interested. All this stuff costs money. We may have to put another fundraiser together at some point. They're a lot of work and not usually a big yield, but everything helps. For now, at least they have each other, they love hanging out together.

— Yeah, they all seem to get along. Why is that little goat so different than the others? I meant to ask you this morning.

— That's Awuchee, means 'Let's Go' in Hausa. He's a Pygmy, with ancestors from West Africa. Hops around like a bunny, he's a riot. Looks like a baby with a beard but he's actually about ten years old. I don't think he realizes how small he is, and the others treat him just the same as the rest.

— He's sweet. Oh, and you started telling me before about the donkeys?

— Yeah, they have a calming effect on horses, that's why I set up Cody's stall between the donkeys and Ginger. Okay … it's four o'clock already. In a few minutes we should start getting everyone

back to the barn, then I wanna see if I can coax Cody into the corral. Tomorrow I'll be showing you how to check and clean everyone's hooves and toes. We have a dental specialist who comes in for everyone's teeth, but we take care of their feet for the most part. A farrier comes every six weeks to shoe the horses. Their hooves have no nerve endings, so there's no pain and it protects their feet from injury.

– Okay.

After escorting all of the animals from the pastures to their stalls, David looked over the checklists in the tack room and swiftly jotted some notes. He said I was free to leave and get ready for supper if I wanted, but I said I'd stay a bit longer. We headed toward Cody's stall. He was standing with his head down a bit, possibly taking one of his little naps. David motioned for me to stay back, so I watched from the aisle as he swung open the pony-wall gate and entered the stall. He left the gate open, and I got my first good look at the majestic horse. His body was a deep-brown with a hint of auburn. His legs, mane, and tail were black, as were the edges of his ears. He had a small white mark on his forehead. David said it's called a 'star', even though it was irregular and looked more like a teardrop. He also had some white markings on the bottom of his legs. His size made me a little nervous, but I tried to stay relaxed while recalling my positive interactions with Ginger earlier. Cody took a treat out of David's hand but the horse's movements were slow and hesitant. David spoke softly to him and eventually was able to lead him ploddingly out toward the corral. Every few feet Cody would stop in his tracks, and David kept murmuring calmly to him until he walked forward again. How could such a huge animal be so sad and so scared? When they finally reached the corral entrance David glanced back at me. I gave him a thumbs-up and headed to my casita for a much-needed shower.

It was close to eight-thirty by the time I finished supper. I hadn't seen Rivka or David in the dining area, but Yusef was there along with the other on-site volunteers. Some of them were gathering in the den to watch TV. I wasn't in the mood for that so I walked out into the dark night, pulling on my jacket. The left side of the moon was lit; it must be in its last quarter. The only light visible, other than from the lodge, was pouring from the barn's tack room, and I walked over to investigate. Had David been in there this entire time? It's been three-and-a-half hours since I last saw him.

I entered without announcing myself, hoping not to disturb the animals, most of whom were probably sleeping. A barely audible sound was coming from somewhere. I stood still for a moment, trying to figure out the source, eventually recognizing David's voice, singing in a language unknown to me. He must be at the other end of the barn. His navy pullover was draped over the back of the chair, and thinking he might want it, brought it with me and slowly made my way down the aisle. Battery-operated lights lined the lower portion of the walls on both sides, and some dim overheads were enough for me to see into the stalls but not disturb sleep. I passed by the alpacas, who were lying down and asleep. Most of the goats were resting peacefully as well. David's voice was more distinct now; he must be with the horses. I passed the donkey enclosure: Liz was sleeping while Luke stood guard. I moved closer to their gate and he came to me. While I patted his shoulder, Ginger stood in her stall with her lowered head facing the aisle, probably napping.

David said '**I know just how you feel, buddy … it's gonna be okay …**' and then resumed the singing. I approached Cody's stall and peered over the gate.

Sweet Jesus. The powerful beast was sprawled out on his side on top of the straw bedding, the back of his head and neck snug against David's outer leg. David sat with his legs outstretched, ankles crossed, his back leaning against the wall, wearing the same jeans and T-shirt he's had on all day. He was gently stroking Cody's glossy neck, smoothing out his mane, crooning a calming lullaby. The magnificent horse was exhaling deeply in regular intervals; the eye that I could see was almost entirely closed. Not wanting to startle either of them, I lightly shuffled my boots. David looked up, melancholy written all over his face. I wordlessly held up his sweatshirt with a questioning look. He nodded while continuing to sing and we both extended our arms until he could grab it. I swallowed hard, quietly left the barn, and choked back tears as I walked back out into the heavenly night.

10. ENOUGH IS ENOUGH

If you do not change direction, you may end up where you are heading.
—Lao Tsu

RIVKA February, 1983 Western Massachusetts

I once had a sweet collection of stone boxes. Most of them were quite small, the largest maybe eight inches wide. There were about fifty boxes in all, from various parts of the world. Some round, some square, oblong, rectangular, one triangular. Diverse colors and striations. Agate, quartz, marble, onyx, soapstone, malachite, and more. Some were a bit clunky, some quite delicate, a couple adorned with inlaid mother-of-pearl. The lids for the hand-carved pieces fit perfectly, but only if you placed them a certain way, like a puzzle, and I marveled at that perfect form of imperfection. Some were gifts from friends and family, some I found during my travels, others I'd bought at flea markets and yard sales over the years. They had no significant monetary value but were precious—my little treasures. The boxes were scattered around the apartment: a few on top of the dresser, some on my little desk next to a neat stack of index cards, many in groups of six or seven on top of the shorter bookcases. I placed them away from high traffic areas like the kitchen where they might topple over or get dirty.

Somewhere along the line the boxes started disappearing. First I noticed one in the bathroom trash, broken. When I asked Rodrigo about it he said it had '**accidentally**' fallen from the desk. I didn't understand how that could possibly have happened, or what he'd been doing at my desk, or why it ended up in the bathroom when there was a trash basket right under the desk, but I let it go. About a month later the lids were missing from a couple of the boxes in the living room. I asked Rodrigo if he knew anything about it, and he said I was being paranoid and why am I bothering him about such stupid things.

Rodrigo was an impetuous man-child when I met him six years ago, and is now a volatile brute. It has finally sunk in that he's a pathological liar and a textbook abuser. I should have figured this out much sooner—I'm a social worker for god's sake, but things tend to become muddled when it's your own life. There were red flags early on: he was married when we met and actually introduced me to his then-wife as his '**house-mate**'; her English was not adequate enough for her to understand what was being said or to correct him. He claimed to be a '**famous**' keyboardist in his home country, yet I was there with him for weeks and there were no gigs to speak of. He kept borrowing money until I had nothing left to purchase a flight back to the States, so he asked his mother for just enough to get my ticket home. He promised he would follow as soon as he got his military papers straightened out, only to find out much later that it was a divorce from his first wife that needed to get settled so that he could marry me.

We had some shared interests, and he seemed sincere when he said he loved me and wanted to spend his life with me. I had ignored the bad stuff because Rodrigo was interesting and fun to be around. In the beginning I thought I loved him—obviously my thick blinders were on. I bought the snake oil.

The scary-crazy behavior increased after we were married. If I don't return home from work precisely twenty minutes after my shift ends he accuses me of cavorting with some imaginary man. He needs constant reassurance, which I give him, but it's never enough. On a regular basis he threatens to kill himself if I ever leave him. One Saturday morning I told him I was going to the Post Office to get some international stamps so we could send a letter to his sister, and he said I'd '**better be careful**' because he knew I was having an affair with the postman.

He never tires of calling me a bitch on a daily basis. To make matters worse, I've lost contact with my friends; Rodrigo makes it next to impossible to maintain relationships with anyone I had once been close with. Social visits are rare and time-limited. My entire life has become centered on his needs.

Rodrigo immigrated on a work visa but didn't actually work, other than the rare, sporadic day job for cash. He pretended to look for employment for a few weeks before the wedding, but then stopped. All of the bills are in my name. I stupidly added him to my checking account, and he goes out and buys things for himself, like a new electronic keyboard set and synthesizer, while I'm struggling to pay the utilities. I need a car in order to work, and now cannot afford to fill up the tank more than three gallons at a time. He's put me in debt. And what does he do all day while I'm working? He's usually watching TV when I get home, no dinner made, no grocery shopping done, nothing whatsoever to help out.

The hitting started a couple of years into the marriage. It doesn't happen often, and he almost always apologizes the next day. It's sometimes a hard whack to the side of my head. Or he'll roughly grab my upper arms and shake me like a rag doll during his screaming rants. One time he kicked me in the stomach as I was climbing into bed. I get through each day by focusing on the minutiae and semi-normalcy of my job, and when I'm home at night and weekends I try my damnedest not to do anything that might upset him. The situation gives 'walking on eggshells' new meaning. His threats of harming himself became threats of harming me. The emotional cruelty is far worse than the physical abuse, though they go hand in hand. Maintaining a continuous state of high alert is exhausting.

This toxic relationship has chipped away at my soul, bit by bit, day by day. I have become numb and pathetic. But the tiny part of the old upbeat and sensible me that's hidden somewhere under all those layers of crap quietly pleads to take action to save myself. Staying is no longer an option.

I thought about calling my father, with whom I've always been close but have kept up only minimal, irregular contact with over the last few years. He has his busy life, consumed with work, which involves a great deal of travel. His small office rental in Manhattan is also where he sleeps. He'd be extremely upset on my behalf if I informed him of what was happening, and there really is nothing he can do at this point. Perhaps my reluctance to ask him for help is also because I'm ashamed of myself for letting things get so bad. Also, I'm worried he'll have another heart attack.

There was no good reason to call my mother, given that she lacks the capacity to assemble an iota of genuine kindness for any sentient being (even her own children), but I did so anyway, desperate to believe there was a remote possibility she might respond with something resembling solicitude. Was it unreasonable for a young woman to seek comfort from her mother without getting belittled or dismissed? Just this once?

Abigail (never 'Abbie') lives and works on Long Island, spends some of her free time volunteering at cultural events (where she can mingle with the fancy-schmancy crowd), and the rest shopping for things she doesn't need. My mother has made it clear since childhood that I was an inconvenient byproduct of an insipid marriage, and I learned my co-dependency skills well from her. She is the Queen of Denial, and when I presented a mild version of what was happening, she predictably said:

— **Well, every marriage is a compromise, you should know that by now. It can't be that bad, dear, you must be exaggerating … Rodrigo is so handsome and charming, I'm sure he'll find a steady job soon. Go out and have a nice dinner together, everything will be fine. Keep in touch, and the next time you're in New York I'll take you to my hairdresser, because we MUST do something to fix that awful hair of yours and give it some style … have lunch at the … shop for some blouses that FIT you … don't know why you insist on wearing frumpy, oversized, shapeless clothing when you have an attractive, svelte figure … and a little makeup wouldn't hurt …**

Yeah, always a pillar of acceptance and support. While I knew it was a long shot, I could have just rammed my head into a brick wall—it would have taken less time and effort. Namaste.

Now that Rodrigo has his Green Card, which as it turns out is neither green nor a card, he doesn't need me anymore. Well, except for the free room and board, but he can crash with one of his mistresses. I don't dare tell him I'm leaving; I'll just let the landlord and utility companies know to cut everything off at the end of the month, which is in eight days. I won't be able to remove him from the joint checking account without his 'permission'; there's no money left in it anyway, so I'll open a new account for myself to deposit my future paychecks. I'll line up a work colleague to help me get my stuff out of the apartment some night when Rodrigo is out at the strip club he frequents. Yes, he actually brags to me about how he can have any woman he wants. I may not have time to gather all of my belongings in what will be a rushed clandestine move, and will probably have to leave most of the furniture, but I'll get what I can. I've already brought a small bag to work containing my passport, birth certificate, a few other important documents, and the one remaining stone box.

11. AT EASE

When a great moment knocks on the door of your life, it is often no louder than the beating of your heart, and it is very easy to miss it.
—Boris Pasternak

HENRY July 5, 2005 Western Massachusetts

> **– What happened to you and your family is terrible, Henry, and you'll always be sad about it. Everything changed, and that's extremely difficult. But sometimes we have to step outside of ourselves in order to move forward. At some point we need to get out of our own way.**

It's coming back to me now, word for word. My caseworker Jean had said this in her hospital office back in 2001, a few days after the second surgery. At the time I wasn't sure what she was getting at; I heard the words with minimal comprehension. Jean knew I was still depressed, even after four years.

Another four years later and I'm living on this wonderful farm. It's only been a week since I arrived and I'm finding my old self again and expanding my horizons. Working with David and the animals has been illuminating, and gives me a purpose. How does one measure happiness? I feel the ground under my feet. I taste and savor the food I eat. I'm no longer coasting through the days while drowning in self-pity. My hand is getting stronger and is hardly a problem anymore—I probably won't need the Band-Aids much longer ... progress on all levels. I'm glad to wake up each morning, and have an unfamiliar sense of peace when I lie my head down on the pillow each night. Good lord, what a blessing it is to be here.

Last night after supper I joined some of the other volunteers in the library-slash-den, as Rivka calls it. A few people had left the premises to join the July Fourth festivities with friends, something that held no interest for me. I avoid the sound of fireworks at all costs—even the reverberation of a car backfiring shakes me back to hell. David was staying at the barn to ensure the animals were okay in case any firework activity erupted in the neighborhood. The movie player was set up and we watched a good film called *Monsoon Wedding*. A couple of the guys inquired about the way some of the women in India dress, trying to figure out how they wrap those saris around their bodies. And asking how people manage to live in a place that gets such heavy rains. I thought they were missing the salient points of the story, but then when one of the main characters stood up to the older man who had abused her as a child, all of us in unison yelled **'You go, girl!'**, so I guess they were understanding the messages after all. And the Bollywood music was a blast.

I checked on everyone in the main pasture. We had finished the morning chores as usual and David said he's planning to see if he can persuade Cody to join the other animals outside. He wants me to hang around a little closer to Cody than I have been, and he's going to ask the same of Nicole when she comes tomorrow. He said that Cody needs to get used to us handling him so he'll respond to all of us, not just David. Makes sense. I've learned the name of each animal and am getting to know their personalities and quirks—serious work but great fun!

Suzy's yellow buggy bounced along at a leisurely pace toward the fields. When she stopped at the fence line I closed the distance between us.

— **Hi hon. You've been summoned by the boss.**

— **Rivka wants me?**

— **Yes, she needs to talk to you in her office. She has to leave right after lunch for a meeting in Springfield, so if you can get to the lodge within the next twenty minutes that'll be good.**

— **Okay, I'll let David know.**

— **Sounds like a plan, see you soon.**

I walked over as David led Cody out, slowly but without hesitation. He seems to be coming along, thanks to David's patience and TLC.

— **I'm not in trouble for anything, am I?**

— **No, dude, I think she just wants to ask you something. It's okay to say no if you're not up to it.**

— **Oh. Okay.**

— **Go ahead over there, I'll see you at lunch. It'll be fine, Henry.**

I washed up as soon as I got to the lodge, then headed to the offices and sat in one of Rivka's chairs. Neat piles of papers and folders took up most of her desk. Lord, please don't let there be any bad news, I've been doing so well here. Or at least I think I've been.

— Sorry about the short notice, Henry, I thought I'd have more time here today but it turns out I've got two meetings this afternoon and three tomorrow, and I wanted to talk with you this week.

— Okay, no problem. What can I do for you?

— Well, I had an idea I wanted to run by you.

— Okay.

— When we first got this property a couple of years ago, you know, to set up the sanctuary, we got so entrenched in all the details to provide for the animals that we knew would be coming as soon as word got out that we could take some, and all the paperwork for that, and then later to set up the kitchen and getting the Volunteer Work Program established, and all that. Anyway, there was something that's remained in the back of my mind, which is that maybe we could have some sort of perennial garden here? Yusef has done a fantastic job with the vegetable plots, but wouldn't it be nice to also have an area with some ornamental plants and flowers? I was thinking somewhere along that rear fence line?

— Maybe near the big red oak?

— Yes! Exactly! Okay here's the deal, Henry. I wasn't sure if you'd be interested, but if you'd be willing to maybe sketch something out for me to look at? We wouldn't be able to pay you for a design, but if you're willing, you could work on it during regular hours, if David can spare you for an hour or so each day. And in the meantime, I'm going to look at the budget again and see if we can scrape up a few hundred dollars to buy some plants, and then you and the other volunteers could do the installation. We have some basic tools here, let me know if anything else is needed.

I was sure this week couldn't possibly get any better, but it has.

— Ma'am—sorry—Rivka. Nothing would make me happier than to make a design for you. When I first arrived here I was getting all sorts of ideas. I was thinking maybe some ferns in the shade of the oak. And masses of flowers to the left of that area where there's sun.

— Oh, this is great, Henry. Listen, I need to tell you something. Are you familiar with Oliver Sacks?

— I'm not.

— He's a brilliant neurologist. Grew up in a religious Jewish household in England, and he's been living in New York for many years. His approach to patients and everything else is a little unconventional, and he was shunned by most of his medical colleagues until someone made a movie based on one of his books, all of which I've read. Anyway, there's a reason I'm telling you all this. The amazing Oliver Sacks goes to our old stomping grounds in the Bronx every chance he gets.

— For real?! Go on.

— Okay. So he's always been interested in all forms of life, beyond humans. And get this, Henry: he has a thing about ferns. He thinks of them as 'survivors'.

— Cool. Because they're ancient?

— Yes, that must be the primary reason. There are fern fossils from three hundred and sixty *million* years ago—I mean, holy smokes.

— That's amazing. They've survived all sorts of storms, literally, through all that time that we can only imagine. And there are so many varieties now.

— Yes! So do you think you can come up with something that would work here? Low maintenance and nothing too complicated. You can check with David about your schedule.

— No, ma'am. I'm doing this on my own time. I'll have something for you by the end of the week.

— Oh, Henry, that's marvelous, thank you. Let Suzy know when you're ready to review it with me and we'll go from there, okay?

— Yes, that sounds great.

To say I was elated would have been an understatement. I immediately called Toni and asked if she or Heather could drop off the boxes and suitcase I had left at their place. I had my sketch pad and pencils here but wanted my grid pad, trace paper, scale, and fine-point color markers. She said she'd bring them tomorrow. I've done only a smattering of design jobs over the last few years and was over the moon to have the opportunity to do this for the farm, even without monetary compensation.

Lunch consisted of a spicy potato dish, green salad, and some specialty crackers and fresh vegetables from our garden. There was hummus and baba ganoush prepared by Yusef, who greatly appreciated my complements. And traditional, melodic Middle Eastern stirrings all around. Yusef explained about the oud, a stringed instrument similar to a lute.

I couldn't wait to share the big news with my new friends. David was eating a late lunch when I hurried out to the main pasture. I called Luke and Liz over and told them about the garden plans. Cody and Ginger were nearby grazing. I kept them in my line of sight while fetching one of the large rubber balls that the donkeys like to play with. We started a little soccer match, and were joined by a couple of the goats: Violet and Kevin. Little Awuchee eventually bounded over to check out the action. Esther strolled closer with the other alpacas right behind her; they lined themselves up along their fence like stadium spectators. Liz brayed with excitement as I talked and laughed and scurried the ball around them. We went on like this for some time when I caught a small movement in my peripheral vision. David was walking out of the lodge to the porch adjacent to his office. He watched us, wearing what I hopefully gauged from a distance to be a smile of amusement and approval.

The rest of the afternoon passed quickly. We took care of the chores, and David seemed pleased about the garden plans and even more so my enthusiasm about the project. He assured me that he'd be able to coordinate the installation, if it got that far, with the animal chores, because the other volunteers would be finishing up the fencing within the next few days. We walked over to the oak and I gave him a general overview of my vision, along with some questions about resources for some wooden slats I wanted to use to create a vertical backdrop for the plantings that would look nicer than the existing perimeter fencing.

— **Unlike you and Rivka I have no artistic imagination, Henry, but I'll help any way I can.**

It had been an absolutely awesome day and I was happy as a clam at high tide.

12. BEYOND THE PALE

A person is sometimes stronger than iron and sometimes weaker than a fly.
—Yiddish Proverb

RIVKA March, 1983 The Northeast

The good news is that when I make a decision about something I act quickly and do whatever needs to get done. I am not one to fold myself into a fetal position and crawl under a blanket; that would be a luxury I couldn't afford.

Immediately upon receiving my next paycheck, I opened a new account, at a different bank this time in case Rodrigo tried to track me or my earnings. I frantically searched for another apartment, and put a partial deposit down on a small two-bed-one-bath place. While initially looking for a studio or one-bedroom, figuring it would be cheaper, there was nothing even half decent available or affordable this time of year. The other reason is that this particular landlord accepts Section 8 contracts, and I had submitted an application the previous day. There was no guarantee that would come through though, and I had to come up with the rest of the deposit within the next few days. In addition to my full-time job at the clinic, I made arrangements to work weekend shifts at the group home that had employed me a few years ago. It paid only minimum wage, but between the two jobs I'd be able to eventually pay off the debts that Rodrigo had racked up under my name and hopefully move on with my life. That was all going to take some time to come together, and I needed cash immediately for food, gas, and the rest of the deposit on the new place. There was also a student loan to finish paying off, but that would have to wait.

I drove down to New York and met with the top-notch folks at Hebrew Free Loan. They approved an emergency loan, with the expectation that I would pay it back within the next ten months. Doable. I then picked up my dad and we drove out to the Island, to the house where my parents had once lived together and which has belonged to my mother since their divorce. My brother and I lived there when we were in high school. Some of my sturdy childhood furniture and other belongings were stored in the garage, so my dad and I loaded up what we could cram into my car. I had told him the gist of what happened without the sordid details. He was quite upset and exceptionally supportive.

The three of us had a pleasant dinner at a delightful Japanese restaurant in town. Despite or because of my state of exhaustion it was a welcome reprieve; I couldn't remember the last time I had eaten out. Or had a full meal. My father and I rolled our eyes and smiled at each other across the table while my mother rattled on about some objet d'art she had recently purchased **'for a song'**. I drove back to Massachusetts late that night, while my dad returned to the city by train. A week later he rented a U-Haul and drove up with more furniture, the rest of my books, and some cash. He helped me get settled into the new place and added a safety guard to the door.

We talked and talked. At one point he apologized for not having tried harder, all those years ago, to move the family sooner to a safer town when I was getting bullied and beaten up at school. (My claim to fame was having been known through-out those elementary years as '**The Ki*e Girl**' as the teachers, all gentile, turned a blind eye and ear.) I never had the heart to inform my father that every time he complained to the school it just made things worse. And he had to contend with Abigail, who, at the time, adamantly refused to be inconvenienced. On top of all of that, he held onto the belief that the neighbor-hood would improve, recognizing in hindsight that it had been a monumental mistake.

We shifted to lighter topics when I served a lunch of PB & J-on-rye and tap water with ice cubes.

– Nu? No caraway? You call this a sandwich?

That got me laughing. Dad knew I always bought the seed-less rye because the caraway would inevitably get stuck in my teeth. Once I actually punctured my tongue while attempting to maneuver one out. The Yiddishkeit purists would *never* go seedless. His teasing was comforting, and a reminder that my old joyous self had a chance of re-emerging. Everything was going to be okay.

The bad news is that after my dad returned to New York I realized I was pregnant from the last time Rodrigo had raped me. At first I thought my body was reacting to all the stress, but I went to an OB who confirmed it. There was no way I was going to allow a potential being to develop inside of me that was not made from love. Thankfully abortion was legal now, so I wouldn't have to resort to a back-alley procedure, which left my friend Sophie with permanent damage to her internal organs just before abortion was decriminalized in New York in 1970. After reviewing all options with the OB, I made an appointment for the following week. I was also informed that I had an STD, for which she gave me an antibiotic prescription.

Rodrigo must have acquired it from one of his girlfriends and passed it on to me. Splendid.

A few days later I experienced a miscarriage. It involved severe cramping and copious amounts of blood, mostly in the form of large, gushing, dark-red clots, akin to five years' worth of heavy menses rolled into twenty minutes. Fortunately I was at home and not work when it happened. I felt relief but also a deep sense of sadness; I knew I would want a child someday but not under these circumstances.

When my brain registered that it was over, I soaked a hand towel in warm water and slowly washed away the residual rivers of darkness from my pale, quivering legs. No caraway. No way to carry me away.

My hormones must have been wreaking havoc, evoking thoughts about a particular chain of events in my life. I considered the possibility that I'm a magnet for needy/freaky/violent men.

When I was fourteen years old I was on my way to work, a summer job at a daycare center of sorts that paid cash, less than minimum wage, off-the-books. It was morning rush hour and all the subway seats were occupied, so the rest of us stood, holding onto the metal bars, packed like sardines as usual. Some guy put his hand under my dress and fingered me. It was sudden and quick and disgusting. I tried to see who did it but that was an impossible task, as I was surrounded by multiple men; it could have been any one of them. And what the hell could I have done about it, anyway? I was wearing a short dress, so it must have been my fault, right? It was 1967 and nearly every female under the age of seventy wore short dresses or skirts. But still, it must have been my fault.

When I was seventeen, I was in the wrong place at the wrong time and ended up in a small, grungy studio apartment with a stranger. He was a decade older and by the time I realized we were alone it was too late; he had locked the door from the inside with a key—I'd learn why immediately—and lunged at me. I remember trying to utter a frightful **'What are you doing?!'** as he shoved me down onto a bare mattress. He raped me, and just when I thought it was over he had other plans. As I attempted to get up from the grimy mattress, which was lying directly on the drab linoleum floor, he gripped the back of my head and forced me to orally satisfy him. He kept one hand squeezed around the nape of my neck, his other hand gripping my shoulder while his ragged fingernails dug sharply into my underarm. Every few minutes he'd temporarily release my arm and gulp down liquor from a bottle on the floor next to the mattress. An open pocketknife stared at me from the floor near the bottle. He kept yelling **'Make it hard!'** and **'Damn cunt!'** over and over. I couldn't scream because his filthy dick was down my throat. The headache-inducing aggressive noise of heavy metal bands blasted throughout the building, so no one would have heard either of us anyway. This part of the rape went on for fifty-one minutes. I am certain of the timing because there was an oversized wall clock with an ugly stars-and-stripes motif just to the right of the door, which was in my peripheral vision.

I kept prodding the cloud of numbness that had seized hold of my brain so that I'd be able to escape when the opportunity arose.

He finally fell back and passed out. My body free now, I retrieved my pants from the floor and yanked them on as fast as I could, then found the key near the knife and unlocked and bolted out the door, sickened and repulsed. Bruises covered my upper body, soreness everywhere. My shirt and underwear were torn, and I had an intense gag reflex that would last for the rest of my life. As would an aversion to men with stringy blond hair. Dirty and broken, I couldn't wait to wash the stench off myself in scalding water. Without any means of transportation, it took an hour of walking on unfamiliar streets through rough neighborhoods in the dark to reach the place I was staying. I have a poor sense of direction and don't know how I managed.

This happened in a working-class city in Connecticut, where I had been visiting a couple of female acquaintances. I gave one of them the CliffsNotes version; she was somewhat sympathetic but not particularly helpful. The next day I decided to call the local police. The response I got was discouraging:

— **Do you really want to come down to the station and file a complaint, ma'am? I can give you the address here, but I'm not sure you're going to want to put yourself through that.**

— **His apartment is in your district and I found out his name—can't you do something with that?**

— **Well no, not unless you file a formal complaint, do you really want to do that? You know, these kinds of things don't usually get prioritized, ma'am, so it's probably not worth your time to come down here …**

Yeah, real effective law enforcement system when it comes to crimes against women. I had walked into an unknown building with some 'friends of friends', so it was partly my fault, right? I was a virgin before last night. If you get raped, does that mean you're not a virgin anymore?

Police departments were initially established in this country to control people of color, primarily Native Americans and

African Americans, an extension of the old Slave Patrols. One hundred and forty-five years later they still can't be bothered with trivial matters like white men raping women and children.

When I was in my early twenties I dated a guy for a few months. I let him move in with me because he was cute and I was an idiot. When I came to my senses and broke up with him he moved back to his brother's place. A week later he knocked on the door and said he had forgotten something. I didn't have a phone in those days and it was ordinary for someone to just come over. Once inside he said he missed me terribly and wanted to move back in. I said I'm sorry but no. His eyes suddenly deadened; he attacked and raped me. He had never been violent with me before. Afterwards he apologized and cried. I told him to get the hell out and never come back. How is it that I've been violated again?

And then yet again, years later by my own husband. But I had married him, so it was my own fault, right? If we enable someone by tolerating their erratic behavior, then we're foolish, but does that make it okay for them to abuse us? Would a shred of dignity ever return to me?

Decades later, the fleeting memories would still bring on the urge to puke.

There have been other traumatic incidents in my life, but none of them were personal: The near-fatal bus fiasco in the high mountains of Greece. The near-fatal four-alarm apartment building fire in Cambridge, an act of arson by the landlord. The near-fatal car crash in rural Maine on a road coated with several inches of solid ice that had not yet been sanded.

Sexual assault is different. It's invasive and intensely personal. It's a violation of what should be the most private and sacred part of ourselves. It's a harsh form of degradation and betrayal, and it happens all the time. Yet we victims, we survivors, are made to feel shame and embarrassment. No one wants to talk about it, including the victims, because talking about something usually makes it more real. Far better to view these events as frightening, incongruous dreams. And it must have been our fault because we said or did something wrong, or our clothing wasn't prim enough, or we shouldn't have been in that neighborhood to begin with, or we shouldn't have trusted someone who seemed trustworthy.

We remain steeped in anxiety and self-doubt because the perpetrators are rarely held accountable. The police are not sufficiently trained in '**these kinds of things**'; they are usually polite but don't want to get involved. And if you survive an attack by someone you actually know—forget it, no one wants to hear about it and it's automatically categorized as '**a misunderstanding**'. Some hospitals now have rape kits, but there is no follow-up even when proper procedures are followed, so most victims don't bother. And the court system is also useless, if it even gets that far, which is rare.

It is the victims who live with the consequences; it is our burden to bear. And only if we're lucky enough to not have been killed by our partner, or an angry ex, or a complete stranger. The short and long-term physical and psychological effects are different for each of us; we have our own unique stories. The aftermath of distress manifests itself in myriad ways, but many of us carry the sadness, the confusion, the frustration, the loss of a piece of ourselves, the helplessness, the shame, the emptiness, the silence. This is the wreckage of misogyny.

It would be many years until I fully understood that none of it had been my fault.

13. ENCHANTMENT

It's better to talk to a woman and think about God than to talk to God and think about a woman. —Yiddish Proverb

JAYCE Late Summer, 1983 Western Massachusetts

— **Honey?**

— **Huh … whah … ?**

— **Honey? For your tea?**

— **Oh! Yes, please.**

She blushed; I must have rattled her. Didn't mean to. Rivka was sitting cross-legged on the large, cushioned wicker chair on the front porch, her flip-flops relinquished to the rough wood flooring. We had concluded an enjoyable dinner with David and my mother, who have since retired to bed. Nina had asked about the divorce and Rivka replied that the final papers were in process with the court and she's feeling considerably better. The wedding band was gone. While the others were in the kitchen I asked her, as casually as I could muster, if she'd like to stay awhile; we could chat on the porch. I'd be returning back home tomorrow and wanted to spend more time with this woman who has captivated my attention since I first heard about her eight years ago. The truth is I haven't stopped thinking about her, and worrying about her, since we finally met in person three years ago. I've seen her a few times since then, but only briefly and never alone. I'm shy by nature but didn't want the night to end. My heart skipped a beat when she said yes.

I opened the door again from the inside and tossed her the small knitted blanket from my mother's couch. Aside from enormous silver hoop earrings, Rivka was wearing a sleeveless black top over worn blue jeans, and had been rubbing her arms, the temperature having cooled considerably since her arrival. I brought out the hot drinks and sat in the other chair. It was close to eleven and the only sound was muffled country music from a distant radio. The air was still. A bit of light emanated from the living room through the window, which was adjacent to the back of my chair, and a few street lights which lined the complex every ninety feet or so. Her deep green eyes and remarkable presence fascinated and stirred me, and without the distraction of other people the focus would be on each other.

— **Thank you for the blanket, and this tea is perfect.**

— **You're welcome. Hey, I just wanted to say … I'm glad you're in a better place now.**

— **Yeah, thank you, Jayce. I don't always make the best decisions when it comes to certain things.**

— **Well, you figured out how to get out of a bad situation, that couldn't have been easy—give yourself some credit, Rivka. Is your new apartment all set up?**

— **Pretty much, you'll have to come over some time. It's close to the Manhan tributary, which is a bonus. No more scary tohubohu in my life, just the usual organized chaos at work.**

She then told me about an ethical issue that arose recently when one of the hospital physicians refused to honor a patient's advance directives. She was still upset about it.

— I mean, the guy had made it crystal clear, both verbally and in writing, that he didn't want to be kept alive on machines if it came to that. And when he had a bad stroke and it came to that, he was kept alive in the ICU for more than two fucking months! Until he finally died. He didn't have any family, just a neighbor-friend, so he and I and my supervisor made a fuss with administration, but to no avail, because there was no existing medical ethics committee, and it probably wouldn't have mattered anyway because doctors are reluctant to contradict other doctors, especially when they're working in the same facility, even though we knew most if not all of them agreed with us. I went to the ICU a few minutes every day to sit with the patient, who was languishing in a coma. If he had lived and come out of the coma, his body wouldn't have been able to function. The whole ordeal was so aggravating. A couple of weeks after he died we got the backstory on this doctor. Turns out he was born with medical problems and his parents were told he might not live long. But he did live, and so it was a 'miracle', and when he grew up and heard the story of his birth he decided he wanted to be a physician. And a devout Christian. So I understand where his beliefs may have come from, but it's not right to force your personal views on someone else, especially someone under your care. From a

patient's perspective, what's the point of doing an advance directive document if it's not going to be upheld by the very people the instructions are for?

Rivka then relayed another disturbing incident from a few weeks ago, involving a sketchy employee at the hospital. She never disclosed names.

— There's a small room at the far end of the hallway in the Geri unit. One telephone, three old chairs. Staff use it to make brief calls or meet with family members away from the busy nursing station, that sort of thing. It was empty so I went in, left the door ajar, and called in a referral to a home health agency for a patient who was getting discharged. Before leaving I stood up and glanced out the window—there was a skinhead with a swastika tattoo and those black varnished tie-up boots crossing the street.

— Charming.

— Exactly. I barely heard myself mutter 'fucking Nazis ...' under my breath and jumped out of my skin when a chilly voice directly behind me said 'Paranoid, aren't we.' My head whipped around and it was one of the lab techs. He was fake-smiling, looked deranged. What was he even doing there?

— God-almighty, Rivka, what a creep, sneaking up on you like that.

— Yeah, I just kind of froze for a beat before gathering my papers, then walked back out to the hallway

**where there were other staff moving about. I tried
to appear calm when I walked past him.**

– Good.

**– So get this: turns out he's a dangerous sicko.
Was arrested last week for sexually assaulting a
bedridden patient at a nursing home, where he'd
been working part-time at night. So he won't be at
the hospital anymore either, thank god. His wife
is a nurse there, she must be mortified—it was in
the newspaper—and there are a couple of kids
at home. Can you imagine finding out that your
father's a perv?**

She made a quick puking motion and we moved on to lighter
topics. Somehow the conversation meandered around to
Rivka hoping she'd be able to purchase a small house for
herself someday, so she could have a yard and plant a garden.
She told me an amusing story from her teenage years about
her dad recruiting her on a hot summer Sunday to help him
build a retaining wall in the backyard, something she had no
interest in.

**– So after three hours of sweaty labor, shoveling dirt
around and lifting those gigantic railroad ties and
trying to figure out how to install them, sawdust
stuck in our hair, my dad said 'Isn't this fun?' I
didn't want to hurt his feelings, so I remarked
about being glad to hang out with him, and
fetched us jugs of cold water from the house. And
the project became complicated because neither
of us knew what we were doing. Every time he**

cut a piece of wood it didn't fit. He had rented a power saw for the weekend.

— So it was measure twice, cut five times?

— Exactly! And even my ever-patient dad got frustrated, so he murmured 'My father's mustache!', which is the closest he's ever come to swearing.

Rivka's husky laugh was infectious. Being with her was simultaneously engrossing and reassuring, as she jumped from topic to topic with ease. My mind filled with various thoughts, like wanting to feel her hands in mine, for starters, when she asked about my work.

— Well, just as in your job, there are several different pieces to it. The teaching part is my least favorite. The kids are fine, and I have the utmost respect for my colleagues, but I don't particularly enjoy being around a lot of people and having to meet new students every year and doing the in-house lectures. When some of them come with me for the field work, that's a different story and is for the most part enjoyable for all of us. Then there's the research that has to get done before we get anywhere close to the excavation phase.

— What exactly do you research?

— We look at property deeds, tax records, census data, old newspaper articles, photos, and maps of specific areas—we sort through all of that and try to resolve any discrepancies. We also sometimes interview local people who may have information, accurate or not, that's been passed down through family or community stories.

— That's great that you include oral history. Wow, that's all quite extensive.

— It is. Some of it gets tedious but most of it's interesting. They call it historical archaeology. I sit in my office, or the library, or the records room and get lost in it … sometimes hours pass without me realizing it.

Without breaking eye contact, Rivka rubbed the base of her ring finger with the thumb and index finger of her other hand. With hasty, repetitive, unconscious motions she was probably reassuring herself that she's no longer bound inside a malignant marriage. Press–pinch-release–press–pinch-release.

— Is all that information-collecting so you'll know where to excavate and what you might expect to find there?

— Yes, that's right. And also to determine if it's a place worth excavating, you know, like if we have enough documentation and points of reference to improve the chances of recovering artifacts and assemblages, which are groups of fragments that are found together. Then the anthropology team figures out the community and societal patterns based on what is found, but that's much further down the line.

— Holy smokes, it's like a puzzle with a gazillion pieces. Okay, now tell me about the excavations.

— Well, there are phases for that as well, lots of prep work. First we get on site and conduct a field survey. It's a risk assessment of the proposed development and dig proposal, as well as an evaluation of the potential significance of what we may find there. We try to keep it non-intrusive because we don't want to inadvertently destroy anything. We review any previous surveys that may have been done of the area, and we try to get aerial photos. There are all sorts of technical aspects to the surveys, and are different based on how large the site is and what kind of information is gleaned from the other parts of the survey. And if it's a specific, purposive survey or a sampling. Then after all that we set up grids along transects. And then we do what's called 'field walking'. There's special training for that, you don't want inexperienced people making assumptions or to miss something that could be important. Geophysical surveys are starting to become more sophisticated and can be helpful and save us some time, there's equipment for that. We have field techs who can assist with some of the grid work and documentation during the survey and excavation phases. Oh, and we have to get permission from the county, the town, the land owner, and utility companies and so forth before we begin any sort of construction, like the structural ramps, which have to be inspected before use. Fortunately I don't have to get involved with that stuff.

— I had no idea that so much was involved … and what a complicated process!

  — I know, it's a lot. And then the digs themselves are hard physical work. I'm only thirty-one, so I'm okay, but there are some older guys and women out there and you can tell it's taking a toll on their backs and knees.

  — Yeah, I'll bet. So tell me about some of your underground adventures.

I don't usually talk this much to anyone, about anything, but she genuinely wants to know.

  — Well, last summer a couple of us drove down to Virginia for three weeks. The team there had already completed most of the survey work and we were there mainly to observe the excavation. The site was in the Alexandria area. I was right there when they uncovered a burial ground of enslaved people.

  — Oh my god. I mean—not surprising, but still. Oh my god.

  — My thoughts exactly. Seeing all those human bones, I felt sick. It certainly wasn't the first time I'd seen skeletons, but …

  — It's not anything one can get used to, knowing what happened to the people who were born into slavery and died like that. The women. The children. The men.

I nodded, and we sat in silence for a few moments. Rivka and I are both sensitive about human injustice of any kind. She got up and took our mugs inside to put some more water to boil. I thought about how easy and comforting it was to be with her. A few minutes passed and she brought out fresh tea for both of us.

— Tell me more.

— Okay. Well this summer I stayed in New York and participated in a survey and dig at the Ithaca Pottery Site, which was set up four years ago. And then I worked at another site near Geneva. The Finger Lakes region has rich Seneca and Cayuga history. They're part of the Iroquois- Haudenosaunee Confederacy, along with the Oneida, Onandaga, Mohawk, and Tuscarora Nations. Unfortunately there's been a great deal of outright destruction and theft of artifacts throughout the area, so it's a bit of a mess trying to figure out what may still have been left underground.

— I'm sorry, Jayce.

— Yeah. Thanks. So we did find some glass beads and bottles, some ceramic potsherds, and larger architectural items like a field stone platform and a stone-lined cellar hole. We even found something that looked like part of a hand pump, which was cool. There were stoneware jugs, and some leather fragments, probably from footwear. And lots of nails and other small metal artifacts.

— Do you know how old these things are?

— Subject to verification, we know that some items are from thousands of years ago, and some are only about a hundred years old.

— So what do you do with the artifacts that are dug up?

— Well everything has to be labelled and recorded and placed in special pouches, and then brought to a place where they're cleaned and stored.

— So it may take a while before they're thoroughly examined and evaluated?

— That's right, but some finds are considered 'hot' and get looked at fairly quickly if there's funding available. Also, sometimes they're deliberately left in storage until more assemblages are gathered from nearby sites.

— Oh, okay, that makes sense. You know, I think what you do is truly important. As sad and painstaking as it may be at times, your work makes other things possible, like giving us a better understanding of those historical cultures—the good, the bad, and the ugly. Makes it more difficult for people, especially whites, to ignore the actions of their ancestors. And for those of us who were born into minority groups, well we can try to come to terms with what's happened to our people, if that's ever possible. And educate others. They need to get the lies out of those children's history books.

— Agreed.

— My father's relatives were murdered in Europe. The neighbors watched them being taken away, some gunned down right on the street, and did nothing. I wonder if those governments will ever acknowledge and try to make reparations for what was allowed to happen. There are neo-Nazi strongholds all over Europe now, still. There were swastikas almost everywhere I went, especially in the cities, but also in a lot of the small towns. And the desecration of Jewish cemeteries, as if the Holocaust wasn't enough?! And will the American federal and state governments ever acknowledge and do something about the ongoing despicable treatment toward indigenous people and blacks and immigrants?! All of the systemic racism, which the police and the courts are part of. When are we going to start righting the wrongs?!? Sorry, I get filled with rage sometimes and have to let it out.

— It's okay, you can vent anytime with me, Rivka. I'm sorry about your dad's family. And the violent antisemitism you endured as a child. I was horrified when you told me and Nina about it last year. I'm glad you can trust me with your thoughts.

— Same goes. I … I wanted to ask you something. About Vietnam. You don't have to talk about it. But can you tell me … was it hideously awful?

— It was. That's an apt description, actually.

— So if someone says 'Thank you for your service', that doesn't even begin to cover it, does it?

— That's right, and no one has ever said that to me, anyway.

— I'm sorry for what you went through, Jayce. I can't even imagine the atrocities you must have witnessed. And I know that when you all came back, you were treated like pariahs, as if you had

started the war, and as if you had wanted to be there. God, you were just a peaceful kid.

— **Yeah, it was bad. So … what were you up to while I was over there?**

— **Let's see, seventy-one and two, right? I was ultrabusy getting high at Grateful Dead concerts on weekends with my commune friends, and taking college classes during the week. And working part time at a JCPenney outlet, processing mail orders for guns and girdles. And trying to avoid getting arrested at anti-war protests and civil rights rallies—went through a lot of cardboard and markers in those days.**

God-almighty, she's funny, smart. and has principles. Rivka has an extraordinary way of understanding things … and people; she groks it all. Being in her presence means getting embraced in her radiance, and it's … well, it's magical. She's gentle. She's strong. She's Rivka.

But I couldn't talk about Nam, even with her. She gets it. Her father was a combat veteran of the Second World War, having served three years in multiple battles around Europe, including Normandy. Evidently he wasn't keen to converse about that part of his life any more than I was.

— **I wish I could stay here talking with you til sunup, but I've got a long shift tomorrow at the group home, so I'd better go and try to get a little shut-eye. Hey, did I ever tell you the name of my weekend employer where at least one badass teenager tries to kill me every time I'm there?**

— No, what is it?

— The New England Home for Little Wanderers.

— Seriously?!

— Seriously. You can't make this stuff up.

We released hearty laughs, followed by sighs. But damn, why does she keep putting herself in danger, even in a work situation?

— **Isn't there someone else on duty with you?**

— **Officially there are two of us there with the fourteen kids. But the guy I usually get stuck working with on Sundays is a jerk, and he takes one of the kids out shopping for most of the afternoon, so I'm there by myself a lot with thirteen unstable teens. And to make matters worse, the kid is a girl who has a crush on him, so he shouldn't be alone with her anyway. I've tried to talk to him about it, but he doesn't care what it looks like or how it affects other people. It'll be fine, I only have to do that weekend gig another few months, then it'll be just the regular forty-hour week hospital job.**

— **Rivka …**

If I had any savings, I'd gladly offer it to her, not that she would accept it. As it is, anything left over from my basic living expenses goes directly to Nina, to help pay for what David needs. We both stood up lazily and Rivka neatly folded the blanket, slid her feet into the flip-flops, and picked up our empty mugs. According to my watch it was close to three in the morning.

— Leave them, I'll take care of it. Thank you for staying tonight, it was an enlightening conversation. Where are you parked?

— Uhh … right there across the street, in front of that beige van. Hey, Jayce? Would it be okay if I give you a hug?

She hugs everyone she knows, it probably doesn't mean anything to her other than friendship. I wish it could go further because I'm still in love with her. Completely. But I can't give her anything more—it's too risky. And we live hours apart; it probably wouldn't work anyway, even if she was receptive to that kind of relationship. Plus, she probably needs time to settle into single life, and I don't want to be a rebound guy.

— Of course.

She approached slowly, gently settled her arms around my waist, and rested the side of her face against my upper chest as I wrapped my arms around her. I could feel her shoulder blades, the ends of her long, curly tresses brushing against the back of my hands. Her faint lavender scent calmed and stirred me at once, her warm and delicate body insisting we remain entwined forever. In that moment I knew with every fiber of my being that we'd always feel safe with one another.

Barely above a whisper she said '**Thank you for tonight.**' We released each other; she picked up her bag and silently walked down the steps to the street. With the rumble of the engine turning over, she turned her head to give a little wave and smile. I waved back and watched her drive away, with an ache in my heart that I knew would not be dissipating any time soon.

14. AN INTRICATE RENDERING

Less is more—more or less. —Ludwig Mies van der Rohe

HENRY July 8, 2005 Western Massachusetts

Balance—Color—Texture—Proportion. Mass—Form—Line. I considered everything and I think it's all reflected here. There are computer programs nowadays that some landscape designers use, but I prefer to do it by hand, the old-fashioned way. Also, I don't own a computer, so it's a moot point. I hope Rivka likes it.

I helped Yusef clean up after lunch because I'm on kitchen duty today, then went to my casita to freshen up and collect the drawings. It was time for the big reveal, on paper, anyway. Rivka and I settled ourselves around the table in the conference room, where we had space to unroll the paper. She brought in a tape dispenser and stapler from her office to weigh down the corners.

— **Oh, Henry, this looks beautiful, and quite elaborate!**

— **I may have gone a little overboard …**

— **No, that's fine, we can always simplify it a bit if we need to. I love the curved edging and the color scheme—every shade of yellow and orange,** complemented by the cool blues—incredible design, Henry. Okay, break it down for me. What's this wall here?

— I thought it would be nice to create a vertical backdrop for the garden. David said we can disassemble some old wooden pallets he doesn't need anymore and seal the pieces to weatherize them, and I'd like to do a horizontal pattern. We can work with however many slats we have and space them out accordingly, so it won't cost anything in materials, except for some nails or wires to attach them to the existing perimeter fencing.

— What a great idea. Is this clematis?

— Yes, but on second thought, any climbing vine requires quite a bit of maintenance.

— Yeah, let's nix that, I don't think it's needed.

— I agree.

— Are those Kerri japonica?

— Yes! See, you *do* remember!

— Well, I only know that because I planted one in my backyard last spring. It grew quickly and keeps re-flowering. And the stems stay green all winter. It looks like you've got three of them here?

— Yes.

— Perfect. And is that some sort of dogwood behind them on the left?

— Yes, it's a Kousa. They eventually grow to twenty feet high and wide, so that'll anchor the garden on that side, with the oak anchoring on the right. I'd also like to get a small Japanese maple if possible for this area.

— How big is this whole plan you've laid out?

— About thirty feet wide by ten feet deep, not including the anchor trees. It can be adjusted if needed.

— Okay. Now tell me what all these flowers are.

— Okay, well of course it will depend on what the nurseries have available and how much money we have to work with, but I'd like to plant some tall daylilies back there, then a combination of columbine, coneflowers, blazing star, and/or salvia in front of the lilies. Then yarrow toward the front here, and some coral bells if I can get them in white. And low blue phlox at the front edge. These are hostas and ferns near the oak, they should do well there. We can use the animal manure to enrich the soil, but we'll need to bring in some more topsoil after we clear the area. There are plenty of shovels and wheelbarrows and bow rakes in the barn, so the only tool we'll need to purchase is an edger.

— Wow, you've certainly thought this through, it's great.

— Yes, of course. Oh, and I also had another idea I wanted to show you.

I unrolled the other design for Rivka, who at this point was beaming with enthusiasm, and perhaps pride? She's the boss here, but she's also a supportive, nurturing person who seemed genuinely impressed.

— Okay, I didn't want to be presumptuous, but I thought this small area up front behind the bike rack could use some sprucing up?

— Yes! The entrance is kind of drab, could certainly use some help. This looks wonderful, Henry. Okay, here's the deal. I can give you four hundred and thirty dollars. The topsoil and any extension water hoses you need can come out of the general maintenance budget, but all the rest has to come out of the four-thirty. The labor is up to you and the other volunteers, just coordinate that with David, okay?

— That sounds great, Rivka, thank you!

— You're more than welcome, and here's the other thing. When you're ready to actually start purchasing stuff, let David talk to the nursery owners after you've picked out what you think you'll want. When in doubt, err on the side of informal simplicity. You'll need to go with David and his truck anyway, and he's the best negotiator this side of the Mississippi. Some businesses are willing to give discounts to nonprofits, so let him work his magic.

— Okay, that's perfect. And if we start reaching our budget limit, I can get smaller specimens that will take two or three seasons to fill in.

– **Exactly. Okay, Henry, I'm so grateful for what you've done here and can't wait to see it all finished.**

– **Me too, and I appreciate the opportunity.**

– **Win-win!**

She initiated a high five and I responded immediately in kind. Lordy, I surely am blessed.

15. BIRDSONG

Life can only be fully understood by looking backward; but it must be lived looking forward. —Soren Kierkegaard

JAYCE January, 1984 Upstate New York

I knew what was inside the package before opening it. My mother had called recently to tell me that Rivka had asked to borrow the old Polaroid and had miraculously transformed the photo of the three of us into a larger, cleaned-up version in black-and-white, using her friend Cal's basement darkroom. She had personally delivered two, one for Nina, in what my mother described as an exquisite silver frame with subtle textured detailing of birds surrounding a cream-colored mat, and the other for David in a simple, modern black wooden frame with white matting. She said that the framing suited each of their personalities and that Rivka had mailed one to me as well.

My first thought was: how the hell did Rivka manage to do this? She's working two stressful jobs, recently came out of a divorce, and is living paycheck to paycheck. Where does she get the drive and time and energy to do things for other people?

What I had not anticipated was how much this would tear at my heart. Alone in the house, I sat at the kitchen table and carefully unwrapped the thick Kraft paper, then slowly removed the box lid. I used both hands to set aside the layers of tissue paper and nearly gasped. There was sweet Chilali in the middle between me and Nina, wearing the oversized Cornell T-shirt I had given her when I first started school here. She was grinning from ear to ear and her head was partially turned to the side, looking up at me. Just before my father took the shot, Chilali had been poking at my ribs, telling me to '**stop being so serious all the time!**', trying unsuccessfully to get me to laugh. At the precise moment the photo was taken, she wrapped her right arm around my waist and her left around Nina's. Of the three of us, Chilali was the one with the unrestrained faith in life. She was filled with silliness and joy on that August day almost ten years ago. I should have laughed. I should have saved her. Dear, sweet sister of mine.

The photo itself was five-by-seven. Rivka had placed a soft-grey mat around it, and a rustic driftwood frame. And there was something else that blew me away. She had placed some marigold petals in varied shades of gold and orange between the mat and glass; they were pressed into the northeast corner, balancing out my height below the northwest. Rivka once told me that marigolds are holy in some cultures, like the Aztecs of Mexico and the Hindus in India, having to do with guiding the souls of the dead back home for a visit. If I remember correctly the yellow represents sanctity, the saffron shade is sacred, and the bright orange is tied to courage and sacrifice. The ancient Greeks and Egyptians valued the flower's healing and restorative qualities. In my own culture the yellows and oranges are a manifestation of the eastern sun (dawn), heroism, determination, heart, and death. We are all connected.

I knew enough about photographic processing to figure that Rivka had to have created a negative from the crappy three-by-three Polaroid, and then painstakingly converted it into a stunning work of art. After some deep breaths, I rose from the chair and carried it upstairs to my room. The pile of magazines from the school's ornithology lab remained in the bookshelf. *Living Bird* was published annually when Chilali was alive, and I also managed to get some old issues dating back to 1962. I always brought some with me when I drove out to visit. She was thrilled having new photos and drawings to look at and try to copy. Sometimes she read the accompanying articles but mostly she loved the pictures. A couple of years ago they started publishing quarterly, and I was so used to collecting and saving them for her that I just continued to do so. I guess I didn't need to do that anymore.

I carefully placed the gift upright on top of my dresser. It would be cherished always.

She picked up on third ring.

— **Rivka.**

— **Jayce! How are you?**

— **Good. Did I catch you in the middle of dinner?**

— **No, not at all, just got home. Everything okay out in Ithaca?**

— **Yes. Rivka, I got the photo and don't know how to thank you.**

— **You like it?**

— **It's beautiful. I don't know how you managed the metamorphosis.**

— **It was my pleasure. I actually tried to make it a little larger, but it was getting too grainy, you know how that goes.**

— Yes—it's perfect exactly the way it is. And I love the framing and mat and what you did with the marigolds … I—it's completely amazing. You— you are amazing.

— Oh no, Jayce, I'm just me. Hey, tell me what you've been up to this dreary winter.

— Well, work's been pretty good. Aside from the usual research, I've been asked by the AIA to contribute an article for their American Journal of Archaeology.

— Ooh, that sounds exciting—what do they want you to write about?

— Methodology. It's not exciting to anyone except a few people in our field who want to have all the technical details spelled out, but that's okay.

— Yes, and it'll be a good addition to your CV, right?

— Uh, yeah, probably, and it looks good for Cornell as well.

— Oh, right. Okay, what else?

— Well I've got another out-of-town project coming up in early spring, probably extensive. Survey and mapping.

— Where are they sending you this time?

— Chaco Canyon in New Mexico. Hopi and Pueblo.

— Holy smokes. It's a massive area?

— It is. There are multiple dig sites but there's been a lot of destruction, mostly from the tourists walking through.

— Oh, Jayce, that seems to be an ongoing problem. Even if it wasn't deliberate, what a shame. So you may be there for a couple of months?

— Possibly through part of the summer, I don't know yet.

— Housing?

— As far as I know there aren't any nearby motels or cabins, so if they can't accommodate us in the dig house we'll probably get set up in large tents, with either outhouses or porta-potties.

— Uugh.

— Yeah, I'm kind of used to it by now.

— I'll bet you have a greater appreciation than most people for the luxury of indoor plumbing.

— Probably. So what's been happening with you?

— Well the good news is that I gave notice at the group home. I have to work this Saturday and Sunday, then the following two Sundays, then I'm done.

— That *is* good news, you've been overworking yourself. What else?

She then told me about a heated argument she had with the hospital administrator yesterday when he found out she had arranged for the services of a professional sign language interpreter for a deaf patient. Evidently this head honcho didn't want to pay for the service, which Rivka explained was necessary. He thought it was fine for the patient's child to handle the go-between.

— It's as if he was deliberately refusing to understand what I was saying. I wanted to scream at him for his ignorance, but I knew he had kids so I took a more personal approach. I looked at him straight in the eye and said: 'Okay, so if you were on a family vacation in Spain and became seriously ill and were taken to a rural hospital where no one spoke English, you'd be fine with your Spanish-speaking twelve-year-old daughter being the one to tell you that you've caught a potentially deadly viral infection that needs urgent treatment? And then subjecting her to all the back and forth questions and answers with the medical staff? Or would you rather have an objective, trained interpreter in the room?' He glared at me, eventually blinked, and then said 'Fine'. You know, like he was doing me a favor by allowing me to do what was best for the patient and family. I think he was more concerned about a potential lawsuit than about doing the right thing.

— The patients are truly lucky to have you, Rivka. You deal with issues on a regular basis that the average person wouldn't even give a thought to.

— Yeah, well I'm never bored, that's for sure. Hey, are you laughing at me?

— No … I'm just picturing you yelling at that administrator in his office.

— Yeah, I wanted to yell, but I kept my cool for the most part. Thanks for listening to my work stories.

— Anytime.

— **Okay, well … we'll talk before your big trip. In the meantime, good luck with the article, and when it's done please send a copy to Nina, okay? So I can read it and she can continue to brag about you.**

This wondrous woman never fails to make me smile. For some reason she deems me worthy of her time and care.

— **Okay. Rivka … thank you again for the photo. For all of it. I don't have the right words to express my appreciation for your thoughtfulness. David and Nina love theirs too.**

— **I'm glad, Jayce, you're more than welcome. And your words are just fine. It's really good to hear your voice. It's … it's always good to hear your voice. I just wish—never mind. Sorry.**

— **What? What do you wish?**

There was a pause before she spoke again.

— **Well … I wish you lived closer.**

Shit. It was my turn to hesitate, and I did. This was the one person in the world I could be totally honest with about everything, even if it was messy and complicated. Everything, that is, except the depth of my feelings for her. I kept it casual, as usual.

— **Me too. My schedule shouldn't be as crazy once I return from New Mexico, so hopefully we can connect at some point soon after that.**

— **I'd like that, Jayce.**

Unfortunately eight months would pass before I'd see her again. I held the photo that night and wept. Thank you, Rivka, for bringing Chilali back for a visit.

16. A BEAUTIFUL GIRL

Whenever I draw a circle, I immediately want to step out of it.
—R. Buckminster Fuller

RIVKA Spring, 1984 Massachusetts

I've been a vegetarian since I was a small girl in the 1950s. It's one of the few things my parents didn't push back hard on. It was more of a personal preference than a moral decision; I mean, what does a six-year-old know about animal welfare beyond feeding your pets? I continue to have a low tolerance for the look and smell of meat at any stage of cooking. So imagine my dismay, along with delight, when Phil, a caseworker from Boston, called to tell me there was an opportunity to meet a half-Vietnamese-half-American eight-year-old girl at a Burger King in Worcester, which was approximately halfway between her current residence and mine. A few weeks ago I had submitted my name to be added to a list of people who would be interested/willing to consider fostering and potentially adopting a child who was 'not perfect' nor an infant. Phil or someone in his office had presumably performed a basic vetting procedure and did not seem to mind that I was a single woman. I didn't expect to hear anything for months, or even years, so this was completely unexpected.

Despite the awkward setting, it was a thrill to meet this lovely girl named MaiYei. Phil bought her a burger and fries and, since the weather was decent, I herded us outside to a patio table, away from the din and odor. We talked non-stop for two hours. I asked about school and what kinds of things she was interested in, and told her a little about my job and described my apartment. She seemed especially excited when I told her that if she decided to come visit she would have her own bedroom.

Phil had given me a brief rundown of the girl's current situation: there was no indication of abuse or neglect by her current foster parents, but she wanted out.

Not much to go on. Phil's a good guy, but he works for the state. Encumbered by the antiquated bureaucracies inherent in government systems, public sector workers, especially when it comes to services for children, have ridiculously huge caseloads and are cubicle-based. They tend to procure the rudimentary demographics but rarely get to actually know their charges. In the world of private nonprofits we have ridiculously huge caseloads and are client-based. The private sector in this particular field tends to have higher standards but lower pay, go figure. To Phil's credit, he said:

– **Just between you and me, I think she'd do better with a mother that doesn't look and act like June Cleaver.**

I had to smile at that one.

So this is what I learned about MaiYei, later to be respelled as Maya at her request when I told her it was a variation of the Hebrew word for water. These observations are based a bit on the initial Worcester meeting but more so on the two weekends she spent at my place prior to moving in permanently:

Maya is extremely bright and eager to learn. She's a bit of a germaphobe, as am I. She has a proclivity toward patterns and order. She is a perfectionist, and seems to put pressure on herself to get things just right. She needs a strong sense of control over her environment, which is a major challenge amidst the chaos of her current foster home, where she shares a bedroom with three other girls. And god only knows the turmoil and mayhem surrounding her birth and all the years since; I'll probably never know the half of it. Maya may not remember much of her first couple of years, but she had to have been affected by the wartime chaos.

She makes detailed lists and then crosses items off. She even thought to bring a full inventory of questions to ask me at the first weekend visit. Her asthma has become easier to manage since the physicians in Boston were finally able to identify and get her allergies under control. She has a low tolerance for ambiguity, particularly in practical matters. For example, when we were getting ready to cook dinner one night, she found a recipe that looked interesting in one of my cookbooks, which are stored in the tall, brimful bookcases in the living room, everything organized by category, which pleases her to no end.

— **What does this mean, 'a pinch of cumin'?**

— **It means just a tiny bit.**

— **But what does that mean, 'a tiny bit'?**

Oy. I pulled out of a kitchen drawer a set of tin measuring spoons, which I've had since the dawn of time; they may have been my mother's. The smallest was one-eighth of a teaspoon and I suggested she use that but not fill it all the way to the top when the recipe calls for 'a dash' or 'a pinch'. She was quiet for a few seconds and then decided that this was a reasonable form of instruction.

I also learned that Maya needs space and quiet at times, who doesn't? She was perfectly content lying on her bed to peruse a book once or twice a day and at bedtime. My kind of gal. She picked out a large tome of children's stories by Isaac Bashevis Singer, whose work I had at one time been an avid fan of and had the fortuitous occasion to meet in 1980 in Manhattan. She also pulled out a nature encyclopedia, and a thick volume from 1944 entitled *10,000 Garden Questions*.

During the first weekend we went to a small local video store (Blockbuster would not make its debut for another couple of years) and rented *To Sir, With Love*. It was one of my favorite movies and she was fascinated with the story and the characters. We ate popcorn and cried when Lulu sang that song at the end. The second weekend, which was longer due to a holiday, we watched two movies: *Fiddler On The Roof* and *West Side Story*, more heartbreakers.

But it wasn't all tears—we giggled often and easily when we talked and when we cooked and when I tried to teach her how to salsa dance. I am crazy about this wonderful girl, who keeps me on my toes. She wants to know how things work and why people do what they do and why the thousands of frog species each make their own distinct sound. She is absolutely delightful.

And she's beautiful on the outside as well.

After driving her back to the Boston suburbs after that second weekend, she gave me a big hug and whispered in my ear:

— **I'm going to tell Phil that I want you to be my Mom.**

— **That would make me very happy, honey.**

And so it came to be.

17. A TANGLED WEB

You can't empty the ocean with a spoon. —Yiddish Proverb

HENRY July 11, 2005 Western Massachusetts

The Eagles' *Desperado* floated out from the tack room. Rivka had given David her old portable radio over the weekend, and he had it tuned to the oldies station. We sang along— knew most of the lyrics even though it was released a short time before either of us had arrived in this world. As a matter of fact, it was David's thirtieth birthday, but I didn't say anything because Peter and Yusef were preparing a special lunch for him, and Rivka had asked me this morning to get David back to the lodge at five minutes after twelve so they could surprise him. If I had known, I would have biked into town yesterday to get him a gift. Maybe I'd sneak back to the casita after lunch to make him a card; that's the least I could do, he's been so good to me. I could try to make a drawing of Cody for him. I was thinking about this while feeding Liz and Luke barley-alfalfa cookies and cleaning their hooves. They would have cooperated without the treats, but I like giving them, and David said it's fine as long as we don't overdo it.

David was across the aisle working with the goats. He told me that Rivka had mentioned at a recent board meeting that she needed someone who knew how to set up a proper website for the farm. As it turned out, the son-in-law of one of the board members is a tech wiz, and after a series of phone calls with Rivka he offered to do it pro bono.

    — **That's wonderful, David.**

    — **Yeah. He'll be coming around next week to take pictures of the animals and staff and the vegetable beds and everything. It's awesome, will make it easier for people to find us. And hopefully spur some additional donations, which are tax-deductible.**

    — **Yes, and the farm will look more like a bonafide, official establishment, which it already is.**

    — **Exactly.**

I checked my watch—it was nearly noon. I was finished with the donkeys and stood there petting them for a minute. Liz likes to be scratched behind her ears and Luke lets me gently rub his neck and head.

    — **Hey, David, ready for a lunch break?**

    — **You go ahead, I'll be there in a few minutes, just wanna finish up here.**

    — **Uhh … actually Rivka mentioned this morning that she needed to talk to you about something back at the lodge. She has an appointment and needs to leave a little after twelve. Sorry I didn't tell you earlier.**

He gave me a confused look but agreed to walk over with me. We washed up and David started toward Rivka's office, but she was already seated at one end of the picnic table with her food tray, along with Suzy and most of the on-site volunteers, plus a few other people whose faces were only vaguely familiar to me. She motioned for him to get his lunch, and when his back was turned she gave me a thumbs up. There were a few restrained giggles, but everyone kept a straight face and resumed talking and eating. The buffet items were fantastic as always, and some upbeat Motown tracks flowed from the kitchen. David returned to the table and placed his tray next to Rivka's; I sat on his other side. She told him that the computer person was going to need his help when it came time to put the website together and they needed to sort out some details regarding how to best present the philosophy of the sanctuary. He said okay, but didn't she have a meeting to go to now? She said it was postponed. He may have started realizing that something was up, but continued eating, nodding to some folks at the other end of the table, which by now was packed full, about fifteen people in all.

A moment later the volume from the CD player was turned down and Peter emerged from the kitchen with a large, enticing sheet cake, covered with fresh berries and candles aglow, followed by Yusef, who carried a cake knife and a bunch of small plates, extra forks, and napkins. Everyone sang the birthday song, while David smiled and shook his head slowly, gracious as the cake was set down carefully in front of him. He thanked everyone, then stood and hugged Peter and Yusef. The cake was as delicious as it looked.

There was no time to get back to the casita; I would work on the card tonight. David and I managed some more chores at the barn, and then led all of the animals outside. Cody seemed to be getting a little better each day, still not mingling much with the others but no longer deliberately avoiding them. And he's not flicking his ears back and forth in high alert as much as he had been. We're both feeling lighter.

In the alpaca pasture David showed me the difference between clipped toenails and those that needed it done. He said it's a fairly easy task with the special clippers and he would demonstrate later on. We watched as Suzy's buggy bounced along toward us.

— **Henry, your father is here.**

— **WHAT?!?**

— **Tall black man, fancy suit, fancy shoes?**

— **How … ughhh …**

— **Hop in, I'll get you back to the lodge. Rivka's chatting him up in her office.**

God, please help me. I washed my hands, taking longer than usual. I haven't seen my father in years, and we rarely speak on the phone; he does a perfunctory check-in every few months. I trudged over to Rivka's office, where he was seated across from her wearing his grim poker face, a striking contrast to Rivka's warm and friendly demeanor. She was going on about the advisory board and the administrative structure of the sanctuary, topics she must have sensed would appeal to him far more than any specifics regarding the animals. I stood in the doorway. Eventually he turned his head in my direction and I barely met his eyes, found myself staring at Rivka's shell bracelet, the one she always wears around her left wrist. It was one of those things that looked like it would make noise when she moved her arm, but it never did. Oddly it was so damn comforting right now, my imaginary oasis in the scorching desert.

— **Henry?**

— **Hello, sir.**

— Why don't you two go out to the back porch, where you'll have a view of the pastures and can speak privately.

— Thank you, ma'am, nice to meet you.

— Same here, and have a safe trip back to Texas tonight.

They stood and shook hands. Rivka can sure hold her own; she doesn't get intimidated by the likes of my father, who tends to lord it over people that he's part of high society. Or thinks he is. I led us out to the long porch. It had warmed to the eighties and was a bit stifling without a breeze. My father kept his jacket on; appearing 'professional' at all times was a higher priority for him than commonsense comfort. There were benches, but we both remained standing.

— How did you find me?

— I called your mother, she told me where you were. I was at a conference in Boston and thought I'd come see you before flying back tonight.

— You rented a car?

— Yes, Henry, I rented a car. So can you tell me what the hell you're doing here?

— I'm taking care of the animals. I'm part of the Volunteer Work Program.

— I sent you to that prestigious prep school so you could move backward to a mediocre state college and become an unpaid farmhand?

I've been a big disappointment to my father, ever since he understood that I was not going to follow in his footsteps and become an attorney. I managed to finish up the landscape design Master's program, but that's not a field he deems particularly respectable or impressive. I'll never live up to his expectations.

— **It's more than that. I'm getting my strength back.**

— **You mean in your hand?**

— **I mean all of me.**

In my heart and soul, I wanted to tell him. I have animal companions and people friends, am happy and safe and my life has meaning for the first time in years. I couldn't imagine being anywhere else right now. But he wouldn't understand. He didn't even glance at my hand. Sometimes I got the feeling that he wished it was me who had died that day instead of Daniel.

I wasn't sure how much longer I could stand there with him in the abyss. I looked out at the goats and donkeys with longing. David had been there with them a few minutes ago but was now nowhere to be seen. Lord, please help me.

God answered my prayer a few seconds later in the form of David To The Rescue in the white buggy. He pulled right up to us at the porch. Praise the lord! For real.

— **Hi, I'm David King, Operations Manager. Henry's supervisor.**

— **James Carter.**

— **Why don't you hop in and I'll give you a tour?**

— **I need to head back soon, flying out from Logan**
  ...

— **We'll do the quick five minute tour, no worries!! Hop in! Henry, why don't you grab the back seat.**

David drove slowly, so as not to stir up any dirt or dust that might accidentally land on my father's ridiculous shiny shoes or his custom-tailored suit. He talked non-stop to my father, pointing out the mountain ranges in every direction and giving him information about this part of the Connecticut River Valley. We passed by the vegetable plots and I told my father about the fresh, organic food served in the lodge every day. He didn't seem particularly interested. Then we pulled up to the big red oak.

— **Henry's designed a terrific garden for this area. We'll be breaking ground later this week …**

My father turned his head and gave me a barely perceptible nod. It was the only moment since his arrival that he acknowledged me in a positive way. David continued chatting away …

— **Everyone's really excited about it. I've gotta tell you, your son has been a great asset here. The animals love him, the staff and volunteers enjoy working with him. You raised a good, honest, industrious man.**

— **Thank you.**

David was surely embellishing, but that was how one charms someone's parents, and it was working as well as anything could possibly work with my father, who had a cold stone where his heart was supposed to be. After the tour, David parked the buggy out front, shook my father's hand, and disappeared into the lodge. I walked my father to his BMW rental, thanked him for coming, and shook his hand. He didn't say anything so I just wished him a safe trip and he nodded. No smile, no parting words.

Back in the pasture I thanked David for the much-needed distraction, and apologized for ruining his birthday.

— **No worries, Henry, you didn't ruin anything. Hey, take some deep breaths, dude, you look like you're about to keel over. I know family stuff can be difficult.**

The breathing actually helped.

— **If you wanna kick off now, there's only an hour or so left—**

— **No, I need to keep working, if that's okay.**

— **Of course, whatever you need is fine. Why don't you go see if Lily's okay, I think Adam was head-butting her earlier. Check her head and sides, make sure there's no damage.**

— **Okay. I'll check all of the goats.**

— **Good man.**

Back at the casita after supper I started on the drawing. The unexpected visit from my father had thrown me for a loop and burst my happy bubble, but I'd be damned if I was going to let it stop me from being who I was and doing what I needed to do for myself. Two steps forward, one step back.

Now another step forward. I think I've captured Cody's glory, his trepidation, and his wish, perhaps, for a new day, when the world might begin to right itself. I wanted to believe that somehow I could help raise his hope. I used a few shades of dark-brown and black and the subtle glint of russet. And the white teardrop high on his head. The thick paper I worked

on was nine-by-twelve, and I had left some blank space above
the drawing, where I wrote:

18. MUTUAL DEVOTION

One plum gets color by looking at another. —Persian Proverb

RIVKA Late Summer, 1984 Western Massachusetts

It was a gloriously hot weekend, and I was taking Maya to meet Nina and David for the first time. It's been a whirlwind of activity—getting Maya settled in, filing the adoption papers with family court, arranging for after-school care, etcetera, etcetera. Lots of crucial details. I had taken a week off of work in order to give her my full attention, and overall she was transitioning well. There were a few freak-out moments, such as when she got frustrated when we didn't find the EXACT shoe style she wanted in the first store, and when she temporarily misplaced the package of hair barrettes she had picked out because they were the ONLY ones that would do. Oy. We worked out a chore-allowance deal and discussed at length what the weekday and weekend schedules would look like. This was a girl who understandably needed to know what the expectations would be as she expanded her world. New people, new school, new way of living. That's a lot for anyone at any age.

The biggest and probably most important discussion we had was about communication. I wanted to make sure she knew moving forward that it was okay to talk to me about anything, even if she thought it might upset me; we would work it out together. With reassurance and love it was an honor and thrill for me to welcome her into her new life, and mine. Ours.

When we arrived, David was lying stomach-down on the living room floor, with coloring books and crayons spread about. Nina and I exchanged hugs, and David jumped up quickly and gave me a tight waist-squeeze. I introduced him to Maya.

— **Hi. You're pretty.**

— **Thank you. Nice shirt.**

— **Thanks. You wanna color?**

— **Um … maybe. Do you have any connect-the-dots?**

— **Connect-the-dots … connect-the-dots … I think there may be some in that yellow book, wanna help me look?**

— **Yes.**

She scrambled down to the floor and immediately became engaged, quietly working with David on the books. She also sorted and organized all the crayons and pencils on the floor, which he didn't seem to mind. At one point they were side by side on their bellies, sharing their masterpieces and occasionally giggling at something the other said or drew. Nina and I caught up with things and then moved into the kitchen to make some iced tea.

— **Nana Nina and I are going out to the porch, if you kids want to join us. It's okay to stay inside, but it's a gorgeous day, may as well enjoy the sunshine.**

A couple of minutes later they were outside with us. David asked Maya if she wanted to run through the lawn sprinkler with him. She wasn't sure what that would entail but was game. She looked at me and I nodded an okay. He advised her to remove her sandals, which she did quickly; he was already barefoot. He grabbed her hand; they ran down the porch steps and made their way off the cement pathway to the lawn. We had a full view of them from the porch, where I reveled in the ninety-degree heat, summer having always been my favorite season. Both kids were thin and fit, Maya an inch or so taller. She was almost ten years old; David had recently turned nine. Due to multiple intermittent illnesses early in life, Maya had lost close to two years of schooling. Fortunately she was able to catch up for the most part, so she and David would both be entering fourth grade at the same time, and at the same school. Even if they didn't become buddies, I figured it would be good for her to know someone when classes would begin in a few days.

Nina and I chatted, watching the kids out of the corners of our eyes. Within what seemed liked seconds, laughter and squealing could be heard throughout the land as the kids ran back and forth and circled the base of the sprinkler. They did this a thousand times and were drenched. I had to shout to get their attention.

— Maya! David! Come up here for a minute!

They did, and I had them both strip down to their underwear. Nina and I wrung the water out of their shirts and shorts and hung them over the railing to dry in the sun. The kids were already back on the lawn, laughing and screaming, along with a few neighborhood children, who must have heard the frenzy and decided to join in. This went on for at least another hour. They were prancing ponies, tiny specks of pure, unadulterated glee on a sliver of earth in a New England valley.

— They light each other up.

— Two peas in a pod.

Nina and I were thoroughly delighted that the kids were forming a friendship, even knowing it could be fleeting at this age. I smiled while imagining the shenanigans they might get into. Nina went inside to prepare some snacks, and the kids finally hauled themselves up to the porch when I made the eating motion from afar. They didn't leave each other's side until it was time to make the twenty minute drive back home. Hugs were exchanged by all.

— Mom, how come David calls you 'River'?

— Oh yeah, it's because when he was learning how to talk he couldn't pronounce my name, but he knew the word river, so that's what he started calling me, and it just sort of stuck.

— That's cute. Hey Mom? Can David come over next weekend for dinner?

— Sure, as long as it's okay with Nana Nina. We'll invite them both.

— Yes. She's kind of quiet but very nice. I like them a lot.

— Me too. Hey, is that David's shirt you're wearing?

— Yeah, he said I could have it because I told him that blue is my favorite color.

— So you gave him yours?

— Yeah, is that okay? He said he likes mine so we switched.

— Sure, honey, as long as it was okay with both of you. You're about the same size so that worked out fine.

— Mom? David said his Uncle Jayce is going to buy him a bicycle the next time he comes to visit. Can I get one too?

— Well, we'll see. Maybe we can all go to the store together to look.

— Yes!!

— Honey, it's not a done deal. We're just going to look, okay?

— Okay.

Maya and David were joined at the hip today, and I was hopeful they'd remain so for years to come. The dots were connected.

19. A RITE OF PASSAGE

Courage is not the towering oak that sees storms come and go, it is the fragile blossom that opens in the snow. —Alice Mackenzie Swaim

RIVKA Saturday Morning, August 1, 1987
Western Massachusetts

Here is Maya's Bat Mitzvah speech. She wrote it completely on her own, did not let me help her prepare, and the Rabbi said she declined his offer of assistance as well. I told her it would be *her* day, and she could make of it what she wanted. I had no idea what she was about to say.

Hi—Shalom. My name is Maya Solomon. I stand here today as I transition from being a girl to becoming a woman. I'm a little nervous because the only other time I gave a speech was for the junior debate club at school. Some of you know me and some of you are here for the regular Shabbat service. I want to tell you a little about my life so far and also what being a Jew means to me.

I was born in the fall of 1974 in South Vietnam. I was orphaned during the war and came here to the United States as part of Operation Babylift in the spring of 1975. There were about thirty-two hundred babies like me that were put on the planes. I don't remember any of this because I was too small. I lived in hospitals and foster homes for the first nine years of my life. The last

foster home was with a huge family. They were nice people but kind of strict and had other foster kids plus their own kids and I never felt like I fit in. We had to go to church every Sunday which I didn't like, mostly because I had no choice about it and also because I was expected to watch over the little kids. Also my foster parents wouldn't help me get into the AP classes in school even though the teachers said I should be in a higher grade. My caseworker from the city came to check on me twice a year, and when I was eight I told him I didn't want to live there anymore. I had to tell him this a few times before he agreed to look for another family. I'm sorry this story is so long.

So when I met my mom Rivka I felt comfortable right away. I stayed with her a couple of weekends to see if we liked each other before I moved in for real. She was smart and kind and funny and didn't treat me like a baby. She gave me choices and let me decide. We talked about all sorts of things and she told me that if I decided to move in that she would talk to the teachers at the school here and make sure I got into the classes that would be 'commensurate with your intelligence and skill level'. When she told me she was Jewish I didn't really know what that meant at first, but over the next three years she showed me by example, which I will get to soon.

I know that my mom has had some rough times in her life. I won't go into details and I'm sure I 'don't know the half of it, and you don't want to know the rest'. That's what she says when she doesn't want to talk about something anymore. But even though there were troubles in the past she has a big heart and always gives me support, no matter what. She calls this 'unconditional love'.

Mom and I are very close with another family. They are Native Americans and their people have experienced centuries of oppression and mistreatment and genocide, just like the Jews. Our cultures are different but we understand each other and spend a lot of time together and learn from each other.

So this is what my mom has taught me about being Jewish:

- Firstly you have to be educated, meaning read a lot and go to school. Also we can learn from our experiences.

- Secondly you need to carry on even when you don't feel like it. You can rest if you had a bad day but you need to figure out how to move on with your life even if you had a bad year. She calls this 'resilience'.

- Also you have to respect other people. Mom told me a couple of things that her father told her when she was a little girl. Zadie Elliot died before I lived here so I never got to meet him, which is sad because he must have been a wise man, like a sage. The first important thing he told her is that 'There will always be people who have it easier than you, and there will always be people who have it harder than you'. Another important thing he told her that she passed on to me is that 'Being smart is a good thing, but it won't shield you from life's complications and struggles'.

- Okay so another thing about being Jewish is that you have to be honest and must always try to do the right thing. Not just at your regular places like school or at your job, but everywhere you go. Also be true to yourself and learn from your mistakes, and that it's okay to make mistakes. Mom calls this 'integrity'.

- Another thing about being a Jew is that you should pay attention to injustices in the world and try to do what you can to help other people. It's called 'social activism'. My mom did a lot of that when she was younger and also still does it.

- And last but not least, she taught me that being Jewish means always remembering where we came from.

So I stand here today, proud to be a Vietnamese-Black-American-Jewess. Thank you for listening to my story. I am grateful to HaShem, and to Rabbi Schecter for being so patient with me over the last year when I kept asking a lot of 'Why?' questions. And also thank you to Cantor Lebow for helping me learn the haftorah singing. Shabbat Shalom.

written by Maya Solomon, age 12
July 1987

20. A SPECIAL GIFT

When I was young, I admired clever people. Now that I am old, I admire kind people. —Rabbi Joshua Heschel

RIVKA Sunday, August 2, 1987 Western Massachusetts

Maya and I were exhausted from yesterday's festivities, and I was still kvelling and buzzing with naches. Heaps of cards and a few gifts were piled on the corner desk in the living room. I went out to run some errands, and upon returning an hour later I heard Maya sobbing in her room. She was sitting on the bed, holding a wad of tissues. She's had some sporadic crying jags in the past, and with the extra pressure recently of the studies leading up to the big day, plus emerging hormones, it was no surprise she was probably feeling overwhelmed.

– **What is it, honey?**

– **Mom, look what the Kings gave me! And they didn't buy it, they MADE it! They made it by hand!!**

Spread out next to her on the white coverlet was a stunning work of art made of cloth, about five feet wide by three feet high, with a few short vertical fabric strips on top surrounding a wooden dowel, so that it could be hung on the wall. There was a depiction of a large bear in the night, with a full moon against the sky. And some trees. It was constructed with a variety of fabric remnants intricately sewn together, mostly in variegated shades of blues, greens, and browns, both solids and prints, and various textures. Detailed beadwork adorned the edges of the bear and moon. Near the bottom, spelled out in embroidery, was:

For Maya With Love From The Kings 1987

- **Holy smokes, Maya, it's gorgeous. I mean truly gorgeous.**

- **I know! I called David and he said the bear is my Native birth totem! It represents strength and confidence and—wait!—I wrote it all down …**

She found her notepad and held it reverently in both hands, tissues by her side, still crying uncontrollably.

- **… and standing against adversity, and the importance of quiet time so I can get grounded and heal. Mom, that's so me!!**

- **Wow, it sure is.**

- **And he said that Uncle Jayce sketched the design, and Nana Nina did the sewing, and David cut the cloth for the edging and backing, and he even lined up the beads before she sewed them on. Look at this, Mom! These are teeny-tiny glass beads! And David went to the fabric store with Nana Nina to make sure she got some blue pieces, because he knows it's my favorite color!**

- **Okay, slow down, honey, do you need the inhaler?**

— No, I'm okay, I used it before, when you were out. And Mom, they worked on it for weeks and weeks! And David said that even though my thirteenth birthday isn't until next month, they wanted me to have this early because Uncle Jayce said it's important to pay honor to my Bat Mitzvah. And you're not going to believe this: Jayce and David wanted the moon to be full, because David's mom Chilali was born during the snow moon in 1959, in February—his dead mom! The Kings wanted me to have something to honor her too so they made it as part of the design, isn't that awesome?

— Yes, that's wonderful. I remember when Nana Nina first told me about her, she said the name Chilali means Snowbird. Wow, this is a lot to take in, honey.

— I know! And there's more!

Oy, I could use a nap.

— So I asked David for Uncle Jayce's phone number. And I called him in New York! Mom I know it's long distance—I'll pay you back out of my allowance.

— No, don't worry about it, it's fine. Were you able to reach Jayce?

— Yes, he was actually there when I called! I know he left the party early last night because he had to make the five hour drive back to Ithaca in time to get ready for work tomorrow morning.

— Yes, and he had driven all that distance on Friday night so he could be with us yesterday. He's a good man.

An extraordinary man.

— Yes, and so listen to what he told me. He said the ancient Hebrew melodies reminded him of his ancient Native music, that it wasn't the melodies themselves but the emotional and spiritual feel of them. He said my singing voice was bright and clear. And he was moved by my speech, he said 'moved', Mom, isn't that amazing? He's always so nice to me … and of course he's happy that I love the wall hanging— he got to see it all finished before they wrapped it up for me.

She was still weeping, but quieter now.

— And get this, Mom. This is the funny part. Uncle Jayce told me that yesterday in temple David was being antsy as usual, and that he wanted to yell out 'Mazel Tov!' every time he thought my speech was winding down, and Jayce had to keep whispering to him 'No! You have to wait until the whole service is over!', and that at one point Jayce had to practically put him in a chokehold so he wouldn't blurt out 'Mazel Tov!'!!

Maya was laughing hysterically along with the tears, and I joined her; we were giddy with fatigue and deliriously happy.

There was an empty wall next to her bed; she had already removed the poster that had been there to make room for the bear.

– Okay, honey, I'll get some nails and the hammer
so we can hang this up.

– And the level, too.

– Of course.

I made it halfway out the door.

– And Mom?

– Hmm?

– Can we go shopping next weekend for a training
bra?

– Absolutely.

21. SHIPS IN THE NIGHT

Certain things catch your eye, but pursue only those that capture the heart.
—Native American Proverb

JAYCE Late Spring, 1995 Western Massachusetts

— Thanks, Jayce. Nothing better than a hot cup of tea in any weather, day or night. Hey, what's all the ruckus out here, is that a city of cicadas on that tree across the street?

— Yes, I think it's the annual species that emerged this year. There are some periodical broods that stay underground for thirteen years, some for seventeen.

— Seventeen years?! Holy smokes, what do they do for all that time?

— They feed off plant roots while hibernating, then finally come out to mate.

— And these are their mating calls? Not very subtle— oh, I'm glad you also find this amusing.

— Yeah ... the males die as soon as the mating is over, then the females die off right after they lay their eggs. They're above ground for only about five weeks, then that generation is gone.

— Huh. I guess we humans shouldn't be taking our cues from them.

— Definitely not.

Rivka and I were sitting out on Nina's porch after dinner, which had been followed by a three-way chat in the living room. It was late, it was dark, I was tired but wanted to catch up some more. And just be with her. We were quiet for a moment, the shrill of insects in the background.

— Have you heard from David recently?

— Yes, he changed his major again, it's poli-sci now. I worry about him sometimes, Rivka, he doesn't stick with anything for long.

— Yeah, he's always been sort of all over the place, has a lot of scattered energy and interests. He'll eventually find his way.

— I hope so. He's a good kid.

— He sure is. Maya seems to have the opposite problem. She's so intensely focused on the bioscience, but then she freaks out if she gets just one question wrong on a test. One question! She'll call me up in hysterics, you know how she gets herself worked up, and it's like the sky is falling because she got a ninety-eight percent and not a hundred. She calms down after a few minutes but thinks the solution is to study even harder, poor kid. David goes to see her in Cambridge at least once a month and they talk regularly—that seems to keep her emotionally in check. He balances her out.

— Yeah, it's good for both of them. Did you know that David chose to go to Clark because it's only an hour away from MIT?

— I suspected that was part of it. Those two are positively something. All through elementary and junior high and senior high, they would see each other throughout the day at school, and then they'd be on the phone in the evenings. And got together most weekends.

— The Dynamic Duo.

— Yes. I can't believe she's twenty, with David close behind. Time is passing us by so quickly, Jayce. We're middle-aged already!

— I know, it's difficult to fathom.

We sat in the stillness and drank our tea. We were both as comfortable with silence as we were with conversation, like the spaces between musical notes, you need both. I wanted to reach out and touch her. I always wanted to reach for her, even when she was nowhere near me on the physical plane.

— I was just thinking about my father.

— It's been almost eleven years, right?

— Yes, good memory! I still can't get over that he died just a couple of weeks before Maya came to live with me. He shared my excitement about

the adoption plans but never got to meet her. He
would have been totally enthralled by her.

— That is a shame. From what you've told me, he
would have been an exceptional grandfather. He
was in his sixties, right?

— Sixty-three. His father had died at forty-eight, just
like your dad, so he thought that any year past that
was a gift, and I guess it was. He was a good man,
so full of life, and wicked smart and funny.

— Like father, like daughter.

She gave me a gentle, modest smile; her eyes misted with the
memory of every soul who has passed through her life. I desperately wanted to hold her hand, to trace all the lines with my
fingers. The map of her world: past, present, and future.

— And then losing Cal two years after that. He was a
true friend and confidant. Maya got to meet him
a few times. He called her *Maya Papaya*, it was
adorable. She made him an elaborate Get Well
card, which he made a big fuss over. She had a hard
time accepting that he wasn't going to get better.
I stopped taking her with me those last months,
he was too sick to have a coherent conversation
for more than a couple of minutes. I'd sit and read
to him on weekends, he liked poetry and short
stories. I'd bring over some Baudelaire and Auden
and Saroyan, you know, stuff like that, and he'd
point to one and I'd randomly choose a few pages.
It was awful, Jayce. He had all those sarcoma
lesions and open sores on his face and body that
people with AIDS get. At least his mother was able

to take care of him til the end. The hospice nurse came in a couple of times a week to do the pain med adjustments, but his mom did all the round-the-clock care.

— Did his father ever come to accept him?

— Not fully, but he tolerated his presence in the house, especially when Cal got too weak to leave the bed. I think his father was of the ignorant mindset that the disease was god's punishment for his son being gay.

— Idiot.

— Yeah, but that's what a lot of idiots thought back then, especially before they heard that straight people were getting it too. He showed up for the memorial service with his wife, so that's something. They asked me to say a few words, probably because they didn't want to, or couldn't.

— Where was the service held?

— At their church, a lovely old brick building with stained glass windows. A few other friends were there I hadn't seen in a while, and some of his former students. We were a torrent of tears.

I nodded. My heart went out to her. How much loss and grief can any of us endure in a lifetime? I grabbed our mugs and stepped inside to put more water up to boil. Once in the kitchen I exhaled sharply, planted my hands on the counter edge, and tried to slow my breathing until the kettle whistled. How many more years would I allow to slide by without telling Rivka what I felt for her? There were plenty of solid, perfectly rational reasons to keep it to myself, but it was becoming increasingly difficult. Fear, fear, fear. If something bad happened to her I wouldn't be able to bear it. Especially if that something was because I messed things up, which I probably would. I'm not suited for a long-lasting relationship beyond family and friendships, and I'd rather get hit by a bus than lose her as a friend. Plus, what could I possibly offer her that comes close to what she deserves? Maybe it's just plain cowardice. Fear, confusion, fear.

— Hey, everything okay? Your mom's asleep, right?

— Yes, all good. Hey, I wanted to thank you for the advice about dealing with that difficult colleague a few months ago.

— You're welcome, did it work?

— It did. He's still a pompous jerk but he's not bothering me anymore.

— That's good. Sometimes we have to over-explain things to people when they don't pick up on regular social cues.

— Yeah, I had already tried to disengage but he wouldn't leave me alone until I spelled it out in plain English. Now he seems to be bothering someone else.

— Yeah. Even the intellectually gifted can be dense about certain matters. I often wish I had followed my own advice about so many things. But of course it's easier to be objective and sensible when it comes to *other* people's quandaries.

— Do as I say, not as I do?

— Exactly! Oh, I meant to ask you, Jayce, how's the house search going?

— Good, as a matter of fact I just put an offer in for a small Craftsman. It's in a wooded area but close to the school and downtown. Needs a little work but has good bones, and there's a covered porch out front, which faces east.

— Fantastic! When do you hear?

Her elbows were raised as she fidgeted with her hair clip, a futile attempt to contain those delightfully wayward curls.

— Probably next week. I don't know if any other offers have been submitted.

— Hopefully you'll get it. I'm pleased for you, I know you enjoy living in that part of the Appalachian range.

— The mountains and lakes. You've got the mountains and the river here in the valley, which is just as awesome, in a different way.

— Yeah. I haven't been to Ithaca since my college days when I used to visit friends going to school there. We'd sit on the floor and listen to BB King and Joni Mitchell for hours on end. Once in a while we'd actually go outside and walk a bit if it wasn't the middle of winter. And I was there for the Cornell Folk Festival in seventy-five.

— Arlo Guthrie?

— Yes! And David Amram, Vassar Clements, and a few other amazing musicians. I had planned to go in seventy-four but never made it.

— Well that's interesting, because I attended in seventy-four, was already living there, but couldn't make it in seventy-five. It was three months before David's birth and my family was in rough shape.

— That's right, holy smokes. That was twenty years ago, Jayce.

— Yeah, so our paths almost crossed in Ithaca, but instead they connected here, indirectly, a few weeks later.

— Huh. Well I'm glad you're happy there. Good luck with the house, let me know how it goes. Oh, before I forget, I scored a couple of Tanglewood tickets for July fifteenth, mostly Vivaldi I think. Would you like to come with?

— Oh, Rivka, I appreciate the invitation, but my summer schedule is too unpredictable to make a commitment, I'm sorry.

— It's okay, another time maybe.

— How did you get the tickets?

— Oh, well my friend Bill from the dance studio— his parents were ushers there decades ago, and so they get season tickets for life. Bill's going to be away in England for most of the summer working on his thesis, so he gave them to me.

— Nice. Hopefully you'll find someone to join you.

— **Yes, that won't be a problem, but you were my first choice.**

— **I'm sorry, Rivka.**

— **No worries!**

We talked a little more and then, as always, she hugged me goodbye. Feeling her arms around me and breathing her in for those few seconds just about undid me. No matter how much I tried to ease my brain away from it, my heart remained heavy and raw. Fear, confusion, fear. I couldn't keep up with the passage of time.

22. INERTIA

No one ever told me that grief felt so like fear. —Clive Staples Lewis

JAYCE December, 1998 Upstate New York

I drove to Stewart Park, at the south end of Cayuga Lake. My people, distant indigenous relations who were part of the Iroquois group of nations, used to live in this serene, beauteous place, in a village they built called Neodakheat. The village and surrounding area were stolen by the Europeans and became a military lot. There was a treaty signed in 1794 to return all sixty-four thousand acres to its rightful owners of the Cayuga Nation, People of the Great Swamp, but that never happened, as New York State completely ignored the terms and objectives of the treaty. Only about four hundred of those indigenous descendants remain in the area as part of the Haudenosaunee confederacy. A long trail of broken treaties between my people and the local and federal governments cast a shadow all over what is now called America.

After parking the car, I ambled across to the waterfront trail and walked slowly along the bank, as I've done numerous times before. No one else was around, probably due to the recent snow squalls and below-freezing temperatures. Wearing my thickest jacket and gloves, I hoped to warm up from the sun and the exercise. Winter is tough on me spiritually; I need to spend time in nature after being holed up inside for hours at a stretch, and it's sometimes a challenge to do that in the cold months. The trees were bare, and every step I took generated a crunching sound, my weight pressing upon layers of snow and ice.

Ten minutes into the trail I heard the unmistakable roar of an outboard motor. As it got louder I stopped and turned to face the lake, which was no longer frozen. I glanced down at my boots, which were now sneakers; the snow was gone and I was clothed in only a T-shirt and jeans, standing dumbfounded on the grass in the warm breeze. The willow trees wore their long narrow leaves, as if it were summer. I looked back up and spotted the source of the sound: a small white watercraft approaching from the west. It was some sort of deck boat with a V-shaped hull, its side painted with **LIFE RESCUE** in neon-green. Rivka was standing in the boat, smiling and waving, her mass of hair and long, lilac-colored summer dress billowing in the wind. She was gripping a narrow metal pole with her other hand. The boat, about thirty yards out, had slowed considerably, the engine noise cut back to a low rumble. I couldn't see if anyone else was aboard or who was piloting. Rivka was shouting non-stop, and with intense concentration I was able to make out her calls: **Swim to me, Jayce! Come on, you can do it! Swim to me! Please, Jayce—it's not too far! Come on, you can do it!** I had to get to her; I needed to save myself, and she wanted me by her side. I stepped over the bank and scrambled sideways down the hill. The lake was deep and I wasn't sure if I'd be able to swim to the boat safely but had to at least try. I began to gauge the distance while entering the relatively calm, midnight-blue water, which was colder than I had anticipated. Dashes of sunlight reflected back up to the clear sky. I could do this; I *must* do this.

Suddenly I was slapped with a familiar noxious odor and surrounded by dead bodies. What the hell?! Dozens and dozens of dead bodies, most of them floating face-down. I immediately recognized the dark-olive-green and tigerstripe uniforms of the U.S. and South Vietnamese Armed Forces. And the black garb worn by the Viet Cong guerrillas, 'the enemy' allied with the north and the Ho Chi Minh troops. Some of the people were wearing civilian clothes, as if they had been going about their day as a farmer, a fisherman, a mother, a child playing with sticks in the dirt in front of the shack they called home. The war had been going on for years, but the villagers had nowhere to hide. There were women, babies, girls, boys, men, old people. Everyone dead, remnants of straw hats floating among them. **No! No! No! No! No!** I screamed at the top of my lungs but wasn't sure if the sounds were actually emerging from my throat or if anyone could hear them. I began to frantically but gingerly turn each body over. First was a teenaged boy wearing a light button-down shirt and dark cotton pants with a cord-tie at the waist. The bottom part of his right leg was missing and he had a pained expression. The next body was a woman with the back of her hair burned off, and what was left of her charred arms tightly holding a cloth sling with a fully intact dead baby inside. She was hunched over, doing her best to protect the tiny, precious child. Next I turned over an ARVN soldier, whose body was torn up from shrapnel, thousands of sharp fragments sticking out everywhere. Next, and next, and next …

I knew I was responsible for their deaths. 'Me', 'You', 'Us', 'Them', what's the damn difference? People killing people, the ravages of war. My stomach roiled with nausea as I moved toward the floating body of an American soldier. I turned him over and it was Andy. Deep-red blood spurted out of the holes in his chest, his pleading eyes fixed on mine. **Andy! No! No! No!**

My head was pounding and spinning, and something jostled my right shoulder over and over—I couldn't move—couldn't pull away from whatever was pushing me. I asked the Creator for help, to bring me to a place of peace, where there was no violence, no killing. The jabbing at my shoulder continued; I clung to a dilapidated raft in the middle of a vast, turbulent sea, and would soon be among the missing or dead … Rivka! Where was Rivka?! Was there a chance I could I swim to her now? No, she would be long gone … I couldn't see anything but the floating bodies, couldn't hear anything beyond my own muffled screams.

It was Molly trying to wake me, her big paw thumping on my shoulder. **Okay, girl. Okay … good girl.** She lowered her paws to the floor but continued staring at me. I was drenched in sweat and self-recrimination, had a terrific headache and raw throat, and got dizzy when I tried to raise myself to a sitting position. Fuck.

It took ten minutes of intentional slow breathing to lower my heart rate and get my bearings enough to rise from the bed. Took some Tylenol for the pounding in my head and a long shower revived me a bit. I changed the bedsheets, put some water up to boil, and opened the side door to let Molly out to do her business, knowing she would stay close. Thankfully it was the weekend and I wasn't expected anywhere. I started opening the bag of coffee beans but decided on tea instead. Rivka had given me a tin of what she described as **'strong but smooth'** gourmet black tea leaves during my last visit, along with a couple of different types of infusers accompanied by a mini-tutorial; she knew tea like nobody's business. The container said *sustainably-grown and hand-harvested—Fair Trade Direct From Kenya,* such a distance it had travelled for me to enjoy. I focused on the shape and feel of the triangular tin, trying with all my might to widen the space between my soul and the continuous visual loop of the nightmare. I wondered about the lives of the people who lived and worked in that faraway place called Kenya, only six hundred miles from Rwanda, where the genocide against the Tutsi took place four years ago. When will it all stop?

I turned the heat up a notch, let Molly back in, and we sat on the couch together. The couch was actually a large futon, which served as a guest bed when laid out flat for the rare visitor. It faced the unadorned picture window at the back of the house, where I had installed a slate walkway in the seven-foot space between the window and the silver maples and paper birches that must have been planted decades ago. The muted greys and browns of the trees and earth were comforting on this dreary winter day. And the stillness. It was late morning and I was grateful to be alone in my own private space, with my dear, loyal dog. There were stacks of work papers to go through, as well as a few bills to pay, but I needed to chill out and recuperate.

The bad dreams were infrequent, and didn't begin until I had finished school. For the first few years after returning from the war I was in bad shape and must have blocked it all out. They used to call it Shell Shock, Trench Fever, Combat Exhaustion, Battle Fatigue. Now they call it Post Traumatic Stress Disorder. I've never been one for groups, and have been able to manage without medication, so I've just let it play itself out.

Rivka once told me that in some of her darkest days, when she was in survival mode, she longed for the simple things, the things that couldn't hurt her. **'In those desperate times, I would conjure up the image of pale-periwinkle petunias, the way their soft petals create a delicate glow in twilight.**

If I concentrated hard enough I could disappear into Claude Monet's garden for a brief moment.' It was a place she had enjoyed visiting, a place she had felt calm and free.

A couple of months ago I had seen an article in the Ithaca Times about the local animal shelter. Having grown up without any pets I was clueless about how to provide for one, but it got me thinking. That same week, one of my research colleagues told me about a **'super canine companion'** he had just adopted, and encouraged me to check out the SPCA on Hanshaw Road, which I did. And fell head over heels for the last remaining three-month-old puppy from a litter that had been left, thankfully with their mother, in the corner of a parking lot near a dumpster. The young man who worked at the SPCA said her siblings had been adopted, and they would look for a family for the mother as soon as this last one was out and into a safe home.

Her looks were exquisite: mostly pale gold coloring with random white spots, a little black around her big floppy ears, and long fur. Evidently she was a mix of golden retriever and border collie, with possibly a trace of Australian Shepherd. When I knelt down in front of the cage she came to me immediately and wagged her tail. I asked if I could walk her around outside in their fenced-in area, so he leashed her up and we all went out. I had already decided I wanted her in my life, and that Molly would be a fitting name (Rivka later informed me that it means 'wished-for-child' in Hebrew). The leash was removed once we were inside the enclosure, and the two of us ran around the perimeter together. She sprung ahead a few times but always circled back around to me.

She had already been spayed and given her preliminary vaccines, so all that was left was to fill out a form, pay the fee, and go buy what she needed. He gave me a list of supplies and let me use a rope until I could get her a proper collar and leash. We drove out immediately to Ithaca Grain and Pet Supply on Seneca Street, where I purchased a plethora of food and treats and bowls and toys and a sturdy brush, plus many additions to the regular basics from the *Getting Started* list. I chuckled as Molly eagerly sniffed every item on every lower shelf. But she stayed by my side, and then jumped into the car as soon as I opened the door. She was energetic and would need a little guidance, which was fine by me; I figured we could and would take good care of each other. She knew instinctively to wake me this morning when she heard, or felt, my stress. At five months old she's only about half of what her full-grown size will be, but is already in sync with my spirit after just two months with me. Holding the tea mug in one hand I pet Molly with the other, telling her what a good dog she was. Within seconds she laid her fluffy head on my lap and closed her eyes. The tea was delectable and helped me remain calm.

After managing to get some work done I felt steadier by late afternoon. I even turned on the radio and listened to an amusing NPR show called *Wait Wait …Don't Tell Me!*, which launched earlier this year and provided another needed distraction. Afterwards Molly and I took a walk in the woods, where I thought about the ancient symbols of the circle and the spiral—the interdependent nature of relationships—between people, and between people and the land. The slow, constant movement of everything around us, the myth of linear time.

We returned to the flashing of the voicemail light. I fed Molly and brought the phone to the couch. It was a message from Rivka:

— **Hi Jayce, it's me—how are you? Listen, I'm having a potluck next weekend, Saturday night, and I** really hope you can come. It's a winter solstice-slash-housewarming party. The kids will be here, and your mom's coming over early to make that stew we all like with the beans and squash. Also, Maya's going to do Nina's hair in a French braid. It's so sweet how Maya is the only person she allows to fuss over her. I know you're not big on crowds, but it's just going to be us, plus a couple of friends, like Bill and possibly Sophie, if she can make it into town. Bill may bring his new significant other. David's bringing his friend Helen from work, because evidently she's not talking to her family right now and has nowhere to go for the holidays, so of course I told him to invite her. I know you're busy, but if there's any way you can drive out it would be fantastic. We're all anxious to meet Molly in person, and to see you, obviously. And you're more than welcome to crash here, especially now that I have more space. We'll do a brunch on Sunday. No need to bring anything, just come if you can, alright? Hope to see you soon. Okay bye.

Naturally I didn't make it. As much as I regretted disappointing the people I care about most, a big piece of me remained frozen with fear and horror and dead floating bodies.

23. THE NEARNESS OF YOU

Love is space and time measured by the heart. —Marcel Proust

RIVKA October, 2000 Western Massachusetts

Friday was a typical workday, in that cases were predictably unpredictable. We were constantly inundated with people who needed support and assistance of one sort or another, and the only option was to remain focused on the task at hand, advocating for whichever patients or family members were sitting or standing or lying in front of me at the moment. I stayed through the dinner hour catching up on paperwork, which was not an unusual occurrence.

Given that there was virtually no time during the course of any weekday to engage in small talk with colleagues, I had no knowledge of the imminent tempest until I heard it on the radio while driving out of the parking lot. It was described as a tropical storm that could become a hurricane and would affect the eastern seaboard and possibly inland. Power loss in these parts was not a big deal and usually short term—it wasn't the dead of winter, and this wasn't Siberia—but best to be prepared. Figuring Walmart might still be open, I headed over to get some batteries for my lanterns, which were sitting somewhere in the garage or utility closet, probably juiceless. Do they take C batteries or D? I can never remember. The store was mostly empty of customers by the time I arrived, as was the battery display case near the checkouts. I schlepped over to the camping/auto department in the back corner of the store and found a couple of four-packs, plus a small flashlight with batteries included. They were all out of coolers, which would have come in handy for storing food, should a power outage last for more than a couple of days.

On the drive home I thought about one of my elderly patients I had spoken with today, and created a mental agenda of follow-ups for Monday.

Max welcomed me with a meow and slow, high tail swish. He knows the routine and doesn't start soliciting for food in earnest until my jacket and footwear are taken off at the front door and I've re-emerged from the bedroom in sweats and socks. He's about eight years old, according to the vet, who said he should be on a diet because he's been overweight since I found him last year wandering the streets and showing up on my back porch most nights. He'd been neutered and well taken care of at some point, but without a collar he appeared to have been abandoned. No one claimed him within the three-week waiting period, so he became mine. On the vet's advice I keep him indoors, which was a surprisingly easy transition for him. I fed him his special food, refreshed his water, and put a large pot of water up to boil for pasta, knowing there was nothing substantial in the refrigerator. It was nine o'clock and I just wanted to eat something hot and settle in for the weekend. Maybe I'd do a grocery run tomorrow if the storm bypassed the area.

Max and I play a game most evenings whereby I sing that ridiculous but catchy Burt Bacharach/Hal David tune *What's New Pussycat?*, and Max responds with a meow at the appropriate pauses when I point at him. He's good company for me. Max, that is, not Tom Jones, who I saw perform at the

Copacabana in 1969 and watched with uneasy confusion as women in the audience took off their panties from under their dresses and threw them onto the stage. The Welsh baritone picked up each one, wiped the sweat from his forehead with them and then tossed them back into the crowd as he continued singing, not missing a beat. I was there for a Sweet Sixteen party. Odd choice of venue by my friend's parents, but it was certainly an amusing, albeit strange, experience.

It was getting late so I called Maya to check in with her while I ate dinner, then went into the sunroom and turned on the TV. Every station had their own version of Storm Warning, Weather Advisory, Storm Team Forecast, Storm Watch, Storm Alert Update, Storm Tracker—okay, I get it, a storm is forthcoming. I had a momentary thought about doing some laundry but was too tired to bother. Max had followed me into the room and was doing yoga stretches on the rug as part of his lengthy grooming ritual. A stack of news articles and human interest stories calling out to me sat on the side table, but I didn't have the energy. Normally I would start popping music into the tape deck but was too worn out even for that. One of these days maybe I'd switch over to CDs, but then what would I do with the hundreds of tapes and records I have? Maya tells me I'm old-fashioned and need to start using modern technology. I thought cassette tapes *were* modern technology; I guess I still have a lot to learn.

I sat and marveled at the kaleidoscope shadows cast by the Moroccan lamp, one of my pride and joys as far as physical objects are concerned. Through no fault of my own, I've lost many precious possessions over the years, so I don't allow myself to get too attached to things. But this table lamp was unusual in that it wasn't constructed of a mishmash of colored glass the way most light fixtures from that part of the world were. Instead, it was a clear glass bowl under a delicate lace of copper cutouts, held together by circular bands and a base of thicker copper. It stood about fourteen inches high. Gazing at the cosmic reflections on the walls and ceiling I thought of Jayce, because my brain tends to get jumpy. I thought about how he doesn't reveal himself all at once, only specks of truth and beauty that shine through the mosaic like flickering stars. You have to encounter enough of the fragments over an extended period of time to fill in the blanks. He's more open with me than with most people; we know of each other's demons and share that vulnerability. But he's remained reserved and wary, even among those with whom he's relatively comfortable.

Jayce walks with purpose and has an innate, astute sense of direction, even in the dark, as if his glorious, lean body had a built-in compass. He can also gauge distances straight away and accurately. When he looks at a person he truly *sees* them; he knows what they're made of. He emanates gravitas and stability. He's smart and strong and gorgeous and I've been in love with him since Nina showed me that picture twenty-five years ago in the midst of a family tragedy. My friendship with Jayce is sacred, and I don't ever want to jeopardize it, and yet … and yet. Cal was the only one I ever told about this chronic, unreasonable crush, which has deepened to a full-on big love. Cal had suggested all those years ago that I '**make a move and see what happens**', but I was never able to bring myself to do so. I've dropped enough hints over the years to fill the Colca Canyon, and Jayce hasn't responded with anything more than casual restraint, so any alternate options fall to him. While I'm pretty sure I haven't imagined the chemistry between us, I've resigned myself to the strong probability that he doesn't see me in a romantic way, or can't bring himself to take the leap. Nevertheless, I like to envision otherwise, foolish as that may be. This unrequited passion never gets old; I will continue to love him quietly, from afar.

I awoke late in the morning, grateful it was Saturday and I could relax, a mindset that didn't come naturally to me but was learning to welcome. While showering I remembered the tail end of last night's dream, which was actually more of a sublime, fleeting vision that appeared amid a transcendental state of consciousness. I was sitting on Jayce's lap in my kitchen and he was holding me in his arms, his embrace warm and reassuring. We were fully clothed but intensely close in a sensual and spiritual way. Why this little scenario occurred in the kitchen of all places was a mystery, but who am I to question something that left me feeling so wonderful? Yeah, like that's ever going to happen. Songs frequently toss themselves into my head, and as I toweled off it was Al Green singing *I'm Still In Love With You*. Of course. Unfortunately, Jayce may not even be single anymore. A few weeks ago Maya mentioned to me that David had mentioned to her that when he called his uncle late on a Friday night he heard a woman's voice in the background. David asked if he had company and Jayce mumbled something about it being **'a work thing'**, so who knows. As much as I want him to be happy, it stung a bit. Thirdhand speculations aside, I did and didn't want to know any of this.

I made a pot of Lapsang Souchong. Removing the smoky, aromatic tea leaves after the requisite fourish minutes, I poured some of the steaming amber liquid into a mug, added gobs of raw honey, and popped an old bossa-nova tape into the player. It was around noon when I stepped out onto the covered back porch. The dark skies and steady rain were accompanied by gusty winds; my neighbor's Tibetan prayer flags were whipping about. The thermometer I had nailed to the post read forty-four degrees, warmer than it felt. Back inside I cranked up the fireplace blower in attempts to overheat the house in case the power goes out. Max was sprawled out lazily on the living room rug without a care in the world. I munched on a dried apricot and pulled out the vacuum.

For each room tackled I sent out a prayer of gratitude for my luck in finding this place: hakarat hatov. When I first viewed the house it appeared to have good bones; the inspection report listed some items needing repair but nothing I couldn't handle. The floors were in rough shape so I had those refinished, and a couple of drafty windows were replaced. All of the cleaning and interior painting I gladly did myself over the course of two weekends before moving in. There was an enormous white farmhouse sink in the kitchen, soft, wide archways delineating the sunroom from the living room, and the laundry alcove from the kitchen, and more space than I've ever had the privilege to live in. Best of all, the immediate neighborhood felt safe. The residents were a mixed bunch, ethnically, gender-wise, and age-wise; in the two years I've been here I haven't seen any swastikas or other terrible things on anyone's body, T-shirt, or fence. There have been sporadic antisemitic and racist incidents in the region, though. What awful shit I went through in my early years, for the crime of being a Jew, and later for the crime of being female. There are hate groups and individuals everywhere; the SPLC keeps track of the hundreds they know about, and once in a fogbow justice is served.

And there have always been sexual predators, their violent acts permeating every level of society, in every country in the world. They are investment bankers, truck drivers, politicians, sports coaches, religious leaders. A supervisor. A family member. A teacher. A landlord. Married, not married. Some prey on children; some hunt for adults.

I'd like to think I've gotten better at heeding the alarm bells when they reverberate in my head, instead of pretending they have no meaning or consequence. In any case, I feel safe in my house, the disquietude no longer taking center stage in my life, and I've been reminding myself that it's probably not necessary to continue maintaining a constant state of hypervigilance. Maybe. Allowing fear to fill so much physiological space while managing a steady stream of anxiety is justified but taxing. All I've ever truly needed was to feel safe. Anything good that is bestowed upon me beyond that is a bonus, tempering the lingering uncertainty. There's an old Hasidic saying from Rabbi Nachman of Breslov about traversing a narrow, perilous bridge, how we shouldn't ignore our fears but we mustn't let them destroy our hope.

Just before one o'clock I unplugged the vacuum, and a moment later the power went out, good timing! Rain pelted the windows, and a quick glance at the bare maple tree in the yard confirmed it was rough out there; several branches had already snapped off, and the wet leaves on the ground were swirling up in a mad rush to relocate elsewhere, the weight of water no match for the strength of the wind. I turned on the portable radio, and the news out of the Amherst station relayed a warning from the police departments that non-emergency vehicles should stay off the roads. So I nixed the grocery trip, no problem; it's not like I was going to starve to death, given that I had some cans and jars of somethings, instant oatmeal, dried fruit, a half-full box of *ak-mak* crackers, some frozen veggies, and leftovers from last night. A feast compared to my poverty years! Besides, I wouldn't be hungry until much later.

Grabbing that pile of reading material from the sunroom, I sat down cross-legged on the living room couch, and Max immediately jumped onto my lap with a thud when his feet landed on the wad of papers. The time passed quickly as I plowed through the articles with my trusty highlighter, scribbling a few notes for a work-related proposal that had been simmering in the back of my mind. I also made a list of minor home projects I'd been procrastinating on: sorting and purging old documents and photos that have been sitting in boxes for years, repairing some of the interior doorknobs, going through my closets to fill a charity bag with clothing that no longer fit and doodads I no longer needed. And maybe defrosting the freezer at some point. Making a list means I'm halfway to actually getting it done, right? I'm ridiculously efficient and conscientious at work, but at home I tend to put certain things off, especially if they're not mentally or emotionally stimulating.

At five I made another pot of tea, Darjeeling this time, and brought in from the bedroom the Herman Wouk novel I had started last night. My parents didn't own a TV when I was growing up, so books became my primary source of entertainment and escape; they still are. I keep art volumes, a few of the classics, and some nonfiction; everything else is returned to the library, traded, or given away. Just as I was delving into chapter seven, my concentration was interrupted by a knocking sound. I sprung out of the couch, jarring Max, and looked through the rain-splattered window glass. Jayce's car was in the driveway—what on earth was he doing here? My heart flipped along with the locks and I opened the door.

— Sorry to barge in on you but Molly needs help, she's hurt. I'm not sure what to do—

— Okay, we'll figure it out. Go get her.

I left the door unlatched and grabbed a couple of towels from the linen closet. Jayce was understandably rattled; he's devoted to his big, sweet dog. Nina hadn't mentioned anything about him coming out this weekend; maybe she didn't know or maybe she assumed he wouldn't be driving all this way in such dreadful weather.

We got Molly situated with an ice pack and makeshift splint, which took some time, and then Max came over to comfort her, wise gentleman that he was.

— **Oh, Jayce, I can't believe you drove in all that mess for so many hours.**

— **I know, it was a challenge. The first stretch was alright. Then on I-88 all hell broke loose from the sky.**

Both of us had vehicles with manual transmission. Great for traction and control, but that's a lot of shifting on a day like this in the wind and rain.

— **Did you even make it out of second gear?**

— **Yes, but never for long … it was first, second, third, second, first …**

We shook our heads. I pulled some containers out of the refrigerator as Jayce entered the kitchen and turned a chair around to face me. He had lifted it from the top rail with one hand and twisted it as if it had the weight of a feather. As soon as he sat down I did an involuntary double take—it was the setting in the vision. *My* man. *My* kitchen. I quickly turned back to the counter as I felt myself flush, the embarrassing symptoms of menopause not helping one iota. Oy—pull yourself together. I'm not sure if he caught me, and didn't want to know. I made a joke about us taking a leisurely walk on the rail trail later and he laughed heartily. Okay, it's all fine.

Jayce's physical and spiritual steadiness permeated all of the molecules in the air and grounded me. We had dinner together by candlelight, and I did my best to not get stirred up, as I inevitably do in his presence. On the one hand it was easy and comfortable to converse as we always have for all these years; on the other hand I had to restrain myself from the increasing urge to caress his face and, well, all of him, really. He was wearing a lapis-blue pull-on sweatshirt over a tee, and well-worn black jeans that he looked fabulous in. His thick, coal-black, wavy hair was tied back as usual, and was significantly shorter than it used to be. In the old days he mostly wore it in a single lengthy braid, occasionally loose. But it was his striking face that had always been my primary focus, in my dreams and in real life. His smooth skin was the color of autumn umber; his strong, masculine features had no sharp angles. A small crescent just above his right brow was visible only at close range, a faint birthmark or old scar. Prominent cheekbones, perfectly shaped ears, always clean-shaven. His warm-brown eyes were like sunbeams on walnut, and when he held my gaze the whole of me liquified.

A band of stunning shell discs circled his right wrist, and he allowed me to examine it up close. I scooched my chair over and he rested the back of his hand in mine as I touched the shells. He smelled like the forest and strength and a hint of warm smoked almonds, a rousing combination. It brought back a memory of the first time we met in person and I had applied a Band-Aid to his bleeding hand. I wondered if he remembered it too … probably not, it was so long ago. But not as long ago as the Chumash people, who Jayce explained have been living on the southern California coast for eleven thousand years. Now *that's* a lot of lifetimes. The discs were held together with a black cord.

Jayce's sleeves were rolled up, and my eyes drifted to the three-inch sunken scar that ran up toward the inside of his elbow, a battle injury, the trench in his skin a tangible reminder of a terrible war. I wished I possessed the boldness to trace my fingers along it, so he'd know that I see him, all of him, and I wondered what other physical scars I might some day have the freedom to discover. Unfortunately the power suddenly came back on and broke the spell. The spell of nearness by a flickering flame, the spell of imagined and real love, the spell of mutual intimacy and unwavering ardor, the spell of dreams and possibilities.

While Jayce went out to get his belongings from the car I fixed up a space for him in the den. The couch in there was huge—long and deep, and would accommodate his full six foot (plus a smidge) frame, which Nina once told me he'd reached by the time he was sixteen. David had slept on it a couple of times and reported it as '**super-comfy**'. He wasn't as tall as his uncle, but it would be fine. Naturally I'd rather have Jayce in bed with me … snuggling, and perhaps engaging in a rapturous noodle dance of the highest order. I took a deep breath in and out and drew the curtains closed.

Back in the kitchen I was about to call Nina, but had to first listen to a message from Abigail:

— **Hello Rivka. This is your mother. You didn't bother to call but I wanted to tell you that I'm fine. I lost electricity for a whole twenty-five minutes, so I missed the first half of *Dateline*. And I ran out of *Clamato* juice. I'm sure if your father were still alive you would have called *him* to check in. I hope to talk to you soon, dear. Goodbye.**

Eye roll—Delete.

Nina and I spoke briefly. She was surprised that her son was in town but glad he was with me. I relayed the message about tomorrow. Molly and Max were still asleep on the living room rug when Jayce returned with his duffel bag. I got a load of laundry going and we shared an enjoyable chat with dessert. At one point I found myself staring at his hand holding the tea mug. His fingers were long and slender, somewhat calloused and with multiple tiny scars, probably from all the digs he's labored on. He had to bend his thumb up high to hold the hefty mug, which appeared small and delicate in those big, beautiful hands. I watched his Adam's apple move as he swallowed and spoke with that smooth, even cadence in that deep, rich voice I would be elated to listen to every day for the rest of my life. Everything about him was intoxicating. I forced myself to snap out of it. Again.

The clock read ten after ten, and Jayce apologetically announced he was going to get ready for bed; he was understandably exhausted. I wanted to give him a hug, knowing I might not see him in the morning, but the moment passed and I didn't. He settled himself into the sunroom and within a few minutes the light in there was out.

I finished cleaning up in the kitchen while the dryer hummed and the clothing tumbled around, a zipper or button occasionally clinking against the metal drum. I cleaned out the litter box, which was tucked away in a corner of the utility closet. With the help of an older neighbor I had installed one of those small, square kitty doors into the bottom of that closet door—ultra convenient for me and for Max, who could come and go as needed without leaving a mess in the house. I swept up quietly and conducted a brief scan of the kitchen and living room to make sure nothing else needed doing, and turned the fireplace blower down a bit.

After using the bathroom, teeth brushed and face washed, I transferred the warm clothes from the dryer into the basket and dumped it all on top of my bed to sort. Cal used to call this task **'fluff and fold'**; we frequented several laundromats in those days together, rating each facility from *One*: Totally Disgusting, to *Five*: Clean and with Working Change Machines and interesting and/or attractive people to look at while we waited endlessly in those hard, molded plastic chairs, me with a book, and Cal scanning the room and checking the status of our clothing every ten seconds. And the presence of weirdos we would furtively discuss, imagining what kind of life they had. **'Maybe a carny ...'**, stuff like that. Oh, Cal, let me count the ways I miss you.

I brought the pile of Jayce's clothes into the inner sanctum of the sunroom, where some dim light was cast from the living room. He was sleeping quietly on his back. Molly and Max were entwined on the rug near the couch, Max's fish toy reposed by the dog's head; he must have brought it to her as a present. Jayce's T-shirt was moon-white against his dark skin. His right arm laid over the herringbone quilt. A five-o'clock shadow had formed and a few silver strands of hair bordered his temples, far less than the salt-and-pepper I've had for years. I put the clothing down on a table and stood for a moment watching the slow, rhythmic rise and fall of his chest. God, he was breathtakingly handsome, a magnificent man with a bruised spirit.

I thought about our outlooks. While we share core values, I'm a cautious optimist and he's a cautious pessimist. He worries that the world will explode if he speeds up, makes direct contact. I worry that the world will fall apart if I slow down, disengage. Neither is true, but those are the defaults we rely on. When we're together, I propel him and he steadies me. Good for both of us old souls, I think. When I'm with Jayce, everything feels right; the messy minutiae of our day-to-day lives is neutralized and all of the big things make sense.

Drifting into that ethereal place where dreams and wishes reside, I relayed a telepathic message through the three feet of air between us: Do you have any idea how much I yearn for you? Not out of any sense of loneliness but because we are meant to be together? Do you know that I hear the tenderness in your voice when you say my name? Do you see me running to you when I fear my own shadow? Can you feel my arms enfolding you in your darkest hours? Do you realize you're my bashert, my zivug—my one and only? That every atom in my body and all the roads in my heart lead to you? Jayce Nakoma King, you are the finest kind. May you get the rest you need.

Steeped in a wistful stupor, I managed to stub my toe—hard—on a chair leg on the way out of the sunroom—**'SHIT!'**—and quickly hobbled though the archway so as not to awaken Jayce with my whisper-swears, collapsed onto my bed, and clutched the sore foot as if my life depended on it, as one tends to do after smashing a body part into a stationary object.

After reading in bed until three in the morning, I finally got some shut-eye. The annoying auto-beeps from the nearby utility bucket-trucks woke me four hours later: Lift—Descend—Reverse—Swivel. On behalf of the workers, those cherry-picker cranes made me nervous. I went into the bathroom to pee and brush my teeth, then donned a robe and tentatively made my way through the living room to the sunroom. The quilt was folded and Jayce was gone, the house seeming particularly empty and sad without him. I entered

the kitchen to put water up to boil and stopped short when
I reached the table. Jayce's beautiful shell band had alighted,
with a note:

Dear Rivka,
Get someone to tie this around your slender wrist.
Have to get on the road, didn't want to wake you.
Thank you for taking care of Molly and me.
Talk soon. Jayce

24. A SPLINT IN A STORM

It is in the shelter of each other that the people live. —Irish Proverb

JAYCE October, 2000

Upstate New York—Western Massachusetts

I hadn't paid much attention to the hurricane warning, except to note that it was expected to hit the Carolinas first and then move north. Many of these storms head back out to sea before much damage is done to the mainland, so I didn't see any urgency to leave on Friday night after work, and besides, I needed a few hours of sleep. So I stayed in Ithaca and didn't head out east until Saturday morning, with Molly comfortably settled onto her blanket in the back seat of my well-used Outback. It was in the low-fifties and overcast; by the time we reached the area just west of Albany we hit torrents of rain. It had been more than three hours of driving and a pit stop was needed, me for caffeine and Molly to do her business. I exited I-88 and looped around to US-20. Having made this trip numerous times over the years I knew the route well: five hundred twelve miles round trip, just under five hours each way in good weather. This was not good weather.

I pulled into the familiar lot of the convenience store in Schodack, which sits along the Hudson. The horizontal winds caused tremendous pushback when I opened the driver's side door. Shit. I pulled up my anorak hood while releasing the door, which the wind promptly slammed shut. I opened the back to get Molly leashed up and out. We quickly jogged over to the grassy area beyond the parking lot. While Molly relieved herself I looked up at the dark skies and wondered how the Mohicans had managed things long ago in this kind of severe weather. And how they were faring in modern times. We sprinted over to the store entrance and I unleashed Molly. The overhang along the front was useless at this point, but I didn't want to leave her in the car. I motioned for her to sit and wait. Inside I quickly used the restroom, poured myself a to-go coffee, and left a couple of bills on the counter when the cashier was nowhere to be seen. Outside, long, narrow tree branches blew around the pavement. Molly was drenched and thankful to see me, though I had been out of her sight less than six minutes. We started back to the car, which was only a dozen yards away, but as we were running the short distance, Molly got tangled up in some large sticks and other debris that had suddenly blown themselves into a pile around her legs. She yelped. I placed the coffee cup on the pavement, climbed over the mess, and picked her up. A minute later I had her in the back seat of the car where we both sat and panted. I checked her legs, which appeared to be okay at the moment; there was nothing left to do but keep on driving. I ran back out and retrieved my coffee, which inexplicably was still upright amid the rubble, and quickly made my way to the driver's seat. We were a little over halfway and it was one-thirty. I was anxious to get to our destination, hoping my mother was okay. And Rivka, who purchased a nice cottage-style house a couple of years ago and had swiftly transformed it into a charming home. They were both self-sufficient, but that didn't keep me from worrying. It was satisfying to cross over the border into Massachusetts, but there was still quite a drive ahead and visibility was extremely limited. Molly had fallen asleep and I turned on the radio. It was difficult to hear the news through the drumming rain and wind; the chatter seemed to be all about the hurricane, which evidently was worse than anyone had anticipated.

Molly woke and began whimpering. There was nowhere to pull over safely so I tried to calm her with my voice and continued driving. She was quiet for a while and eventually fell back asleep. It took intense concentration to navigate in the storm; even with the wipers on high speed I was barely able to see much ahead, and had to maintain a firm grip on the steering wheel to avoid swerving from the wind and wet tar. We finally reached MA-9, the last forty-two mile stretch. We arrived at Rivka's house around five and I pulled into her driveway, in front of the small, detached garage where hopefully her Forester was parked and protected. Leaving Molly in the car momentarily, I sprinted up to the front entrance and knocked hard, glancing at the mezuzah on the post at my eye level. My concern for Molly had reached a high peak. The two locks clicked open, followed immediately by the inward swing of the thick wooden door.

— **Jayce! Come inside!**

— **Sorry to barge in on you but Molly needs help, she's hurt. I'm not sure what to do—**

— **Okay, we'll figure it out. Go get her.**

I was falling apart but knew we had come to the right place. I raced back to the car and carried my big loyal dog into the house. We were both soaked through. Rivka had put a towel on the floor in front of the fireplace in the living room, where a couple of battery lanterns provided additional light. I carefully laid Molly down on it.

— It's her left front leg.

— Okay, sweetheart, I'm going to touch you gently
    … yeah, that's the spot, it's a bit swollen.

— That's how she was whimpering in the car.

— Okay. I'll find something in the freezer we can use.

She turned on a lantern in the kitchen and fished out a bag of frozen peas. She inserted that bag into a larger clear one and carefully placed it on Molly's leg. We sat on the rug on either side of my dog.

— How long have you been without power here?

— About four hours. Are the traffic lights out?

— Yeah, it's a mess out there. Downed trees everywhere.
    I'm sure the mountain road is closed.

— Yeah, and I'll bet the Oxbow is flooded, and all
    those roads in Holyoke that are down by the canal.
    Good girl, Molly … you're going to be okay.

Rivka ran her hand slowly across Molly's side and back, from the top of her head to the base of her tail, over and over, telling her what a good girl she was, and that she knew what it felt like to be hurt, and that things would get better soon … I watched and listened intently as she soothed the dog. It was working on me as well.

— Jayce, why don't you take off your jacket and
    boots, leave them by the door. I'm right here with
    her, it'll be okay.

— Oh. Okay. Hey, your cat's been sitting there just
    staring at Molly this whole time. Max, right?

— Yeah, he's waiting for us to finish fussing over her so he can come over and offer comfort. He knows she's in distress.

— Should we give her some aspirin or something?

— I don't think it's safe to give her human painkillers or anti-inflammatories. There's no phone service so we can't call a vet for advice, not that we'd be able to find anyone open now, anyway. But I think we may need to stabilize her leg.

— Like a splint?

— Yeah, sit here and keep the bag on her, I'll go look for something.

— I made a mess of your floor with the boots.

— No worries. I'll be right back.

I was starting to feel better and Molly seemed calmer as well. Rivka always knew what to do in any situation, one of her many innate talents. Max was still sitting and staring. He was a large black-and-silver tabby, with sparkling green eyes like his person, but a lighter hue. Rivka reappeared a minute later with a flat, wide wooden spoon, a small towel, and some thin strips of cloth. We worked together to wrap the towel around Molly's leg, place the spoon against it, and tie it together in three places—not too loose, not too tight. Molly whimpered intermittently but seemed resigned to her situation.

Max must have figured we had concluded the emergency procedures; he walked over and started licking the side of her face. It was both comical and touching to observe their interaction. Molly seemed a bit bewildered for a few seconds, but then stopped crying, released a sigh, and welcomed Max as he curled himself into a giant fluffball against her belly.

— Okay I think she's good for now. Fortunately my stove is gas so I can heat up some leftovers. How long were you on the road?

— We left just after ten this morning. And I didn't sleep much last night.

— Oh, Jayce, I can't believe you drove in all that mess for so many hours.

— I know, it was a challenge. The first stretch was alright. Then on I-88 all hell broke loose from the sky. But yeah, any kind of food would be appreciated.

— Keep me company in here. The big furry creatures are fine, just let them sleep. I know you're probably worried about Nina, but she's most likely safe at home. We'll call her as soon as the power returns.

— How do you always know what I'm thinking?

— Well, not always, but probably because we've known each other for so long.

— Hey, something smells good. I apologize for not helping, Rivka, I've kind of melted into this chair.

— You're fine, nothing for you to do, just relax.

Rivka had a simple, rectangular teak table in the kitchen, with built-in leaves that could extend out for extra guests. One side abutted the wall; each of the other sides had a chair, one of which I had turned to face her. She found a jar of marinated artichoke hearts, and had heated up pasta with vegetables and pesto sauce. We washed it all down with ginger ale, and the meal revived me for the time being. She was admiring the shells that were banded around my wrist and gestured to get a closer look. I reached out; she held the back of my hand with one of hers and moved the tips of her fingers over the thick, flat discs with the other. My wrist tingled from her touch, and the sensation quickly vibrated through the rest of my body.

— **It's beautiful, Jayce. What kind of shells are these?**

— **They're Chumash from the southern California coast. The indigenous people have been there for over eleven thousand years.**

— **Holy smokes. Were they used as barter?**

— **Yes, wampum—sometimes just decorative and sometimes as money.**

— **Each shell is unique, so many shades of white, sand, oatmeal, complementing each other. Did you make this?**

— **Yes, just drilled a hole in the centers, then strung them together.**

— **Simple, rustic, gorgeous.**

Her nearness always had a potent effect on me, and it was disconcerting when she released my hand. Interrupting my thoughts further was an unexpected high-pitched rumble, marking the electric power surging back to life. The small lamp on the kitchen table lit up, erasing the intimate mood of the candlelight. We both stood and I brought our empty bowls to the sink.

— Take your clothes off.

— Excuse me?!

— Your clothes. They're all full of shmutz from the storm, and I'll bet they're still damp. I'll do a load of laundry now while we have power.

— Oh—okay. But you don't have to do my stuff, I should get going and see if I can get to Nina's.

— Don't be ridiculous, Jayce, you're not going anywhere tonight, it's too dangerous. Do you have a change of clothes in your car?

— Uh, yes. I'll go get them.

— The switch for the outdoor light is above that half-moon table by the door. I'm calling Nina to tell her. Hopefully she has power.

— Okay, tell her I'll swing by in the morning but I have to get back to Ithaca by tomorrow night.

— Okay.

By the time I returned, Rivka was in the kitchen hanging up the phone.

— She's fine. I told her what happened with Molly and she's glad you're staying here. Evidently the worst of the storm is over but some of the roads by her place are blocked from the downed trees and utility wires— she said there are all kinds of emergency trucks trying to clear things.

— She sounded alright?

— **Yes, especially now that her heat is back. She's
going to bed soon.**

— **Okay, good.**

— **You can use the sunroom to change. I set up some
bedding on the couch in there. I'll throw your jacket
in the wash too, just empty the pockets, okay?**

— **My anorak can be washed in the machine?**

She gave me her '**Seriously?**' look, which instantly answered
my question. I removed my wallet and keys from the pockets and felt my mouth form a smile as I walked into the sunroom, which was located behind the living room, separated by
an arched cased opening and filled with lush houseplants. The
small bathroom off the sunroom had a sink, toilet, and penny-
round tile flooring; a stack of sage-green hand towels rested
on a shelf just below the mirror. I stripped down to my boxer
briefs, and then decided to toss those in the heap as well. I
changed after a quick wash-up and brought everything to Rivka,
who was already busy loading up the machine in the alcove
behind the kitchen. Beyond that was a door leading to the raised
back porch, which had a few steps descending to the backyard.

The tea kettle whistled. I turned the burner off and pulled
two mugs out of the cupboard while she yelled out '**Earl Grey!**'
and then '**Halvah! On the counter next to the honey!**' referring to a sweet tahini-pistachio confection that she declared
she got hooked on when she spent all those months in Israel
long ago; I found it delicious as well. Molly and Max were still
fast asleep in the living room, where two walls were lined with
packed-full bookcases. I started looking through an exhibition
volume of amazing Robert Polidori photographs from Cuba.

We discussed those while the washing machine hummed and we enjoyed the dessert. We also chatted a bit about our jobs, and the kids, who by some strange phenomenon called time, were now in their mid-twenties. David was working down in New Jersey while Maya was furthering her education in Boston.

The power went out and turned back on after a few seconds. It was only a tad past ten but I was losing steam. When Rivka got up to transfer the wet clothing to the dryer, I told her I needed to crash.

— **Of course, Jayce, you must be exhausted. There's a sheet and quilt and a couple of pillows in there, but please let me know if you need anything else.**

— **Thank you, I'm sorry, I just can't stay awake much longer. I'm going to take Molly out back so she can empty her bladder. Oh, and thanks for setting up the bowls for her.**

— **My pleasure, she's such a sweetie.**

— **She is. Max is special too, I'm glad he's here.**

— **Yeah, we both have good companions. Hey, I'm sorry I don't have any coffee in the house for the morning. If I had known you were coming …**

— **No problem, I'll get some at my mom's.**

When I woke in the morning, a weak fragment of eastern light was making its way through the gauzy linen covering the windows. I remembered when Rivka had found a bolt of fabric on sale and said that curtains were easy to sew. Max was sprawled out on the rug next to the comfortable large couch I had slept on, his head nestled into Molly's armpit. Those two were quite the pair. I moved the quilt aside, sat up and stretched, used the bathroom, put on my boots, and carried Molly out to the yard.

The wind had ceased and the heavy rains had lessened to a drizzle. Emergency crews in loud trucks were at work nearby trying to remove tree limbs and other detritus from the roads. Back inside I tested the electric blower on the gas fireplace; sure enough it was still working. I took a quick shower in the main bathroom, where an array of plant-based soaps and shampoos were lined up on the ledges, including a large bottle of Dr. Bronner's lavender all-in-one, Rivka's enticing scent since I've known her. I used a frothy almond-milk soap.

After dressing I entered the living room, where Molly was sniffing the towel that she and Max had initially slept on. The flooring throughout the house, save the bathrooms, was pine planking, which Rivka had paid someone to sand down and re-stain a rich brown. There were attractive, neutral-colored thick wool and cotton area rugs in the living room, sunroom, and bedrooms. The house was significantly larger than her previous place and she seemed to be happily settled here. There was no dirt anywhere; she must have quietly swept up the mess late last night.

I had Molly lie on her side so that I could slowly remove the splint ties. The swelling was gone; it must have been a sprain or strain, and I planned to get her thoroughly checked out by her vet in Ithaca. She had a slight limp when she tried to walk, but no more whimpering.

My freshly laundered anorak was hanging on one of the iron hooks by the front door, and a neat pile of now clean and folded clothing sat on the table in the sunroom. I packed my duffel and looked around before heading out. I had briefly visited a couple of times since she bought the place and was impressed but not surprised by all of the delightful things

Rivka's collected. In addition to the bookcases, the pale-pewter walls were filled with framed folk art and colorful tapestries from her travels, everything arranged with balance and harmony. There were unusual lamps, candelabras, and all kinds of small, interesting pottery pieces, many of them abstract depictions of an assortment of animals. I picked one up and indulged in the smooth roundness of the glazed clay in my palm. A person could spend months here just looking at everything—it was like a homey museum.

I peeked into Maya's room, where the Bat Mitzvah bear displayed itself on the wall above her bed, which was topped with neat stacks of clothing, papers, and folders. A large black-and-white photo of her and David from their trip to Italy last year hung on the adjacent wall. They were grinning ear to ear, the Trevi Fountain directly behind them spouting recycled water from the aqueduct. Rivka had given them a list of some of her favorite places, mostly coastal towns and villages, none of which the kids went to. They preferred to hang out in the big cities, and Rivka reported that for weeks and weeks upon their return they would close every conversation with '**Ciao!**' She sometimes rolled her eyes at their silliness, but we were both pleased that they remained close.

At the end of the hallway was Rivka's bedroom. The door was ajar about a foot, and I couldn't help but gaze through the space. Her reading glasses and carpal tunnel brace were atop a stack of books on the night table, which was to my immediate left. The bed was on the other side of the table. She was sleeping on her back, one arm bent at the elbow above her head, the other draped over her sternum and the crumpled corner of a quilt the color of eggplant. Her face was turned toward me, those deep, mossy eyes resting beneath the lids. One leg was bent up while Max slept against the other; he must have sauntered in while I was showering.

Rivka's dark curls fanned out over the pillow. Part of the quilt had made its way over the edge of the bed, a small portion held between her ankles, which were covered with thick, loose socks. She told me many years ago that she's had sleeping problems since around age five, which coincides with the beginning of the physical assaults at school. Well, she may have lost her wrestling match with the quilt, but she appeared relaxed and peaceful now. I made out her familiar gentle curves under a long-sleeved shirt the color of amethyst and heather-grey sweat-shorts that came to her knees. Her physical form from head to toe ... her spiritual essence ... these were things of beauty I would never tire of. I was sorely tempted to lie down on that bed and hold her close and feel her warmth and breathe her in while she slept, our bodies melding effortlessly. Instead, I turned away, forgoing another chance to learn the sacred songs of Rivka Solomon.

A few days later, back in Ithaca, I would discover a small envelope tucked into the pile of clothing she had washed. Inside was a set of keys on a five-inch length of knotted twine, and a note in her unadorned writing:

Jayce,
I hope that Molly is on the mend.
As my Sephardic ancestors would have said:
Mi kaza es tu kaza. Anytime you're in town
and need a place to rest and unwind,
please feel free, whether I'm home or not.
Safe travels, now and always.
R xo

Oh, Rivka, if you only knew.

25. A SEARCH FOR A BROTHER

Blessed are the flexible for they shall not be bent out of shape.
—Marsha Petrie Sue

RIVKA July, 2002 Nova Scotia, Canada

> — Bingo! Riv, I may have found something, but it's hard to see the entries without a magnifier. Who invented these machines, anyway?

> — Long before computers, it was all we had at the time to condense newspapers and magazines. Did you turn that dial on the bottom all the way to the right?

> — Yeah … let me try again … okay it's a little better now. 'Deed Transfer—J. Solomon to L. Smyth—District Municipality of Guysborough.' If it *is* him, it looks like he sold the house or the land or whatever it was in March 1993.

David and I sat in adjacent Microfiche booths in one of the back rooms of the Spring Garden Road Memorial Library in downtown Halifax. We were going through old newspaper listings, primarily focused on property transfers and obituaries. Maya was settled at the large wooden table behind us, carefully perusing the phone books of each Nova Scotia district. We were looking for information that might lead us to the whereabouts of my long-lost brother Joel.

It had been a while since I'd taken a road trip. This one was fourteen hours each way, not including stops for food and gas. I had asked Maya and David to join me, and we found a four day slot that worked for all of us. I wanted the company, and also, since the debacle in Greece many years ago, I wasn't keen to drive on any of those hairpin, cliffside roads where even low, useless, tinfoil guardrails may have been an afterthought. Not that we'd have much time for the Cabot Trail or anything extensive like that. But still, best to have the kids with me, and I was relieved they could do it. I wanted to see if I could locate Joel, who's been out of our lives since … well it seems like forever.

Arrangements were made with one of my neighbors, whose cat I looked after last summer when he was at the Cape, to feed and check in with Max. A gracious friend of mine let us crash at her house on Maranacook Lake on the way up. We were currently staying at the Dartmouth Hampton Inn, just outside the city here, and we'd be heading back south the day after tomorrow.

Joel was nineteen when he dropped out of college and retreated to Maine. That was in 1974. My parents worried, but my brother had always followed the beat of a different drum, so they figured he'd eventually run out of money and/ or come to his senses and return to us at some point. He never did return. The last time I saw him was in the fall of 1989, fifteen years later. I had managed to track down his phone number, and not a moment too soon. Shortly after our depressing little reunion in Hotzeplotz he headed even farther north to Canada, or that was his plan, anyway. The remote Maine town of Shirley Mills, which boasted sixty-two residents at the time, was 'too crowded' for him. Go figure.

- So that was nine years ago that he sold that property.

- Yeah. I'm gonna see if I can use their phone.

- Okay, sweetie.

Like me, David was resourceful and intermittently driven. When an idea takes hold he goes for it. In the meantime, Maya reported that she could not find any listing for Joel, either in the White or Yellow Pages, in any of the districts, which included the surrounding islands. Oh well, it was worth a shot. We strolled over to the ladies room, and a few minutes later we all returned to our makeshift office. David had his business face on.

- Okay, here's the deal. I spoke to the realtor who handled the sale. He never actually met Joel in person. He couldn't tell me much, but he opened up more when I told him I'm also a realtor.

- That's great, David!

- Well, yes and no. It sounds like it was in fact your brother, because this guy's assistant saw him when he came in to sign the final papers, and described him as tall, skinny, brown curly hair, thick mustache. Like the picture you showed us.

- Yup, that's him.

- Okay. So Joel bought a small parcel of land near the village of Guysborough in 1990. It's in the far northeastern end by the Canso Strait, which divides the peninsula from Cape Breton, about three hours from here. He paid cash, less than an acre so only about a thousand dollars. This guy was under the impression that Joel was planning to build a house on the property but for some reason never did. Maybe he couldn't deal with the complex paperwork for permits, evidently there are extra hurdles when you're not a Canadian citizen. So he sold it for about what he had paid for it three years earlier. I asked about a forwarding address, which he was reluctant to give me. I heard him rustling some papers, and he said it looks like the check was sent to a post office box in Newfoundland. He couldn't tell me anything more.

— Newfoundland, oy ... okay. Well as splendidly rugged and panoramic as I've heard it is, we're not going there. Thank you, David. At least now we know he was still alive as of nine years ago.

We found a vegetarian-friendly restaurant nearby and devoured a late lunch. Maya had a thousand questions about Joel. Didn't we all.

— So what was your brother like when you were growing up? He's three years younger, right?

— Yes. He was quiet for the most part. Liked to take things apart. He once dismantled a radio with all the tiny components and somehow managed to put it all back together. He was about seven at the time.

— Huh. Did he have normal conversations with you and your parents?

— Uhh … yeah, but he tended to be in his own little world. He hung out with our dog and cats more than he did with us.

— Is he autistic or something? Or do you think he has a mental illness?

— I don't think he would meet the clinical criteria for an established mental disorder or even a mild level of autism. He's more like an oblivious space cadet, an introverted version of my mother.

— Oh, like totally self-absorbed?

— Yes. And a lack of awareness. He wasn't bratty, although one time when he was about twelve he was pissed off at our mother about something and swung a baseball bat through his bedroom door. That was the only time I witnessed him overtly angry. When I last saw him … let's see … he was in his thirties, and I had to practically beg him to let me drive up to see him. That was the weekend I dropped you off to stay with Nana Nina. Then when I got there he was as passive as he'd always been. Not once did he ask how I was doing or what was happening in my life—bubkes. I told him a few things anyway, but he didn't seem interested. He's just incapable or unwilling to have a meaningful conversation or to step up for anything or anyone unless it benefits him directly.

— So he's the opposite of a mensch.

— Exactly. When our father died I had no way to get hold of him. So he wasn't at the funeral, he's never met you two—I mean it's ridiculous. I asked him 'Wouldn't you have wanted to be at dad's funeral?' He said 'No, what for?' Nothing *happened* to him when we were growing up that I know of. He didn't get any of that antisemitic crap that I went through, because he had light hair when he was little and no one knew he was my brother, and a few other Jewish kids started going to the school by then. Our mom can be difficult, as you know, but our dad was a good man, and neither of them abused him. I just don't understand why he cut off all ties with the family. And with civilization.

— Did he ever meet your psycho ex-husband?

— No, Joel was gone by then. He doesn't know about that part of my life.

— Did he have any girlfriends or boyfriends?

— Actually he did have some girlfriends. They were nice and pretty from what I remember but never lasted more than a few weeks, except for one who was weird like him and that relationship lasted a year I think.

— Do you know how he supports himself?

— Well I asked him that when I saw him thirteen years ago. Evidently he had acquired some carpentry skills, and he knew masonry as well. So he was doing chimney repairs, some construction, odd jobs. His house was quite small but he had built it himself, which was impressive. He didn't have luxuries like an indoor bathroom, but he had set up a pump to access water from a well, and a small refrigerator, and electricity, I think from a battery-operated generator. And the house seemed solid, albeit basic, like a rustic cabin. There was a decent wood-burning stove in the kitchen that heated the whole place. He said that the only reason he had a telephone was so he could get work. People would call him to request help with some project they were working on. Folks in rural areas tend to be self-sufficient for the most part, and they barter a lot with their time and skills.

— You stayed there overnight?

— Just one night. He gave me a ratty blanket and I slept on the plywood floor in the kitchen. I used my jacket as a pillow, it was like camping out.

— Wow. Hey, mom? Maybe you could hire a private investigator to try and find him in Newfoundland.

— Hmmm … not an unreasonable thought, but I don't think he wants to be found. He could easily obtain my phone number if he ever wanted to, it's a public listing.

— Your mom's right, honey. Sometimes it's best to let sleeping dogs lie. Or, in this case, leave sad, strange brothers alone.

I nodded slowly. David spoke up again.

— Well, maybe he got lucky and found a woman who's as spaced out as he is and they're living happily on a mountaintop somewhere.

— Exactly.

We walked around Victoria Park and the Public Gardens and talked about the word 'family' and all of the things that can mean. I told them about the Yiddish term mishpucha, which refers to the extended family network and close friends. Both kids are sensitive and thoughtful when it comes to these kinds of discussions, and I was comforted by their presence. We sat on a bench and looked out on the lawn, whereby Maya informed us about the carbon-based chemicals called green leaf volatiles that create the smell of freshly mown grass. She constantly amazes me with her knowledge and profound understanding of things that are way over my head.

Our hotel rooms were across the hall from one another and each had two double beds. That night Maya slept in David's room instead of mine. She's a grown woman now and can do what she wants. Besides, David was still recovering from 9/11, the terrible day that upended his life just a few months ago; I imagine he appreciated a warm body close to him, someone who cares about him deeply. Maya sweetly asked if I was okay before she gave me a tight hug and collected her toothbrush and Hello Kitty pajamas. I told her honestly that yes, I was fine. I didn't mention that I was weary from all the questions that had no answers and was grateful to be alone with my book.

The next day we ambled around the Art Gallery of NS, an interesting museum with a classy gift shop, where David purchased an exquisite pottery bowl for his Nana (with whom he's been staying temporarily, to her delight) that was made by a local indigenous woman. The artist incorporates sweetgrass into her pieces before they're smoke-fired. They wrapped it in tissue paper and a fancy box with the museum logo embossed on the top. Nina will love it.

We regrouped at the car, had a hearty, delicious lunch, and then walked around for another few hours in the sun, although even during the day we needed light jackets. At some point we got hungry again, so we settled ourselves at a plastic table and shared some snacks from a local vendor in lieu of a proper dinner. Then we did the boardwalk stroll with ice cream cones. It was still quite humid, the temperature having dropped to the low sixties, and the ever-present Atlantic breeze had me frequently shifting my body so I could access my dessert without hair covering my face. I should have brought a headband or something.

It was common for Maya to be the recipient of admiring stares and double-takes in public, and this trip was no exception. Confident but humble, she does not realize the scope of her striking beauty. People seem curious about what mix of ethnicities she was created from. She is Everything, I want to tell them. She is my daughter; she is extraordinary; she is Everything.

By the time Maya and I finished our showers and made our way to the self-serve breakfast area the following morning, David had already eaten and was perusing a *USA Today*. The fog lifted as we chatted at our window table. We finished packing, checked out, and loaded the car for the long journey home. At my request, David took the wheel for the first leg of the trip. Our plan was to stop in Saint John, New Brunswick, where they filmed *Children of a Lesser God* in the eighties. I settled into the passenger seat and looked out at the awesome scenery; it had been a bonny few days by the water. Maya sat in the back, diligently reorganizing her belongings.

David informed us about the thirteen Mi'kmaq First Nation communities who have been living on Nova Scotia for thousands of years. In Halifax it's primarily the Métis and

Inuit. He said that there are about twenty-five thousand indigenous people living on Nova Scotia, which is about 2.7 percent of the total population. Jayce had probably given him that information when he heard about our planned trip. I had done a little research myself and knew that the African Canadian population on the peninsula was 2.4 percent, many of them descendants of enslaved people. Unsurprisingly, the Jews were a minuscule 0.2 percent. Most of the minorities lived in or near the capital. I suppose that, for some in this maritime province, the stunning topography and friendly people compensated for the lack of diversity.

— **I noticed tons of Scottish and Irish names in the phone books.**

— **Yes, a lot of people came here from that part of Europe starting in the seventeenth century due to war and religious discrimination. And famine. The landscapes are quite similar. Scotland, and what is now the American continent, were actually connected until sixty million years ago.**

— **Really?**

— **Really. More than 92 percent of the Nova Scotia population is made up of white Christian Europeans. The minorities are spread out across the peninsula but a lot of them live in the Halifax area.**

— **Huh.**

We were quiet for a few minutes while David got us onto the main road heading out.

— **David, I wanted to run something by you.**

— Mom, is this going to be another one of your sueñitos?

— It is, honey.

— And you don't need me, just David, right?

— Correct.

— Okay, then I'm going to put my headphones on and chill out back here.

— Okay.

A sueñito is a 'little dream'. In the course of time that I lost the small bit of conversational Spanish I once knew, Maya had become fluent. She was also teaching herself Ladino, which some of my paternal ancestors had spoken, and after a few visits to the National Yiddish Book Center in Amherst said that in the future she may want to learn Yiddish as well. She knew a few words from me that had integrated themselves into everyday speech, but that was a far cry from reading and writing it. She also recently hinted that she'd like a guitar (for her birthday in a couple of months, perhaps?) so that she could teach herself how to play. All those hours listening to my 'ancient' Dylan and CSNY and Muddy Waters and Segovia tapes evidently provided some inspiration. Osmosis, I guess. Maya was self-motivated, had a good ear for music and languages, excelled in all academic pursuits—quite the polymath.

— I have a couple of questions for you first.

— Sure.

— You're still enjoying the Vet Tech courses, right?

— Definitely. I really hope I can find a job working with animals when I finish the program.

— Okay, good. And you were able to get your realtor license transferred to Massachusetts?

— Yes, there's partial reciprocity so all I had to do was take the state exam, which was similar to the one I had taken for New Jersey. I've been doing a bit of buying and selling part-time, because I'm supposed to stay 'active', plus I need some income while I'm in school. It's not much, because it's all split commissions, but I figured I can always fall back on that if the animal thing doesn't pan out.

— Good thinking. Okay, so … you know that Danco Modern place, I think it's Route 5?

— Just north of the Jewish cemetery?

— Yes. I was there a couple of weekends ago with Maggie. She wanted to buy one of those ergonomic lounge chairs—they're very comfortable, by the way. So as we were leaving I noticed a For Sale sign pointing down one of the nearby dirt lanes, you know how there's some farmland in that area? We did a quick drive-by, and it's a sizable piece of property, I think it said 8.7 acres. There's a gigantic barn and a lodge-type structure. The barn especially gave me that strong, warm energy.

— Yeah, you have that intuitive gift that kicks in at unexpected times and places.

— Yes, I wish I had paid more attention to it in my younger years.

I proceeded to tell him my ideas about establishing a sanctuary for animals that had been abused, neglected, or abandoned.

And setting up a volunteer work program, loosely based on the kibbutz model of communal living, with which I was very familiar: labor in exchange for room and board, in an atmosphere of kinship, collaboration, and goodwill.

- **So … a refuge, but not a petting zoo … and not a homeless shelter.**

- **Right. More like a safe place for humans and animals to land. Second chances for everyone involved.**

- **What about your job at the clinic?**

- **Well I'd have to keep working there until we get some initial funding. I would put a down payment on the property out of my personal savings if you can negotiate a decent price. We may be able to get some multi-year grants, but eventually we'll need to become more self-sustaining. I have some ideas for that as well, but first things first. You'll be finishing up school soon, and I think I'd like to do something else while I still have the energy. We both have a lot of skills that can be put to good use. Look—I realize this all sounds a little bit insane, but wouldn't it be phenomenal if we could pull it off?**

David took his eyes off the road for a nanosecond to give me a bright smile. Thankfully he had inherited his mother's good looks, as well as her verve and playfulness. He's resilient like his uncle and his grandmother who raised him. Our wheelhouses complemented each other and I knew we'd make a solid team. I also knew he wouldn't agree to something as significant and potentially life-changing as this out of loyalty; it was speculative and he had to want it as much as I did. He chuckled as his eyes went back to focus on the road. He gave himself a moment before speaking.

— I agree, Riv, it sounds a little insane. Let's do it.

We let the magnitude of the decision sink in, which took all of three seconds. The two of us revved up and bounced and sang along to some classic Earth, Wind, and Fire, which we blasted out of the speakers for a long stretch while the midday warmth beamed down on us from the open sunroof. At some point, Maya reminded us that we were due for a pit stop. She was giggling; joy is contagious like that.

Is there a prayer for brothers who are in self-imposed exile? I wasn't sure. But I did know I wouldn't be chasing after Joel anymore.

Onward! It was now time for some pivotal planning for the sanctuary, and I was eager to get started. And thrilled that David was willing to organize and run it with me. At the risk of putting the cart before the horse, I silently recited a sheheckeyanu of sorts: Yevorach esek zeh b'shefa, sisug, berachah, v'hatzlachah. May this venture be blessed with prosperity, happiness, and success.

26. AN EXCAVATION

But such is the irresistible nature of truth, that all it asks, and all it wants, is the liberty of appearing. —Thomas Paine

JAYCE Sunday, June 26, 2005
New England—The West Coast—Southeast Asia

A few weeks ago, Rivka called and asked if I might be willing to accompany her daughter to Vietnam sometime over the summer. Maya wanted to see if she could find any blood relations, dead or alive, or anyone that may have known either of her biological parents. Rivka knew that this trip would cover an immense geographical, emotional, and spiritual expanse, and that it was a big ask. She insisted that I think about it for a few days before making a commitment. The last thing I wanted was to dig up old, painful memories, but I suspect that's precisely what Rivka thought might be healing for me. And, of course, keeping Maya calm and safe. Maya communicated to me directly that she also thought it was a good idea for her to be with someone she trusted, and that knew the region (which I didn't really, not anymore), someone who would stay with her **'if I freak out'**. I also said yes because it was the first time, in all of these years, that Rivka asked anything of me.

The journey would be seventeen days, including the lengthy round trip travel. We sorted out our passports and visas, and I arranged for a driver-guide-translator through the Vietnamese embassy in D.C. This person would also be responsible for organizing our accommodations, which might need to fluctuate. I purchased the air tickets, and Rivka sent me reimbursement for Maya's share in the form of a check that I hadn't yet deposited before leaving Ithaca. She knew I would have been insulted if she tried to pay for both of us. True to form, there was a note in the envelope expressing gratitude for me having taken care of the details, and for agreeing to do the trip. David, my mother, and Rivka had all volunteered to keep Molly with them, and while there were no doubts that each would take good care of her, it made the most sense to have her stay with Nina, who had finally retired last year and was perhaps the one who would most benefit from the companionship of my dog during this time period.

It would take forty hours of travel each way, including stops in Chicago, San Francisco, and Singapore. God-almighty, as my mother would say. Actually that *is* what she said when I gave her a copy of the flight schedules after arriving at her place yesterday. She had never ventured outside of Turtle Island and could not imagine ever doing so.

At six in the morning I arrived in Easthampton. Rivka opened the door in a tank top, rumpled pajama pants, and disheveled hair, alluring as always. The band of shells I'd left with her five years ago circled her left wrist—does she sleep with that on? Maya's luggage was near the door. She was back in the kitchen preparing fresh coffee for us in to-go cups. Rivka spoke softly:

— **Thank you for doing this, Jayce. No matter what happens out there, it's going to be okay.**

— **You mean for Maya?**

— **I mean for both of you.**

Where she gets her unwavering faith I'll probably never know. She gave me a quick, high-powered hug. Maya came into the living room, exchanged brief, heartfelt goodbyes with Rivka, and we headed out. As we moved onto the ramp for I-91 southbound, Maya smiled and said she's sure that as soon as we had closed the house door, her mom would have started in with the Tefilat HaDerech, the Hebrew wayfarer's prayer for a safe journey.

> — **When she first adopted me I asked if she prayed often. She said no, usually only on special occasions. That customarily she just says them in her head, and in her heart, knowing that it may not help, but it won't hurt, and that 'perhaps it might nudge things along in the right direction, so why not?'**

> — **Makes sense to me.**

> — **Me too. But I think she prays for other people and never for herself.**

> — **You're probably right about that. But it seems she's happiest when the people she cares about are safe and happy, especially you.**

> — **Yeah. I sure lucked out.**

> — **As did she.**

An hour later we left my Subaru at the Park'N Fly in northern Connecticut and took their shuttle van to the Bradley terminal. After checking in and moving through the security lines we boarded the first flight. Security at all airports had ramped up significantly since 9/11, though I wasn't sure how realistically effective all the extra searching and other protocols were.

Maya had packed a few small rolls of toilet paper for us in the one suitcase we checked, which was filled with her larger toiletries, extra clothes, and lady things I knew nothing about. She had me add a couple of my less-important small but bulky items; everything else fit into our carry-on bags. I verified that she had her inhaler and albuterol vials on her; she even had a note from her physician and an extra prescription in case we ran into any problems. Maya was, unsurprisingly, a meticulous planner and packer.

Now that we were actually on our way I was having second thoughts, but did not allow them to take root. There was a palpable fear of what might be uncovered, both in my own past and Maya's. She was a full-grown adult now (how did *that* happen?) but was my responsibility nonetheless. She and Rivka were family as much as David and Nina were and I would see this through for both of us. For all of us.

The layover at O'Hare was brief and hectic. The subsequent five hours to California were tolerable, even pleasant. Maya and I reviewed the tourist tips she had researched about our final destination in Southeast Asia. No shorts that didn't cover the knees unless on the beach. A large scarf or loose shirt for Maya to cover her shoulders if we entered a sacred place. Only bottled beer or purified drinking water, no coffee unless you see it made in front of you. No feet pointing toward an alter. No finger pointing at worshipped gods. No crossing arms. No fooling around with the chopsticks. No raw veggies. No iffy fish or meat. Shoes off at the door of any private home (Maya and I normally do that anyway). No photographing people unless you had their permission. Last but not least, don't bring up the subject of the war; *they* can bring it up, but not you as an American.

She had brought a list of common words and phrases and their pronunciations, which we practiced while in flight. Xin chao! (sin chow!), Tam biet (tarm byeet), Lam o'n, Cam o'n ban, Vang, Khong. Hello, Goodbye, Please, Thank you, Yes, No. After a few rounds we received a sign of encouragement from a young Vietnamese-American woman seated in front of us, who looked back and gave a thumbs up through the narrow slit between the high-backed seats. She would later inform us, as we were all waiting at the baggage carousel upon arrival, that she was a second generation immigrant living in San Jose with her family, and that she worked at her aunt's nail salon. She said that Tippi Hedron's manicurist personally taught her aunt the trade at a refugee center. Then she and Maya had an animated discussion about hair styling tools and products.

Maya knew I disliked crowded places and, whenever possible, would steer us toward sparser corners of the airports we passed through, if we were going to have to wait awhile and not allowed outside, where it was probably just as packed. Crowds could become cyclones of confusion. We purchased soft, warm pretzels and used the restrooms after we changed terminals and arrived at our new departing gate. Once we were seated and settled in on the plane I was fine.

The third of our four flights was eighteen hours in the air from California to Singapore. This large plane had a three-four-three layout for economy class, and we were in the center section. I managed to get an aisle seat for myself so my legs wouldn't be too cramped. Maya was on my right. There was a young Asian couple to *her* right, their two young children with their grandmother on the other side of that aisle, so that they could all see each other. On the other side of the left aisle closest to me were two British men in their forties, their laptops already propped up on their tray tables. A twenty-something Asian woman in a pink hoodie was in the window seat next to them, fidgeting with whatever was in her tote bag.

After adjusting the overhead vents, retrieving books from our carry-ons, and buckling ourselves in, Maya and I chatted about her employment situation. She had finished up her doctorate in microbiology a couple of years ago. Both of us were in fields that center on complex, technical specificity, hers even more so than mine. Naturally she had remained at the top of her class in all of her academic training, had completed several internships with work-study and scholarship programs, and at least one fellowship that I knew of. She had spent the last year-and-a-half working at a research lab in Worcester, leaving that job a couple of weeks ago, partly because, in spite of the good pay, it had become somewhat monotonous, and partly because she wanted to take three months off so that she could get some time and space to weigh her options for the future. And to take this trip. She was getting lucrative offers from all over the place, including several prominent research facilities in Europe. When she told me what Denmark was offering I just about choked on my water.

— **Maya, that sounds almost too good to pass up!**

— **I know, right? But I don't think I could handle living so far away from mom and David and everyone.**

— **Would you consider doing it for just a year maybe?**

— **They require a three-year contract. Same for that position in The Netherlands. And there are those teaching positions at MIT and the hospital in Worcester. Those are the closest to family so they're very appealing. And there are some good jobs in**

Pennsylvania as well. I can't see myself anywhere in the Midwest or even California right now. And those are just the ones that have contacted me without me having even applied! And there are probably some good options at Princeton.

— It's great that you have so many choices.

— Yeah, but it's too many choices! It's overwhelming! My supervisors from the last two jobs said they'd be happy to be strong references for whichever positions I decide to apply for.

— Good. Now tell me about the different taxonomies.

Maya explained about the classification systems used for proto-zoology, immunology, and everything in between. We then had a lengthy discussion about the many types of pure, exploratory research such as evolutionary microbiology, as well as applied research techniques in the medical and agricultural fields. She provided details about so many categories and sub-categories that I now had a much better understanding of her chosen discipline.

— Well I can tell you what it was like teaching at Cornell, but each field and school is different. I can see you doing extremely well at whatever you decide, and teaching offers more of a variety of experience, as opposed to being in one room, one place, all the time. You'd have a balance of interactions with students, colleagues, and maybe still get to keep your hands in the research aspects.

— Yeah, that does sound good. So many things to consider, it was good to talk it out. Thanks, Jayce.

— Anytime. That's what sort-of-uncles are for.

— You're the best sort-of-uncle I could ever ask for.

We had been in the air for quite some time. The stewardesses (I think they're called *flight attendants* nowadays) came around with snacks, which were more substantial than those tiny bags of peanuts they dole out on the domestic flights. We read quietly for a while and used the restrooms, as much to stretch our legs as to relieve ourselves. I checked my watch: it would be another fifteen-and-a-half hours until our expected arrival in Singapore. And then another changeover. God-almighty indeed.

Maya and I returned to our books. Coincidentally, we had each brought memoirs. She had the newly released *The Glass Castle* by Jeannette Walls, and I brought Frank McCourt's *Angela's Ashes*, which I regretfully had not made time for at home, where I'm always busy with technical manuals, anthropology reports, and archaeology journals. We had each tucked an extra paperback into the checked bag as well. If we ran out of reading material before returning home, we could always swap, like Andy and I used to do … Andrew Gold, my first true friend.

~ ~ ~ ~ ~

Rivka once told me that she was born on the day that Edmund Hillary and his mountaineering Sherpa partner, Tenzing Norgay, climbed to the top of Mount Everest. It was the twenty-ninth of May in 1953, and they were the first to make it all the way to the summit, the highest place on earth. Rivka was born in a mutable mode, her spirit directed at concluding each season and helping transition to the next.

I came into this world a year earlier. Like my mother Nina, I was born of the earth; we are twenty-two years and four days apart. We are of a fixed modality, which embodies each season fully. My father Elan was born of water, protective and sensitive but unable to find a solid foothold for himself on land, his cardinal form aimed at starting a season but going no further. I am Nipmuck and Wampanoag on my mother's side, and Narragansett on my father's. My birth totem is the beaver; in the western form of astrology that would be Taurus: solid and dependable, set in our ways. It's interesting to think about how the planets were aligned when we came out of the womb into this physical plane and what that might mean. How much is fate and how much is random chance? Our core character traits and tendencies may be set at birth, but as adults we are free to make decisions that will determine our life path. *Some* decisions, that is. Others are made for us. The ancient Greek philosopher Heraclitus said that 'No man ever steps in the same river twice.' The riverbed remains mostly unchanged but the water keeps on flowing.

Back in 1971, the year I turned nineteen, none of this metaphysical pondering mattered. The only thing that mattered was the date of my birth, the sixth of May. The military draft was in full swing, and I had neglected to take any action to avoid it or get a deferment.

My life up until then had been fairly simple, and I was taking time off before applying to colleges, working intermittently painting houses with an acquaintance from high school and living with my parents and sister. My folks had no savings, so college was going to mean filling out a multitude of financial aid and loan solicitation papers in addition to the regular school applications. I had considered joining the Peace Corps but hadn't bothered to fill out the forms for that either. Conscientious Objector status was unobtainable unless you had longstanding ties to the Quakers or Mennonites, so that was not an option. I had considered backpacking around Europe, something a lot of kids were doing back then, but did not make decisive plans, not that it would have saved me. Some young men were fleeing to Canada, which I had also given some thought to. The very notion of anyone being forced to participate in any sort of military operation was sickening, but the reality of the situation for me personally did not sink in until it was too late. My hesitance to put forth a concerted effort when it was most needed, to prepare for what might lie ahead, ended up costing me.

I was against the war, of course. I had always abhorred any kind of violence, and this particular war, American involvement in Vietnam's civil war, was irrational and built on deceptions and lies, which came as no surprise to me. My people, and most other minorities, were so used to the government shitting on us that this was just one more event in a long history of events created by dysfunctional and cruel systems. 'All men are created equal' as long as they are male and white and Christian and have monetary resources.

More than forty-five thousand Americans had already been killed in Vietnam, and twice that number had deserted. I was well aware of the massive anti-war protests that had taken place in Chicago and elsewhere in the preceding years. Some of the people who organized and attended those rallies came from families who had the financial means to enroll them in higher education classes or pay off a doctor to write a fictional medical or psychiatric diagnosis so that they wouldn't have to join up. I was both envious and slightly resentful of people who could do that. Jimmy Carter, on his first day of office as president in 1977, pardoned all of the draft dodgers, but back in 1971 no one could have predicted that. I would also learn many years later that forty-two thousand Native Americans served in that war, many of whom were killed in action. I would not cross paths with any of them directly during my training or in Vietnam. We weren't good enough to be treated with respect in our own American towns, or by our government, but were deemed good enough to fight in a senseless war, 'to show American power to those North Vietnamese Commies' and 'protect the American way of life'. Indigenous people were not even granted access to the U.S. Bill of Rights until 1968, but politicians thought it was fine to risk *our* lives for something we had no interest or stake in and would never benefit from.

I had already been classified as a 1A – Fit To Serve. Tiny pieces of paper with each day of the calendar year were individually placed into small plastic capsules, which were then tossed into a large glass bowl. Each one would be extracted and assigned a number from one to three hundred sixty-six. On the fifth of August the lottery was held for my birth year. This was a bingo game I didn't want to win. The highest number called was ninety-five. Mine was fifty. The reality quickly sunk in; there was no getting out of this. I was to report to Fort Benning in three weeks. My parents and sister were devastated. *I* was devastated. And the fun had yet to begin.

The ten weeks I spent in Basic Combat Training, aka Boot Camp, were nothing short of bizarre and frightening. On the border of Georgia and Alabama, Fort Benning was a huge complex with thousands of people working and in various stages of training. Everyone was in some sort of uniform; I had no clue what all of the insignia patches were about and didn't care.

Day One they shaved off all of my hair. First, with scissors, they cut off the braid, which had grown all the way to my lower back. Then I was given a very short buzz cut. The whole procedure took just minutes. Don't they know we Indians need our hair?! It's a sacred symbol, an important spiritual connection to our ancestors and the Creator! Of course they didn't know, and if they did they wouldn't have cared. It wasn't just demeaning, it was saying Your Culture Doesn't Matter, You Don't Matter. As it was, I didn't speak any of the languages of my people; that was all lost from forced assimilation long before my parents were born. And now I no longer had the power and strength of my hair; I wasn't myself anymore. I may as well have been dead.

We were issued army fatigues and rucksacks and duffel bags and all sorts of equipment and paraphernalia. Some of the boys were new conscripts like me. I was assigned to a ten-person squad, and we would often train with three other squads, forming a platoon. There were lots of blacks but mostly whites, and we came from all different parts of the country. The black guys tended to be quiet, speaking in hushed, polite tones with each other. A couple of them gave me a subtle welcoming nod, their expressions neutral. Some of the white guys were noisy and obnoxious. After hearing them interact with each other I was astonished by how many seemed to be illiterate and of low intelligence, probably high school dropouts. It was clear that a few were juvenile delinquents, perhaps ending up in the army because their parents couldn't tolerate them at home anymore.

And then there was the yelling—the loud, startling voice of the drill sergeant barking out orders—commencing before sunrise each morning and continuing throughout the day, every day. All activities had to be done a certain way, including menial tasks like rolling our socks and cleaning the barracks. There were multiple inspections. Everything was so tightly regimented that I couldn't breathe freely. There were the night drills and the push-ups and the marching and the running and the crawling and the rifle training and the ground fighting exercises. I thought I was in decent physical shape before I got to BCT; I was wrong. Lots of repetitions, and more yelling. My head and body ached like never before. It didn't take long to determine what was required of me: Obey all orders, immediately, and without any interference from my own thoughts.

'FORM UP!! 'FALL IN!!'

We had a minuscule amount of free time. Whenever possible I walked around outside, desperately craving the sky and trees and air, without someone screaming in my face. During Week Four I took a different route, and came upon a large field where dogs were getting trained. It was called the Scout School. There were mostly German Shepherds, and a few Labrador Retrievers. I learned later that most of those dogs would be sent to Vietnam with their handlers, and were used to detect mines, ambushes, traps, and tunnels, saving many lives. I would have liked to have been one of the handlers, or one of the dogs; anything would have been better than my current predicament.

'PLATOON, HALT!!' 'COLUMN RIGHT, MARCH!!' This was going to be a long, rough haul. My spirit was half broken before I even set foot in Nam.

My memories were thankfully interrupted by the flight crew coming around with sodas and juices and then full meals. Maya filled me in about the unstable upbringing of the author described in the book she'd been reading.

— **Yeah, families come in all different shapes and colors and sizes and oddities.**

— **Yeah, but she got herself educated and became a successful journalist and writer. She persevered!**

— **She did. She persevered.**

The food was satisfying. We eventually got to stretch our legs an hour later after they collected our trash. Maya went back to her headphones and book. I went back to ... 1971.

~ ~ ~ ~ ~

Memory is a tricky thing. Much of what I experienced in the year I spent in Vietnam was so horrific that my brain still can't process it. My body and heart absorbed it all; some things you can't unsee no matter how hard you try, the monstrous leviathan of the past still weighing heavily on me. Some images return in short bursts, clear as day and in a blaze of color. Others, the really bad ones, come back in a jumbled sequence of black-and-white filmy fragments, pieces of events mixed together one on top of the other and all at once, along with the acrid stench of death and destruction.

There were about twenty of us that completed BCT at the same time in early November. We were deployed to various bases in Vietnam, some to the Cambodian border in the south or the Laos border in the north, some to the DMZ. Five of us were sent to Long Binh Post, a large base twelve miles northeast of Saigon. I learned quickly that we had been distributed to the units where soldiers had been killed; we were the replacements. We didn't know it at the time, but fewer and fewer replacements would be sent; we would be the last to remain at the base until it was turned over to the ARV on the eleventh of November in 1972.

I was assigned to a seven-person squad, given a preliminary schedule, and pointed toward the sections of the base where I'd be bunking and training. Long Binh was so massive that I never actually saw most of it except from a distance. It was shaped like an irregular triangle, where over fifty thousand people were spread out among the sprawling grounds, including some South Vietnamese, mostly women, who had been hired to do cleaning and other jobs. Some ARVN-uniformed men served as interpreters. There were buildings for engineers, medical staff, intelligence operators, clerks, aides for high-ranking officers, and other non-combatant personnel, all of whom had access to various amenities that were off-limits to us regular grunts. I later heard they even had an active, unsanctioned brothel over there, amidst the various 'clubs'. In a different area was the Long Binh Jail, referred to as *LBJ* or *The Stockade*, an overcrowded military prison with such harrowing conditions that it became notorious for inhumane treatment of its own people, most of whom were black soldiers. Things improved somewhat following a riot in 1968, after which an upgraded facility was built and guards were better trained.

There were tall, manned lookout towers all over the place, and piles of sandbags surrounded the structure foundations. I spent my first afternoon accompanying a soldier on ground perimeter patrol. We walked as he told me about how the base had been attacked three times in the past, the first being in early 1967 when the VC breached some of the barbed wire fencing by the ammunitions dump and destroyed much of the high-explosive artillery projectiles. He assured me that they were better prepared if an attempted enemy attack were to happen again. I asked about the oily-musty smell in the air. He said it was mostly from Agent Orange; **'It's everywhere, you get used to it.'**

That first night at the barracks, Andy Gold introduced himself to me, the only person in the squad who made any effort to offer a welcome. There was something about the way he stood there shaking my hand that exuded goodness, intelligence, and humility, a genuine person I could have a conversation with. He was skinny like me and almost as tall. Had been in-country for five weeks, and didn't want to be there any more than I did.

We found a few moments to speak more privately outside. Andy told me that most of the soldiers would be wary of my presence until I proved myself as someone they could rely on out in the field. He said that assignments off the base were '**not fun**' and could last for days at a time, or much longer. That '**Sometimes you start off in one place and end up in another.**'

Andy also warned me about a guy named Krozeg, who was housed nearby but not in our platoon.

— **He's a prejudiced bastard who uses derogatory terms for all minorities and lives to taunt us. Don't let him get under your skin, Jayce. He's usually with his sidekick, Coin, a dolt who laughs like a hyena at everything Krozeg says.**

— **Thanks, I'll keep an eye out. I'm an expert at ignoring people like that.**

— **Good, me too. I guess we've both had a lot of practice.**

Over the next few days, usually at mealtime, Andy and I shared stories about our lives back home. He had grown up in Philadelphia and had no siblings.

— **My paternal grandparents sent my father to the States from Poland when he was ten years old, shortly after their older son died of diphtheria. They had already emigrated across the border from Germany. Anyway, they wanted to get my dad out of the country before the Nazis finished rounding up all the Jewish families. They didn't** have enough money to get out themselves, so they sent him alone to live with a distant cousin. He grew up with them in Philly. Never heard from or saw his parents again.

– That's heartbreaking, Andy.

– Yeah. Europe was a horror-fest in the thirties for Jews and their friends, and of course everything got even worse after that. Anyway, my dad is a good guy. He's been working as a postal carrier since before I was born. Not very ambitious, but his attitude is that he just wants to live a normal, uncomplicated life, which is understandable. We always did stuff together on the weekends when he didn't have to work. In the summers we'd drive out to the local and regional baseball games, where my dad would cheer and clap. He loved those games, and then we'd stop at the diner on the way home for a milkshake. In the winters sometimes we'd get up before dawn and take the train into New York, spend the day in one of those big museums and then go to Katz's or the Carnegie Deli and eat gigantic sandwiches before taking the train back home.

– That sounds like fun. What about your mom?

– Oh, she's great too. Her parents also came from Poland. She was born in the States, had polio when she was a kid so she walks with a limp, when she gets tired she uses one of those canes. She cooks a lot, and my dad fixed up a rolling

> bar stool so she can work right at the counter preparing her noodle kugel and home-made bread and pickled vegetables. And all kinds of soups. Sometimes she works as a substitute teacher at the elementary school, which is only a block away, she doesn't drive.

— My mother doesn't drive either. So you didn't go to college? Is that how you ended up here?

— Yeah, my parents say I'm good with numbers and should go to school to learn business accounting, but I'm not sure that's what I want to do. I've always read a lot, all kinds of stuff, and I especially like philosophy, but what kind of job would I be able to get from studying that? I don't know, man. If I was home at least I could start figuring it out. Fucking draft …

— Fucking draft …

It was the beginning of dry season, and I had found a friend that I wasn't looking for but desperately needed.

~ ~ ~ ~ ~

Virtually all of our missions were Search and Destroy. Find the enemy and kill him. I received extra rifle training on the M-16, and the M-1911 pistol, which was primarily used by officers but was told to get familiar with '**just in case**', and different types of grenades.

> — You've got exceptional aim, King. Keep at it until you're more comfortable holding it and can reload

quickly. The Cong are brutal. If you see them, kill them before they kill you. If you're ambushed, kill them before they kill you. No hesitation. Got it?

Those words turned out to be true, and probably saved my life, although there were times I wasn't sure if it was worth trying to stay alive.

Soldiers were off elsewhere on the base moving and prepping the large equipment for rockets and missiles, as well as the M-60 machine gun, which required a team of three to transport, load, and fire. The nearby Bien Hoa Air Base functioned for multiple branches of the U.S. military, with their planes and armaments and operations. So many weapons of war.

As ground infantry we were out in the field almost daily, usually on various patrol assignments, which lasted anywhere from a few hours to a few days. So far I had been lucky; we heard the sound of firefights in the distance on a couple of occasions but were not called in to directly engage. I got the sense that operations were not well-organized. As busy as we were, time passed in a slow grind. I loathed every minute off base and counted the days I could return to the States, hopefully fully intact in body, if not otherwise.

Late on a Saturday morning in January, just as we were getting ready for lunch at the mess hall, O'Malley, our Staff Sergeant, told us we needed to go with Shaw and his squad **'into the city to investigate the incident'**, referring to the killing of two of Shaw's men the night before last. O'Malley would not be joining us, which seemed odd, but we always did what we were told, quickly gathering our supplies for what would hopefully be a short outing. There were six from our squad and only four left in Shaw's, so the ten of us piled into the truck with our rifles and empty stomachs for the twenty-five minute drive into Saigon. We remained relatively quiet, sensing that Shaw was seething. All we knew was that two American soldiers, both in-country for only a few weeks, had been shot at close range while out for what they thought would be a fun night of drinking and boom-boom on Tu Do Street, Saigon's red-light district. Neither Andy nor I had ever been there.

Shaw had the driver park on a side street and instructed us to take our rifles, leave the rucksacks in the vehicle with the driver, pile out, and follow. On the main road Shaw approached a group of three prostitutes who were hanging around waiting for business. When they saw Shaw's hardened jaw they quickly realized that this was going to be a different sort of business meeting. He assumed a domineering stance and began speaking quickly to them in English and broken Vietnamese, the volume of his voice rising steadily every few seconds. The women, who were dainty and actually appeared to be in their late teens, responded in Vietnamese and broken English. They all wore mini-dresses and gaudy jewelry. Shaw wasn't getting the answers he thought were due him, and grabbed one of the girls roughly by her left shoulder and marched her a few yards into the alleyway. She was the one who had been saying **'Don't know! Don't know!'** while the other two had been more subdued during the initial 'interrogation'. Tolner, one of Shaw's soldiers who had known the victims briefly, stood guard over those two, rifle at the ready. The rest of us stood a few feet back, at the corner of the street and alleyway. We knew that some prostitutes were informants for the VC, or for us, or both. There was no sure way to know who the enemy was when many wore civilian clothing. A lot of the VC lived in the extensive underground tunnel system and emerged mostly at night, but many were hiding in plain sight in the city and villages. I gathered from Shaw's yelling that he was trying to get the name of the village where the alleged VC killer lived. God-almighty—he could dislocate her shoulder if he didn't loosen his grip. Suddenly he pulled out a pistol, placed the barrel against the side of her head, and continued screaming at her. She was clearly terrified and blurted out something that must have been the information she thought he was looking for. How can anything you say when your life is being threatened be considered accurate? The cocky, malevolent Shaw didn't care; this was his version of 'interviewing a possible witness or co-conspirator'. Only when he put the pistol away and removed his hand from her shoulder did the urine trickle down the inside of her leg. I averted my eyes immediately and we all walked quickly back to the truck. Andy and I exchanged **what-the-hell-just-happened?** looks.

Shaw told the driver our new destination and we were on the road again. As usual, it was close to ninety degrees and humid. Monkeys dotted the Saigon streets and stole food right out of people's hands if they weren't paying attention. We passed signs in Vietnamese, French, and a few in English that I assumed were to attract the foreign soldiers. Bicycles and motorbikes were everywhere. Women of all ages walked around the city with quang-ganhs, the long bamboo shoulder poles with a basket attached to each end. Some were carrying produce from their family's farm to sell, while others were transporting arms and ammunition for the VC. What a strange and frightening place this was.

About thirty minutes out of the city we reached a checkpoint, where an ARVN soldier reported that there were land mines up ahead and it wasn't safe to proceed, so we needed to detour. This was par for the course in any travel; there was danger lurking everywhere. We turned around and headed back, eventually pulling over so that Shaw and the driver could consult their rudimentary maps. After some back and forth between the two of them, a decision was made to take one of the dirt roads as far as we could; then we'd have to hike the rest of the way. On the country road we passed a minuscule house that had a twenty- foot bomb crater in lieu of a front yard. It was another forty minutes before we reached the end of the drivable part of the unpaved lane. Everyone but the driver got out and began walking, this time with our half-filled rucksacks of about thirty-five pounds, and the ever-present rifles.

This unexpected expedition turned out to be a good four miles, and involved wading through the sludge of several large rice paddies, which not only was uncomfortable and slow, but left us vulnerable to attack on all sides. We walked single file, because mines were sometimes planted along the sides of rice fields, sometimes in the middle. The water came up to our knees in some areas; what I didn't know then was that my feet would never thoroughly dry out and would remain sore for the duration of my deployment. But alas, the heat, humidity, and wet conditions were the least of our problems.

We finally reached what remained of a small village. Hundreds of the rural, once- tranquil communities had already been partially or completely destroyed, either burned down by American troops or the VC, or bombed by the NVA. A few people were milling about, mostly women, small children, and a couple of elderly men. There were several rusty bicycles haphazardly strewn on the dirt.

Shaw ordered us to round up any males we could find between the ages of ten and sixty so that he could 'talk' to them. We had three minutes to bring them to the side of a dilapidated building that had probably at one time been the village center. There were four small huts, all with thatched roofs and on short stilts, just a few yards of space between each structure. Andy and I teamed up, went over to the furthest shanty, and climbed up into the doorless entry. The woman inside was standing, holding a baby. She appeared alarmed to see us, and quickly uttered a word that we didn't understand while maintaining eye contact with us. There was a motion in my peripheral vision. Andy followed my gaze to a prepubescent boy in an orange T-shirt who was partially hidden behind a bamboo screen. He stared at us between the slats with fear in his eyes. Andy and I silently made a joint decision in that moment to pretend we hadn't seen him. We stood there with the woman for a few more seconds, then turned around and exited.

Tolner had located a boy of about fourteen, and one of the other soldiers brought another boy, also a teenager. Tolner kept his rifle pointed at them while standing a few feet behind Shaw, who was 'talking' to them. '**WHICH ONE OF YOU FUCKING GO*KS WERE AT TU DO ON THURSDAY NIGHT?!**' Neither of the boys responded. They stood tall with slightly confused and defiant expressions, trying to appear tough like the full-grown men they might eventually become. It wasn't clear if they even understood what Shaw was saying. Shaw tried again, in English and broken Vietnamese. Suddenly Tolner swung his body around sharply to the left and aimed his rifle at a boy in the distance who was running away from the compound toward a grove of trees, a boy who couldn't have been more than eleven years old, a boy in an orange T- shirt. Tolner shot him twice in the back, and he fell face-down onto the dirt. No movement—he was certainly dead. Shaw gave a short nod to Tolner, as if he had done something dutiful, something patriotic, something good. Andy and I glanced at each other and swallowed hard.

Shaw returned his attention to the two teenagers whose backs were against the wall. It was like a fucking shooting gallery where no one wins any prizes. Indeed, Shaw decided unilaterally, and without any rationale, which of the two kids seemed the most guilty, as if it was beyond the realm of possibilities that neither had anything to do with the Tu Do incident. Shaw pointed his rifle at the one on the right and I flinched when he shot him in the chest. The dead boy's scrawny body crumpled to the ground while the other boy remained standing silently with tears running down his face. Shaw pivoted and led us back the way we had entered the village. Just before we reached the first rice paddy, he yelled out **'Eye for an eye, that's how we do it, boys.'** Then he went on to equate the villagers with the pig excrement that is sometimes used as fertilizer in the rice fields.

Andy and I had been warned by one of the weapons instructors that we would most likely be faced with **'questionable circumstances'** and to keep our mouths shut or we could get killed by our own men. He had said something similar regarding AWOL, **'if you ever think about it'** … if you get caught you will either be killed, or go to jail if you're lucky, and that if you *weren't* caught, you would end up dead anyway because you'd be hiding out in a village or jungle, and bad things will happen; no place was safe.

We got back to the base in time for a late dinner, but I could barely touch anything on my plate. We were tired, sweaty, and still wet from the knees down, but none of that discomfort compared to the sickening feeling I was experiencing with increasing frequency as the weeks went on. I thought we were supposed to be helping these impoverished farming families, not terrorizing and killing them. No wonder O'Malley had stayed behind. He must have known that Shaw had a short fuse and didn't want to be a part of, or a witness to, his revenge.

On the way back from the mess hall, I walked a few feet off the path and vomited into the sand until some of the anguish inside of me from Shaw and Tolner's malicious lunacy subsided. Andy waited, and then we both got ourselves cleaned up at the outdoor showers. The dreadful situation I was in created an exigency, and I summoned BrownWolf while lying on the cot that night.

BrownWolf first came to me in the dream realm at the age of four. When I told my mother about it all those years ago she had explained that he was my spirit helper, and that first vision was analogous to a meet 'n greet. Now, in Vietnam, I needed him badly. He appeared after a few moments, standing sideways in front of me on his slender legs, his head bowed low. His coat was beautiful, with black and silvery-white splotches mixed in with the predominant dark-brown—in a pack of a thousand I would recognize him. He lifted his head and turned it so that he could look directly at me with his golden eyes. He apologized, then lowered his head again, focused on the ground. He seemed terribly sad that he couldn't help me in that moment, and then disappeared. Perhaps he discerned a reservoir of strength in me that I didn't see in myself.

~ ~ ~ ~ ~

It was small comfort to be back at the base after a mission, but certainly better than out in the field, where everything was completely unpredictable and extremely dangerous. One morning, after another sleepless night, I was walking around the base before patrol duty and came upon a small KEEP OFF THE GRASS sign rising a few inches out of the sand. It was white with black lettering, and made about as much sense as this damn war, because there was no grass anywhere, only a small tuft of weeds a couple of yards away.

Everyone called each other by their surname or a nickname. Everyone except for me and Andy, and a down-to-earth character named Earl Harris who Andy introduced me to. Earl hailed from Detroit, had a broad nose and face, skin the color of ebony, and usually sported a durag he had made from a torn T-shirt. There was a three inch horizontal scar above his right elbow. He was all of twenty-one, a couple of years older than Andy and me.

Earl filled us in about his origins. His father earned a good living as a blues singer, '**one of the best in the country**', but left the family when Earl started kindergarten, the same year his mother lost her clerical job at one of the car factories when the assembly lines closed down there in the 1950s. ' ... **I've probably got some half-sibs out there.**' His mother was left alone to raise their three kids. Earl's brother Eugene was now twenty-three, already married and with a child; Earl indicated they'd never been particularly close. He was fond of his sister Alice, who had dropped out of high school and became a drug addict.

> — **So Alice was seventeen and strung out on heroine when she gave birth to a baby boy. I was with her in the hospital and they let me go to her room after the delivery. She was in bad shape, but the kid looked good and had lots of thick black hair on his little round head. Alice named him Jamal, because it means beautiful. Beautiful Baby Jamal. I got to hold him for a few minutes. But they took him away because no one in the family could take care of him. I begged my mother to bring him**

home and promised to help, but she said no, it was too much for her. I was twelve at the time. So they took him away and sent him into foster care. Alice went back to livin' on the streets and no one knows if she's still alive.

Andy and I exchanged a quick glance; neither of us could imagine the circumstances he was describing.

— **Sorry, Earl.**

— **That's rough, Earl.**

He nodded slowly and looked down at his boots.

I felt fortunate in that moment. Frustrated that I was in this hellhole participating in futile warfare, but fortunate that I had family back home that cared about me. Mail service was slow, but every few weeks I received a letter from my mother, sometimes with my father's signature under hers, and always accompanied by notes and drawings from my little sister Chi-lali, which inevitably made me smile. One was a rudimentary sketch of the bedroom we shared, with our narrow beds against opposite walls and a low dresser between them. She had included the plaid pattern of my blanket and the flowers of hers and, best of all, had drawn the lava lamp sitting on my side of the dresser that she had given me a couple of birthdays ago, and, on her side, the little wooden fox I'd given her for *her* birthday the February before I was drafted. The fox was her spirit helper; she had known this since she was three. My mother said that they missed me, and that she wished she could send a hot meal of **'good food'** to Vietnam, but of course that was not possible. She mentioned the continued anti-war protests in the States, and tidbits about their life back in Connecticut, such as splurging to buy a used television set, a first for our family. One of Chilali's notes said **'You are the best big brother! Please come home!'** with little sketches of birds and butterflies in the margins. She was too young to understand that it wasn't my choice to be here. Periodically I'd send letters back through the PX, mostly so they'd know I was still alive. I never told them what was really going on in this part of the world.

In May of 1972, halfway through my deployment, I received a marvelous twentieth birthday gift from the family. It was a small paperback entitled *Invitation to Archaeology* by James Deetz. My mother knew of my interest in the subject and managed to find it at a library sale. I read it cover to cover several times; it gave me something to look forward to, if I were to make it home in one piece. Andy read it as well, and we discussed some of the contents: 'Culture is Learned Behavior … Culture is Patterned … Society is the Vehicle for Culture …' I was fascinated by the text and illustrations and was grateful to have a friend to share it with.

~ ~ ~ ~ ~

A lot went down on the eighth of June. With American support, the South Vietnamese Marines engaged in a large, intricately planned operation at the My Chánh River against the PAVN's Easter Offensive attacks that had been ensuing for weeks. In another area, north of the DMZ, American jets bombed a rail tunnel following B-52 air strikes against North Vietnamese strongholds.

In our region, on this same day, the South Vietnamese Air Force dropped four napalm bombs over Tràng Bàng, twenty-eight miles northwest of Saigon. Innocent civilians and South Vietnamese troops had been mistaken for the enemy, who had begun to infiltrate the area in the days prior. Our platoon was called in to assist. When we arrived and saw the devastation it was difficult to know where to begin. There were rows of bodies along the side of Highway 1, some burned beyond recognition. Noxious soapy gasoline fumes permeated the air. Dozens of wounded were crouched down or standing or running on the road toward us, away from the fire and plumes of smoke. For a few seconds Andy stood, frozen, muttering '**Holy shit …**', while Earl paced in a slow, tight circle, surveying the wreckage and murmuring '**Jesus fucking Christ …**'. We got word that Cu Chi Hospital was already filled to capacity, so we would need to transport the remaining refugees to Barsky Hospital in the city for the medical care they urgently needed.

A girl of about seven approached us. I poured some water into my canteen cup and held it to her mouth; she took a few sips. Her entire body was shaking; parts of her hands and one of her arms had burns, and she held a badly injured infant, probably a sibling, probably already dead. Earl gestured an offer to take the baby, but the girl shook her head and wouldn't let go. It would have been too painful on her skin to pick her up, so Andy led her to one of the buses and got her situated. Along with other soldiers, we repeated this scenario quickly with about twenty more children and women, a few of them clinging to each other. Many of them continued screaming in pain, some were silent, some were crying; all were in shock.

I remembered from a war history class that, in addition to the obvious severe full-thickness burns, exposure to napalm can cause rapid loss of blood pressure, respiratory problems, loss of consciousness, and death. There were a couple of medics with us, but this was far beyond their scope of training, and in any case they didn't have the equipment and supplies necessary to treat these kinds of internal and external injuries. As we made our way to Saigon, Andy kept his arm lightly around the little girl, who continued to clutch the motionless baby. Earl was encouraging the people near him to drink water from his canteen cup, while singing in a soft, melodious tone in attempts to soothe them. If there had been any way to make the bus go faster I would have done it. A small boy near me was patting the face of his mother, who appeared to be passed out, the back of her head against the wire-covered window. The burns on her left leg looked horrendous, and I wasn't sure if she was still breathing. I gently took the boy's other hand and he crawled onto my lap, collapsing into my chest. He whimpered throughout the entire ride as I cradled the back of his head with my hand and wondered in terror how any of this could have happened.

~ ~ ~ ~ ~

The composition of the squads and units shifted often, as fellow soldiers were killed, wounded, reassigned elsewhere, or completed their tour of duty. Morale was at an all-time low, not that it was ever decent. Some of the officers seemed to be drinking excessively whenever they were at the base; there must have been an endless supply of beer. Some of the grunts were smoking opium or shooting heroine every chance they got. Between the druggies, the FNGs, and the erratic nature of missions, every moment off base was perilous. There were too many unknowns and you had to function with an acute level of situational awareness in order to have even a chance of survival, all senses on high alert, every single damn second.

In early July our platoon was flown by two Hueys to a clearing, from which we hiked single file into and through a dense jungle in the mountains, a section that had not already been defoliated by Agent Orange. Intel was limited and sketchy at best, but we were given the coordinates of possible enemy activity and told to set up an ambush. In reality, we became sitting ducks for *their* ambush.

We had decided not to bring our flak jackets, which were actually eight-pound vests made from layers of ballistic nylon. As it was, we each carried eighty- pound rucksacks plus extra ammo, and the vests would have been too heavy and hot. Besides, they would not have protected us from bullets, only some shrapnel and other small debris, and would have greatly inhibited our movement.

Combat duty in a Vietnamese jungle is not something one can ever get used to. The physical setting alone was enough to unnerve you. There were all kinds of venomous snakes, scorpions (that evidently can live in any environment), and leeches that left bloody welts on our skin. Once in a while we'd come across a huge tarantula, and spiders the size of volleyballs with hairy, spiky legs. Bees. Horseflies. Bats. Add to that all kinds of other strange things crawling around the tree trunks, so much so that if you rested your back against the bark you were bound to get an unwelcome visitor. And, of course, the omnipresent mosquitos, for which we were required to take anti-malaria tablets. Many years later it became public knowledge that those pills were actually toxic to some people, who in the meantime were misdiagnosed or went undiagnosed for decades. We also kept mosquito repellent in our helmet band and had to keep applying it to any exposed skin. The jungle was surreal, akin to being in the middle of a multi-dimensional, deeply saturated oil painting, and not in a good way. My normally-keen sense of direction evaporated in that place. It was hot, humid, eerie, disorienting, and frightful twenty-four-seven.

We started off with twenty-three men. There were two squad leaders, O'Malley and Ortiz, and a Second Lieutenant named Evans. Anderson was our radioman, LaPere our medic.

All were decent, reliable guys and all engaged in direct combat with us. There wasn't much activity the first few days, and we spent most of the daylight hours searching for entrances to the complex VC tunnel system, so we'd *maybe* have a better idea of the direction we *might* be attacked from when the Cong snipers ventured out after dusk. But some of the entrances were 'false', set up to fool us. The real ones were usually booby-trapped with snakes or bamboo spikes, in case anyone dared to lift up the small door on the ground. All bunker openings were heavily camouflaged. There were hidden punji pits (later to be banned internationally) and all kinds of traps everywhere, jury-rigged by the VC, as well as 'toe-popper' land mines that were left over from American troops who had been in the jungle before us. Wilk usually ran point, so he was first in line and used a handheld, unreliable metal-detector stick before taking a step onto the slimy ground. We all looked out for telltale signs of possible traps and mines buried under the surface, creating an excruciatingly slow process when hiking in the sauna-like jungle for miles. To further complicate matters, the VC guerrillas sometimes used rubber soles that made it appear like they had been walking in the opposite direction of their actual path, making the discovery of any footprints a puzzle.

On the fifth night there was a thirty-minute-long firefight, during which four of our guys were badly injured; they would need to be evacuated in the morning. The helicopters could not safely reach anywhere near us unless it was daylight, and even then it was extremely dangerous for them, above and beyond any weather concerns. Farnsworth had lost the use of one arm from a multitude of bullet wounds. Miller suffered knee damage and could no longer walk. Clark's chest was in bad shape; he was barely breathing. Narecki had lost most of his left ear. LaPere, who was kind and always remained calm when treating fellow soldiers, bandaged them all up and administered morphine. Eight of us carried the four of them a half mile to the clearing at daybreak, pre-arranged by Anderson. It was doubtful that Clark would make it.

Naturally there were no replacements, so we were down to nineteen. So far Andy, Earl, and I were okay. We had an unspoken pact to try and stay alive for each other, if not for our individual selves; we were brothers in this.

The annual southwest monsoon caused daily torrential downpours. We were constantly afraid of running out of ammo and water, never knowing when we'd get a delivery of resupplies. If we were lucky it was four days; usually it was longer. The army had replaced the heavy C-rations with slightly-less-gross freeze-dried 'meals' that smelled like dog food, and you had to mix water with the powdered substances after disinfecting the liquid with iodine tablets. We often went days without food, saving the water to drink; that was far more important. Years later it would come to light that all of us had been exposed to Agent Orange; it had already contaminated the food and water systems throughout the country.

In addition to the desperately-needed 'fresh' water, ammo, dry socks and anti-fungal powder, each of us were given an accessory packet containing toilet paper, a few cigarettes, matches, and chewing gum when the crates of resupplies came in. Usually it was the same Huey that took away our dead and wounded. It was too risky to smoke once the sun went down; even if you tried to hide the glow it could be seen by the enemy, so we indulged occasionally during the day to stave off the hunger, which worked for about ten minutes.

Three weeks in we took turns bathing in a stream of water, five or so at a time. It would be the first and only chance we'd get to use soap. It was good to feel clean, even if briefly. We then pulled our filthy uniforms onto our still-damp bodies and carried on.

Every few days we moved to a new location, and each undertaking was treacherous. Don't get injured or killed while walking. Don't get injured or killed while marking out a new safety perimeter, which sometimes involved the planting of frag mines along the edge. Don't get injured or killed while digging a foxhole. If we made the move at night without any starlight, we held onto the ammo belt of the guy in front of us.

We generally slept in shifts, but it was rare for any of us to doze off for more than an hour at a stretch; there was too much adrenaline pumping through us. We would lie down or curl up right on the wet, mucky ground, or in an equally awful shallow trench we had dug for ourselves when we lacked the energy to dig a proper foxhole. I can't remember why there were no hammock provisions. We always kept our poncho hoods on to protect us from critters; it was better than nothing. We heard that the bite from a two-inch brown scorpion was worse than the bite from the six-inch black ones. This was our life—keeping track of all the minutiae while feeling helpless and trying to stay alive.

After hiking several miles uphill one day in hundred-degree heat, we sat down to rest. Earl placed himself on a fallen log, and within seconds felt something on his back. He quickly jumped up while O'Malley rushed over, and with the tip of his bayonet removed a twenty-inch-long centipede just before it reached Earl's neck. He flung it a few feet away and Stinson came over and chopped up the aggressive creature with his machete. O'Malley said that even if the centipedes don't bite you, their legs are venomous. God-almighty. I gave Earl one of my Marlboros and tried to get him to sit on the ground next to me but he was too shaken up. He paced in a small circle while flailing his arms in the stifling air, muttering a stream of expletives about the '**fucking-wacko-creepy jungle animals … in the middle of the boonies … none of the fellas back in Detroit are gonna believe me if I try to tell them about this fucking-crazy-creepy Nam jungle shit**.' We all shook our heads in agreement. Even the guys who had grown up in agrarian regions of the States were astonished by the assortment of menacing wildlife in the jungle. Eventually Earl stood still, and after a moment began to chuckle softly. We all dissolved into laughter and couldn't stop. Needing to keep the volume down on the off chance we'd get attacked in daylight made us crack up even more, until our ribs ached and our sore eyes teared up. Earl finally lowered himself next to me and I patted his back. Andy gave him a stick of gum and told him that we would always remember this incident, and that he'd organize a reunion for us in Philly just to recount it. We'd call it *The Best-Worst Day in the Jungle*, and his mom would gladly make delicious soup and casseroles for all of us, or we could get pizza. Earl shook his head and then nodded and we were all completely delirious, from hunger and exhaustion and the fucking-crazy-creepy Nam jungle shit.

There were more firefights, always after sundown. The VC guerrilla snipers would send bullets flying at us with their Russian-made AK-47s from about forty yards away. We would immediately drop to the ground and fire back with our rifles and machine guns aimed at the general direction of where we thought the enemy was; it was hard to tell in the dark. We had been trained to 'shoot at the lowest part of the visible mass', but there was no visibility! We had to keep pausing to reload and would keep this up until we were reasonably sure they had retreated. Sometimes it was twenty minutes, sometimes much longer. It was always incredibly loud, the ringing and vibrations remaining in our skulls for hours afterwards.

Even during the day, even if it wasn't raining at the moment, scant light reached us on the ground. One morning we tried to bring some levity to our situation by creating a fake menu consisting of our favorite dishes from back home. We went around and each of us named something, resulting in a multi-course meal of appetizers (Dunbar said that his mom knew a hoity-toity lady who called them 'hors d'oeuvres'), entrées, sides, drinks, and all kinds of desserts. It was an excellent distraction, but made us hungrier than we already were, and left us with a deep longing for the small comforts of civilian life, which I would never again take for granted.

Andy, Earl, and I endured minor injuries from the sporadic firefights. Bullets grazing our skin, and small slivers of shrapnel entering our bodies from the night the VC hurled some sort of explosive device in our direction. Earl pulled a thin slice of shrapnel out of the back of my right shoulder as it was burning through my skin. We couldn't use flashlights, but he managed and I was grateful.

We were the lucky ones. There was an hour-long firefight during a lightning storm one night at two in the morning. Severe injuries were suffered by Ragsdale, Wilk, Porowski, and Garnier. Garnier had been hit by large shards of shrapnel all over his chest and bled out before we could get him medevac'd. It was disheartening to lose him; I was sorry for his family, and for his pregnant fiancé back home. LaPere had done what he could for all of them, but having to wait several hours for the medevac chopper did not help the chances of recovery and survival.

We were down to fifteen. One afternoon the rain stopped and most of us pulled our ponchos off, if only to breathe in the hot, sticky, stale air a little better. We were standing around scouting for low terrain so we could set up yet another base camp. Suddenly a bunch of red ants fell from a high leaf and landed on Andy's head. He felt the stinging immediately and leaned forward while frantically trying to get them off with his hands. He was swearing until Evans told him to close his mouth to keep the insects out. I quickly removed Andy's shirt and shook it out hard several times while Mayhew swiped Andy's torso, neck, and hair to get the ants off and away.

The very next day, Hall was lying on the ground taking a nap when a krait viper wrapped itself around one of his boots. Becker, who was sitting close by, jumped into action and got the snake to curl itself around his rifle. Its head was getting too close to Becker's hands so he dropped the gun. Ortiz calmly walked over, gently poked at its thin form with a piece of tree branch until it slithered away, and wordlessly handed Becker's rifle back to him. Hall slept through it.

Ortiz was smart and built like a compact truck, on the short side and all muscle. This was his third tour of duty—he said he was unable to adapt to civilian life and kept signing up because **'This is the only world I can handle right now.'** He also told me that the last time he was in a Vietnamese jungle he saw a water buffalo, and there were monkeys throwing rocks at his squad.

Our sadness and desperation increased daily. Two more guys were badly hurt one night. Stinson was showered with mortar shells on his back and arms; his helmet had holes and dents but his head seemed to be okay. It was a different kind of shelling than usual and we wondered if the attack had come from the guerrillas or from the more organized VC soldiers.

LaPere rushed back to the foxhole to grab his kit and then went over to help Stinson. The firefight continued and they managed to hit LaPere's right arm with bullets, his good arm, the arm he used all the time to bandage us up. He had been afraid to do more damage to Stinson by moving him out of harm's way and now they were both injured. Shit. It was another ten minutes until quiet set in.

Silence in the nighttime jungle was intense; we could barely see each other but could hear each other breathing and the pounding of our own hearts.

Stinson and LaPere were medevac'd late in the morning. After getting them into the Huey, we followed the reek of death and discovered a group of decomposing bodies along the tree line by the clearing. A dozen young VC were sprawled about, including a couple of females, though it was difficult to tell. They all wore the usual black loose-fitting garb and square-patterned scarves, their brown ammo holders still wrapped around their torsos. Most of their eyeballs had been plucked out by wildlife and there were maggots all over them, a gruesome sight. All weapons had been removed from the area. Ortiz surmised the bodies had been there a few months, most likely shot by one of our helicopter door gunners in response to an attack when they were trying to land. These dead kids were 'the enemy', but they all came from families. Why hadn't their relations come to collect their bodies? Maybe there was no one left to collect them? I was thoroughly tired and demoralized; everything was so damn confusing.

I didn't know how many people I may have injured or killed; none of us did. How can I live with honor when my very survival depends on participating in pointless warfare?

Our numbers had dwindled to thirteen. While we had all received basic first aide training, things would be much more difficult without LaPere. Hours and hours of hopelessness, the presence of Earl and Andy my only solace.

A few nights later, Dunbar walked out to the perimeter to relieve himself. It had been quiet, but we were on full-alert as always. On his way back to us, his leg got caught in a trap, its rusty metal claws imbedded just above the knee. He screamed out and fell to the ground; I could only imagine the pain. The trap was big enough to ensnare the leg of a fucking elephant. His howling made us a target. Earl and Ortiz immediately retrieved shovels, the ones we use to dig trenches, and began trying to release Dunbar from the trap. The rest of us had already formed a half circle with our backs to them, ready for the VC bullets, which came swiftly. We fired back. A few minutes later Dunbar was free of the trap but his leg was sundered. Earl and Ortiz stayed with him and applied a tourniquet; we all knew Dunbar would need an amputation. As the firefight continued, Anderson ran toward the foxhole to strap on his heavy radio to alert HQ and request support, with Evans on his heels. Anderson's job was exceedingly perilous—in the jungle he couldn't get reception without extending the antenna the entire ten feet, making him an easy target, even if he tried to keep his body low. We continued to get rained with bullets, which eventually became sporadic. In the silent pauses I could hear the static of the radio but no voices. I ran back to the foxhole and found Evans, unharmed but tearful, crouched over Anderson, who had been killed instantly by VC bullets while Evans had been trying to help him strap on the fifty-four pound radio with the ridiculously high antenna. Shit, we had lost another really good guy.

Evans didn't waste any time. He fiddled with the equipment and lifted the hand piece and made contact: ' ... **no**

**medic, no RTO, no reinforcements … no supplies …
cannot sustain … get us the fuck out of here … well then
send a Cobra if you have to so the Huey can land safely!
… yes … 08:00 … Roger that.'**

After six weeks in the jungle only eleven of us returned to
Long Binh intact, our bodies heavy with exhaustion. But we
were alive. And we hadn't become POWs, a fate worse than
death. Was that the silver lining in all of this?

~ ~ ~ ~ ~

We got word that the U.S. government had told its citizens
that there were no longer any American ground combat troops
fighting in Vietnam. Lies upon lies.

One Sunday afternoon when we were off duty, Andy and I
dragged a couple of rickety lawn chairs over to the side of the
barracks. We removed our sweaty shirts and leaned back with
our books, grateful to pass the coveted time in the relative safety
of the base and for the temporary reprieve from rain. Simon and
Garfunkel's *The Sound of Silence* crackled through the loudspeak-
ers. Ten minutes in, Krozeg stuck his head out from the far end
of the building and approached slowly, stopping three feet in
front of us. He snapped his ugly square mug and thick neck both
ways to make sure no one else was within earshot.

  — **Well what've we got here? The No-Speaky-In*un
    and the Nig*a-Lovin'-Ki*e, tellin' each other
    bedtime stories. Ain't that cute …**

I don't rile easily, but this was at least the fifth time Krozeg had
spewed his vile hate directly at us. Usually he just looks our way
and mutters snide remarks until Coin lets out a snarky cackle. I
was tempted to provide a retort and wished for him to return

to Texas with his tail tucked between his legs, but we took the high road and ignored him as usual. That evening, Andy mentioned the incident to Earl.

— **Don't worry, fellas. One of these days someone will beat the crap out of that asshole, he sure got it comin'. But it won't be me—Krozeg's not worth gettin' in trouble over.**

We shook our heads in full agreement. Then the three of us sauntered over to where movies were periodically shown on the base and watched a black-and- white version of *Mary Poppins*. Other nights, if none of us were on patrol, Andy, Earl, and I sat around playing cards. Andy would inevitably pose a question, usually focused around the same theme.

— **So why are we really here, Jayce? What greater purpose are we serving?**

— **I don't know, Andy. But I've come to realize that not everything's a sign from the fucking universe.**

— **You mean sometimes a rose is just a rose?**

— **Yeah, and what I wouldn't give to be able to smell a rose right now.**

Then Earl would chime in.

— **Well if I had a sweet-smellin' rose I would give it to a sweet-smellin' lady.**

— **Anyone in particular, Earl?**

— **Nah, but when I get back home I think I'll look for someone to be with, a nice, pretty lady that'll watch over me. And I'll take her out dancin' and treat her right. But first I gotta get a good, steady**

job, like drivin' one of them Detroit city buses. And maybe I'll try to find Baby Jamal, make sure he's okay, y'know? He'd be about nine years old now. Maybe they'll let him come live with me, if he wants.

— **Those are good plans, Earl.**

— **Thanks, fellas. Alright, enough chit-chat. Either of you boys got an ace?**

A week later, with only eight days short on his countdown calendar, Earl was out on a convoy security detail and got blown to smithereens.

~ ~ ~ ~ ~

Andy and I had lost our sense of humor, but so far we hadn't lost each other.

The eighteenth of September was muggy, gloomy, and confusing. I don't remember all the details of that day, just the broad strokes. After completing some on-base duties, five of us left mid-day for a highway patrol assignment. Andy had suffered a sprained wrist a couple of days prior but had fashioned an ace bandage around it from a cloth strip and insisted he was fine. He was almost giddy with the knowledge of only fifteen days until his turn for the Freedom Bird. I urged him to stay back at the base but he said '**No, Jayce, I can shoot with either hand, I'm good. We're staying together**'.

There was a full unit of Quan Sats already on-site when we arrived. They were the uniformed South Vietnamese military police, and they said that a land mine had just destroyed an ARVN tank but there were no casualties and they didn't need us. After Ortiz communicated with HQ we turned the truck around and drove to another location, whereupon we walked a half hour to join a handful of fellow soldiers who were planting a circle of mines around a VC bunker that was believed to still be in use. We worked carefully, and at dusk began the hike back to where we had been dropped off, hoping we wouldn't have to wait long for a truck to return us to base.

The road was only forty feet up ahead, at a higher elevation than the path we'd been walking. We heard a thud as we approached, followed by a small explosion a second later. We assumed the grenade had originated from the other side of the road in front of us because we weren't close to any enemy hiding spots behind us, or so we thought. The VC were in a thicket of eight-foot-high elephant grass more than a hundred feet behind and to our left. How could I have missed that? Was my guard down because a speck of sun had not yet dipped below the horizon?

We realized too late that the grenade had been thrown as a distraction. As we dropped to the ground the bullets were already flying toward us and we were facing the wrong direction. We quickly squirmed our bodies around amidst the low weeds and small piles of tar chunks and other debris—leaving us virtually unprotected—and positioned ourselves about six feet apart. The firefight continued for just a few minutes but it felt longer; it always did. When the gunfire stopped, our ears still ringing, Andy said he thought one of the guys down the line may have been injured from the initial explosion, and he was going to check on him. Before I could yell for him to stay down, he was up and running. He must have figured the firefight was over and lacked the patience to crawl. I found out later that his rifle had jammed and he wasn't able to fix it (because of his injured wrist?), and knowing Andy he probably reasoned that he hadn't done his full share in the firefight and wanted to help afterwards any way he could. God-almighty.

It happened incredibly fast but in slow motion. A loud spray of bullets landed in Andy's chest and he fell onto his back, his helmet dislodging as he hit the ground. I screamed his name and frantically scurry-crawled over. I put pressure on his wounds with my hands and what was left of his shredded flak jacket, but knew it was futile. Ortiz waited a few beats after the gunfire stopped again and rushed up to the road for help.

Andy's eyes remained fixed on mine as he made a herculean effort to speak, his voice a rattling whisper at the edge of the precipice.

- **Jayce … where do we go … when we die?**

- **I'm not sure, my brother, but I know it's peaceful there. And I promise to come find you when it's my turn.**

He managed a weak smile, his pupils widening as he took his last two shallow breaths. Heavy, clear liquid drops were falling onto my hands, still splayed across his bloody torso. Only when I raised my eyes to the night sky as the medic checked for a pulse did I realize it wasn't raining. I stayed there, crouched over Andy, until Ortiz touched my shoulder. '**King, we need to move him now**.' I nodded slowly, helped them carefully place my friend onto a stretcher, and watched as they took him away.

Utterly despondent and soaked in sorrow, I summoned the courage of my ancestors to get through the remaining fifty-five days of my deployment.

Upon returning to civilian life it would take three years for my hair to grow back. It would take a lifetime for my heart to become whole.

27. PROVENANCE

A day of traveling will bring a basketful of learning.
—Vietnamese Proverb

JAYCE Late June—Early July, 2005 Vietnam

It was seven on Tuesday morning local time (late Monday night back home) when we found ourselves at border control in the still-under-construction international terminal at Tan Son Nhat airport. Maya reminded me that it's not called Saigon anymore—it's Ho Chi Minh City. I would always link it with the old colonial name. The airport abbreviation code is SGN, so I'm not the only one. U.S. airlines began to resume flights to Vietnam just six months ago; they had not operated these routes since 1975.

We were awaiting our turn for the customs desk, where the inspector would examine our visas and ensure we weren't bringing in any contraband or excessive cash. In the area behind the security check-in stations were a few people greeting the arrivals. I quickly spotted Trai, the gentleman with whom the embassy contracted to be our person. He was holding a handmade sign:

King
MaiYei
Jay

Close enough—time to rock'n roll. As soon as clearance was completed we approached and introduced ourselves. Trai (surname Tran) seemed like a happy-go-lucky guy, and

280

welcomed us with smiles, cheerful hand shakes, and a solid command of the English language. Maya noted the muggy heat as we followed him out to a small tan sedan. Trai appeared to be in his early forties, midway between Maya's age and mine. He acknowledged that we were probably tired from the long trip as he drove us to our modest hotel in an outskirt of the city to settle in. He gave us the choice of starting our search today or waiting until tomorrow—I deferred to Maya, who opted to not waste any time.

The hotel room was actually a clean two-bed-two-bath suite, which was perfect for us—we each had our own space but were in the same unit, which Maya had requested and that Trai was able to find and book for us at a reasonable price.

Over breakfast at the main-level restaurant, Trai told us he had a wife and a teenaged son. '**I taught him how to use computer and now he is with it all the time when he comes home from school until he goes to sleep … my wife has to tell him to stop and come eat dinner.**' This was a good-natured complaint from a devoted family man. I was curious but didn't dare ask if his parents were still alive. Maya and I gave a brief synopsis of our respective careers when he inquired, and then we got down to the serious business at hand.

> **— Okay, now I tell you what we do for next two weeks, yes? I already research all the papers for the children like you who fly to America. The documents are not so good … and no papers for the plane evacuations, but I come up with leads to help us. Now that I see you—with the dark skin— we will have more problems.**

Maya and I exchanged a glance; she was certainly aware of the bigotry that permeated so much of society, but as far as I knew she hadn't experienced overt racism directed at her personally (with the exception of a minor incident in kindergarten when a classmate told her '**My brother says you have ch*nk-eyes**', neither girl understanding at the time what that was.) So this was new to her and she appeared a bit frightened. We knew the prejudice was not coming from Trai; he was simply informing her of its existence here. I tried to reassure her; Trai did as well.

> **— It is okay, let me explain more. You are Amerasian, but the dark skin means you cannot pass at all for regular Vietnamese. Here they call you 'con-lai'— means 'half-breed', or 'bui doi'—means 'dust of life'—means not civilized. It is good you were evacuated because there is much discrimination here against all the mixed races, not just the dark skin, especially in 1970s and 1980s but still some now. Means when we go talk to people some will close door on us, you understand? Mostly the older ones. But also means we can narrow search to see if anyone knows of the woman—your mother— who was with American soldier with the black skin. This is good. Complicated ... bad and also good, you understand?**

Maya nodded, retrieved her inhaler, shook it, and took a long puff.

> **— Please, MaiYei, no one will hurt you, it is just some people might refuse talk with us, okay? Also, I have to say we do our big search but no promise.**

**I do this before with other American children and
I have many contacts, so I do my best and maybe
we have success, but no promise.**

— **Okay, I understand, thank you.**

Back in his car, Maya sat up front while I stretched my legs in the back. During the drive Trai asked if we knew of Celine Dion, and after a couple of clarifications ('**singer from Canada? ...** ***The Prayer?***') Maya figured out what he was asking, and then he began to hum, sporadically interrupting himself to point out a landmark along our route or a building in the city skyline. Trai was a small man with a big personality. We would quickly and gladly adapt to his compressed pronunciations.

We spent close to two weeks driving to and from many locations, mostly apartment buildings in and around the city, as well as some rural villages. Trai must have spoken to well over two hundred people, with Maya and I standing quietly behind him. Some, indeed, slammed their door when they saw us. Maya had appreciated the advance warning, but it was putting a strain on her—sometimes needing the inhaler—sometimes leaning into me for a reassuring side-hug; it's difficult to not take those incidents personally. I imagine my presence also seemed odd to people: tall and sepia-toned with braided hair. Along with the ebullient Trai, we made a peculiar trio.

Every few days we'd take a break from the search and do touristy things, like explore the Saigon Opera House, the Jade Emperor Pagoda, the Thien Hau Temple. Maya's favorite (mine as well) was the day we took a ferry to Can Gio Mangrove Biosphere Reserve and hiked around to see the flora and fauna of the wetlands. I experienced a moment of unease when we reached views of the nearby forest, but let it pass and focused on Maya, who was delighted to take everything in. Despite the occasional panic attacks she was open to new adventures, something I greatly admired. I was proud of her for setting this trip in motion, bravely looking for the missing pieces of her past.

The old, enormous Ben Thành Market would have been too crowded for me during the day with all the indoor vendor stalls, but we did take a nighttime, outdoor stroll there. Trai advised us not to buy anything, and another day took us instead to a less expensive but better quality store, where he helped us select and purchase small handmade items for our mothers back home. We also bought a joint gift for David, whose thirtieth birthday would occur while we were flying back to the States.

Trai accommodated our interests and pointed things out from a distance, like the people doing tai chi in Tao Dan Park, and one afternoon we made an excursion to Yunnan Province to see the massive rice terraces. We avoided the war-related attractions. He knew from my visa application that I had been here before; there was no need to discuss it.

I tried to reconcile the sights and sounds of today's Vietnam with those I remembered from decades earlier. The noxious smells were mostly gone, and I reminded myself that danger was no longer lurking from every direction. Views of the mountains revealed lush landscapes. Even with the almost-daily downpours (for which we had brought packable hooded rain jackets at my suggestion), most of the scenery was picturesque, including the many palm varieties that lined the roads, the ancient tamarinds, and the vine-covered teak trees in the highlands. I thought of the thick, spiny, low-hanging 'Wait a Minute' vines we had to avoid in the jungle, but the memory dissipated just as quickly as it had come, a detail that was no longer useful.

It was extremely hot—some things don't change. Downtown Saigon still bustled with people and hordes of slow-moving motorbikes and scooters, but it was cleaner and more cosmopolitan. Most of the farming refugees had come to the city area after the war and worked menial jobs to survive. There seemed to be less poverty, but Trai informed us that there was a lot of income inequality, creating a wide divide between the rich and poor with no true middle-class. He said he was one of the few lucky ones in that he had steady work as a guide; he'd never live like a king but could afford all the basics for his family and that's all he cared about. There had obviously been numerous infrastructure efforts made throughout the country; even the villages seemed nicer and easier to access, though there were still plenty of bomb craters in the countryside that had not been filled in. My memories were safely tucked away but not forgotten.

Trai kept a supply of rice cakes in the car so we could snack between meals. He made sure that any food we consumed was safe and said he was relieved we had no requests for the 'exotic' dishes that some Americans want to try. **Some people think they have culinary adventure, yes? But then they get sick and ruin the whole trip. It is good to try new things, but only a little and nothing crazy … American stomachs can't digest some of the foods.**' Maya said that some Americans are just plain stupid. Trai said there are stupid people from everywhere.

During all the outings, Maya and Trai conversed nearly non-stop with each other; I was pleased she felt so comfortable with him. I would usually wander off, in my head or physically, but never far. After each unsuccessful search visit, and there were many, Trai would hustle us back to the car and reassure her—'**we keep trying, okay?**'—and then distract her with unrelated topics, like asking what snowflakes feel like when they fall on your bare skin, and how does she pick out things in the big stores back home when there was so much to choose from? Most of these conversations, when I paid attention, were quite amusing. One day he taught her the lyrics to a song made popular by Celine Dion—he *really* liked Celine Dion. I knew that his access to world news and culture was limited due to heavy censorship; nearly everyone in Vietnam had a TV but all of the programming was government-sponsored or government-sanctioned. Trai had regular contact with foreigners, so he had more real-life experience and knowledge than most citizens.

On the eighth of July we made multiple house and apartment visits as usual, and in the early evening found someone with a viable lead. It was an older woman who glanced at Maya, and after lots of back and forth with Trai said that she thinks that someone related to Maya's biological mother may still be living in or near one of the apartment complexes in a different district on the other side of the city. There were many neighborhoods within each of the twenty-four districts, so this seemed an impossible task, but Trai was hopeful. He cross-referenced the family name of Ly with the spotty orphanage records … it was a common surname but this woman just confirmed it, so that was promising. When we returned to the car, he said we will continue the search in the morning, and that his wife was expecting us all for dinner right now. It was Friday night and we were scheduled to leave the country first thing Monday.

The meal was delightful, as was Trai's wife Kim and their fifteen-year-old son Viên. We crowded around the table in their humble apartment and ate delicious vegetarian versions of bo bia (spring rolls) with spicy peanut sauce, and rice with fresh stir-fried vegetables flavored by a tasty coconut-scallion sauce. Kim spoke minimal English, and we knew sub-minimal Vietnamese (which I felt bad about, but at least we were proficient with chopsticks). Viên was fluent and talkative; he told Maya privately that we were **'very special'** because this was the first time his dad had ever brought clients to their home. After some blessed coffee, Trai took us back to the hotel and said we'd continue the search early in the morning. We were running out of time.

Trai picked us up on Saturday and we headed to an area we had not previously covered. After about four hours we got another lead. Maya was stirred up as we grabbed a quick lunch at Trai's insistence. We hit the ground running again and by mid-afternoon hit pay-dirt.

Inside the unlocked gate of a three-story apartment complex was a courtyard. A few plastic utility pails were lined up neatly against one wall, and a rundown wooden bench took up space on another side. Trai approached a gentleman about my age, who as it turned out was the superintendent for the building. He knew all the tenants but, as luck would have it, that knowledge was not needed. As soon as his eyes landed on Maya, coupled with Trai inquiring about the Ly family, he motioned for us to wait and ran quickly inside to get his wife. After some verbal commotion she entered the courtyard, looked at Maya, and gasped. Then she began crying and opened her arms wide while Trai translated:

– I know who you are ... come here, child.

Her name was Chi (surname Ly) and she was the younger sister and only sibling of Maya's biological mother. After hugging Maya tightly we were ushered inside the little apartment off the courtyard where Chi and Tenh lived. Trai translated the flurry of words and emotions as Maya and Chi smiled and wept.

> **— I thought I would never get to see you again. I am very happy … you are beautiful just like your mother and father … you tell me everything I tell you everything.**

And there was much to tell. With all the jumping back and forth between time sequences I paid close attention so that I'd be able to help Maya make sense of it all later on and to provide some context—it was a lot to take in even if emotions had not been involved.

Chi told us that the name of her sister—Maya's mother—was Liên, which means water lily. She was a good big sister to Chi and was 'a happy girl—I think you say *bubbly* in English?'. She was born in 1953 and they grew up in a small village (which no longer exists) about twenty miles south of Saigon. Liên met Maya's father Neil in April of 1973 when she was working at the U.S. Embassy, where the DAO (Defense Attaché Office) was housed after becoming operational, a couple of months before the withdrawal of U.S. military forces at the end of March that year. From what I could piece together, with the assistance of Trai, Neil was not in the armed forces—he was an American civilian Department of Defense employee with some sort of 'technical' expertise. Chi had met him but did not know his surname or what part of the States he was from or what exactly his job had entailed.

> **— Liên and Neil were in love. It wasn't just casual boom-boom. He wanted to marry her and bring her to America, where she would be safe from the war and where they could start a family. He**

had plans for them. He said after they arrive in America he would have access to money to get me and our parents out. It was very bad here back then. He wanted us to all be in America together.

— **Did your parents meet him?**

— **Oh yes. At first our dad was skeptical, because he wanted to protect her. And he had never met a black person before. But then he recognized that they truly loved each other. Also, Neil was respectful to all of us. He was shy and not pushy.**

— **Did he know your language?**

— **Only a few words, but he had a little book of English-Vietnamese translations that he always carried in his pocket, and also gave one to Liên so they could communicate with each other and our parents. He brought us treats when he visited. Neil was good man. And smart.**

Chi said that Liên realized she was pregnant with Maya in late February of 1974—they had spent a few days together in December. It was not planned but she was happy. Neil was also excited but they both felt the increased urgency of emigrating so she could give birth in the States. Neil had already submitted the papers for Liên to get out, and he had said that if he could get her on a plane before he was allowed to leave himself that she could stay with his family until his contract ended. She wasn't thrilled about it but agreed that it was the safest plan under the circumstances. He assured her that his family knew about her and they would be accepting. His father was a World War ll veteran (when troops were segregated) and understood about wartime circumstances.

We had been sitting around a kitchen table, which was situated in what appeared to be the only living space, aside from a bedroom and bathroom off to the side. Chi said something to her husband, whereupon he rose to retrieve a small black-and-white framed photograph of Chi and Liên, ages six and nine respectively. It was the only surviving photo of Liên. Maya and I noted the resemblance to her biological mother—the expressive, perfectly round face, the nose, the warm smile. The black skin, textured hair, and full lips were inherited from Neil. Maya said her eyes must be a combination of both. Chi nodded and allowed me to take a photo of the photo; I also took some of Chi and Maya and Tenh. Maya's newly-found auntie and uncle did not have any children of their own, so there would be no biological cousins to meet.

Maya was hesitant to ask but wanted—needed—to know about her parents' deaths, which Chi eventually got around to. Trai was sensitive to the situation as always and remained patient. Maya reached for Chi's hand, which she took.

— **In early June, when Liên was five months along, they still didn't have clearance to leave the country. They were both frustrated about the paperwork hurdles and anxious to get out. One day Liên went into work as usual, and could not find Neil. He wasn't allowed to talk about work with her, and it wasn't unusual for him to be elsewhere occasionally, so she tried not to have much worry. But then the next day he was still gone. She looked and looked all around the building, wherever she was allowed to go during her quick breaks. She**

asked for him at the DAO office, the room where he usually sat at big desk. They knew who she was and finally one of the men took her into hallway and told her that Neil had been sent to Bien Hoa Air Base the day before and had been killed along with another American when the PAVN fired many rockets onto the runway. The man was friend of Neil so she knew he was telling truth. She said he was filled with apologies. Liên was devastated but she kept working to help support the family. I think maybe also she thought Neil would appear, like a miracle, like maybe it was all a mistake and he was still alive. So every day she goes to the same place where her future husband used to work—it was very difficult and she cry every night.

Maya and Chi were both tearful again and Tenh got up to prepare green tea for everyone, a little reprieve from the sadness. We all took turns using the tiny bathroom, and then Tenh and I sat quietly outside in the courtyard for a few minutes to finish our tea. It was drizzling but we didn't care.

— **So now the rest of story. I am sorry to tell you, MaiYei, but you have right to know. You were born in our village—too dangerous to go to hospital. Your má loved you very, very much. We all did. My family had nothing and it was terrible time in the country but we all had love for you and took care of you best we could. One day our father was sick. Our mother and Liên stayed with him but he said I must take you with me to nearby village to someone he knew—they sometimes**

barter for supplies. Father was spiritual man and sometimes he knew when something bad was going to happen. So I go on bicycle with you in the wrap. Not big trip. Liên and má do their usual chores in village while I'm gone. Then VC come and shoot everyone in our village and burn down. Don't know if target or why our village. Everyone dead—terrible. I scream and scream and cry. Then take you back to other village. This was in December when I just become eighteen years and you were three months. I hold you all the time and thinking about my whole family dead. There was no milk to feed you now that your má gone. People I stay with nice but they also have nothing to help. So after a few days I take you to orphanage in Saigon, the Catholic one because it looked clean and I know they can take care of you. Many babies there. Wanted to keep you but we had nothing and also you would be shunned because you are the mixed-breed. So I tell orphanage your name and birthday. They write down on little paper and attach to your blanket.

Chi confirmed Maya's birth date as the sixteenth of September. I thanked the Creator for a small piece of paper pinned to a baby blanket. I'm sure Maya did as well. She used her inhaler as we listened to the rest of the story.

— **I was sad but knew you would be safer than if I tried to keep you. Had plans to come see you whenever I could, and maybe when the war was over I could take you back and raise you. I went to orphanage in April and they say they got all the**

babies on the evacuation planes. I was sad again but also knew you would be safe. And pray hard you have good life in faraway place.

All of us were tearful, including Tenh and Trai, both of whom knew of many similar stories. It was late. Chi said we were to come back the following afternoon, our last day in the country. She wanted to hear more from Maya about her life, and would tell her anything else she wanted to know.

True to form, and in line with her excitement (along with the emotional fatigue), Maya composed a list of additional questions she planned to ask her auntie Chi. She asked me to add some, which I did, but also advised her to listen to any stories Chi wanted to share—that was just as important.

Trai picked us up late Sunday morning. Maya wanted to bring something special to Chi and Tenh, so we went to an upscale shop where Maya purchased the largest gift basket they had. It held an array of cookies, little cakes, fancy table napkins, and fruit. Trai laughed with approval and said it would last them many weeks.

It was another productive visit. At one point Tenh and I left the apartment to give Maya and Chi some privacy, leaving Trai with them to continue translating. Tenh brought me around to one of the apartments he had been cleaning before new tenants arrived, and I helped him with wall-prep and painting. Neither of us spoke the other's language but we managed well, Tenh full of smiles when he realized I had some skills.

Dinnertime rolled around and it was time to go. Chi presented Maya with a tiny decorative ceramic vase, painted green with pink flowers and delicate brown stems, less than two inches high and wide. Chi apologized for not having anything of Liên's to give her. Maya glanced at me across the table while holding the bibelot in her palm—her auntie and uncle were of modest means and she wasn't sure what to do. I gave her the slightest nod and she accepted the gift graciously, saying that she'll keep it on her dresser where she'd see it every day and think of her Vietnamese family.

There were tearful good-byes. It had been a thrilling, albeit tiresome, couple of days for Maya. Trai had managed to find a needle in a haystack so that she could learn about her roots. She used the inhaler a couple of times that night, but said she was okay, she just needed to begin to process everything. All in good time.

28. RELEASE

Each of us is more than the worst thing we've ever done.
—Brian Stevenson

JAYCE July 11, 2005
Southeast Asia—The West Coast—New England

- Jayce … Jayce … Jayce! Wake up!

- Fuck. Sorry, Maya. Did I wake you?

- No, it's six in the morning. I've already taken my shower. We're meeting Trai downstairs in an hour to go to the airport. You were having a bad dream—you sounded scared. You were yelling 'Andy'? Like over and over.

- Shit. Alright. I'm awake now, thanks. I'll get ready.

- Okay. Then we'll finish packing and check out at reception. We can grab some coffee downstairs before Trai gets here.

- Sounds good. Sorry about that, didn't mean to frighten you.

- It's okay.

- Hey, do you have any Tylenol?

It was hot, muggy, and misty as I sat on a bench outside, facing away from the bustle of the hotel and into the distance—trying to create a little quiet for myself as I looked at the past in the cold, hard margins of memory. Maya sat a few yards behind me, and I heard Trai approach while exchanging pleasant greetings with her in Vietnamese.

— **Where is Jay?**

— **Over there.**

— **He is okay?**

— **I think he may be a little sad this morning.**

— **Ah, okay, I go talk with him. You stay here with luggage. We leave ten minutes, yes?**

— **Yes.**

Trai sat down beside me.

— **I'm sorry, Trai. I'm sorry for everything that happened here.**

— **No, Jay, not your fault, not your big rock to hold. Problems in Vietnam started before I was born. I was only seven when you were here. We didn't blame the American soldiers, even the cruel and stupid ones. We put blame only on your government, and the north here.**

— **It must have been terrible for you and your family.**

— **Yes, but you must listen. You had no choice. Government send you here. Good men like you, I know you probably wanted AWOL. Most AWOLs got killed ... look at MaiYei's father—he didn't**

even do the AWOL and he probably wasn't forced to come here and still he got killed. I am glad you are alive. MaiYei is glad you are alive and I am sure more people back home. You are good man and you must live good life, okay?

— **Thank you, Trai. You're very kind.**

— **It is because I know who you are inside. The guardian spirits listen to us—before and now, and tomorrow.**

I nodded, shook his hand, and we all headed to the car. Maya was quieter than usual while Trai gave us instructions for future communications. Maya could try to send a package of non-prohibited items directly to Chi and Tenh if she wanted, and they *might* receive it, but they didn't have a computer so any important correspondence, including photos, should be sent directly to his personal email address. He would print it out and translate for them in person. He was completely trustworthy and we knew he'd take care of it. He said that no matter what, he wanted us to stay in touch. Maya promised she would—a friendship had formed.

As we got closer to the airport Trai began singing softly. Maya joined in and the volume swelled and they belted out the *Titanic* theme song—what else would it be? Those two were something else. Maya was still weepy when Trai led us into the departure terminal and pointed to the security line. He was tearful as he said goodbye, and told us we were **'most interesting and best clients'** and he would miss us. I handed him a huge tip, which I know he'll appreciate when he opens the envelope after we're gone. He was worth double his weight in gold.

Maya was chatty on the first, short flight. She wanted more information about her father, and I suggested she follow up with the DOD but not to get her hopes up. Even with a surname it would be difficult; without one they were unlikely to do the extra research. But it was worth a try.

We had some time during the Singapore layover, where Maya cajoled me into entering the butterfly garden with her, where I distracted myself from the fact that we were actually *in* a butterfly garden *in* an airport by taking photos of Maya giggling when a bunch of the insects landed on her.

During the second flight, the long one heading east toward the States, Maya asked me who Andy was. I gave her the short version: that he was an exceptional person who tried to find meaning in everything, that he had a keen sense of humor, that he was ambidextrous, that he would sing along to *Leaving On a Jet Plane* whenever it came out of the speakers at Long Binh, that he had done a Bar Mitzvah, that we could always read each other's thoughts, that we had an infrangible, unbreakable bond, that he had been killed. It hurt to talk about him but I didn't fall apart.

— **You were both so young. Did you ever reach out to his parents after the war?**

— **Uh, no. I was badly shaken for quite a while after returning to the States. I didn't want to think about anything that happened, couldn't deal with any of it.**

— **Yeah, that's understandable. But what about now? Maybe one or both of his parents are still alive— they'd be about Nina's age, right? In their mid-seventies?**

— That's about right.

— I know it's a sensitive subject, but I'd bet they'd like to meet the person who had been their son's good friend, the one who cared about him and knew him at the end. Maybe you could track them down—y'know full circle and all that?

— You sound just like your mom when you say things like that.

— That's a complement, right?

— Definitely.

— You said Philly, right? You can probably make a list from the online phone book and make some calls … I'll help if you want.

— Thanks, Maya, I'll think about it.

And think about it I did.

After a hearty meal, Maya went back to reading and making lists.

In a liminal state, I took some deep breaths and called for my ancestors. Molly rose excitedly from the floor in front of the couch, where I had been reviewing an archaeology journal. I followed her out of the house to the back, where my beloved BrownWolf was waiting. He led us through the trees to a small bridge that arched over a stream. On the other side was a large wooden platform in a clearing. We stopped and watched the people there mingle: some standing, some relaxing in lounge chairs, all enjoying the sun and music. A faint, delightful aroma emanated from the lavender meadow in the distance. My mother Nina was conversing with an elderly gentleman who looked vaguely familiar. Rivka was dancing with her friend Bill. A young man with thick black glasses poured Maya a refreshing drink. David was his usual jovial self, chatting with friends who responded with laughter. It was a joyous scene.

BrownWolf turned his stately body, focused his eyes on mine, and said that an eagle would be coming soon to visit. I understood and thanked him for his guidance. The Creator, the Great Spirit, was watching over me. Over all of us.

The contents of my brain churned round and round for the remainder of the journey. One by one I peeled off the coarse layers of things and thoughts I no longer needed, until the dissonant chords faded away. Solid plans were formulated before we touched down at Bradley.

29. SPELLBOUND

It doesn't cost anything to look. —Yiddish Proverb

HENRY July 12, 2005 Western Massachusetts

In mid-afternoon, David and I were cleaning the stalls while the animals were still in their pastures. A female voice called out his name and he immediately dashed outside.

— **Maya, honey!!!**

The most beautiful woman I had ever seen was running toward him. She jumped into his arms and circled his waist with her legs as he spun her around. They graced each other with multiple, rapid face kisses before she slid down. Obviously thrilled to see each other, I assumed she must be David's girlfriend. We've had numerous conversations over the last couple of weeks amidst our developing friendship, but the topic of relationships wasn't something we covered; I never brought it up after he told me he'd lost someone on 9/11.

Watching and listening intently from where I stood, I wanted to meet her but didn't dare intrude.

— **Missed you like crazy.**

— **Me too, honey.**

— **I have sooo much to tell you.**

– Good, I wanna hear everything. We'll have to connect later if you're not too tired.

– I slept through most of the last two flights, I'm okay.

– My uncle's alright?

– Yes. We each had some rocky moments but we're good.

– Did you drop your stuff off at your mom's?

– Yeah.

– Okay, I'll check in with her and find you right after dinner. You may wanna talk to her privately first?

– Yes, but I can do that and then tell you both the long, detailed stories at the same time afterwards— she'll be fine with that.

He nodded, caught my eye, and gestured for me to join them. Good lord, I hope I didn't smell too much from the barn work. Removing the glove from my right hand, I carefully leaned the pitchfork handle against the siding with my left; I would look like an incompetent fool if it fell over.

– Maya, this is Henry. He's been my reliable right-hand man. The animals love him, the goats and donkeys follow him everywhere.

– Oh yeah? Nice to meet you, Henry.

– Nice to meet you as well, Maya.

Her delicate hand formed a solid grip. Flawless black skin, significantly darker than mine. Thick, course, jet-black hair that was parted on the side and smoothed out into a wavy, stylish bob. Deep, dark eyes that took everything in. A spectacular combination of Amerasian features. Small gold earrings, I think they're called studs, if I remember correctly from the bits and pieces about female grooming and attire I had learned while living with Heather and Toni. A cobalt-blue T-shirt and tan, slightly rumpled, lightweight cargo pants adorned Maya's petite frame. Water sandals wrapped around sturdy feet. A faint New York accent. She maintained eye contact with both of us, and her smile filled a five mile radius.

— **Okay, I'd better get going. Unpacking and laundry and getting my land legs. Nice to meet you, Henry.**

— **I'll see you in a couple of hours, honey.**

— **Okay. Ciao!**

She gave David a peck on the cheek and I returned her wave as she pivoted to leave. We stood there on the dusty earth, side by side, like a couple of mute Neanderthals, and watched her walk away. She headed toward the lodge; she must have a car out front.

— **She's quite glamorous, David.**

— **Sure is. And incredibly smart. Like Albert Einstein-kind-of-smart.**

— **She's much prettier than Albert Einstein.**

— **Yeah.**

I had countless questions but was unable to formulate them at the moment. David put me in charge while he went to the tractor supply/feed store, instructing me to follow the usual routine and assuring me he'd check on the animals later on.

The following morning, after we got the alpacas, goats, donkeys, and horses outside, David said that the perimeter fencing was just about complete, which meant that the other volunteers would be reassigned to the animal care starting tomorrow. Which meant that David and I could go to the plant nurseries in Hadley on Friday, and then I could break ground for the garden over the weekend. He planned to give me two volunteers to help with the digging, planting, and all the other needed tasks, barring any complications or issues with the animals. I was excited about this, though I'd miss working full time in the barn and pastures. With three of us we should be able to get everything done within a week or so, depending on the weather. I didn't mind working in rain, but wouldn't expect the others to follow suit. In any case, I'd be reviewing the design tonight so I'd be fully prepared for our shopping trip.

The magnificent Cody continued to improve each day, what a relief. David had expressed surprise and appreciation for the birthday drawing, and said it was '**too nice to keep in the barn**', so he brought it to his RV.

At lunchtime, the other volunteers were enthusiastically talking about '**Music Night**'—it was going to be tonight. Tonight?! '**Maya's back from her trip**.' Maya?!? I was even more confused now than I was yesterday. I vaguely remembered Suzy mentioning something when I first arrived at the farm, something about Rivka's daughter. Was Maya Rivka's daughter?!

Music Night was now the talk of the town. One of the volunteers, a hip guy with long dreads named Jamal, said he would be bringing his bongos. Everyone was going to be there, in the den-slash-library right after supper. Okay … okay. I wanted to look nice for the party, but didn't have any special clothing here, or anywhere for that matter. I would take my usual shower before supper and would have to make do with one of my button-down shirts and jeans.

What a night it turned out to be! I couldn't take my eyes off of Maya as she sang tunes from various genres. She made a disclaimer in the beginning, reminding all present that she was not a professional musician. It didn't matter. She had a silky, melodic tone and played the guitar well, encouraging everyone to sing along, which we did. She referred to the sheet music in front of her on the table for some of the chord changes. Lots of clapping during and after every song. All the volunteers were crowded into the room, along with David, Rivka, and Yusef. One of Yusef's daughters was there as well; evidently she and Maya already knew each other and sat together, with David on Maya's other side. They were in the far corner of the room on the low couch, while the rest of us were in chairs, some of which had been brought in from the conference room next door.

Jamal's bongos on Marvin Gaye's *What's Going On* and a bunch of other tunes added depth and flavor. They did a jazzy version of Leonard Cohen's *Dance Me to the End of Love*. And *The Peace Song* by Jesse Colin Young. And some James Taylor: *You Can Close Your Eyes*. Then Dylan's *Don't Think Twice, It's All Right*. Someone requested *Wishes* by Lari White, which I had never heard before. It was a simple country song with a slow waltz tempo about unrequited love. Jamal set the bongos on the floor and sang in perfect harmony with Maya, using one of the lyric sheet copies that were passed around. Everyone liked it so much that they sang it again.

To top off the wonderful session, Maya and Jamal did the call-and-response of Antonio Carlos Jobim's *The Waters of March*, which I knew from childhood; I actually remembered most of the words, which was quite a feat since there were about a dozen verses. My mother used to play both the Portuguese and English versions, which were produced in Brazil and became available on records in the U.S. a couple of years prior to my birth. She also had the Stan Getz - Joao Gilberto version that was released in 1976, a couple of years *after* I was born. So I sang along as best I could—Maya looked over and beamed at me, seeming pleased that I was familiar with it. The last stanza streamed and settled into me as it never had before. It was about the promise of a new season, the assurance of good things to come. It was precisely how I'd been feeling since I arrived at the sanctuary, and I would remember this night always.

Maya was in deep conversation with David as she returned her guitar to its case, but glanced up and graciously thanked us for coming as we filed out of the room. I caught up to Rivka and told her how impressed I was with the music and we chatted for a minute; she was clearly a proud mama. I then helped Yusef clean up the coffee cups and other stray items in the kitchen, and learned that his daughter Tazeen, nicknamed Taz, had been a high school classmate of Maya and David.

Jamal and I walked together back to the casitas. I knew from a lunch conversation with him last week that he had been at the sanctuary for two months, and that he had fallen apart last year when his nineteen-year-old son died of a drug overdose. Tonight our conversation focused on bossa-nova, Afro-Cuban tempo patterns, the energy of sound and rhythm, and what a bussin evening it had been.

Alone in my room, I thought about how lucky David was to have Maya in his life, and how he deserved to be happy, and how fortunate I was to be here. I said a prayer of thanks to the lord, and sleep eventually claimed me. My dreams were filled with joyous music, and the crystal clear image of the dazzling and wondrous Maya smiling up at me.

30. A MORASS OF DESPAIR

The biggest mistake is you think you have time. —Buddha

HENRY July 15, 2005 Western Massachusetts

Nothing went as planned. First, we had to postpone the trip to the nurseries because David had obligations off-site all afternoon. Also, deep-cleaning and reorganizing had to get done in the barn, and repairs were needed on some of the interior pasture fencing in preparation for the upcoming rotation. It was all hands on deck.

We completed the morning chores, and just before breaking for lunch David relayed the general assignments for the afternoon: three outside to work on the fencing and monitor the animals, three of us inside the barn.

Over cheese platters and gazpacho, Jamal and I exchanged anecdotes about Howlin' Wolf and Robert Johnson, both from Mississippi. Then Larry explained why the Huacaya alpacas that we were taking care of had such clean and fluffy fleece: no lanolin. The fleece of the less-common Suri alpacas was also lanolin-free, but their wool was different and appeared as crimp-less, matt-less long silky dreads. He had learned all of this from a book in the library-slash-den.

No one lingered after the meal; we were all eager to get everything done, and done well, before David returned this evening. We took our responsibilities seriously.

After pulling out the grain bins and making notations on the inventory checklists, I joined Larry and Jamal in the stalls, which were undergoing a thorough washing. The troughs had already been cleaned and sanitized before lunch. We needed to lay fresh bedding in each of the enclosures, so Jamal went to the tack room to get straw from the loft. The top of the ladder was secured to the bottom of the storage loft, and we had all been up and down at some point, thankful that the ladder never swayed; it was a twelve foot drop.

The periodic thump of large bales hitting the wooden planks was followed by a different sound: a thwack accompanied by an unexpected loud, short, low-pitched grunt. I hurried into the tack room to find Jamal sprawled out, facedown on a three-string bale, which had landed intact with the twine holding its dense rectangular shape. He was moaning and breathing hard. Good lord! I told him I was going for help and yelled out for Larry to stay with him. I ran like lightning to the lodge.

Between panicked, panting breaths I apprised Rivka of the situation. She motioned for me to come with her while relaying something in short-speak to Suzy as we rushed out front to grab a buggy. She asked questions on the way: Was Jamal able to speak? Could he move his legs? His arms? I didn't know anything except that he needed assistance. She said it's okay, that I did the right thing by immediately seeking help. Then she muttered something about getting **'a friggin' phone line out there …'** She was sharing my worry.

We got to the barn in no time and all the volunteers were surrounding Jamal; they must have witnessed my frantic state a few minutes earlier and knew something had happened. Rivka leaned in and laid a gentle hand on the back of Jamal's shoulder. He was still moaning.

— Tell me where it hurts.

— Chest.

— It looks like you're able to move your neck?

— Yeah. Neck's okay.

— Good. Do you think anything's broken?

— Don't know.

— Okay, we need to get you checked out at the hospital.

— No. Please.

— We have insurance for everyone at the sanctuary so don't worry about that. If you're able to get on your feet I'll drive you there.

— No, please … no hospital, I'll be okay.

— Oy. Jamal. These are your options: if you can stand and walk, I'll take you. Otherwise I'm calling an ambulance.

— No, no ambulance, I'll get up. Give me a minute.

Rivka had me sit with Jamal in the back seat of her car. He was still holding his chest and breathing heavily. He apologized to Rivka, saying it was his fault, that he had misjudged where the edge of the loft was and had pushed the bale over while his arms were still wrapped around it, thinking he had a few more inches. She told him that accidents happen, it wasn't his fault, that she knew he wasn't trying to teach himself how to fly. He said it hurt to laugh and apologized again for the inconvenience. He whispered to me that he doesn't like hospitals. I tried to reassure him.

The ER was moderately busy. Rivka pointed to a short row of empty chairs, where we sat and waited. She gave the desk staff whatever information they needed (she had asked Jamal for his birthdate on the ride over: he's a dozen years my senior), and eventually was able to get an ice pack for him to hold over his chest. She sat with us awhile but rose a couple of times to remind them we were still waiting. Finally they called us and the nurse positioned Jamal semi-upright on a narrow bed in one of several, small adjacent spaces with wraparound curtains. He was still clutching the ice pack to his torso. A physician walked in and the nurse quickly removed the pack and wielded a pair of scissors to cut the front of his T-shirt, starting at the bottom in the middle.

— No—please! It's a vintage Marley!

Indeed the faded coral-colored shirt boasted a charcoal silk-screened image of a beaming, probably high-on-weed, Bob Marley. Rivka was on the other side of the bed and quickly signed 'wait' to the nurse, who lowered the scissors. Rivka asked Jamal if he was able to sit up a bit, which he did. She lowered the guard rail and sat on the edge of the mattress behind him. She rolled up his shirt while telling him at every step what she was doing, including moving his dreads out of the way and when to try and extend his arms. From the other side I helped get the shirt over his head, and became startled.

Dozens of deep, faded scars covered Jamal's shoulders and upper back, most of them small and round, like old burn marks. Sweet Jesus. I'm naive about some things, but this was horrifying—even *I* knew that someone had hurt him badly long, long ago. Rivka noticed them as well and we shared a brief, somber glance, knowing not to say a word. She stuffed

Bob into her tote bag for safe-keeping, and helped Jamal into a Johnny top, leaving the front open.

Jamal leaned back against the pillow while the physician asked him questions related to pain level as he pressed a few spots on his chest and abdomen. X-rays were ordered and someone came a few minutes later with a wheelchair to whisk him away to Radiology.

I sat back down in the waiting area with uncontrollable tears. My father had repeatedly told me growing up that I was '**too sensitive**' and needed to '**toughen up or you'll turn into a goddamn white pansy**.' My mother would counter with '**Leave him be, James—he does well in school, he's a good kid, he doesn't need to play sports** …' In any case, I became self-conscious about crying but it happens occasionally, usually unexpectedly. I had removed my glasses to wipe my eyes when Rivka reappeared in the seat next to me and offered a small pack of tissues from her bag.

— **Thank you. I should have gotten there sooner.**

— **The tack room?**

— **Yeah. I should have been there.**

— **You mean so you could have been crushed by the heavy bale *and* Jamal?**

— **Uh, well, no, I guess that doesn't make sense. It just pains me to see him hurt. If I had been helping him maybe it wouldn't have happened.**

— **Henry. Our emotions often have nothing to do with rational thought. Is this about more than Jamal?**

Of course it was, but I didn't fully realize it until she asked. My throat was tight so I just nodded. She put an arm around my shoulders in a maternal fashion. I couldn't remember the last time my own mother had done that.

> — **It happens. It's going to be okay. Look, they're bringing him back. Why don't you keep him company while we wait for the X-ray results.**

An hour later we were in the CVS parking lot on King Street in Northampton, waiting for Rivka to return from her mission to purchase a couple of large ice packs and ibuprofen for Jamal. The doctor said there appeared to be some hairline fractures but it was mainly swelling and bruising, which will take a week or so to heal. Of paramount importance was that he hadn't punctured a lung or any other internal organs. He was tired but seemed to be breathing easier.

> — **Thanks for getting help and staying with me, my man.**

> — **You're welcome. You scared the heck out of me.**

> — **Me too. I'm glad she took me to the ER, it wasn't as bad as I'd feared.**

> — **Rivka's a good lady, she takes care of us.**

> — **Yeah. She said I should rest up for a few days and then she'll put me on light duty. And hot-damn— she saved my Marley. The farm's a good place, bro, it's like a Promised Land.**

> — **It is. Most of my depression melted away the minute I arrived.**

> — **Ditto.**

– Hey, do you want me to bring a tray of food to your casita when we get back?

– Thanks, my man, but I'll be okay eating at the lodge.

Everyone rallied around Jamal at supper, including David, who wanted everyone's input about implementing additional safety protocols, and we would continue the discussion in the morning. I verified with Jamal that he had put the ice packs in the freezer compartment of his casita fridge.

~ ~ ~ ~ ~

My mother Diondra was beautiful—still is—but she lost her mojo the afternoon that Daniel was killed. Her spark died along with her youngest child. He was her Miracle Boy—there had been at least two miscarriages between my birth and his, a span of five years. She doted on him, often excluding me, which I tried not to take personally. He was my cute little brother and I indulged him as well. His favorite cuddle-toy was a stuffed dinosaur named Rex, and I had taken it upon myself to ensure it was on his pillow waiting for him each night while my mother bathed Daniel in the tub down the hall. As soon as his pajamas were on, he'd clutch Rex and climb into bed, ready for sleep in the company of his tan friend with the oversized head and beady eyes.

Growing up in a Louisiana suburb was mostly easy for me, and, I realize now, quite sheltered. My mother's family had money and lived in the Tremé neighborhood of New Orleans, just north of the French Quarter, until the area was razed for highway construction. They travelled in the social circles that dominated black cotillion classes and Ethiopian debutante balls. Diondra's mother, my Ayate Essie, came from a line of Ethiopian farmers and had a strong influence on me. We were together several times each week, and as soon as I could walk she introduced me to the art of planting and pruning and weeding and harvesting the flowers and vegetables at her house—that was our thing, just the two of us. Afterwards we'd sit in old rocking chairs on her back porch, admiring our work and making plans while drinking iced bunna, a spicy coffee concoction that she would have prepared earlier. Once in a while she'd change it up and give me a glass of thick barley and fruit juice, which she called yebesso duket.

I had my grandmother's dense, kinky hair, which I always kept short. Hers was quite long, often held together by a colorful cotton headwrap. At home she'd usually wear an equally lively patterned dress, her large and calloused feet steady on the ground. She donned more conventional attire in public at my mother's urging, who'd tell her '**We can be proud of our heritage like you instilled in me but we need to look proper and fit in.**'

One time Ayate Essie took me to the Botanical Garden in City Park to show me what neglect, decay, and vandalism did to a once-thriving green oasis. I remember feeling confused and forlorn about that.

Even after moving up north, my mother and I visited often. My grandmother had the financial resources to hire a groundskeeper but preferred to do it all herself, although when she had a stroke in her late fifties she did have someone mow the vast front lawn. She passed at the age of sixty-seven, three years after we buried Daniel. She called me to her deathbed and said she'd had enough of this world, and that I possessed a natural gift for horticulture and must remember everything she taught me, and to continue generating new ideas. I promised I would, and have kept that promise with the same passion and patience that she taught it. If only I could get my business off the ground. Dear lord, I miss her.

My father rose from a lower station in life. My mother fell in love with James when they met at the hospital where she was employed as a registered nurse. Along with some sort of scholarship for minorities, he was working his way through law school by doing a stint as a security guard. Diondra's parents initially objected, but at some point surrendered to their daughter's wishes, possibly because she was already pregnant with me, a detail that everyone in the family vehemently denied in defiance of the math.

Twelve years into their marriage, my parents decided to move to New York with the prospect of better job opportunities. I was eleven-and-a-half, and Daniel was six, when we settled into the second floor rental of a three-story Victorian. Unlike most other Bronx neighborhoods, which were saturated with poverty, violence, unsavory graffiti, and loud boomboxes, our house was situated on tree-lined Perry Street near the Mosholu Parkway, a relatively quiet, safe area.

~ ~ ~ ~ ~

The following morning I knocked on Jamal's door. His plans for the day included making coffee in his casita, taking a shower, lying around with a book, going for lunch at the lodge, taking a nap, and lying around until suppertime. Sounded sensible to me—he needed to rest. The image of his scarred upper body had imprinted itself on my brain. I was relieved that he was okay. Now. He was okay now.

David and I headed out to the nurseries immediately after the midday meal. I was thrilled, of course, and had brought along my lists and ideas and backup plans in case we weren't able to get all the plants and bushes I had envisioned. It was

Saturday and we would have a good three hours in Hadley to look and choose and wander around heaven while trying to stay focused. We loaded up huge bags of topsoil and made arrangements for some more to be delivered on Monday. Some of the smaller plants were carefully placed on top of the bags, and David followed my lead in stabilizing them by keeping everything level and tightly packed. The rest of the cargo bed got filled with the remainder of our purchases, also packed methodically and securely. A fun, successful outing, and I couldn't wait to get started on the sanctuary garden. On the ride back we discussed which of the other work volunteers he could free up to help me. I updated him on Jamal's progress, which was a relief for David as well.

— **Could have been a lot worse.**

— **Yeah, thank goodness it wasn't.**

— **Yeah.**

David invited me to the RV that evening. He said that Maya would be there and it was her idea; she knew that he and I were friends and wanted to get to know me better. He informed me that Maya would pick up some ice cream, and I should not bring anything, '**just come over after dinner.**'

Maya's idea? I was still unsettled from the debacle with Jamal and from my own family memories, but very much looking forward to the visit. I deliberately said nothing about the invitation to the other volunteers, not wanting to cause any potential awkwardness, though they'd probably be fine with it and there was talk about watching a movie.

The RV had a small kitchen, a tiny bathroom, and a large bed in the back. I was pleased to see the drawing of Cody on the counter, newly framed and leaning against the wall. Maya complemented me on my illustration skills. I thanked her and asked how she learned how to play guitar. It took effort not to get distracted by her refined beauty; she smelled good too. We chatted while David poured iced tea for everyone, the cold drink reminding me of my childhood in the south. Maya told me a little about her recent trip to Vietnam when I inquired about where she had been, and I would learn the full story at a later date. David and I sat across from each other on either side of the small pull-down table while Maya spooned out mint-chocolate-chip ice cream (for David and me) and raspberry sorbet (for herself) into white melamine bowls, and then sat down next to David. Only a few inches separated the three of us, but it was a comfortable kind of closeness.

When it became my turn to talk about life circumstances, I said I didn't know where to begin, to which Maya responded **'From the beginning'** while David said **'Anywhere you want, dude'** at the same time. So I began with some context, including how pleasantly shocking it was moving to the northeast where things were far less segregated. Racism was alive and well, but people from diverse backgrounds worked together in businesses, something rarely seen in the south. I left out the part where my father had always told me that I should **'never get into a situation where you're the only black person in the room'**, a ridiculous notion. I told them how disorienting it was to see for the first time the humongous commercial and residential superstructures throughout New York City. In New Orleans, people were occasionally squeezed into small spaces for short periods of time, but in New York the towering buildings were on top of each other, and everywhere. It was something I eventually got used to. Same for the northern winters.

In response to a question from Maya, I informed them that slavery was not discussed at home or in the schools when I was growing up (shocking but true), that I didn't know much about it until I got to prep school as a teenager (embarrassing but true).

David asked politely if my **'different kind of hand'** was something I was born with; he had seen me with a Band-Aid the first few days on the farm, but that would not have necessarily explained anything one way or the other. I said no, and proceeded to tell them about that terrible day, the day I keep getting pulled back into. The day that, if I replayed it in my head enough times, might have a different ending, though I knew that was impossible.

Once I began opening up I couldn't stop.

It was the last day of July in 1997, a Thursday. Daniel had graduated from high school a few weeks earlier (unlike me, he had been allowed to attend public school, the rationale being that NYC education was superior to Louisiana's, which was true), and he was registered to begin law school at Fordham in the fall, for which he'd be commuting to their Lincoln Center campus. There was some ambivalence, and he had asked my advice a while back, whereupon I told him he should study what he wants and not heed to any family pressure. In my father's eyes, the Miracle Boy had become The Prince.

My father was at work as usual but my mother had switched shifts with one of the other charge nurses at the Montefiore Medical Center in the nearby Norwood section. She was home and expecting us for supper at six. I was twenty-three years old and already living in Massachusetts, but had taken the Peter Pan bus down to visit my parents and Daniel for a couple of weeks. In the early afternoon he went to play basketball with a couple of friends (another reason our father didn't hassle him much), while I had gone to the NYBG to walk around for a few hours—an awesome place where new plant species could be discovered, touched, learned about.

I skipped over the part where I had been waiting at the bus stop outside the NYBG, chatting with a young woman who may have been flirting with me, and missed the bus. I didn't actually miss it, I just, uncharacteristically, chose not to board when it arrived, knowing it would be at least another twenty minutes until another would turn up that could bring me relatively close to my parents' place. She was waiting for the Fordham shuttle and we were enjoying our conversation. If I had boarded the first bus would things have turned out differently? If I had arrived earlier would it have been *me* that my mother sent out to the local bodega to buy raisins for the cookies she planned to bake?

— **So I got off the bus around five and was walking the few blocks back to my parents' apartment. As I got close I saw Daniel dart down the front steps and turn right onto the sidewalk. I was only about fifty yards behind him but the view was partially obscured by a mailbox and some overgrown bushes. I jogged past those and was about to call out to him when a teenager suddenly appeared from the cross street on the right. He stood directly in front of Daniel, facing him, and withdrew a small pistol from a paper bag he was holding. Then a loud bang—he shot Daniel. He just shot him! What the hell?! I reached my brother in a split second and started to grab him from behind. He was shorter but more solid than** me. His arms had gone limp … it all happened so fast. He collapsed onto me and we landed on the pavement together, both face- up, the entire weight of his body on my chest and legs. My right arm was also pinned, but my left hand covered his chest, where his heart was. Then two more bangs, one right after the other—that teenager shot Daniel in the chest again! The two bullets went through my hand. What kind of person does such an evil thing?! Who was he? How could this have happened?!

Maya rose to retrieve a contraption that David explained was an inhaler for her asthma. He indicated that I should finish the story as Maya sat back down.

— I had hit my head pretty hard when we fell back, and started to pass out when those last two shots were fired. I remember the burning sensation in my hand and the anguish of not knowing if Daniel was dead or alive. I also remember hearing my mother's spine-chilling scream from inside the apartment— she must have been at the big bay window, which didn't open but offered a full view of the street and sidewalk below. I was in and out of consciousness and heard emergency vehicles approaching, while my mother was leaning over us whimpering 'my babies … my babies …' And I vaguely remember hearing things from the EMTs like 'faint pulse … his hand's blown up … they're brothers … '. My mother went with Daniel in the ambulance while a police cruiser took me to the same hospital, but I didn't know any of that until the next day.

David and I sat quietly for a few beats while Maya refilled our iced teas.

— Well, fuck, Henry, that's a lot to unpack. Keep going, tell us the rest if you're up to it.

— Okay. So I woke up in the hospital on Friday—it must have been lunchtime because staff were moving those metal carts around with the food trays. My door was open and they were talking in the hallway about a toddler who had died from eating powdered cocaine. Drugs were being sold out of a childcare center and the kid had found some on the floor.

David and Maya shook their heads.

— Well, you know, it was the Bronx. Anyway, my hand was heavily bandaged and my head also hurt and I desperately needed to know about Daniel. There were wires and tubes attached to my right arm, hooked up to monitors with those little screens, and one of them to a bag filled with liquid hanging upside down. Some older guy was sleeping in the bed by the window. Someone brought in food and I asked if my mother was around. They said no, but a couple of minutes later a nurse arrived. She said I had a concussion and that they had performed emergency surgery on my hand the previous evening but that my vitals had stabilized and I would be alright. I asked about Daniel and she said she didn't know, but a cop was on the grounds wanting to talk to me. I was kind of in a daze. She helped me sit up, and then stand to shuffle over to

the bathroom with all that stuff still attached to me and the metal pole with the medicine. Then she got me back to the bed, gave me some pills, and encouraged me to eat something.

I took a breath and noted David's furrowed brows and a tearful Maya. I asked if they'd had enough and they said no, to please go on. It had been eight years, but it was the first time I was telling the entire story to anyone. Despite the sadness, I was unburdening myself to people who were listening intently. This was far better than ruminating over it on my own.

— I had a little soup and a few bites of a cold grilled cheese sandwich, which helped with the dizziness. I gave them my parents' phone number and asked that they call, but it seems my parents either weren't home or weren't answering. Why weren't they at the hospital? I finally got some answers when Detective Blume came in. He was a middle-aged guy with a gentle voice, gave me his card and we had a lengthy conversation. He pulled a chair over to my bed and told me that Daniel had died, they had tried to revive him in the ambulance but he was gone, 'I'm sorry, son.' He said that my mother had stayed until my surgery was finished and then went home, and that my father had been at the hospital earlier that morning when I was still asleep but left to go to work. Work?! Detective Blume had me confirm that neither Daniel nor I knew the shooter. Then he asked me to tell him what I remembered, which wasn't much. He said one of the neighbors heard the screech of the getaway

car on the side street, but no one got the plate number. He explained that it was most likely an initiation test for someone who wanted to join a gang. 'They have to prove themselves.' He asked for a physical description, which was difficult because I had only seen him for a split second: a kid maybe sixteen, about five-seven, white or maybe Hispanic, with a grungy wife-beater shirt and newish blue jeans and a brown belt and a black-and-red bandana tied tightly around his forehead. Detective Blume asked about tattoos, which prompted me to recall the lengthy cross running up the inside of the kid's left arm, and possibly a swastika on the right side of his neck. Detective Blume told me to call him if I thought of anything else, and that he was sending a sketch artist over to try and get a visual of the shooter's face and tattoos. He said it was unlikely they'd be able to locate and arrest the perp, but there would be a permanent record of the incident and they would try. What he didn't say was that a case involving victims of color was never prioritized— even I knew that. The detective was a good guy but everything would just go into a file.

– Yeah, that sounds about right. Sorry you went through all that, Henry.

– Thanks.

– So your parents didn't stay together?

– No … they kind of stopped talking to each other after that. Neither of them would give *me* the time

of day either, which was frustrating because I was grieving too. I felt so alone and cast out. My father was still angry at the world as usual but he also lost the will to be a husband or father. A couple of months later he quit his job and moved down to Texas to join a group practice with someone he knew from law school. My mother stayed on for a while—she really liked her job at Montefiore but was alone in that big apartment and eventually moved back to Louisiana to live with my Ayate Essie. She got a nursing job at Tulane and stayed in the house even after her mother passed. I had returned here for school, which I think was good for me. I wasn't eating or sleeping much but somehow was able to focus on my classes and did well. And I worked part-time at Cowls Building Supply until the last reconstructive surgery in April.

Maya and David nodded. Then we talked about a few things of a more pleasant nature and they gave me brief hugs goodnight. It had been a comforting visit.

~ ~ ~ ~ ~

Throughout childhood I attended church every Sunday at Diondra's insistence. My father and I, and later, Daniel, were expected to wear starched white shirts under our suits, shoes shined and bodies clean, and we did. Our mother wore beautiful dresses and fancy shoes and amazing hats, some with feathers attached. We were considered a good, stable family, and we tried to live up to that image. In some ways we were, and pieces of the ritual were fun, especially when a little girl my age named Amina sat with her family in the adjacent pew—we'd eye each other and swing our legs and giggle until one or both of our parents told us to sit up and settle down, jolting us out of our reverie. I never attended a service again once I was sent to prep school. Other than the energetic gospel music, I had neither the interest nor understanding of what all the fuss was about. But my mother remained a true believer.

Shortly before she returned to Louisiana, I took the bus down to New York for a weekend visit. I told my mother that I wanted to talk about Daniel, that we had never talked about him since he died, that we had never talked about that day. It was the only time I allowed myself to feel anger toward her. She hesitated, glared at me for a few seconds, but then agreed to sit down and exchange memories that never should have been repressed. We both cried while looking at old photos and reminiscing about my brother as a sweet baby, as a rambunctious toddler, as an easygoing fourth grader, as a studious high school honors student, as an eighteen-year-old young man full of promise on the day he was senselessly killed.

— **Did Jesus love Daniel?**

— **Of course he did. Still does.**

— **Then why did He let him die? What kind of god allows that to happen? Why didn't He protect him?**

— **I don't know, Henry. I don't know.**

— **Then why do you still go to church every Sunday?**

— **Because if we say your brother's name, he is with us. And church is where I want to say his name. That's where I can feel him by my side. And I have to keep praying for his soul.**

That was the first and last time we spoke of Daniel.

31. A CLARIFICATION

Can't nothin' make your life work if you ain't the architect.
—Terry McMillan

HENRY July 17, 2005 Western Massachusetts

We started on the garden this morning and I was in good spirits. Everyone had gone to the lodge for lunch and I was about to join them when I spotted the gorgeous and effervescent Maya walking across the field in my direction.

– **Hi.**

– **Hello, Maya.**

– **So this will be a garden?**

– **Yes, hopefully within the next week or so. Lots of prepping for now.**

– **Wow, that's fast. Nice. Well I'm meeting Taz for lunch but wanted to stop by first to tell you that I, um, I like you, even though you're kind of nerdy.**

I've been accused of being 'weirdly traditional' before. And a couple of kids have called me an 'Oreo', inferring (like my father) that I'm not black enough. But not nerdy, not that I know of, anyway.

– **You're a microbiologist and *I'm* the nerdy one?**

— Touché.

— I like you too, Maya. And I appreciate you and David being so supportive last night.

— I'm glad you told us what happened.

— Me too. So was it the glasses that gave me away?

— Well, yeah, maybe you need new frames that don't have to be held together with electrical tape. And those clips you use.

— My carabiners? What's wrong with carabiners?!

She was teasing me, giggling softly. And that smile—lordy.

— Well, nothing, but most people don't have so many. And all the colors. And sizes.

— I only have about a dozen, plus a set of three I hardly ever use because they're very small. They each serve a different purpose, see? This one hooks the work gloves to my jeans so I won't misplace them.

— Okay, then I'll stop making fun of them.

— I'm glad we've reached an understanding.

She was still smiling, but a thought was brewing in that brilliant brain of hers; she seemed a bit nervous. Should I say something? What would I say? I waited. Come on, come on, please talk to me, Maya.

— Um … Henry. I'm trying to tell you that I like you. I mean I like-like you.

Is she saying what I think she's saying? I'm not particularly adept at translating signals, or even words in plain English sometimes, given that I've never been in a stable, long-term, amorous relationship, only a few Friends With Benefits with women who released me as soon as someone they *really* liked came along. But Maya, oh my lord.

— **Are you saying … uh … aren't you with David?**

— **Oh! Um, no. David and I are super close but we've never been romantically involved. We're not together-together.**

I vowed then and there to never make assumptions again. Good god and everything holy.

— **So does that mean I can ask you out on a date?**

— **Yes, I'd like that.**

— **Great. But you'll have to drive, I don't have a car or license.**

— **I know, David told me, that's okay.**

Her sweet laugh stirred up my insides, and our eyes remained locked together as my heart catapulted over the moon. We made tentative plans and she hurried off and it's a miracle I was still standing upright.

On my way back from lunch I sang *Oh Happy Day,* recalling how the Edwin Hawkins Singers were ostracized because churchgoers danced to their music—some uppity pastors thought it was disrespectful of Jesus. Daniel said Jesus would have been delighted to dance to that song, even if it hadn't been about Him.

I spotted the goats in the pasture—something was off. As I got closer they began bleating loudly and running toward me. Turned out Adam had a gold sweatshirt over his head, wrapped around one of his horns. He and the entire herd met me at the fence line asking for help.

— **Good lord, Adam, what did you get yourself into? Did someone leave this on the fence rail? There you go, buddy, better now? Let's go find your little styrofoam tube tips. I know they look stupid, but they're less stupid than you running around with a shirt over your eyes or getting stuck in the fencing. I'll issue a scolding to whoever left his clothing within reach.**

He thanked me and ran free, the other goats following. The donkeys had been looking on from a distance, as had the alpacas, who now all returned to their busy schedules of grazing and sniffing the air and each other and living the good life.

I was more than a little excited at the prospect of courting Maya. If this is what true love feels like, I'll hold onto it and never let go. I hungered to share my elation, but figured I should be discreet about the source. That evening, when David and all the volunteers were at the lodge eating supper, I spent a few minutes at the barn. Some of the animals were already asleep, some just beginning to settle themselves in for the night. My entire body vibrated with Everything Maya. I told Liz and Luke, my loyal associates. I told George and Awuchee. I told Willow and Frieda, while Esther looked on with skepticism. Cody was peacefully napping so I discussed my first-date plans with Ginger, who seemingly approved with a muzzle nudge to my shoulder. And so it began, happiness abounding.

32. AN INTERVENTION

Truth is not a crystal that you can stash away in your pocket, it is an infinite liquid into which you fall. —Robert von Musil

JAYCE August 27, 2005 Western Massachusetts

It was seven in the evening and I had an appointment at the farm. I was about to put my house up for sale—nothing was keeping me in Ithaca anymore beyond the comfort of the predictable—and had asked David to check property options in Hampshire County. I would miss the landscape particular to upstate New York, but beauty was to be found elsewhere, and I felt stronger for having made the decision. I'm not a multitasker and was already overwhelmed by the process. I had asked him to gather the information quietly and not discuss it with anyone, including Maya, with whom he normally shares virtually everything. He agreed and always kept his word.

Upon arrival I walked around to the pastures, avoiding the lodge where workers were probably gathered for the evening meal. David and Rivka had created a terrific setup here—I was impressed each time I visited. Molly immediately trotted over to the horses, who sniffed their hellos through the fence; they knew each other well by now and David had given his okay.

Henry was engaged in earnest discourse with the goats as he led them into the barn. When I met Henry a few weeks ago I immediately recognized him from the vision—the part with Maya in the sunlight—so I knew they were somehow connected. He was a bright, affable guy with the courteous dialect of a Southerner folded into the straightforward demeanor of a Northerner. Presently he was waving a four-fingered hand in the air to keep a hovering mosquito at bay.

— **Hi Jayce. David had to run an errand, he'll be back shortly.**

— **I can come back in an hour.**

— **No, please stay. His exact words were: 'If my uncle gets here before I return, don't let him leave.' Hey, Molly is so chill, Ginger and Cody walked right up to her …**

We chatted for a few minutes until David showed up. As the sun lowered on the horizon, Henry left to unload the truck and get the horses inside; he had explained that occasionally they stay out late in good weather. Molly greeted my nephew by rolling over for a belly rub.

— **Hey, Unc. Sorry about the delay, had to get to the feed store.**

— **They're open this late?**

— **No, but they left our stuff in a big, covered bin outside for me to pick up. Glad you're back in town—I have a few things to show you. The listings are in the RV, but I wanted to throw something into the mix first.**

— What do you mean?

— Well … I was wondering what's going on between you and River.

— What are you talking about? There's nothing going on.

— That's what I thought.

— David, what is it?

— Look, Jayce. I know you're a private person, and I was hesitant to bring this up, but you and Riv have been circling around each other's orbits since I was born.

— And …?

— Well? Do you love her?

— Of course I love her. She's been our close family friend for—

— No. I mean do you love-love her.

I knew what he meant the first time but didn't want to answer. It was none of his damn business and I hadn't even begun to figure out what to do about any of that, and each year that passed … well, it would just pass.

— David.

— Listen, Unc. I've seen the way you look at her. And I've seen how she gets all flustered when she looks at you. Riv's constantly asking about you—she tries to sound nonchalant. Ridiculous—the two of you. All these years.

She looks at me that way? She asks after me that way? Am I clueless? Have I been selfish?

— **David, by the time I finally got to meet her in person she was married.**

— **Yeah! And she got rid of that scumbag decades ago!**

— **Keep your voice down.**

— **No one can hear us. Even the barn is too far away.**

— **Look, David. I appreciate your concern but I don't think Rivka needs a man complicating her life, especially me.**

— **Oh, and you've made that decision *for* her?**

I was getting annoyed but he had a point. Then again, he didn't know how difficult these things were for me. Or maybe he did.

— **David, please.**

— **Look, Jayce. You're my favorite uncle.**

— **I'm your *only* uncle!**

— **Exactly! And I want you to be happy.**

— **Why would you think I'm not happy?!**

— ***Are* you? Because I'm pretty sure that being moderately content is not the same as all-in full-on true happiness. And you're right—Riv probably doesn't need a man. She's a complete person and has her shit together. But wouldn't it be … something … marvelous? Stellar? The completion of a full circuit?**

— **Does she know you're talking to me?**

— **Hell no, she'd probably throttle me with disapproval.**

I'd been entertaining the same thought.

— **Do you remember when Nana let me spend two weeks with you in Ithaca the first time, that summer I turned eleven?**

— **Of course I remember. We had a lot of fun.**

— **We had GREAT fun. And remember when you took me on that trail—the one with the stone steps and those awesome waterfalls?**

— **The Cascadilla Gorge.**

— **Yeah. And I kept rushing ahead?**

— **You were a little wild back then and I had to keep calling you back. I was worried you'd get hurt.**

— **Right. Well this conversation is *me* bringing *you* to that big iron gate by the trail. Now it's *your* turn to run through it.**

The katydids were just beginning their nocturnal chorus as we stared at each other for a long moment. Misty-eyed, David unleashed barely-contained frustration.

— **Unc. Do you have any idea what I would give to have just one more day with Nomi?**

A slam to the heart. Nomi was his big love, killed on 9/11—unimaginable—incomprehensible. Nomi's grandfather had barely survived the brutal conditions of an internment camp in Wyoming, one of many 'relocation centers' for Japanese-Americans during Word War ll. Two generations later his lovely twenty-six-year-old grandchild died in a terrorist attack. David and Nomi were living together when the unthinkable happened. God-almighty. I took a step forward and pulled David in, held him as he wept quietly into my shoulder.

— **Alright … alright, David. I hear you.**

We stood there together, in pain and familial love.

— **If you have feelings for River, then go get her. Do it soon. And don't fuck it up.**

— **Thanks for the vote of confidence.**

We shared half-smiles and bloodshot eyes. I turned to leave, my canine companion by my side.

— **Hey Jayce?**

I pivoted around.

— **Molly's not the only one who loves you unconditionally.**

I paused, nodded, and headed out. It wasn't until the next day, while driving back to Ithaca, that I realized I hadn't got the house listings I had come for. The laughter came quickly.

33. A DISAGREEMENT

Labyrinths are designed to get you found. —Wavy Gravy

HENRY September 4, 2005 Western Massachusetts

Over a delicious Moroccan brunch at Amanouz Cafe, Maya gave me a lesson about the helix. I could barely keep up with her half the time but loved her silky voice and always learned something. I had taken the day off because she'd be starting her teaching job at MIT and we didn't know when we'd see each other again, something that caused my insides to twitch. She talked about the corkscrew shape and how it curves around a fixed axis, and proceeded to befuddle my brain with terms like helicoid surface, Cartesian coordinates, intertwined helices, parametrization, chirality, and torsion. I perked up when she mentioned ferns.

— **Spiral shapes are found in the DNA of every living organism. It's a symbol of resilience because it's extremely stable and can tolerate harsh environmental changes. Think about it, Henry. Ferns, vine tendrils, antelope horns, snail shells, human fingerprints, weather patterns, galaxies. I had a lengthy discussion with Jayce about it when we were on our trip. He said that many of the ancient symbols of his people were circles and** spirals because they represent our life journey 'in search of the center' and embody the connectivity between humans and the land and sky. Swirls are their tribal migratory patterns, and both single and double spirals have been found on cave walls and ancient Native American pottery, images of wind and water and so forth. He mentioned something about the legend of the whirlwind. A few architects have even adopted the shapes for their buildings.

– The Guggenheim.

– Yes!

– Well now I'll be thinking about spiral shapes when I plan my next garden project.

– Yeah, it's pretty cool stuff. I'm going to try and incorporate some of it into my curriculum.

– That's a great idea. Can you videotape your lectures so I can watch them when I get the sudden urge to learn something deeply complex? Or when I'm missing you?

– Henry, I know you're worried, but we'll be fine.

– Okay.

– Want to go to Raven?

– Definitely.

We held hands while walking the few blocks toward the other end of downtown Northampton. (We hold hands! We're a couple!) Maya's mom used to take her to the small used bookstore often, and said that Rivka would sit in one of the large armchairs up front for a full hour perusing large art volumes while Maya browsed the shelves out back. Today she chose two books, and I found a vintage botanical reference manual. We paid and were strolling along one of the quieter back streets when I raised the issue that had been on my mind.

— **I wanted to talk to you about something.**

— **Okay.**

— **Well … we've been seeing each other for almost two months now, and you know how I feel about you, Maya.**

— **And it's mutual. I told you on our third date that I knew you were my bashert the first time we met.**

— **Yeah, that was so great the way you explained it—destined soulmates. Okay, well since we've been getting serious, I thought it would be proper for me to talk with David and your mom and make sure I have their blessing to keep this going.**

— **What?! Our relationship is between the two of us, not anyone else!**

— **I know, but they're both protective of you and I thought it would be wise to get their blessing.**

— **We don't need anyone's permission to see each other!**

— **I wouldn't be asking for permission, just their blessing.**

— **What's the difference?!**

— Uh … I don't know, Maya. I'm just trying to do the right thing here.

— Oh my god, Henry. I appreciate that you're overly polite to everyone, it's one of your charming attributes. But I think it would be ridiculous to involve them in OUR relationship. Our friends and families will either support us, or not, and we don't need to ask for their approval.

— Are we having our first major argument?

— Uh, yes, I guess so. And it won't be the last, we haven't even slept together yet.

Good grief. It's been on our minds but we've waited, given that a location with complete privacy has not been available. Plus we both wanted to take it slow— in theory, anyway. As for our conversations, Maya does not shy away from conflict, which is a good thing even though it terrifies me. I'm learning that it's okay to disagree and we can talk it out.

— Alright, well I won't speak with them if you think it's a bad idea.

— You're free to talk to anyone you want, but it just seems silly and completely unnecessary. Besides, they're both very fond of you and are happy for us.

She couldn't have mentioned that sooner? I don't always understand her, but I sure am crazy about her. Perhaps we're like the linked strands of the double helix.

Back at the literal ranch, I stood in the perennial garden, proud of my design and the work we put into bringing it to life. Everything had filled in well. The powder-blue Speedwell was no longer in bloom but still impressive, and the staggered Sky Pencil plantings in the back added the perfect touch of evergreen; they looked like miniature Italian cypress trees. I noticed a small patch needing some extra mulch, which I'd take care of tomorrow. Rivka had purchased (with her own personal money, which David said she didn't want anyone to know) three dozen high-quality solar lights, which she had me install where I thought best. They provided soft stipples of what she called 'cosmic illumination' in the evenings. From start to finish, this project has been a resplendent collaboration.

I couldn't help but wonder what Daniel would have thought of the sanctuary. Growing up, our exposure to farm animals was limited to picture books; he probably would have been as astonished as I was meeting them for the first time. I conjured up his grin and laughter.

Just before suppertime I swung by the barn. Rose had been under the weather; Jamal and Larry were taking turns administering the medicine the vet prescribed after the initial injection when he was out here a few days ago. Rose was not especially enthusiastic about this particular enterprise, so they mixed the liquid with her favorite oats and a little yogurt. Someone had to sit with her four times daily to ensure she ingested what she needed. Jamal was perched on a stool in the corner of the alpaca pen, hand-feeding her the messy mixture from a bowl.

— **That's a big girl. You're gonna keep gettin' better, yeah? Yeah. You're a gentle warrior, aren't you, Rosie?**

She continued gazing intently at him with her enormous sapphire eyes.

— **Henry, my man! Good day off?**

— Yes, but I missed these awesome critters.

— I know, they tend to tug at your heart, don't they?

— They do. Rose is looking better, even since yesterday.

— I know, check out her fleece, my man. Softer now, and the pretty brown splotches look more pronounced. When she got sick it affected her whole body it seems.

— Yeah, she definitely looks healthier.

I remembered what David had said about most of the animals arriving at the sanctuary with lice or worms or pneumonia, all kinds of maladies. And their insides filled with fear and sadness. They're not struggling so much anymore.

Jamal began singing Otis Redding's *Sittin' On the Dock of the Bay*, but with impromptu lyrics:

Sittin' on the bench in her pen
Givin' sweet Rose her medicine, yeah
Sittin' on the bench in her pen, in the baaarn …
Knew I shoulda braided my dreads
Cuz some bits o' straw are stickin' to them, yeah
Sittin' on the bench in her pen, at the faaarm …

It struck me that, despite whatever terrible things Jamal had experienced in his forty-three years, he had not been broken beyond repair.

Nor had Rose. Nor had I.

34. ABUNDANCE

Nothing is worth more than this day.
—Johann Wolfgang von Goethe

HENRY September 6, 2005 Western Massachusetts

A handwritten note taped to my casita door from David said I should report straight to Peter in the kitchen at eight-thirty after breakfast. A little odd, but we all helped out where needed and occasionally diverted from our regular duties.

Maya had driven out to Cambridge yesterday and I missed her already. She was sharing an apartment with another female science teacher and they'd be starting the fall semester today. I was rooting for her and knew she'd do well, even if a panic attack developed; she always managed to get herself through those.

I made myself some toast and coffee at the lodge and tried to relax. Peter arrived just as I finished washing my cup and, with my nod of approval, put Roberta Flack on low. He explained that he came in early to prep and wanted an extra set of hands because he needs to leave at lunchtime for a dentist appointment (that part turned out to be true). He had me wash and dice lots of potatoes, radishes, carrots, and peppers. I'm not as fast as he is but can hold my own, my malformed left hand having adapted well to various tasks. We laughed hard while sharing stories about the lengths the goats go to in order to avoid puddles.

— I swear, Henry, it couldn't have been more than half an inch deep. They walked all the way out to the fence line and back so their hooves wouldn't get wet.

— I know, I've seen them do that. They're tough as nails about most things but not when it comes to an itty-bitty puddle.

— You got that right. Hey, nice job on the front entrance.

— Thanks, it was quick and fun. You've seen the big garden out back, right?

— Yes, but it's been a few weeks. Let's go out there as soon as we finish up in here, okay? You can give me the lowdown.

— Sure, let's do that. About one-third of the flowering plants are in bloom at any given time, so it'll look a bit different now. But there's a good variety of foliage so it'll always be attractive, even in the cooler months. Rivka wants to get an extension built onto the existing paved path to reach the garden, making it more accessible to people who use a wheelchair or walker.

— Good idea.

— Have you seen the big acrylic mirror David installed on the exterior of the barn?

— No, is it for the alpacas?

— Yes. They've all checked it out, but Pearl and Frieda have used it the most so far. Pearl stares at herself for ten minutes at a time. We're not sure if she recognizes herself or if she thinks she's made a new friend.

— Oh, man, that must be a crazy sight.

— It is.

Peter laughed but kept glancing up at the clock. At nine-thirty he instructed me to cover the bowls of freshly sliced veggies with plastic wrap, and said it was **'time to get out there.'** We headed toward the garden, where a small crowd was gathered in a section of the curved gravel edging up front, between the big oak and the midpoint. Yusef, Nicole, David, Rivka, Suzy, and all of the work volunteers quietly watched us approach. I couldn't read the expression on their faces.

— Peter, what's going on? Why is everyone here?

— We arranged a little surprise for you, everyone chipped in. Don't stress, okay?

— Okay.

Now I was really stressed. As we got closer, Rivka stepped forward.

— Henry. You created a beautiful space here at the sanctuary, something beyond what any of us could have imagined. You knocked it out of the park, and we thought it deserved a special commemoration.

Behind her, everyone moved over a few inches to either side. The parting of the Red Sea.

A pedestal stood three feet above the ground, a sturdy stake holding it in place. Mounted onto it was a thick, rectangular bronze plaque. Classy, with raised lettering and a simple border. I looked down and held my breath.

**Memorial Garden
Dedicated To
DANIEL CARTER
1979 — 1997**

It was all I could do to remain standing and force myself to breathe. Of course the tears began flowing, and despite choking up I looked everyone in the eye and nodded, so they'd know for sure they'd done a wonderful thing, the best gift in the world, a thing so thoughtful it would carry me through the rest of my days.

— **There's something else, Henry. My Uncle Jayce couldn't be here today but he found an Apache blessing and dictated it to me. I hope Daniel would approve:**

May the sun bring you new energy by day,
may the moon softly restore you by night,
may the rain wash away your worries,
may the breeze blow new strength into your being,
may you walk gently through the world and
know its beauty all the days of your life.

Overwhelmed by the sacrosanct force of love and kindness surrounding me, I approached David first and thanked him with a hug. Then Rivka. Then each and everyone else. When I embraced Jamal he whispered '**It's all good, my man**.' Everyone was smiling and tearful. When David good-naturedly said '**Okay, now everyone back to work.**' we all laughed.

They returned to their respective duties (Suzy and Rivka via the yellow golf cart) while I stayed behind an extra minute to admire the plaque. Dear lord, how fortunate am I?

The perennial garden was now truly complete and would endure for many years to come. I couldn't fix what happened to Daniel, but this is where I could say his name.

35. MOMENTUM

If I know what love is, it is because of you. —Hermann Hesse

RIVKA Thursday, September 8, 2005 Western Massachusetts

- — I can't believe how big and beautiful it is. The animals are going to flip out, David.

- — I know, right? Mike listened intently when I told him what we needed. He asked good questions, including measurements. And look—they installed a bunch of those short, chubby wheels on the sides, so when we rotate pastures we'll be able to tow it. They came up with that on their own.

- — Holy smokes, I am beyond pleased. This is even better than I could have imagined. You obviously did a great job working with Mike.

- — No, he and his class did the design. I just told him what I thought would work and Nicole and I suggested a few tweaks once they initially drew it out. But I had no idea it would translate into this.

We were standing around goggling at the brand new shelter/ play structure that had been built by the Northampton High students. In a stroke of serendipity, the father of one of the school kids happens to be the wood-shop teacher at one of the local schools, and when he came to pick up his daughter from the farm a couple of months ago she told him that Nicole, not knowing what Amy's father did for a living, had mentioned that the animals would benefit from a better structure than the one they'd been using. So after a lengthy meeting with David the following day, the thoughtful and enterprising Mike Reed made this the summer project for the kids who were enrolled at the school for extra credit or to make up for lost work from the previous term. He charged us a nominal fee for the materials, and provided all the labor at no cost to the sanctuary. It came to fruition in a phenomenal way, and Nicole had contacted the Hampshire Gazette, who sent a reporter and photographer, as well as the regional TV station, who had *their* reporter and videographer. Win-win-win! It was a splendid, sunny morning, in the mid-seventies, and photos were taken of Mike and his wood-shop kids, about nine in all, and then another, of me flanked by David, Nicole, Suzy, Henry, and four of the remaining work volunteers standing behind us (one of the guys didn't want to be in any pictures). They also took a couple of wide-angle shots of the staff on one side of the structure and the construction group on the other. I gave a brief speech expressing our gratitude. It was like a ribbon-cutting ceremony, but without the ribbon and scissors.

Henry was adorable, barely able to contain his excitement; at one point I thought he might start doing cartwheels. I knew he was eager for the animals to check out their new playhouse, which would also serve as a shelter, so while the media people were still there, he and Nicole went over to the barn, and after a couple of quick trips were able to get all the goats and donkeys into the pasture. Kevin, Violet, Julia, and George immediately began jumping up and down the ramps, followed shortly by Lily and Adam. The small but mighty Awuchee hopped up and down the lower tier like a mini-pogo stick, eliciting more unrestrained smiles. Liz and Luke eyed the new structure with cautious interest and accepted lots of petting from all of us, including the high school kids, who were eminently proud of their work and visibly touched that the animals enjoyed it so much. A few of the boys and girls were teary-eyed, reflecting the emotions of all of us witnessing this special moment.

Back at my desk in the lodge, there were two voicemail messages. The first was from Sam Shapiro, a gentleman I had met at a social work conference a few years ago. Sam was a smart, pleasant widower who lived in the Old Country (Queens) and called intermittently to ask me out on a date, under the guise of discussing work-related issues. We had a healthy, mutual professional consultation thing going on, but toward the end of virtually every phone call he would inevitably bring up something about him visiting the sanctuary, and did I know of a decent hotel nearby, or that I really should visit him the next time I was down in New York, he can put me up for a few days, no problem, and we could go get egg creams at the diner (*that* was almost enough for me to say yes) because he knew that, along with real bagels, chocolate egg creams were the only other thing I missed about New York since my father died. Flattering, but no, thank you; Sam was a good guy but I wasn't attracted to him enough to embark on that kind of relationship, and I didn't want to lead him on. I would return his call another time.

The second message was from Jayce. Jayce! As always, I melted at the sound of his voice and could barely get through the message, because my immediate impulse was to climb all over him in person with zest and zeal. But I digress. It was a simple request to call him **'when you get a chance'**. And it's a new number; he just got a cell phone yesterday. A mobile phone! I don't even know how those things work, though both David and Maya purchased theirs recently. I'll probably be the last holdout. I called him back immediately.

— **Hi Rivka.**

— **Hi—how did you know it was me?**

— **Your office number pops up—it has Caller ID.**

— **Oh! That sounds good. I should probably get that for my home phone. Are you laughing at me?**

— **Yes, you're even further behind the times than me. You may already have the service, but you need to buy a phone that has a display window.**

— **Oh, okay, I'll have to look into that. So ... how are you—what's up?**

— **Well, I umm ... I'm in town and wanted to talk with you, but privately, not when you're working.**

— **Okay, sure, do you want to come over tonight? I can put something together for dinner.**

— **Tonight?!?**

— **Yeah, Maya's flown the coop, so I'll be alone at home.**

— **Oh, okay, that would be great. But my mother's expecting me for dinner. Can I come over afterwards?**

— **Of course. How about eightish, is that good?**

— **Yes, that'll work.**

— **Jayce. Is everything okay?**

— **Yes.**

— You're not sick or anything?

— No, I'm fine.

— Okay, then I'll see you later. And bring Molly.

— Okay, I will, see you tonight.

— Okay bye.

— Bye.

I didn't know what to think. Is he really okay or does he have some awful disease? He sounded so serious. Well, he always sounds serious. If he's not sick, is he coming over to tell me he's getting married to some divorcee out in Ithaca? Or that he's moving to some remote island far, far away? Oy. I saw him briefly a few weeks ago when he and Maya returned from Vietnam and he seemed alright, but what do I know? He drove back to Ithaca, though Maya said he was planning to come out here again 'soon'. Evidently soon was now.

While attempting to take a hiatus from my unhelpful nervosity, Suzy walked into the room. We have adjoining offices with a shared wall and door, like those adjacent hotel rooms that can connect on the inside. Suzy was grinning.

— Did you just win the lottery?

— No, but the sanctuary did.

— Tell me!

— Look at this, Rivka. A five thousand dollar private donation. I have no idea who these people are.

I looked at the letterhead. And the brief typed paragraph. Then back to the letterhead.

— Suzy, this is great! But I don't understand … why

would a group of lawyers in Houston, Texas be interested in our little—

We simultaneously gasped.

— **Whoa … holy mackerel. Okay, listen to me. It says they're doing this anonymously. So not a word to anyone. Not anyone on the Advisory Board. Or the BOD. Or even David. Anonymous means anonymous.**

Suzy made the My Lips Are Sealed gesture.

— **And when you start putting the annual report together, just add it to the donation list without any identifying information. Okay, do up the usual Thank You letter and forward it to me. I'll jazz it up and we'll send it with some photos of the sanctuary that aren't already on the website.**

— **Maybe include one of the garden and memorial plaque?**

— **Exactly what I was thinking. This is such good news. Even though it's most likely a one-time donation, it's something, and will be of great help. Remember—anonymous.**

Some people don't know how to love out loud. But they find another way.

It was seven when I arrived home, still elated about the new animal structure, the PR tied to that event, and the unexpected donation to the sanctuary. I popped Pink Martini into the player; their music fit my cheerfulness and I wanted that mood to extend for as long as possible. After taking care of Max's food and water, I indulged in a quick shower, anxious to be ready for Jayce's visit and not wanting to smell like animals, not that he would care. Dinner would have to be figured out later, priorities first. I put on my age-defying faded blue jeans and a cute black top with spaghetti straps that lined up perfectly with my bra and cami straps. If it got chilly later I could always add an overshirt. I may be fifty-two but I'm far from dead. I brushed my teeth, inserted my favorite moonstone earrings (which, according to my gem and mineral reference manual, would help channel my 'divine feminine energy'), and sort of tried to fix my unfixable hair.

In the kitchen I put some water up to boil and opened the window to let in a breeze from the back of the house. There was a knock; I glanced out the front window to make sure it was Jayce's car in the driveway before opening the door. As thrilling as it always was to see him, there were drifting thoughts that something might be wrong. Of course I would be there for him no matter what, but would rather get run over by a train than for anything bad to happen to him.

The sleeves of his chambray button-down were partially rolled up; his usual black jeans and wide-banded plastic sandals completed the outfit. His thick, shiny hair was loose, skimming his broad shoulders and still damp from a shower. He gave me his slow smile, which immediately undid me. His deep-set eyes had some wariness … no more than usual, but still … kinahora—please don't let there be anything amiss.

– Hey.

– Hey.

As soon as I reached out to pat Molly she entered the living room and began sniffing for Max, who sauntered out of my bedroom to welcome her. Jayce left his footwear on the inside mat next to mine and followed me into the kitchen, where

I prepared tea for both of us. We chatted briefly about the unseasonably warm day and he smiled when I told him about the new play structure at the farm. The music had run its course, the furry creatures were in another room, and now it was just the two of us.

Jayce sat in a chair facing me. I was always taken aback by his physical presence, no matter the occasion. Too antsy at the moment to sit at the table with him, I perched on the stool, leaned my back against the rounded edge of the countertop, rested my bare feet on the wooden bar that existed for that purpose, and faced him. He was clearly apprehensive to begin telling me whatever he was going to tell me, so I raised my eyebrows, braced myself, and waited on shpilkes.

— **Okay. There's something I should have told you a long time ago. I think ... well the trip back to Vietnam gave me a new perspective, and some clarity. I was always afraid of ruining our friendship, and I still have that concern, but I'm going ahead anyway. Do you remember, back in the eighties, when you told me about the *Shoah* interviews with the Holocaust survivors that you watched until you 'couldn't take it anymore'? And that one of the things that left an impression on you was how some of the concentration camp survivors talked about how hope was the thing that got them through the atrocities? Hope that they'd make it out alive, even though their family members had been killed. Hope that the world might someday be a better place. I thought about that a lot. I thought about how amazing it is that with all the awful crap you've had to deal with in** the past, and I'm sure I 'don't know the half of it', you didn't allow those difficulties to ruin your life. You still see the good in people and you're patient with everyone you meet.

— Well, not necessarily every—

— Rivka. Please.

— Sorry.

— And I realized that the only time I've ever truly felt hopeful was when I've been with you. Your exuberance is infectious, and you're so knowledgeable about all the things that really matter.

— No, there's so much I don't—

— Rivka.

— Sorry.

— I love that you juggle a hundred thoughts in your head at any given time, but you're still present in the moment. I love that even though it takes you an inordinate amount of time to locate your car in any public parking lot, you can trace the music and migratory patterns of the Romani over centuries. I love that even when you mutter a string of expletives when you're having technical frustrations, you don't give up. I love your descriptions of the terraced cliffs on La Gomera and the caves in Belize and the penguins on the Falkland Islands. And the folk dance you learned in someone's backyard in a tiny Croatian village. I love that you knew way back then about Johnny

Cash advocating for Native Americans, and that when you came back from Peru you were worried about those people who live on top of that mountain in poverty with no way to get down for supplies. I love that you wear mittens in the winter and boy sneakers in the spring. And you're still in contact with the foot-and-mouth-painting artists you met in Israel. You see the possibilities in everything and everyone. Look at the way David has turned out, in large part because you gave him the confidence to be who he is and were always there for him in ways that Nina and I didn't know how to be. Stop shaking your head, I'm not finished. And Maya … well she's something else entirely, you raised her beautifully. I love your look of pure delight at the simplest things, like moss clinging to a rock or the view from the bridge of the rising moon. Being with you is a magical odyssey—you're a force of nature, Rivka.

He broke eye contact with me for the first time since he'd started and sipped some tea. I picked my jaw up off the floor and swallowed hard; I was verklempt. I was also thirsty, but didn't have the capacity in that moment to do anything normal like hold a mug, let alone try to drink from one.

— Look. I don't know much about relationships, but I pay attention, and I know that every time I'm with you it's like being enveloped in a warm sea of bright wildflowers, and you always bring me back to myself, the part of me that still cares about being alive in this world. We have Greeting Hearts, what my people call it when kindred

spirits unite. But the way I feel about you is more than that, because I'm also wildly attracted to you in a physical way, always have been. Rivka—shit. What I'm trying to tell you is that I've been in love with you since the beginning. I love-love you, as the kids would say. And I'm in the process of selling my house so that I can move to this area. I've sent out some feelers and there's consulting work for me here, and I can travel to supervise digs in other regions if need be. I want to be closer to family, and to you. You live in the biggest part of my heart, Rivka, and I don't want to spend the remainder of my life without you in it. So I was thinking … hoping … asking … if maybe you'd like to spend more time with me, in whatever capacity you're comfortable with, of course. I'm not sure I deserve a chance … I realize it may be too late … but I'd like to see if we can make a go of it. And it's okay if you don't feel the same way. I wanted you to know this, no matter what the future brings. So what do you think?

Oh. My. God. That was better than a courting flute. What do I think?!? Seriously?!? With my entire body trembling, it took four slow, shaky steps for me to close the gap between us. I carefully placed myself sideways on his lap as he circled his warm arms around me. My head rested in the curve of his neck; the rest of me sunk into his chest, where his muscles could be felt through the soft fabric of his shirt. I couldn't speak. His left hand ran slowly up and down my back as he gently rocked me. His familiar earthy-almond-forest scent was dreamy.

— **Happy tears?**

I managed a tiny nod and tried to compose myself.

— **Here, you can use my sleeve.**

Something resembling a muted chuckle-whimper came out of me. I straightened my torso enough to release my right arm and raise it to wind loosely around his neck. My free hand traced the smooth crescent above his right brow, and the contours of his gorgeous face. His misty eyes were full of love and relief and anticipation.

— **I love-love you too, Jayce. I always have.**

He tilted his head back a fraction, closed his eyes, and held me tighter. His eyes opened to look intently into mine, and we stayed like that for a moment while my right hand got lost in his luxurious hair. Our lips found each other and latched on. We danced with slow deliberation through the prelude, savoring every blissful second, getting to know each other in this new way. I vaguely heard some purring and moaning, probably flowing out from both of us. Minutes passed and eventually we had to come up for air. He gently pressed his forehead to mine and whispered my name. His strong, protective arms around me felt like home, and all was as it was meant to be. I kissed him again, this time more urgently, while the Neville Brothers' version of *Fever* coursed through my veins. We kissed like we meant it, because we did. After another few minutes, or maybe an hour, we reluctantly paused again.

— **I'm sorry it took me so long to tell you. I hadn't realized … I thought I was protecting both of us. Was afraid of losing you altogether.**

— **You could never lose me—it's okay … everything's okay now.**

— Thank you for not giving up on me, Rivka. Hey, by the way, yours was the first incoming call on my cell phone.

— Ooh—do I get a prize?

— Only if you want one. You can claim it at any time.

— At my earliest convenience?

— Yes.

Our laughter sparkled all over the kitchen while we held each other. Everything felt deliciously exciting, and as comfortable as a well-worn sweater.

— Jayce, am I hurting your legs?

— Uh, no—maybe—I don't know … that's not the part of my body that's screaming for attention right now.

— Shall we retire to the bedroom?

— Definitely, I've been planning to carry you in there. Just as soon as I can remember how to walk.

Okay then.

I was awash in the astonishing, rich sensation of peaceful happiness. Our love was true; we were each other's reason to rejoice. I held on tight. L'naytzach n'tzachim—forever and ever.

36. EPILOGUE

Out beyond ideas of wrongdoing and rightdoing there is a field. I'll meet you there. When the soul lies down in that grass the world is too full to talk about. —Rumi

HENRY Saturday, June 23, 2007 Western Massachusetts

– God-almighty, I worried those two would never figure it out.

I followed Nina's gaze down to the lawn and garden area. A garden that I designed with pleasure and that Jayce and I installed last summer. Rivka's hand rested lightly on Jayce's back as he leaned in to listen, then nodded before she walked off and he resumed his conversation with one of the other men. I was on Nina's left. Suzy was sitting to her right and had sputtered a laugh at her comment. We were relaxing in Adirondack chairs on the new back deck at Rivka's house. Actually, it was Jayce's house now as well.

Maya had woven Nina's long silver hair into an intricate, elegant braid, and she wore a pretty blouse with teal embroidery. About eighteen of us were gathered this afternoon for what Rivka called a **'smallish-double housewarming-slash-summer solstice-slash-bon voyage party.'** She appreciates things that can serve more than one purpose. In any case, there indeed was much to celebrate.

Al Jarreau sang *We're In This Love Forever*, a slow, easy tune from Rivka's old collection; she had put me in charge of the music. For her recent fifty-fourth birthday, with the assistance of Jamal, Maya and I had a bunch of her old phonograph records and cassette tapes converted into CDs. She had amassed an impressive, eclectic compilation, organized by genre and larger than what many DJs had at their disposal before digital technology took hold. Some of the jazz and classical albums had once belonged to her father.

Pitchers of iced tea and sangria sat on the sideboard, along with an array of tasty treats prepared by some of the guests. The bowls and platters were covered with adorable netted tents to keep the bugs out. Yusef had shared with Nina a recipe for one of his Lebanese eggplant concoctions, and they've had some lengthy discussions about growing and preparing beans for consumption. He donated the seedlings for her raised herb and vegetable garden.

For the rest of the yard, Jayce and I kept the existing plants and added a colorful arrangement of lilacs, salvia, and bleeding heart. Puffs of blue hydrangeas, groups of blue and salmon geraniums, fuchsia gerberas, and purple coneflowers. And the woodsy, herbal fragrances of lavender and rosemary when you rub your fingers into them. I had been granted free rein and a decent budget. Jayce was especially pleased that I had included lavender in the mix. He said '**Everything you chose belongs here.**' It meant a lot to me.

Rivka's original back porch had been enclosed and insulated so it could be converted into an office for Jayce. She said they don't refer to it as a man-cave because it's filled with sunlight. They rerouted the back exit from the kitchen and had a large deck built, overlooking the joint backyard. As soon as the bijou house next door came up for sale, Jayce put a deposit down so his mom could move in. He said it was kismet that the neighbor left when they did. Rivka called it a miracle of miracles. Nina said the true miracle of miracles was her son and her friend merging their lives in the fullness of time.

The communal backyard was now fenced in on all sides, with a gravel area in the far corner for Molly, who was currently lying at our feet on the sunny deck. She was approaching nine years of age and still active in her chill way. Last week David staked a pink plastic flamingo into the ground in Molly's corner as a joke to annoy his uncle. Rivka thought it was hilarious and it stayed.

To the right of the circular stone fire pit, Bill was showing Rivka, in slow motion, some dance steps from a class she had missed. It involved arms serpentining around waists while legs moved forward and backward. Maya and Taz were next to them in bright sundresses, trying their best to follow along.

~ ~ ~ ~ ~

A close friend of Jayce's named Marty Gold was visiting. He's a widower from Pennsylvania, an engaging man. He drove up a few days ago to house-and-pet-sit for Jayce and Rivka during their upcoming two-week trip to Costa Rica. Marty is Nina's age and they're forming a friendship. Maya thinks he'll be good company for Nina when Jayce and Rivka are away, and that they'll be sharing some meals together. Maya hopes he'll stick around in their lives, because he's already becoming a de facto grandfather to her. Marty is fluent in Yiddish and has been teaching her pronunciations and witty idioms. She peppers him with questions and he seems to enjoy it.

~ ~ ~ ~ ~

I finally got my driver's license at the age of thirty-two. Nina said I shouldn't feel bad because she didn't get hers until she was almost fifty. Maya had initially tried to teach me, but after a few lessons, during which she kept calling me a '**Nervous Nelly**', she proclaimed she'd run out of patience, so I signed up for professional Driver's Ed classes. David sold me his old truck for next to nothing, which enabled me to broaden the scope of *Carter Landscapes*. Things got jump-started when Hector hired me to design a space for their large side yard. Suzy had shown him the perennial garden one day when he picked her up from work at the sanctuary, as I was nearing the end of my six-month term there. I didn't drive back then, but I rendered the design and referred him to a local, family-owned company to do the purchasing and planting. Word spread, and within a few weeks I had designed gardens for several of their neighbors. Now that I have the truck I usually do it all myself. Enough requests come in to keep me busy during the spring, summer, and early fall, and enough income to keep up with the rent year-round on my apartment, which is located just a few minutes from here in Easthampton. I think Ayate Essie would be proud.

~ ~ ~ ~ ~

Activities at King Solomon Sanctuary have expanded. A small pre-fab greenhouse was assembled so that Yusef can plant seeds on-site and not have to rely solely on the setup in his basement. He grows looseleaf lettuce, kale, spinach, and some root veggies in there during the cold months. David made arrangements with the nearby River Valley Food Co-op, so Yusef brings them a portion of the harvest year-round, providing extra income for the farm. The sanctuary is on their vendor list between Katalyst Kombucha and Mapleline

Farms. Some of our crop is donated to the Northampton Survival Center.

Like me, Cody is doing well; you wouldn't guess that he'd suffered through a dismal time. The sadness never goes away completely, but we are no longer adrift.

An alpaca named Tina has joined the herd. A homeowner with limited space thought it would be 'cute' to have one as a pet, not understanding that they're pack animals. It took Tina a few weeks to learn to share hay and gain socialization skills, but she fits in well now. She and Rose have bonded.

Esther still spits at the new people.

I know all of this because I'm at the sanctuary most Fridays, running the donkey therapy program. Yeah, it's a thing now. Rivka heard about a place in the UK that helps people with different abilities and/or high stress levels, and David contacted them to get details. We started out with what Rivka called the 'pilot program' once a month, and a waiting list grew quickly so we now do it every week. (David fills in on the rare occasion I can't make it.) The program is called *Stand By Me* and is structured to accommodate one person at a time, along with a family member, friend, or caretaker. Rivka trained me in the importance of confidentiality, and writing a brief progress note after each forty-five minute session.

We have the 'guest' stand or sit on one side of the small pasture (or a portion of the horse corral that we cordon off in bad weather for this purpose) and wait for the donkey(s) to approach after calling their name(s). Then the person can gently touch and talk with them. In addition to Liz and Luke, another set of donkeys arrived from Save Your Ass Rescue in New Hampshire. David gave me the honor of naming them; I chose Ruby and Rick and everyone approved. We usually have two donkeys at a time for a session but sometimes all four.

We host a variety of guests, each of whom is allotted up to eight visits. A quiet young veteran with PTSD who served in Afghanistan has been coming; he's adjusting to his leg prosthesis. There's a boy with developmental challenges whose mother said that being with the donkeys is the only time he's calm. She had me take a picture of him with Ruby, his favorite. A woman in her fifties with terminal cancer told me about her decision to end the grueling chemo and radiation treatments she'd been undergoing, and it's the only trip she makes out of the house each week. There's a trans college student who said there aren't many people who accept them as they are, **'so this is my primary support.'** An elderly man comes in with his daughter, who pretends to be the designated guest. She reported that he's been depressed since his wife and most of his friends have died, so he 'tags along' for her 'de-stressing' sessions and it seems to be benefiting them both. She said that hanging out with any combination of Liz, Luke, Ruby, and Rick has brought laughter back into his life. He calls her most nights to talk about them and keeps asking what day of the week it is so he can count the days until the next Friday. A pre-teen girl from Haiti who is losing her sight was initially fearful of the donkeys, but her father, who accompanies her, eased her into it, to the point where she will now initiate ball-playing with them. It's been an ongoing, outstanding learning experience for me. And the donkeys are jubilant with the extra attention and treats.

Rick and Ginger seek each other out in the pasture. The spunky spotted donkey and the sweet tangerine horse trot around together, sometimes breaking into a gallop. Their capers make quite a spectacle. Liz and Luke remain inseparable.

~ ~ ~ ~ ~

Jayce and I got to know each other at a deeper level during the many hours spent together installing the garden and the raised bed for Nina. He taught me alternate ways to lay out a grid. I taught him how to layer and fold in the natural compost and fertilizer.

Jayce is erudite, serene, and reserved. He gradually opened up, like the slow unfurling of a fern frond. He has little interest in small talk, but we eventually exchanged thoughts about religion, historical events, racism, antisemitism … his calming presence balancing out the weight of our discussion topics.

— **Long before we arrived, so much had already happened. Things we know about, things we don't. It's all in our lifeblood, even if we're unaware of it. Generation after generation of community, family, the lands we come from. The cycles of life and death … those patterns are swimming around our bodies from dawn til dusk. Adversity and hardship, but also, perhaps, good fortune. If we're lucky to have inherited some useful strengths then we can experience moments of inspiration and discovery.**

He said there are countless injustices in the world, that we cannot rely on karma to obliterate the souls of our enemies, but must act with good intent nevertheless. He had my rapt attention.

— **But it's not always simple. Sometimes we unexpectedly find ourselves in a quagmire, forcing us to make a split-second decision about whether to protect ourselves or our loved ones at the expense of something or someone else. That 'someone else' might be an innocent bystander,**

and that 'something else' could very well be everything you know to be true and right.

– **Betraying your principles in order to stay alive?**

– **That's right. It's a terrible thing to be faced with, Henry.**

Lord, have mercy. There was no doubt this man knows of what he speaks. Impossible choices. I nodded, the air falling silent as he turned away for a moment. I didn't press for details, changing the subject with a question about the smudging ritual Maya had mentioned.

– **Ah, yes. Nina did a white sage-smudging of herself and the house prior to moving in. We used one of Rivka's large abalone shells as a bowl. It's common practice among indigenous cultures in the western hemisphere, especially North America and Canada. It's a sacred cleansing, to get rid of any negative energy. The smoke connects us to the spirit world, so it can be part of a prayer ceremony. Most people use sage, but some use sweetgrass, cedar, or tobacco.**

Jayce went on to describe essential oils that can supplement a smudging ceremony, like juniper berry, peppermint, thuja … which I found fascinating. He said his mother remembered at the last minute to open some windows so the smoke alarm wouldn't go off! And that when they finished, he installed the housewarming gift I had brought over: a large wooden wind chime, which isn't actually a chime at all, but does spin, the thin, stacked teak slats rotating around a central dowel, forming a spiral. Jayce hung it from the edge of Nina's back porch ceiling and attached the bottom to the top of the railing, providing some privacy and visual interest when she's out there. As soon as I'd laid eyes on it at the Cottage Street art show I knew Nina would appreciate it. When presented to her, she called me '**a thoughtful young man**.' And she let me hug her for the first time, perhaps acknowledging, after nearly two years, that my intentions with Maya were honorable; she protects her own, blood or not.

I did not ask Jayce about the rugged scar on his forearm. He didn't ask about my hand. There was no need.

Jayce is of my parents' generation, but we were both in our early twenties when our younger siblings died. Sitting on the ground with water bottles during one of our sporadic breaks, I told him about the set of five notebooks I found unexpectedly in Daniel's dresser after he was gone, all chock-full with drawings of people—faces mostly—and hands. Page after page. I hadn't known he was teaching himself how to draw, or that he had that kind of talent, and my mother was just as surprised when I showed her. I imagine he had kept them hidden because our father would have disapproved.

Jayce told me about Chilali's pastime of drawing delicate birds, then slowly tilted his face to the sky.

— Do you know about the V formation?

— Not really, tell me.

He explained that it's only the large, strong birds that fly in the V: ducks, geese, seagulls, cranes, swans, ibises, pelicans, cormorants, sometimes crows. As the lead bird flaps its wings, lots of small circular air patterns are created, which the other birds take advantage of. The vortices make long migrations energy efficient, with each bird flying slightly behind and to the side of the one in front of it so there's less wind resistance.

— **But it gets tiring for the bird in front, so they switch off from time to time, minimizing the need to stop and rest. The lead bird lets itself fall back and another one takes over.**

— **So it's a perfect form of cooperation that they do instinctively?**

— **Yes, and not only does flying like that conserve energy, it's also how they keep track of one another and avoid collisions within the flock.**

— **Why don't smaller birds do this?**

— **Because their wings move too frequently and erratically. Their shorter wingspan necessitates a higher vertical degree of flapping, so they can't create the upwash of a rotating vortex like the large birds.**

He described the five different wing shapes, each a form of adaptation to the birds' environments. There are those with long and narrow Active Soaring wings, enabling seabirds like albatrosses to maintain low-speed flight without much flapping, especially over water. Eagles and vultures have the broader Passive Soaring wings that allow them to rise higher and catch the hot-air thermal columns with the wide 'slots' between their primary feathers. The Elliptical wings of ravens, doves, sparrows, woodpeckers, and other species are short and rounded, enabling quick take-offs and tight maneuvering in confined spaces like dense vegetation. Swifts, falcons, terns, and sandpipers all have High-Speed wings, which are slender and pointy, optimized for sustained speed. Lastly are the Hovering wings of the hummingbird, kestrel, osprey, and more. Hummingbirds can flap their tiny wings up to eighty times a second. When I asked how he knew all of this, Jayce said he **'learned a little about birds'** long ago from material published by the ornithology department at Cornell.

By the end of that day my brain was saturated with details about aerodynamics, the planform of wings, the vane asymmetry of primary feathers, and the airfoil formed by the secondary flight feathers so the bird can rise up. I asked a ton of questions as usual and was the eager-to-learn 'Grasshopper' to Jayce's humble, wise, and patient *Kung Fu* monk.

One cloudy morning as we spread the mulch, Jayce asked if I had had a religious upbringing. I told him about the gospel music, the only part of Sunday church that carried meaning for me. He nodded.

— **Music is vital, no matter what you believe in. Virtually every known culture has created their own form of rhythm and melody. Some prehistoric flutes were found in European caves. They were made of bone and ivory and are more than forty thousand years old.**

— **Amazing! What about you—were you exposed to special music growing up?**

— **Not much, because a great deal of our culture has been diluted from assimilation. But I know that my people have prayer songs for all the important things. Prayer songs for health, for planting and harvesting, for war, for peace. For love ... for**

sorrow. There are prayer songs for courage, for protection, for hope, for survival.

— **Wow—the crucial things.**

— **Definitely.**

~ ~ ~ ~ ~

When she's not busy cooking and gardening, Nina spends her time crafting. She knits up a storm—winter gear, sweaters, blankets, and so forth, using natural-fiber yarn. She also creates extraordinary, personalized tapestries for people who hire her to make something with particular themes, often for marriages, births, a move to a new home, and other special life events. Beads and shells are sewn onto some of them. She uses Rivka's old sewing machine for the borders and backing; everything else is done by hand. She also sews cotton and jute tote bags, where she incorporates appliqués of indigenous themes like double curves, animals, swirls, and unique geometric patters. Everything Nina generates is high-end. She's not interested in the craft fair scene, but she gets enough requests through the grapevine to pay her utilities and help with the mortgage on her little house, which I imagine Jayce is taking care of but it's none of my business.

~ ~ ~ ~ ~

David eventually found his second bashert. He arrived in the form of Leo Levin, a large-animal veterinarian. Maya said you can have more than one bashert, especially if the first one died. One day last year, when I was at the sanctuary working with the donkeys and chatting with David, he checked his watch and said he needed to leave immediately.

— Gotta go see a horse about a man.

— Don't you mean … ?

— Nope!

He chuckled all the way out of the barn, leaving spurts of effervescence in his wake. There's more to the story, but it's not mine to tell. Suffice it to say he seems immensely radiant in the relationship, happy as a clam at high tide. Leo's a secure, solid guy, on the quiet side, a fitting counterpart to David's outgoing presence. Maya and I sometimes join them for a double date.

Inside Jayce and Rivka's sunroom is a photo from six summers ago of David and Nomi, the two vibrant young men smiling broadly at the camera in their New Jersey kitchen. They were cooking a stir-fry and discussing the idea of adopting a rescue cat. Maya had taken the picture while down for a weekend visit. A month later, on a Tuesday morning that initially seemed like any other weekday morning, Nomi and two thousand nine hundred and seventy-six other innocent people were killed. Most of them left this world in prolonged panic and anguish, engulfed in the flames of evil. David said that his first big love will always be in his heart, but he's ready to start a new chapter; Nomi would have wanted him to live his life.

~ ~ ~ ~ ~

Maya and I are going strong. It's been difficult living two hours and seven minutes apart, not that I'm counting. We see each other as often as possible, usually with me driving out to Cambridge on a Saturday and returning home on Sunday. Sometimes she'll come stay with me for a whole weekend, during which time we'll also visit her mom and David. Our nightly phone calls mainly consist of listening to the minutiae of our respective days and boosting each other up. And occasionally squabbling about stupid things. I'm the luckiest guy on earth.

At Maya's request, we flew down to New Orleans last year so that she could meet Diondra, who remains a shell of her former self but was able to carry out the niceties of hosting weekend company. Upon leaving, my mother said ' **I like her, she makes you happy.**' On the flight back, Maya whispered '**I still want to meet your father someday, even if he is an unpleasant prick.**'

My adoration of the brilliant, beautiful, and brave Maya Solomon is boundless. We can step into each other's dark, confusing places and share our sadness of the past, our concerns for the future. We have things to sort out, like where we want to settle down and what that will look like; we're in it for the long haul. My lavish love for Maya is infinite, but I know she's not mine to keep. She's mine to love for as long as she'll have me.

~ ~ ~ ~ ~

So we are gathered here today, while the sun moves along its highest pathway in the sky. We are the interconnected circles of those we rely on and care for most in this life, the people we gladly show up for in all the seasons. I've found my herd. The mountains surround and protect us.

I think about the ancestral memories that Jayce spoke of, how they are embedded in our marrow, our neurocircuitry filled with the people and places we came from. The gifts we've inherited, the unspeakable things, the songs buried deep in our heart. We are all of it. The ongoing genetic research is providing a scientific explanation for what many have known all along. Our relationships transcend time and place; everything exists in relation to everything else. Each of us matters.

Sometimes we have to go back in order to move forward; sometimes we need to push forward so we can look back. And, as Jayce explained, everything hinges on your reference point. **'If you're on the leeward side of a vessel, you could drift too quickly and eventually run aground. But if you're standing on the lee shore of a landmass, you're already facing the wind.'** There must be as many circuitous routes as there are inhabitants of the world. No one can predict what will happen next. But for now, in this steady, sturdy beat of my life, I am present and awake in the new hope of respair, blessed with riches beyond measure.

How is it that some of us make it through and some do not?

Perhaps it's all in the wing feathers.

A few songs from
MAYA'S PLAYLIST
(for voice and acoustic guitar)

Better Than Ice Cream 1993 Sarah McLachlan

Blackbird 1968 John Lennon/Paul McCartney

Can't Find My Way Home 1969 Steve Winwood

Cry Me A River 1953 Arthur Hamilton

Dance Me To The End Of Love 1984 Leonard Cohen

Fast Car 1988 Tracy Chapman

How Deep Is The Ocean 1932 Irving Berlin

The Lee Shore 1970 David Crosby

Love Has No Pride 1972 Libby Titus/Eric Kaz

Make You Feel My Love 1997 Bob Dylan

The Nearness Of You 1938
    Hoagy Carmichael/Ned Washington

Overjoyed 1979 Stevie Wonder

The Secret Sun 2003 Jesse Harris

Shower The People 1976 James Taylor

Summertime 1935 George Gershwin/DuBose Heyward

The Waters Of March 1972 Antonio Carlos Jobim

Where Peaceful Waters Flow 1973 Jim Weatherly

You Don't Know Me 1955 Cindy Walker/Eddy Arnold

ACKNOWLEDGMENTS

Much of the *Before We Arrived* story takes place in what is now Hampshire County, Massachusetts, where people of Indigenous tribal and non-tribal communities have been living for thousands of years. I would like to honor the Nonotuck, the Nipmuck, the Wampanoag, the Pocumtuck, and all of the original inhabitants of the region.

With infinite love to my wonderful family and friends, near and far. Thank you for believing in me and cheering me on. Extra gratitude for holding me steady as I rode the waves goes to Jeanne Flottemesch, Joshua Pine, Cindy Rubin, Eleanor Rubin, and Sara Snyder.

An exuberant shout-out to the womenfolk at The Village. I admire your resilience, your humor, your generosity of spirit. It is an honor to be part of the herd.

Special thanks to the adventurous Maryanne Banks for information about the parks and trails around Ithaca, New York, and for your encouragement along the way.

Special thanks to Judith and Ari Cohen for assistance with some of the Hebrew transliterations. Todah rabah for your steadfast support.

Special thanks to Athey Thompson for allowing me to use your gorgeous poem, and for writing it.

Special thanks to the war veterans who have shared their stories, and to those who cannot. Thank you to James Cusick, former Lieutenant with the US Navy, for taking the time to correspond. I am exceptionally indebted to John A. Robinson, former Corpsman with the US Navy and First Marine Battalion in Vietnam, for reviewing my chapter about the combat experience, providing additional details, and giving me the green light.

Immeasurable thanks to the lovely and multi-talented Megan Gentile for your outstanding ongoing technical support, and beyond.

Special thanks to the Tudryn family at Noodle Neck Farm for allowing me to hang out with your darling, fluffy alpacas; they are the sweetest.

Special thanks to Tricia Hamilton, Sierra Hirsch, and all the folks at Jefferson's Safe Haven, a magical animal sanctuary filled with precious sentient beings. It was an honor to meet your menagerie of rescues.

Special thanks to David Brule, member of the Nehantic Tribal Council and President of the nonprofit Nolumbeka Project, for the work you do to preserve the sacred land and Indigenous history of New England.

With gratitude to Dr. Ursula McMillian and the surgical team at Cooley Dickinson Hospital, for your skills and kindness when I needed both.

Special thanks to Mahendra Singh for channeling Henry to illustrate Cody, and for the marvelous cover design.

Last but never least, I want to acknowledge marginalized people everywhere, and all victims and survivors of trauma. The ones who came before, and the ones who will come after.

Jodie Pine
(she/her)
2025

DISCUSSION GUIDE

for *BEFORE WE ARRIVED*
by Jodie Pine

Themes

- Loss of a sibling/child/parent
- Loss of a close friend or partner
- The meaning of 'family', biological and found
- Responses to personal trauma—immediate aftermath and over time
- Relationships between family/herd members
- How race, religion, and culture inform our views and how we navigate through the world
- Randomness vs. Fate vs. Choice
- Genetic vs. Environmental
- The universality of pain and suffering
- Second chances
- The function of dreams and visions
- The potential healing power of animals

Questions

1. When we first meet Henry he is sad and aimless. Do you think he would have eventually found his way to a happy life if he hadn't gone to the sanctuary?

2. Jayce works at a job that holds great meaning for him, but is haunted by the past and on some level deprives himself of living fully. Has fear, anxiety, or self-doubt ever inhibited you from welcoming potentially positive opportunities or connections?

3. Rivka decides to establish a personal relationship with Nina after her professional role of assisting the baby comes to an end. Given their differing ages and backgrounds, why do you think the two women are drawn to each other?

4. All three of the central characters are well-educated and have some insight about themselves. Does this factor in to how they manage their struggles?

5. How do each of the narrators relate to their respective nuclear family members? Do some of those relationships change over time? Explore the differences in the tone and milieu of the households they grew up in.

6. Each of the main characters was born into a minority family, as were many of the secondary characters. What are the theoretical and real links between individual and collective/generational traumas and strengths?

7. While there can certainly be overlaps, people respond to traumatic events in different ways. Have you had first-hand experience with tragedy? Did your perspective of yourself and/or your view of the world change because

of it? Did this result in a shift in your life priorities or relationships?

8. Maya and David form an instant bond at a young age. What does their closeness mean to each other as they grow into adulthood? What are the salient components of a healthy relationship?

9. *Before We Arrived* was written in alternating-first-person using dialogue and internal monologue. Are there any differences between how the primary and secondary characters see themselves and how others view them?

10. Jayce is attached to Molly, Rivka and Max are buddies, and Henry is smitten with Liz, Luke, and the other farm rescues. Have animals played a role in your life? What can we learn about the dynamics between animals of the same or different species?

Award-winning author Jodie Pine grew up in New York and set about writing after a lengthy career in human services. She can usually be found in the Connecticut River Valley—drinking endless cups of tea, listening to Cuban salsa, and daydreaming about sea turtles. *Before We Arrived* is her first novel.

Visit her website at https://www.jodiepine.com.